SUNDOGS AND SINNERS

Amy Krout-Horn

Sundogs and Sinners

This is a work of fiction; any resemblance to actual persons, living or deceased, is purely coincidental.

ISBN 978-1-7334448-6-6

Library of Congress Control Number: 2019954187

Cover art by Carises Horn

For my dear friend Dawn, who has taken this wild literary
road trip with me from its beginning,
and for my Ladies of the 80's: Gabriella, Nissa, Janice, Melanie, and
Shelly, who have had my back through five decades'
worth of peaks and valleys.
I love you, my sisters. Together, women rock the world.

Chapter One: Exotic Flowers of Fargo

Angela Sorenson parted the white silk robe at the neckline and dabbed the sweet-scented oil onto each collar bone before sliding her fingertip lower and swiping what remained along the top of one full breast. She plucked the crystal atomizer from the dressing table, tipped the heart-shaped cut-glass bottle until she felt the perfume's thick wetness against her finger, and, pulling the slick, cool fabric from her shoulders, she slowly circled each bare nipple. Suddenly, every breath brought the seductive scent, loosing thoughts of hot sugary sand, salt, citrus, and sweat-drenched bodies writhing in erotic bliss beneath tropical sun. She opened her eyes from the all-too-brief fantasy and looked into the towering oval mirror framed with gilded jasmine vines. They were her favorite flower, her favorite perfume, one of the only aspects of herself that she had chosen to retain openly.

She assessed her reflection, pulling her arms free from the robe's sleeves until she sat, her waist encircled in snowy silk, and she could admire the reconstructive surgeon's clean, precise accomplishment. She sat more erectly and pulled her shoulders back. She was pleased with the way her natural C cups no longer showed the gravitational weight of time and motherhood, and that the scars had all but disappeared.

Moving the round stool with the rose crushed velvet pad away from the mirror, Angela stood, untied the robe, and examined her lower belly, again satisfied with what she saw. Among affluent suburban women and the plastic surgeons who loved them, it was referred to as the "mommy package:" lift, tuck, liposuction. Most claimed that the procedure was for them and solely rooted in their own perceptions of body image, but Angela had never lied to herself about the reasons behind her choice. Guarding this truth, she told others that she did it for her husband Lars; not because he had asked or insinuated, but because he never would do either. For that, and all the other innumerable reasons linked to his unquestioning, unyielding love for her, it seemed logical that she would grant him the gift, the illusion, that time lost had been retrieved.

She took the atomizer and poured another drop, which she painted across the milky flesh of each inner thigh, and then replaced the glass stopper, setting the bottle among the cluster of Chanels, Diors, Valentino, and Shalini: a tangible collection of birthday wishes from her parents, the honorable Judge and Mrs. Kenneth Erickson. The tokens subtly reminded their daughter that they wished her to be someone else, someone more sculpted out of their own cold WASPish white marble. Angela sat, drew the silk kimono back around her nakedness, and moved the stool closer to the mirror. She studied her reflection for a long moment before she lifted the boar bristle, silver handled brush to her shoulder-length curls and swept the bangs away from her forehead so that she could see the other scar.

Ten years since she had seen its source. Ten years since she had taken the baby and fled from Minneapolis. Ten years since her old moneyed Fargo family had made their conditions clear in the form of a legal contract. After she had signed it, they allowed Angela back into their financial fold.

She lifted a French manicured nail to the jagged, quarter moon of tissue, hidden just inside the hairline of her left temple, and pressed hard against it. There were so many ways that someone you loved could hurt you. She dug the nail a little deeper, testing it, secretly wanting to feel something, but *those* kinds of wounds healed, became numb patches. Perhaps all wounds did. She let the honey-colored hair fall back over her face and laid the brush on the dressing table.

She and Lars were getting away for the weekend, although, at a glance, one might wonder what they had to get away from. Life in the Osgood neighborhood, with its perfect vista of newly constructed mini-mansions, lush green golf course, and housewives who felt safe in wearing diamond tennis bracelets while walking their Pomeranians and Shitzus, was by no means stressful. Regardless, Angela looked forward to Las Vegas. She loved the unapologetic way gross excess was wrapped up in neon and rhinestone. It was just one giant gaudy, absurd present, waiting to spill forth its eccentric contents. Angela couldn't wait to pop the lid.

Boredom. That's what she was getting away from, what she had forever been trying to get away from, what had, when she was eighteen, driven her as far off the path that her parents had planned as she could run. At least that was what she'd told herself at the time.

***

Maybe things would have transpired differently had the seventeen-year-old Angela been able to see beneath the seventeen-year-old Lars' blond, beige, blue-eyed layers, had she been able to separate the young man from his contrived country club etiquette, navy blue sport coat, and that orthodontist straightened, ultra-white smile that he flashed across their parallel plates of bloody prime rib every time she bothered to glance his direction. *That* Angela had been too busy strutting her inner rebel around. She had applied fuchsia streaks to her hair just an hour before the thousand-dollar-a-plate fundraiser organized by her mother, slid a gold ring onto her lip while in the ladies' room, and wore a "nice girl" cashmere cardigan, intentionally shrunk in the dryer, unbuttoned almost to the navel. Under it, she sported a purple lace bra and a message scrawled in matching ink between her breasts in small curling letters not unlike the lace itself.

"If you are close enough to read this I'll fuck you."

That Angela had taken one look at *that* Lars, and decided he was everything bland and bourgeois that she had grown to loathe. She saw her parents, his parents, the spawn of every martini-sipping, golf club-swinging, charity fund-raising, Bridge-playing adult Angela had ever known. He sat across the banquet table, his mother the cardiologist and his father the neurologist flanking him, and Angela had wanted to thrust her sterling silver meat knife through the tidy knot of Lars Sorenson's pin-striped necktie.

***

Angela rose from the dressing table, tied the robe, and crossed the plush taupe carpet, rounding the pair of wing-back chairs and round glass table that faced the fireplace, which she had lit before her bath, although the early May air had risen above forty degrees. Absently, her hand drifted over the silk king-size duvet as she passed the foot of the four poster on her way to her walk-in closet. Once surrounded by enough clothes, shoes, scarves, and handbags to stock a small boutique, Angela paused, as she often found herself doing when entering this space. The room resembled the one attached to the room in which she had grown up, only that one had a small window that looked out on her mother's prized rose garden. Angela had spent many of her teen hours crouched beside it with a cigarette, the Waterford diamond-cut ash tray lifted from her father's study balanced on the sill. Her mother had fired a cleaning woman because of that missing crystal, an injustice to which young Angela had stayed silent.

Her mother had a closet as large and as overflowing as this, too, and it was to that clandestine location that Angela, at fourteen, had taken the gardener's son, a sixteen-year old with potting soil under his nails and the smell and stain of cut grass on his deeply sun-tanned skin. Angela had pulled her mother's floor-length mink from its sacred place in the climate controlled little room and spread it on the floor, and there, atop a garment that cost more than his father's annual income, the gardener's son was given the virginity of the district judge's daughter. The coat—like the swiped crystal, the garish hair dyes, the lip ring, the trashed Volvo, the announcement that she wasn't going to college—elicited silence from her father and denial from her mother.

Angela surveyed the section of walk-in where her outerwear hung. No furs in this closet. Her daughter would have to wage rebellion on one of the buttery leathers. Angela did a slow rotation as she surveyed the dimensions of the well-lighted space that was, to her now, a rectangle of decent-sized closet. Ten years ago, she had, as a stipulation of her father the judge's ironclad contract, been confined to a residential room this size at Hazelton. There, Angela pretended to overcome an alcohol addiction, and her twitchy roommate, a cokehead supermodel, pretended that Angela did not exist.

Prior to rehab, she had lived in a smaller place, a back room of a run-down Minneapolis apartment. Unlike the recessed, soft lighting of her professionally designed walk-in, that room had no overhead; just a chipped ceramic table lamp with a cracked plastic shade and a bulb with a higher than recommended wattage that had turned the unbroken side of the shade a yellowish-brown. On one wall a double mattress laid directly on the floor, a battered crib sat against the opposite wall, and a scarred blue milk crate, turned upside down, sat between, the glaring light source at its corner. The room had a closet about the square footage of a very tight public toilet stall.

Angela sometimes used to hide there, spine pressed to the rear wall, knees pulled to chest, hands clasped behind her lowered head, trying to block out the noise with her forearms, until the craziness crested and receded back into the state of tense leadenness more commonly shared by the apartment's many occupants.

After the door got ripped off its hinges, the closet no longer served as a panic room, but it didn't matter, because by that time Angela had long since graduated from outside observer to active antagonist. Whether on the delivering or the receiving end, bloody noses, broken fingernails, bruised cheeks, gave her something she craved. It gave her visibility. Angela quickly learned that men couldn't look away, couldn't pretend that you weren't standing right in front of them, couldn't nod inattentively at your words without ever taking their eyes off the screen or the red-head at the end of the bar or a volume of West's North Dakota Century Code Annotated, not when you swung a cast iron fry pan at their ribs. She received full attention when she had a man flat on his back, his hair soaking up a half pitcher of beer off some dive's linoleum, while her knee crushed his groin. In the same vein, Angela decided that a man had to look at you before he slapped your face. Rage behind his fist was a raw, real emotion, unharnessed molten energy that he didn't hoard behind high walls. He shared it with those whom he hated, but, more often than not, he shared the brutal by-product of his accumulated frustration with those whom he loved.

In that far-off Minneapolis apartment, distanced more by years of therapy than by memory or miles, a man named Dave Bordeaux and the girl he always called Angie had looked at each other, had shared with each other, and, in the most awful of ways, loved one another—again, and again, and again.

Angela had come full circle, back to the world of walk-in closets, Waterford crystal, wealthy white men and their wealthy white wives, and, without Lars, she might have sacrificed sanity at the point of her re-entry, but he told her that he had been waiting a long time for the return of that bold, long-legged blonde whose gold-ringed lip pouted beneath a slender perfect nose, insolence that belied baby blue eyes, and soft curls the color of thick honey streaked with magenta war paint.

***

"*I* can read that," Lars had said on that night, so many moons ago, when he found Angela behind one of the golf course out-buildings as she smoked an American Spirit. She was sitting in an abandoned electric cart, one patent leather black pump propped on the dash, the wool satin-lined skirt high on her bare skin, revealing the tight lacy elastic of a garter-less stocking. She blew a mouth full of smoke in his face and scowled.

"Read what?" she said, as if annoyance could cancel out the obvious.

Lars stepped in front of the cart and leaned close until the toe of Angela's shiny shoe pressed into his inner thigh. She didn't move her foot. They locked eyes, so similar in color they could have been gazing into a mirror, and Lars placed his index finger so close to the scrawled purple ink between Angela's breasts that she could feel heat on her skin, although he wasn't actually touching her. Neither looked away, each challenging the other to react.

"That," he said and, without taking his eyes from hers, lightly pressed the fingertip to Angela's warm skin. "I can read that."

"Really," she said. "And what does that say, Lars?"

She drew his name out long and slow, making it sound as ridiculous and mundane as she presumed he must be. She thought the challenge would thwart him; the socially acceptable teenage sons of North Dakota doctors, especially ones named Lars, only used that hardcore word under certain circumstances that mostly involved their male friends.

Even Angela's mother, on the single uncomfortable occasion that she spoke to her daughter about sex, referred to it as "making love," which, when considering her parents' iciness towards one another, seemed like a ludicrous, fanciful choice of terminology.

But Lars Sorenson had kept looking at Angela, never flinching, never faltering, his cheeks never flushing, as he spoke the line. When he reached the word, he drew it out, just enough, and then hit the last consonant with a soft click. At the sound, a tiny breaker flipped and Angela felt the tingle travel all the way to the toe she still had pressed against Lars' leg.

Taking his finger from her chest, he said, "It would have been more dramatic with a comma."

Fire rushed into Angela's face; she broke eye contact, and pulled her foot off the dash, slamming it down on the cart floor.

"You're an asshole," she said as she buttoned the cashmere sweater.

He laughed.

"Why am I an asshole? Because I have an eye for punctuation or because I'm the one who responded to your advertisement? By my look," he said, tugging at the ends of the tie, "you probably thought that I'd be the last guy. You probably think I'm too Fargo for you, right?

She took the last drag of her cigarette, stubbed it out with the toe of her pump, and kicked it off the golf cart's rubber floor mat, into the gravel.

"You're too Fargo for Fargo," she said, exhaling the smoke as she began to climb out of the cart. "Now don't you have a Young Republicans rally or something that you should be running off to?"

Lars stepped from in front of the cart and blocked her exit. Scowling, Angela considered the meat knife/tie knot idea again. His wholesome, boyish face was now shadowed by a darker, more resolute expression and the blue of his eyes took on a gunmetal cast. They glinted with a kind of sardonic sexiness that, at least for the moment, intrigued Angela enough to mentally drop the deadly cutlery.

"Before you run off to a rave or Lilith Fair or whatever else you might be having to get off to," he said, "tell me one thing."

She glared at him but made no attempt to leave. He brushed a finger in a line over his own dirty blond hair, pointed to his bottom lip, and then gave a single nod in her direction, saying, "All that ... is it really you? Because from where I stand, it looks like a PG-rated, totally played-out version of a teen rebellion."

She clenched a fist, thinking how good the curved silver handle of that meat knife would feel in it, and what a real bitch it would be to lift blood stains out of his starched, snowy white dress shirt. Lars smiled, keeping the perfectly straight pearly whites hidden this time.

"I'm sure your Fruit Stripe hair and lip hardware pissed your parents off … big time! But if you were really serious, you would have made it permanent."

Angela's face burned and she slid across the seat, but Lars' long legs allowed him to easily follow, and he barred Angela's escape again. With one hand on the metal armrest and the other on the dash, he stared her down, his words slowing her more than the physical barrier.

"Beautiful girls don't need distractions like that to get people to look at them. And I know that you know this already, because otherwise, that shit in your hair wouldn't wash out in two to three shampoos, as we both know it will, and …."

He reached over and gently slid the fake ring from her lip and stretched it until it fit on the tip of his little finger. Once again, the touch had created sensation that traveled far beyond her mouth, and for that, Angela hated him more, hated herself the most.

"You're beautiful."

He should have kissed her then, should have taken that moment as Angela froze under the phrase, but he hesitated, appearing confused by the sadness that, for a split second, twisted her exquisite face. In that instant, young Angela Erickson had flown into the darkness, away from Lars, the first person who had ever called her "beautiful."

***

Angela turned at the sound of Lars' voice and found him standing in the doorway of the closet. He wore a charcoal gray suit jacket and burgundy tie, a pair of Ray ban aviator sunglasses peeking from one pocket.

"Ready for Vegas, baby?"

Angela nodded as he wrapped his arms around her waist, lowered his lips to her neck, and breathed in the familiar sweetness, a sweetness so intense that he could almost taste it on his tongue.

"You could have anyone," his father had said, when Lars had told him that he wanted to marry Angela. "She's very—"

"Beautiful," Lars said.

"—complicated," his father finished.

Complicated or not, Lars' father had seen that his arguments were futile; his oldest son would propose to the woman, with or without the heirloom diamond his father had promised him. In the end, Lars had walked out of Dr. Sorenson's dark wood paneled study, the black velvet box that cradled his grandmother's one and a half caret diamond set in white gold filigree tucked safely in his jacket pocket.

Angela never knew of the conversation between Lars and his father, but she didn't need to—her in-laws' disapproval was a thorny undercurrent that had never softened.

Lars kissed her again, this time on the mouth. The kiss quickly deepened, and Angela felt it reaching inside, curling towards, yet not quite touching, the pool of heat in her belly. The diamond, the house, the clothes, the trips, the white Mercedes, all paltry trinkets when compared with what she had brought him. Lars believed that Angela had given him love. She had given him her trust. Angela had given Lars the sweetest gift of all. She had given him a daughter.

Chapter Two: Undiluted

"Can I wear your pink Uggs?" Jasmine asked, fishing a boot from under the edge of Rosella's desk.

Rosella stuffed another pair of skinny jeans into the suitcase that lay on the floor in front of her, folded a periwinkle tunic sweater, laid it on top of the black jeans, and turned on her knees to look at Jasmine, who held the pink suede against her chocolate brown corduroys for assessment.

"Oh, yeah. Those would look *so* excellent! Did you bring your silver ballet flats?

"Yes … and the scarf."

"The black infinity?"

"Of course."

"Which one?" Rosella asked, eyeing the blue tunic. "The gauzy one or the one with the metallic thread?"

Jasmine rolled her eyes, smiled, and said, "Silver flats, metallic thread. Duh."

Rosella found the other Ugg under the suitcase lid and tossed it to Jasmine, saying, "OMG, I'm totally wearing that to Festival of Nations. Unless …."

Jasmine pulled on one of the pink boots.

"Unless what"

Rosella bit her bottom lip and then said, "Unless you planned on wearing them Saturday."

She *had* intended to wear the shoes and the scarf that day, but since she already had on Rosella's Uggs, she would have felt guilty admitting it.

"They're all yours, Ro." Jasmine said and reached down to adjust the tops of the boots around the legs of her jeggings before walking over to the full-length mirror that hung on the back of Rosella's bedroom door.

She frowned, as she always did when she took the first peek at her complete reflection. Her face was too round, her shoulders too broad, too square. She had a decent waist and her butt wasn't flat or fat, so it passed the test. But her legs were too short, in her opinion, and although Ro said how lucky she was to already have such great boobs because, according to Ro, her own chest resembled that of a boy with two really bad mosquito bites, Jasmine didn't feel comfortable with the way they drew unwanted comments from their junior high male classmates.

Overall, she thought her body resembled that of a well-endowed Oompa Loompa and the pink boots were just adding to the perception. She retreated from the mirror and flopped back on the bed with an exasperated sigh. Rosella jumped up and grabbed something from a cedar box on the antique oak dresser.

"Here," she said, holding out pink shell Zuni inlay earrings with silver dangling feathers and a bracelet that matched. "Get your Indian on, girl."

Jasmine looked up at the tall willowy girl with the shiny black pixie cut and wide animated smile. She was wearing her favorite statement T-shirt-of-the-month: Hello Kitty with a puff paint arrow shaft that Ro had added jutting from the center of the cat's forehead. Jasmine loved that wicked sense of humor and often wished she had the courage to pull off daring things like that, but Ro seemed to fit in her skin, seemed to own her wit; skills which Jasmine had yet to master. She took the jewelry, slid her own small gold hoops from each pierced lobe and replaced them with the long showy feathers before pressing the cuff bracelet onto the side of her wrist. She turned her head from side to side and asked, "Too much?"

Rosella reached over and opened the plastic clip, letting Jasmine's wavy brown hair fall between her shoulder blades and then used her fingers to fluff it out.

"Damn, Jas, you've got great hair. You need to trash all these shitty things," she said as she flung the offending accessory over her shoulder.

It hit the wall and made a small rip in a Justin Bieber poster that Ro had also modified using black and red Sharpies. The pop icon now had curved horns, demonic eyes, a pointy goatee, and a long, forked tail that swept up over one shoulder, the end in the singer's hand as if it were a microphone. Below, in Gothic-looking script, Ro had written, "All Hail Bieb-elzabub!" Both girls cracked up simultaneously when they saw the torn paper dead-center between his legs.

"Oh, crap." Jasmine snorted in fits of laughter. "You've awakened it."

"We'll have to bring it a blonde, blue-eyed virgin to appease it. Who should we sacrifice?" They looked at each other and in unison said, "Taylor Vander Schmidt," and then fell into further hysteria.

***

Taylor VanderSchmidt—not to be confused with the two other girls and one boy in their homeroom who also were named Taylor—was Cheney Middle School's seventh grade self-proclaimed "it" girl. Wherever she was—on the back of a horse, in figure skates, bent into a pretzel atop a yoga mat, or with a vegetarian lasagna in front of her—was where everyone was supposed to want to be. Taylor upheld this place on the social dais by keeping a swarm of adoring clones around her at all times.

Taylor and Jasmine had started Kindergarten together, attended the same birthday parties, jumped rope with all their female classmates at recess, and dined on the same chicken fingers at the same lunch room table. When Taylor and Jasmine's parents had cocktails on Saturday nights, the girls played Barbies and My Little Ponys and watched Disney and Harry Potter movies together.

But at the dawn of sixth grade, a seismic shift in social dynamics took place. As if they had special, highly sensitive predictive equipment, some girls felt it coming and secured their positions close to Taylor. Others formed their own, lower-rung circles. A few, like Jasmine, obliviously began the first day of middle school believing that every girl was still her friend, every boy was still unimportant, and every open seat was still available.

"I'm saving that for Amber," Taylor VanderSchmidt informed on the first day of middle school when Jasmine approached the cafeteria table where Taylor sat sipping on a bottle of water and nibbling on a protein bar.

Jasmine then moved towards an open spot across the table, but Taylor shook her head, and with a sticky pink lip gloss smile that did nothing to sweeten her tone, said, "Actually, they're all saved."

After finding the same situation at other tables, Jasmine had finally dumped her tray full of pizza and chili cheese fries at a distant satellite location at the far edge of the noisy lunchroom. From this limbo locale, Jasmine had slowly learned, as the initial days of middle school slid into the first week, the lesson that some girls had mastered much earlier. Taylor's table was at the center, where everyone could see her and everyone exiting the lunch line could be seen. It created maximum accessibility for the "in" crowd to either giggle behind their hands about what a girl was eating, what she was wearing, and what her hair looked like, or give a girl a friendly little wave as if to say, "You're not completely irrelevant, but you're still not one of us." In the most prized of the possibilities, Taylor VanderSchmidt gave the nod and a girl was invited to sit upon the limited number of Princess Vander Schmidt's unoccupied sub-thrones.

Usually, Taylor's crowd wore the same pencil skirt with boots, or half ponytail or Juicy jeans or bangle bracelets, and, always, the shiny wet bubblegum smiles. Jasmine knew that she could try to follow their trends; her mom, in an attempt to nudge her forward in life, could fix her up with a pair of their polka dot leggings or frilly white peasant blouse or floral print jeans, but, without the permission of the Princess, these desperate ploys backfired badly. Jasmine's mother had driven the final nail into her daughter's outcast coffin with a simple handbag purchase.

"Is that a Dooney and Bourke?"

Jasmine had turned from the sink in the girl's bathroom to find Amber, Kirsten, and one of the lesser Taylors clustered close like cattle before a severe winter storm. Kirsten was pointing a candy cane striped nail at the purse hanging from Jasmine's shoulder.

"I think so," Jasmine said as she dried her fingers on a paper towel and prepared to leave the restroom. "It was an early Christmas present."

Amber gave a snarky little laugh and said, "You think so? You think it's a Dooney and Bourke? You don't know? That's too tragic."

That might have been ammunition enough for Taylor and her mean girls, but it got worse—much, much worse. For as Jasmine walked out, Taylor VanderSchmidt walked in with an identical Dooney and Bourke strapped to her body. There was a weird little standoff as each girl registered the other's brand-new status symbol, and then Taylor's brow wrinkled, her candy cane hand still pressed against the door, as she shoved passed Jasmine without a word.

Retaliation had taken less than twenty-four hours. It probably had taken less than twenty-four minutes before Jasmine felt the impact. She trudged through the following days under the weight of whispers and stares as Taylor waged an all-out war, the effectiveness of her propaganda machine so replete that even a few of the teachers seemed to look at Jasmine with a kind of repulsed sympathy.

Adopted. Alcoholic mother. Half-breed Indian. Fetal Alcohol Syndrome. Brain damage.

Taylor spun the delicate truth with vicious lies so successfully that Jasmine began to question everything that she thought she knew about herself and her parents. When Lars brought her home a fluffy white kitten after she had casually mentioned how much she liked a certain celebrity's furry feline, Jasmine wondered if it was compensation for the fact that Lars was not her birth father. When Angela had a glass of New Year's champagne, Jasmine wondered if her mother had relapsed. When Jasmine received a B on a Natural Science exam, she wondered if her mother had quit drinking while she was pregnant. But most of all, she began to wonder about the Ojibwe man who had vanished without a trace from Jasmine's life when she was a toddler. She had no memory of him, no pictures, no contact. Angela never spoke of him and had once said that he might be dead. If he was still alive, Jasmine wondered if he remembered her, wondered if he missed her, wondered if he cared at all. Alienation gave her plenty of time to ponder these things. Loneliness gave her ample opportunity to pretend to read a novel while she picked at a plate of cafeteria spaghetti and daydreamed about the paternal family of which she knew nothing.

Finally, she went to her parents and asked that they tell her more about the man she knew only as Dave. Straight away, she could tell that they were divided on the subject.

"What would you like to know?" Lars had said, his face warm and open, seeming ready to broach any difficult topic that would ease his adopted daughter's mind.

Angela had been far more reluctant and had placed a firm grip on her husband's arm, as if she were reeling him back into safer waters.

"I think you know everything that you should know," Jasmine's mother said carefully, and then added, "at this time."

Later, when her dad tapped on the bedroom door and stuck his head in to say good-night, Jasmine seized upon the chance and said, before he could avoid the question, "Dave … my birth father … what was his last name?"

Lars exhaled heavily, swallowed hard, and paused. Obviously torn, he lowered his voice and asked, "Why do you want to know, Jasmine? Are you looking for him?"

"No, Dad," she said. "I just want to know … for myself. That's all."

Closing the door behind him, Lars sat on the edge of her bed, his forearms resting on his knees, hands clasped, head turned to look at his daughter in the soft light of the reading lamp. "Okay," he said, as he ran fingers through his thinning hair. "Because I don't think searching for him would be a good idea, at least not until you're a little older and better able to handle what you might find."

Jasmine nodded as she stroked the little white mound of kitten named Katniss that slept on the pillow beside her. Lars' eyes drifted from his daughter to the textbooks piled on the floor next to the bed. She had wrapped each in a protective jacket constructed from brown packaging paper, decorated each with chains of bright flowers, hearts, stars, and rainbows, all neatly drawn in neon and glitter marker, and, in the center, just below black letters indicating the book's subject, she had written in capitalized block, JASMINE SORENSON.

Lars' gaze traveled to a framed photograph that sat on a shelf among the girl's collection of seashells and a pale blue blown glass dolphin. During a trip to Florida, he had hired a photographer to capture the shot of Jasmine and Angela, both in lavender eyelet sundresses and straw sunhats, seated beneath an arch overgrown with climbing jasmine flowers. Filtered light fell upon their faces: Angela's milky, flawlessly smooth, Jasmine's golden brown from days spent on the sands of Siesta

Key.

His mother-in-law's only comment, and the fact that Jasmine overheard it, still singed the edges of Lars' thoughts, causing lines to cut into the corners of his mouth. When they had given the woman a copy of the beautiful portrait, Jasmine's grandmother had said, "The girl is too dark. Didn't you make her wear any sunscreen at all?"

Lars turned back to his only daughter, his only child, the only child he would ever have, and said, "Bordeaux. The last name is Bordeaux."

***

Rosella brought Pandora up on her iPad and was belting along to a Lana Del Rey song, when Jasmine shouted, "Remember when you gave VanderSchmidt that awesome nickname?" Swaying with the minimalist movement of an I'm-too-hip-to-dance Goth, Ro yelled back, "Oh, yeah. Bitch totally had it coming."

***

Day one of seventh grade marked the beginning of the end of Jasmine's social isolation with the entrance of a new girl. Rosella Bachman had transferred from the Minneapolis Public School System, which gave her clout and a certain city mystique that preceded her arrival. This provided Rosella an edge in the Cheney cafeteria social gauntlet, so Jasmine wasn't overly shocked when she witnessed Taylor VanderSchmidt assessing and then waving the new girl over. The shocker came when the new girl, who had obviously noticed Taylor's gesture, kept walking, never making eye contact with anyone, until she reached the No Man's Land where Jasmine sat. Rosella smiled, introduced herself, and then knocked down the door of Jasmine's outcast world with a single question.

"Hey. my fine red sister, can I sit with you?"

Somehow managing to keep the tuna salad from falling out of her open mouth, Jasmine had nodded, and then, to her own surprise, carried on a reasonably coherent conversation through the rest of lunch.

On rare warm Fargo days, most students congregated outside until the bell rang. Normally, Jasmine hadn't taken part, but when they had deposited their trays, Rosella had grabbed her arm and said, "Let's go breathe some of that wholesome farm fresh North Dakota air."

When they stepped onto junior high's version of a prison yard, the VanderSchmidt Gang was already positioned, ready for a confrontation. No one shunned Taylor and got away with it—especially when she was sporting her new three hundred dollar designer cowgirl boots. Like a procession of parade ponies, they clomped across the courtyard, Taylor at the lead, chomping her bubble gum bit. Rosella spotted their approach, glanced over Jasmine's shoulder, and said, "Oh, God, here she comes, little Taylor Not-So-Swift."

VanderSchmidt reined up when she reached them, Amber, Kirsten, Lesser Taylor, Bailey, and Regan halting in a tight semi-circle behind her. Flipping the end of a pigtail between her fingers, Taylor said, "You're Rosella, right?"

Jasmine held her breath and tried not to leak nervous laughter.

"My friends call me Ro."

"Okay. Ro," Taylor began.

"You can call me Rosella," Ro interrupted.

"Whatevs," Taylor said, her slippery smile slipping a little. "So you're Native American."

Ro glanced Jasmine's direction and raised a brow as if to say, "Watch this."

"We prefer American Indian."

"American Indian then?"

Jasmine watched a devilish glint grow in Ro's dark pupils.

"Actually, we prefer indigenous."

"Indigenous?" Taylor said, as if the meaning of the word had flown right over her quite pretty, but quite empty, head.

"Yeah," Ro said, pointing at Jasmine with her chin. "We're Native American."

Regan snorted and Taylor snapped her head to the side and shot the girl a deadly look. Turning back to Rosella, Taylor angrily yanked a pigtail hair free from her sticky strawberry coated lips, and, still determined enough to steer into the skid, said, "What tribe?"

"I'm from the Whatthefucksittoya people. How about you, Jasmine?"

Jasmine rapidly unraveled Rosella's run-together words, and despite herself, she started giggling. When Taylor and the others stood for a long moment with identical perplexed looks on their faces, Jasmine only snickered more. She was almost certain that she had peed a little when Taylor shook her head and said, "I've never heard of that. Where's *that* tribe from?"

"Here, there, all over," Ro replied, as she gave Jasmine an inconspicuous nudge.

Taylor stabbed her stare into Jasmine as she directed another question at Rosella, her intent cuttingly clear as she asked with the kind of sweetness that causes cancer in lab rats, "Are *you* a full-blood?"

Ro sighed. Jasmine could tell that her new friend was quickly growing tired of playing games with someone who had the cultural sensitivity of a flagpole.

The cooler term is "undiluted."

Just as it had begun to dawn upon Taylor that the girl was messing with her, the bell rang.

"Nice getting' to know ya'," Ro had called in a sing-song falsetto, as Taylor Not-So-Swift and her boot scooting bevy trotted away.

***

Ro and Jas had been solid ever since; one rarely spotted without the other. And by the close of their first week as seventh graders, they both knew that they would be besties for life. Rosella and her two younger siblings had been adopted as infants: Ro's sister from China, her brother from Russia. Ro liked to joke that she was the family's only domestic.

"My birth mother dropped me off at a fire station in Bemidji, said she couldn't take care of another one. It's legal to do that, no questions asked. I suppose it's better than getting left in a dumpster or out in the woods or something. Mom and Dad brought me home to Minneapolis when I was a month old," she had confided.

Jasmine admired the matter-of-fact way that Rosella could talk about it, a way that didn't make Jasmine feel sorry for her as much as it made her feel that it was simply another indestructible girder in Ro's secure construction.

"I'm adopted, too," Jasmine had heard herself say after Ro finished, as if the other girl's self-possession had swung open a secret hatch and invited Jasmine to step into the space beyond, a space into which Jasmine had never ventured. "My dad adopted me when he married my mom. I was three."

It had felt strangely good to share this fact about her life, as if saying it out loud clipped loose the razor-sharp barb that Taylor VanderSchmidt had affixed to it. Jasmine also felt it was an admission that bonded her and Rosella more securely. When Jasmine told her that she had been born in Minneapolis, Rosella came up with the beginning of an elaborate story.

"Maybe your birth father was up in Bemidji … walleye fishing or moose hunting or something very 'Northern Minnesota' like that. Maybe he and my birth mom hooked up," Ro started.

"And then he returned to Minneapolis empty-handed because city Indians aren't good moose hunters. My mom was there and felt really sorry for him, fed him dinner, and—"

"Bang! Knocked up!"

They had fallen into fits of giggles then, neither girl imagining that their tale could contain any truth.

***

Rosella squeezed in a short denim skirt and some tan fringed toe sandals, flipped the carry-on roller bag's lid shut, and tried to zip it closed. Her mother had given firm instructions that only one bag per passenger would be allowed in their minivan if everyone was going to ride comfortably all the way to the Twin Cities. At that point, Ro had suggested that they strap her sister to the rear bumper so that the older girls would have enough space for shoes.

Friday night to Sunday night, that's it. How many costume changes do you teen divas think you need?" Mrs. Bachman had teased.

Ro perched atop the bulging luggage and asked Jasmine to help her drag the zipper the last few inches. When they finally finished the difficult task, Rosella parked the bloated bag next to Jasmine's in the hallway.

Ro tapped the thumbs-up icon on a Halsey song before logging out, packed the iPad away in a tie-dyed case, grabbed Jasmine's hand, and said with her brand of contagious enthusiasm, "Come along, Miss Sorenson. Your experience on the Bachman Bunch Family Fun Tour is about to begin."

Jasmine snatched up the Dooney and Bourke bag and followed as excitement and an undergrowth of unexplainable nervousness began to bloom in her stomach.

Chapter Three: In the Shadow of a Ghost

The Strip lay far below, and, although the clock read three a.m., Las Vegas' radioactive-like glow still rose, reaching into the hotel suite's sitting room and bathing Angela in its low man-made light. She pressed her forehead to the cool glass, a wall of window separating her from the world beyond. She closed her eyes and imagined the desert and all the unfortunate missing individuals some said it held in its barren rocky grip. Behind her, in the other room, she heard Lars sigh in his sleep, and she opened her eyes, turned from the window, and quietly shut the door between the rooms.

If he awoke, he would ask Angela if she had remembered to pack her prescription and when he found out that she had, he wouldn't understand why she had chosen not to take it. Sometimes she welcomed the insomnia. Sometimes she liked to allow her thoughts to fight it out for an invitation to these somber after-hours parties. Sometimes she preferred the anxiety that came with lucidity over the velvety-soft slowness of the Xanex. Her husband couldn't accept any of these explanations.

She sat on the love seat and pulled her bare legs under her so that the extra-large hotel robe served as a throw. She and Lars had had a good evening: lobster, a bottle of Crystalle, a streak of luck at the Blackjack table, a lavish burlesque show that afterwards that prompted Lars to stop the elevator between floors and shove his hands beneath Angela's skirt with a urgent, heated dominance. He rarely showed that kind of aggressiveness, but it was a show of power that she constantly craved. Dinner, superb; champagne, excellent; and the sex ... better than what she had grown to expect, but when she felt the sudden jerk from sleep that always proceeded the restlessness, Angela sensed right away that her ghosts were not going to let her break even.

She propped a velvet, gold-threaded throw pillow beneath her head and surrendered. As was their custom, the ghosts all came at once—the living ones, the dead one—and cluttered her mind with a ticker tape blizzard of random memories, until, after a while, one took shape from the fluttering bits and stepped forward out of the storm. Tonight it was the dead ghost. Tonight it was Adam.

***

Adam and Angela Erikson had been born into a family that had assigned their positions within it generations before their conceptions. Compiled of lawyers, politicians, and land barons and the demure women of wholesome values and peaches and cream beauty who were chosen to bear their progeny, the family name carried predestined tracks for its sons, and sometimes, to a lesser degree of importance, for its daughters.

Even as an infant, Adam possessed this knowledge. In every baby picture, he looked directly into the camera with a magnetic charisma that seemed too well-developed for someone so young. From the clarity of Adam's keen blue gaze to the slight curl of his lovely little lips, he exuded a regal confidence that said he was more than prepared to embrace his destiny.

As Adam Erikson grew, he exhibited all the fine physical features of his mother, the former Miss North Dakota, and all the intellectual prowess of his father. He was a golden child who met, and then exceeded, all his parents' expectations. Much to his father's delight, the boy took to the water and by his fourth summer could lap the Erikson's pool. A former collegiate swimmer, the proud father swam alongside his son, never letting the boy touch the far wall first until the boy's growing strength and the man's waning vitality crossed as descending and ascending lines upon life's unseen linear graph.

The year that Adam swam the length of the pool for the first time, Angela was born. Like Adam, Angela was a beautiful baby, but, unlike her sibling, she seemed to sense the world around her as a dreamy water colored, frivolous thing. To her, everything was framed with intangible edges she could not grasp hold of, and the silliness of it all precluded Angela from taking any of it seriously.

With each year that passed, the differences in the Erikson children's personalities became more apparent. Adam studied karate and earned belts in quick secession. Angela displayed an average ability in a gymnastics class. The A honor roll always included Adam's name. Angela managed to keep most of her marks above a C. From the beginning, Angela was red ribbons and silver medals to Adam's blues and golds.

Initially, their parents were able to conceal their disappointment about this disparity, dredging up as much enthusiasm for their runner-up as came natural for them with their champion. But then one day, Angela's mother placed all her thin-shelled maternal hopes and ambitions for her daughter into one basket: the Little Miss Red River Valley Pageant.

***

Angela tucked folds of hotel robe more snugly around her cold feet and stole a glance at the honor bar's contents. Massaging the knot forming in her neck, she reminded herself that the one thing that she had inherited from her mother could have toxic consequences. This time, she would resist the lure of the liquor, but the memories remained relentless.

***

"Shoulders back. Chin up. Smile … no wider. Show some teeth." Her mother had drilled, as eight-year-old Angela practiced yet another deliberate stroll across the parquet floor of the Erikson family's music room.

Her mother followed her, fiddling with the velvet bow of Angela's cocktail-length pageant gown and bulleting more commands with each step.

"Now, turn—not that fast. You want to allow the audience, and especially the judges, time to see you. That's better. Don't lose the smile … good. Now walk to the piano … gracefully seat yourself … that's right. Keep smiling."

Suddenly, Angela's mother threw her hands up, her voice turning from stern to stormy. "Oh, my God, How many times must I tell you? Do not wipe your hands on your skirt."

Angela began to explain.

"It doesn't matter if they perspire. A proper lady does not dry her palms on her clothing."

For Angela and her mother, Susanne, it had been like this for months. They had gone through hours of tedious fittings of the custom dress: tier upon tier of carnation pink silk, lace, velvet, and cut-glass beads. Every morning, her mother put Angela through the nerve-racking stage promenade lessons. In the afternoon, Susanne subjected the girl to countless attempts at the right hairstyles and the best make-up effects. In the evening, Angela's mother made her recite complicated phrases aloud in order to learn proper word enunciation so that the introduction and interview would flow flawlessly. Angela's least favorite aspect of the forced pageant march were the hours at the baby grand trying to perfect the simple sonata her mother had chosen as Angela's "special talent."

As the event drew closer, Angela gained a greater sense of its immense importance through her mother's increasingly obsessive behavior. The night before her beauty pageant debut, her mother had toted her own pageant scrapbooks into Angela's room. Lovingly, she spread them out on the girl's bed and opened the plastic pages. Sipping her third post-dinner gin and tonic, Susanne shared her fondest memories with her daughter.

"This is the sash they place over your shoulder when they crown you," she slurred ever so slightly, running a fingertip over the golden letters. "My tiara is in my closet. We'll look at it tomorrow."

Angela had reached to touch the sash's shiny material, but her mother quickly turned the page, taking the prized memento out of Angela's reach. The next pages were filled with pictures of Susanne as a girl, her flaxen locks resembling those of a Shirley Temple doll, a Hollywood-worthy smile below glowing pink cheeks, enchanting blue green eyes, the Little Miss Red River Valley sash draped over pale lavender taffeta, gold plate and rhinestones sparkling atop her proud head. Susanne stared at her child-self longingly, took a drink from the rocks glass, and spoke almost in a whisper as if she were more in conversation with the girl in the photo than with Angela.

"The beginning of it all," she said. "At fifteen, I took Miss Teen Fargo; sixteen, Miss Cass County; the same year, Miss Teen North Dakota."

She closed the album and reached for the largest, leather bound volume which contained an eight by ten glossy of a twenty-year-old Susanne slid into the cover frame as a bit of alcohol slopped onto the bed's coverlet and she said, "I was in my second year of college. I had just met your father at the Gamma Phi/ Sigma Chi mixer. He had recently been accepted into law school and he told me that he would have tried out for the Olympic swim team if it weren't for his commitment to his future career. He asked me what my plans were and I said that I intended to become the next Miss North Dakota."

Angela had silently watched her mother ceremoniously open the album as if it were her Ark of Covenant, and gently touched dried roses preserved beneath yellowing plastic.

"And I did," she said, enunciating every syllable with a disquieting mixture of resentment-tinged pride. And then the pride faded, but a low-level defiance remained as she continued, "I also told him that I was going to marry a lawyer."

Then Angela's mother had scooped up the many pages of her past accomplishments and embraced them tightly to her breast as she looked down at Angela, who, by mere appearances, was a convincing replica of the bygone beauty queen. Beaming the superfluous smile that Susanne Erikson shone upon anyone who might judge her, she said, "You are my daughter. You will do well. Do you understand, Angela? You will do well."

Her mother's words rang more with the force of a demand than with confident encouragement, and as Angela responded with a skittish, uncertain nod, she couldn't help but think that the smear of red lipstick that marred her mother's grin looked a lot like blood. When her mother had told Angela to get some beauty rest—making a small kissing sound in her daughter's direction because she still cradled the pageant books—and left the room, Angela crawled from atop the cream lace coverlet and found the remnants of Susanne's drink sitting on the thick pile of ivory carpet beside the bed. Angela's mother had chosen to decorate the room in all off-white tones, hints of gold accenting certain hardware; the drawer pulls, the fixtures, and part of the crown molding's design featured its rich metallic luster. It was an impossible environment for a child to keep pristine, but it was expected, nonetheless, and the wet ring forming beneath the forgotten gin and tonic might leave a stain like the one Angela had accidently created upon Susanne's favorite French provincial tea table. Lifting it from the plush patch of ivory, Angela carried the crystal glass into the adjoining bathroom. Within the brighter light of another white and gold space, the partially melted ice, clear liquid, and bloated lime wedge suddenly seemed sacrosanct in Angela's pale slender hand. The red print of her mother's lip adorned the rim, and, in a spontaneous ritual of mother/daughter, and in some holy spirit of desiring that the two might become one, Angela placed her mouth to the crimson impression and drank. It hit her tongue, bitter and sour, and it vaguely evoked the olfactory memory of pine needles. It burned a little on its way down, but Angela resisted the urge to gag, letting the sweet override the other lingering flavors, until the chalice was empty.

As a lovely new warmth began to spread within her, Angela practiced the scrapbooks' winning smile, the mirror reflecting an image haloed all in white and gold, and, for that beautiful moment, Angela felt as if she really was Susanne Erikson's daughter. She felt as if she would do well. She felt her mother's wishes and her own wishes become one.

But as the sun rose the day of the pageant, the feelings had been replaced with a nervous stomach, a mild headache, and all Angela's previous inclinations towards apathy.

Back stage, as Susanne hovered over her with a curling iron, a comb, and a bottle of maximum hold hairspray, Angela slid into her typical mode of detached observation and watched the curious creatures around her. In Angela's estimation, there seemed to be three types of mother/daughter duos. The most noticeable were the hardcore pairs consisting of different variations on a girl sassing about their make-up case and a mother snapping that her peevish offspring was displaying dreadful posture. Next came a nicer brand of child whose vocabulary included "please" and "thank you," was happy about her participation, and whose mother would remain proud regardless the outcome. The last subset consisted of mothers shoving towards a vicarious win and their hapless little daughters dragging shyly behind. Although the hardcores' icy glances gave the impression that, in the beauty category, the former Miss North Dakota's daughter had the cut-throat competitors, both young and no-longer-young, a bit unnerved, Angela could only relate to the other quiet girls, shackled in ribbons and bows, each anxiously awaiting another dreaded dose of maternal disappointment. At least she hadn't begun to cry like some of them, although Angela had wanted to ever since her father announced over his usual black coffee and grapefruit half that he wouldn't be coming to the event.

As happened all too regularly when it came to Angela's activities, a massive case load and up-coming trial preparations would prevent her father from leaving his study all weekend. "Don't pout, Angela," he had said without moving his attention away from the Wall Street Journal. "Your mother will be there. That's what is most important."

The void that lay between Susanne's obsessiveness and Kenneth's obliviousness was a lonely place, a place that's terrain never felt quite solid, a shaky place where Angela knew she could not win. Had either parent shifted attitude towards center, everyone might have felt more victorious, but it seemed as if her parents hadn't visited middle ground on anything for some time. For a while, Adam, with all his academic and athletic attributes, had drawn them towards one another, the shared pride a platform for their compatibility, until Angela noticed Adam had begun to slowly separate himself from their mother, while more and more he looked to their father for cues. Suddenly, the unspoken rules had been drawn up: Adam's future belonged to Kenneth, Angela's belonged to Susanne, and each parent seemed to clearly recognize who would win. While Kenneth quietly reveled, Susanne quietly resented, and the marital chasm widened under long stretches of their silence.

From second row center, flanked by sets of parents, Angela's mother sat rigid as a steel rod, held her breath behind a beauty queen smile, and kept her hawk eyes peeled on the spotlight's harsh circle. Angela moved tentatively across the stage, and, maintaining a twisted half-smile, stopped within the cold white light and introduced herself in a shy whisper as a local morning radio host, dressed in a rented tuxedo, held the microphone. Following pageant protocol, he then asked Angela what she hoped to be when she grew up. In the audience, Angela's mother closed her eyes, heat starting to rise into her cheeks, as seconds ticked by and her daughter looked down at the toes of her dyed-to-match pink satin shoes. Another dozen deafening ticks of the clock went off, before she heard her daughter's voice, too loud and almost drowned out by feedback, say, "Adam."

Startled, Angela pulled away from the microphone and dried her hands on the gowns voluminous skirt like a meat cutter wiping grime on a butcher's apron.

Low chuckles rose from the audience and the host kindly asked, "Adam from the Bible?"

The hardcore mothers released a cruel collective sigh of relief that this was not their child making a fool of herself, making a fool of her mother. Angela's mother gripped the arms of the auditorium seat as Angela shook her head and continued to ball silk and lace in each fist.

"Adam," she said, the host drawing the microphone back just in the nick of time and preventing another shriek of feedback, "my brother."

"Well, Angela," the man responded with radio-quality tone and enthusiasm, "as an older brother myself, I think that is a very nice answer."

Polite applause rose from the crowd. Angela hurried from the stage, too young to comprehend that the brittle part of her mother that the woman had tried so hard to preserve had just crumbled to dust inside its yellowing cellophane shroud.

Following a piano performance pockmarked with stops, starts, wrong notes, and a forgotten bar or two, Angela was given a small plastic silver cup mounted to a black plastic stand affixed with a sticker:

LITTLE MISS RED RIVER VALLEY PARTICIPANT

Angela and her mother rode home in a frozen, dead silence. When they reached the house, her father was not in the study, but in the pool. He and Adam cheerfully waved, and then had taken another lap. Susanne had taken a gin and tonic to the closet where the souvenirs of a successful youth laid in a row like glossy rectangle grave markers. Angela had taken the unmentionable memento of the day back to her unwelcoming, lifeless room.

***

Angela considered returning to bed, and then , realizing that she no longer wanted sex nor sleep, decided it better to "let sleeping men lie."

Wasn't that the spin Adam had put on the old adage that far-off summer twilight when he and Angela were teens and had snuck past the rattan chaise lounge where their father napped, half-glasses low on his nose, an open Tom Clancy novel pitched on his chest like a pup tent?

Through Angela's thoughts, her brother's ghost stirred an icy finger round and round. Had it been a bottle of their mother's Bombay Sapphire hidden in Angela's straw bag or had Adam lifted one of Kenneth's bourbons from beneath the family's beach house stocked bar? The cold, dead stir stick swirled faster and faster.

Had Susanne been there that evening, or had she been off at the club, taking another private lesson from a twenty-year-old tennis pro?

Adam's spectral finger stopped spiraling and poked cruelly at the most tender hidden folds of Angela's horrid, hoarded recollections.

Time had mixed a chaotic cocktail of details, and Angela had spent hours of therapy in an effort to untangle fact from fiction, the guilty from the innocent, and the *what if* from the *what was*. Her psychiatrist encouraged Angela to "let herself go there," telling her that Angela the adult could now face and deal with what Angela the fourteen-year-old girl had not been well-equipped enough to battle.

With the memory of poor dead Adam at the helm, Angela the adult took the suggested cleansing breaths, stretched full length upon the hotel settee, closed her eyes, and left Las Vegas.

Chapter Four: After the Sea Swallows the Sun

"What do you think you're doing?" Angela had whispered with a saccharin-sweet lilt that late summer early evening when she walked in on Adam squatted beside the liquor cabinet, covertly sorting through the bottles.

He twisted around to find her leaning behind the bar, her arms crossed, a surprised, yet gratified, look on her young, pretty face. Quickly scanning beyond his sister, he saw that their parents weren't lurking close behind and growled, "None of your business. Get lost."

"Are you stealing booze? Are you going to that party down the beach?"

"Shut up, Angela. Keep your voice down. Dad's asleep on the lanai."

She noticed the open slider that connected the living room with the screened patio, and knew she had Adam right where she wanted him. She turned the volume up a quarter notch, saying, "Why? Is there something that you don't want him to see?"

Alarmed irritation caused Adam to grab the hem of her denim cut-offs, pull her to the floor, and press a hand over her mouth.

"Yes," he hissed. "I'm going to a party. And, yes, I'm borrowing a couple of bottles. Now, please, act like you didn't see anything, stay quiet, and get out of here!"

She nipped a pinch of flesh on the meaty part of his hand and he yanked it away.

"Take me with," Angela whispered. "I'm totally bored. Mom wouldn't let me go to the club with her and Dad's obviously dead to the world. I want a little fun."

"Hell, no. I'm not dragging my thirteen-year-old sister to a party with me. What kind of loser does that?"

"The kind of loser who gets caught red-handed by that sister. And I'm not thirteen. I'm fourteen."

Adam rolled his eyes and snapped, "Who cares? What's the damn difference? Thirteen. Fourteen. You're still not coming with. Got it?"

"Oh, Dad," Angela suddenly sang out in loud falsetto, "Adam has something he wants to show you."

He tried to grab her again, but she shoved his hand away and hopped out of range.

"Okay, okay! You can go. Just please be quiet."

Angela stood and grinned down at her brother.

"Don't worry. I won't embarrass you. I can hang with your crowd, no problem."

Unwrapping a hot pink stretch band from around her ponytail she shot it at him before she headed up the stairs, adding over her shoulder, "I'm going to change. Be back in a sec."

Her return raised his eyebrows. In the looks department, she certainly wasn't going to equal social suicide for him. Her long blonde hair flowed loose over her suntanned shoulders. She wore a short red floral spaghetti strap sundress. A gold necklace held a sparkling chandelier pendant that drew the eye downward to the supple crevice between her high firm breasts. Her excellent make-up job only added to the effect. She could easily pass for seventeen or eighteen; an acknowledgement that she could see both impressed and disturbed Adam, as she motioned for him to lay the contraband alcohol inside the straw beach tote and she nestled a blanket around the glass bottles. Sometime, while he had been busy actively ignoring her existence, his baby sister had moved far past anything that resembled babyhood, and if Angela's attractiveness had drawn his attention, then who knew how many hormone- and alcohol-charged males were going to hit on her? She knew it was a situation Adam had never considered, and therefore, had never prepared for. This entire Florida excursion had, from its conception, kept Adam just shy of settled.

The Eriksons usually took their annual trip to the family's Siesta Key vacation property during winter break, but that year Susanne had decided that she and the children should spend the summer there as well. She had taken up tennis again after her introduction to the country club's newest instructor and thought that picking up his intensive lessons again in early June would improve her physical and mental health. Adam and Angela's father hadn't blinked at the plan, said that he would try to fly down on weekends, and contacted the Sarasota club, pre-paying for his wife to receive instruction three times a week.

Adam wasn't as enthusiastic as their mother.

"Why can't we go to Europe again," he had questioned.

"This is for your mother," his father had said dryly. "Take one for the team, son. I promise, next summer, Spain, Italy, France, wherever you like."

Kenneth had given his wife a cool, knowing glance before concluding with, "For now, enjoy the beach while your mother enjoys her tennis pro."

Angela, not caring where she did the time, had merely shrugged and went to pack her Louis Vuitton luggage.

Adam glanced at Angela again and began to question her. Did she fully understand the kind of attention she was bound to attract? He stopped when she glared at him as if addressing a presumptuous stranger. She didn't look to him for brotherly advice; in fact, if anything, she had grown to resent most everything about him. The lofty pedestal upon which their parents had placed him created the rift, but he was to blame for having never stepped down off of it, never having reached out and pulled her onto it, never having the inclination to share the limelight.

Angela pointed at the note pad next to the cordless phone and, as she peered over his shoulder, Adam grabbed a pen, hurriedly scribbling Laslow's BBQ, Home at 12, Angela with.

He propped the message against the charger base and they quietly left through the front door, rounded the house, holding their breath as they passed by the screened porch where they could hear their father still snoring behind the heavy perfumed curtain of sweet green night blooming jasmine. Cautiously, they negotiated the narrow path that lead onto the beach.

Mountainous pink clouds pressed down from above, the Gulf of Mexico thrusting huge curled white teeth skyward, until the sea finally found the sun's edge and slowly swallowed the light, one wet mouthful at a time. Angela removed her sandals and walked through the warm ebbing tidal pools. A few paces ahead, Adam moved over the firm packed sand, broken shells crunching beneath his purposeful stride. In the distance, heavy bass beat an electronic pulse, signaling the heart of their destination, and Adam's pace quickened the closer they got to it. Suddenly, he slanted away from the water, towards the dunes and the cover of tall sea oats and grass, waving for Angela to follow.

Angela and Adam didn't know the group of kids they had been hanging out with as well as the ones she and Adam had known since they were little, the ones like themselves whose affluent parents owned cold weather get-away houses on the key. Like the Erikson kids, they were all the very white, then painfully pink-skinned children who played together through the cool sunny December and January afternoons, until their private prep schools reconvened and they returned to their frozen homelands. The summer kids, including the alluring Miss Jenny Laslow, were mostly locals, with a smattering of European youth that rotated from week to week, and those like Adam and Angela, whose parents were, for one reason or another, spending the season apart. Gregarious as usual, Adam had dived right into the alternate summer social scene and had taken up with Jenny's brother Brian and his collection of surfing, sailing, and jet skiing compatriots. Angela mostly stayed on the fringes, observing. Though Adam traveled in a more strait-laced circle back in Fargo, and the constant casual consumption of beer and weed kept him grappling for new excuses for not partaking, Angela could tell that Jenny's arrival on the scene had blurred Adam's moral code considerably.

"Here," Adam said, and took the bag off Angela's shoulder, pulling a bottle from it and twisting the top until the seal popped. "I need some."

Angela had seen him share a Heineken with their father beside the pool once in a while, and in recent years they both had been allowed a glass of wine with holiday dinners, but beyond that, she had assumed that her swim team captain, future valedictorian brother was part of the D.A.R.E. crowd. Adam put the rum to his lips, took a long pull, swallowed, and then, as if the liquor had punched the air from his lungs, sucked in a ragged breath. He offered the bottle to her and wiped his mouth on his bare wrist. Making mental notes of all the tiny cracks forming in her brother's pedestal, Angela accepted the bottle, took a small sip, decided she liked it just as much as she liked Adam's recently revealed flaws, and took another drink, this time a little more. Before they placed the bottle back in the bag, they both downed another generous swig, and by the time they mounted the bleached steps of the Laslow's deck, Angela felt giddy and Adam appeared god-like.

Brian and Jenny Laslow's mother and her top-notch divorce attorney had carved out a settlement that included the multi-million dollar beach front home, and since their mother often spent long weekends in Belize with one or two of her latest, as Jenny called them, "boy toys," the Laslow teenagers made excellent, felonious use of the spacious dwelling at every opportunity. The house oozed the too obvious excessiveness that older money Like Angela and Adam's parents would have found vulgar. Every room had a television and a telephone, including bath and powder rooms. The great room on the upper floor and the family room below it had the largest screens money could buy, both equipped with stereo surround-sound. Fully stocked bars were part of each floor as well. There were no rare books, precious oil paintings, or pieces of antique Venetian furniture. An interior designer had selected the few abstract pieces that hung on the walls like large-scale examples of a child's finger painting, Cosmo and TV Guide seemed to be the home's only reading material, and ultra-sleek leather, chrome, and glass were featured throughout. That night, every square inch of the hard-edged ultra-modern space vibrated with deafening techno dance music and raucous young laughter.

Adam separated from Angela immediately, but not before grabbing the half bottle of rum from her bag along with Jenny's favorite, Gray Goose. As Angela watched, he nudged his way through clouds of smoke and resistant layers of sweaty bodies, asking the few people that he recognized if they had seen Jenny. Once Adam had abandoned her, Angela suddenly felt conspicuous standing with the large straw bag on one shoulder, so she retrieved the last bottle, set it on the broad cedar rail beside her, and nonchalantly dropped the bag onto the sand below. Taking the bottle by the neck, she looked at the label, and, relieved that Adam hadn't stolen any of Susanne's wretched gin, started to remove the seal from the second bottle of rum, this one a golden Bacardi.

"Can I get you something to mix that with?" a tall, tan boy asked, gently exhuming it from Angela's hand like they were old friends and peeling the plastic free. "I'm Clay. And you are?"

He had on black and orange board shorts and a loose-fitting tank with the Mr. Zog's Sex Wax logo on the chest. His hair was brown and wavy, and the summer sun had splashed blond highlights in all the right places. Angela couldn't exactly judge his age, but she was fairly certain that he had five or six years on her. Feeling bold and a little flattered that a more mature boy had approached her, she told him her name, and they weaved their way towards the outside bar where he procured them both big plastic tumblers filled with ice and a two liter of cola. Inside, the music broke for a second, something glass shattered against the tile floor; somewhere, a girl shrieked, a bunch of guys laughed, whistled, and applauded, and a raunchy 2 Live Crew number started up on the multi-disc player. Clay maneuvered her back towards the deck's stairway, and suggested they go down to the beach, where some of the party's guest overflow spilled.

"It's quieter down here," he said. "We can talk."

As their feet hit the sand, the house's flood lights illuminated the small tattoo on the handsome surfer's outer ankle, just above the strap of the Nike athletic sandal. Angela recognized the Greek letters. Sigma Chi, the same letters engraved into her father's fraternity ring. Suddenly her interest in the older boy inexplicably folded in on itself, leaving him far outside the small tight knot of longing caught behind her ribs, and, with her words tripping over one another, she told him that she needed to find her brother. Before the boy named Clay could respond, Angela had snatched the rum and darted back up the stairs.

Like Concord wine spattered across the snowy surface of a linen napkin, Adam Erikson's sober system quickly clouded under the stain of more alcohol. Angela spotted him as he wandered through the party. Every so often, he got sidetracked by random girls latching onto him for spontaneous frenzied groping, grinding, and tongue grappling as hits of Ecstasy rolled over certain sects of the eclectic crowd in wanton waves. For long moments, it appeared as if he forgot why he was there, why he had come, who he was looking for, and then he would clutch the vodka in his fist, the name Jenny would swim slowly to his lips, and

Adam would forge on clumsily across the chaos. From a safe distance, so that he wouldn't know she was there, Angela followed. Somewhere, in his searching, someone had lifted Adam's rum, and, as the evening wore on and people told him that Jenny had left, while others said that she had just returned, but Adam hadn't spotted the reason for whom he seemed to be willing to risk everything, Angela could see him playing with the vodka's seal. She sipped rum from the bottle she still carried and wondered if he needed a swallow of additional courage. She wondered why Adam seemed so drawn to such a wild girl. She wondered why he didn't seem to notice all the other, less elusive girls that were stroking him with their eyes as he passed through the crowd. But then Jenny's wide Cheshire mouth, her cat-like hazel eyes, her long brown mess of spiral curls, and her taut aerobically toned body invaded Angela's thoughts, and she shamed at the idea that, in some dark, secretive way, Jenny Laslow attracted Angela, too.

When Angela watched Adam mount the stairs to the third floor, she waited ten rapid breaths, three swallows of rum, and followed.

Upstairs, at the end of an empty hall, Jenny's loud laughter punched through the closed door of the master bedroom. Adam didn't bother to knock before seizing the gold olive shell-shaped handle and entering the ex-Mrs. Laslow's inner sanctum. Heart leaping in a crazy double-time dance, Angela crept towards the open door, knowing what she wanted to see, but afraid of why she wanted to see it. Dipped in shadow, she swept away the final flecks of fear, knelt so that one ear pressed against the golden shell, and peered beyond the crack in the door.

Jenny lay sprawled on her side across the California king, a three-inch section of raspberry pink drinking straw held to one nostril, an oval mirror reflecting a half dozen lines of white powder positioned in front of her. Some guy with gel spiked dirty blond hair, a forest green Ralph Lauren button-down, and his hand on the girl's sixteen-year-old ass, sat at the edge of the bed beside her. Her eyes re-focused on Adam as she lifted her face from the tray, snorted several times, and curled an index finger in a beckoning command. Adam moved closer and Jenny addressed her current company coldly, saying, "Thanks for the blow, baby. I'll catch up with you later."

She plucked his hand off her ass as if she had just discovered a fat palmetto bug crawling along her flesh and waved him off. He rose, shot Adam a knowing look, and turned to leave. Angela scurried across the hall into a linen closet while the spiky-haired boy slunk away. When Angela heard his stony footfalls on the stairs, she exited the hiding place, and, relieved to find the door still ajar, quietly took up her voyeuristic position once more.

Jenny patted the rumpled spot the guy had just vacated and purred,

"Far-go … rumor has it, you've been hunting the party for me. That true?"

Adam sat and laid the Gray Goose on its side next to the mirrored offering bestowed by her last worshipper. He drank her in as she sat up and reached into the nightstand for a pair of nail scissors, which she used to remove the plastic seal from the vodka. She wore a black bikini top interwoven with metallic gold thread, matching T-back bottom, and a diaphanous black shawl adorned with gold beads and sequins tied low around her jutting hips. The cavernous room's dim light did nothing to soften the jaded hardness of her face. Tugging the stopper free, Jenny raised the bottle to her lips, slowly running her tongue around the circumference before she drank, licked her lips, and offered it to him.

"Bump plus booze equals balance," she said and then exploded into spasms of hysterical laughter.

Judging by the vacant look on his face, Adam couldn't seem to fully process what she found so funny, but he smiled anyway, taking a swallow of clear alcohol, and then giving it back to Jenny, who set it on the nightstand. Angela crouched out of their sight lines, watching, her stomach fluttering with forbidden anticipation. Jenny fell back onto the coral satin comforter, her hand carelessly shoving the tray of cocaine towards the foot of the bed. Her huge bottomless pupils stared up at him as she said in a throaty, taunting, coolly confident whisper, "You didn't stalk me all night just to bring me a bottle of vodka, did you, Far-go?"

It was Jenny's brand of antagonistic uninhibitedness combined with a rough-edged, slightly tawdry appeal that had attracted Adam, attracted Angela, attracted so many, perhaps too many. She seemed to bully the very air around her with boisterous volume, and her eyes never lost their look of challenge that seemed to assert, "I'm going to beat you. I'm going to bang you. Either way, I'm always on top." Angela was sure Jenny was the complete antithesis of every soft sweatered, sweetly shy girl with whom Adam Erikson had experienced his limited amount of half-clothed, lights out, sexual pleasure, and although something about her felt dangerous, cruel, and vaguely repulsive, he obviously wanted her nonetheless. He grew hard, as Angela watched Jenny's gaze locked down on the fly of her brother's khakis.

"Not just vodka, I see," she said, as she reached behind her neck and loosened the bikini ties so that the shiny black Lycra fell away from her stiff pink nipples.

"Not just vodka," Angela heard him repeat, the words slurred like his head had sunk beneath an unseen wall of water.

Jenny's stare took on a reptilian quality as her eyes flitted from him to the tray and back again before she claimed the oval of glass, balanced it on her torso so that the undersides of her breasts rested over its edge, and said, "You're a really nice northern boy, Far-go. And I love to turn really nice boys bad. Want a little snow storm?"

Quick as cobras, her legs wrapped around the backs of his knees and pulled him towards her. To Angela's surprise, but also to her jealous pleasure, Adam, the perfect Erikson child, accepted the straw and knelt between Jenny's open legs, the rip currents of rum and vodka that rolled through his veins apparently telling him that it was okay, that everything was okay, that anything was okay. The rum throbbing through Angela's body agreed.

As he inhaled the trail of white that ended a quarter inch from Jenny's naked breast, Angela tingled, wondering if the drug made her brother feel as good. When he lifted his face from the mirror, it took on a comical expression, as if he had an overwhelming urge to blow his nose. Angela bit the back of her hand, squelching laughter, as Adam frantically rubbed his nostril. Jenny laughed at him; his first-timer's reaction presumably giving her a sense of well-seasoned superiority. Angela smiled at the older girl's reaction, feeling the laughter still locked in her own throat.

Jenny moved the cloudy mirror out of the way and, with a savage serge, shot upward, seized Adam by the shirt, and towed him down on top of her. Her wide mouth closed onto his, her tongue and teeth working mercilessly, as her hands tore at his zipper.

In that instant, Angela knew that she had an opportunity to leave, to separate from the strange desire that she knew she should not feed, to pull herself away from the quickly crumbling edge of moral acceptability. She swallowed hard. She had known all along this was the reason Adam had wanted to come here. She had known all along that this was the reason she had followed. There was still time. Angela could be downstairs, on the beach, with Clay, sinning in simpler ways, but the purr that began in her brain and traveled like a million moth wings across every inch of her skin kept Angela hidden in the shadows.

When Jenny had Adam's pants unfastened, she rolled him roughly onto his back as she yanked pants and boxers to his ankles, pulling each of his cross trainers off, the laces still tied, and throwing everything in a heap onto the floor. Angela crouched so close she could have reached out and run a finger over the silk of Adam's underwear, and something welled up, hot and hazardous, making her want to feel the fabric on her flesh.

Tearing away her own scant clothing, Jenny mounted him, her ass brushing against his full erection.

On all fours, Angela crawled farther into the room, her bare knee sliding over the boxers as she took cover behind an overstuffed chair, her eyes never leaving what was unfolding on the bed. There was no going back now, and Angela could feel tiny pieces of herself turning to stone, turning to water, turning to fire.

Jenny leaned in, and Angela shivered, imagining the smell of cigarettes and alcohol. The sharp bones of Jenny's pelvis dug into Adam, and Angela pressed her fingers deep against her own thighs. From where she knelt, Angela could count the scattering of freckles that were littered over Jenny's chest and the faint birthmarks along Adam's upper thigh, and Angela's pulse drummed faster, her fingers itching to trace what her eyes tallied.

Suddenly Adam's features shifted, a sickening slush seeming to roll through him, and he grabbed at his abs. There was such a distasteful, all-consuming neediness masked behind Jenny's compulsive, violent sexual approach, and, as Angela's admiration swelled, Adam's face darkened as if he suddenly wished he hadn't found Jenny after all. Her knees crushed tighter on his lower ribs, and she dragged the mirror back, propping it on Adam's chest.

"You're so cute, I'm going to let you have some more."

Again she laughed at herself as if it were the funniest thing, and then she shoved the pink straw into his left nostril, pinched the other shut, and tilted the mirror so that some of the coke drifted onto his neck like a thin layer of powdered sugar.

"Snort," she demanded.

With the sharp edges of the plastic straw cutting into his inner nostril and Jenny's finger denying oxygen to the other side, he had little choice but to breathe in deeply. With the second line, his body jerked and slackened, jerked and slackened, as if it had become the cage where the coke and the booze were slugging it out for control; one yanking him skyward, the other shoving him to the ground.

For a moment, Angela felt apprehension thread its way through the pleasure, but she remained frozen behind the cover of furniture.

Jenny tossed the mirror aside and slid down Adam's body until she was positioned with her muscled calves vice locked on either side of his hips, the apex of her spread thighs teasing him with its nearness, but she hovered, denying entrance. Angela's breath caught and she felt molten fragments flying free, melting back together, breaking her apart, fusing her together.

Tsunami-like, everything rushed through Adam, too, and any last remnants of control were stripped away, the obvious need for release bringing it all towards an unavoidable imperfect storm. Jenny lightly rubbed herself over the tip of his penis and then pulled back again. He let go an agonized groan and she averted her narrow eyes to the warm stickiness hitting her inner thigh. She gave a disgusted, impatient little huff before bolting off of him.

"It figures," she said with such a nasty note that it might as well have been her nails cutting across Adam's face. "That's what I get for partying with losers."

His only rebuttal came as a hot explosion of vomit onto the coral comforter's satin surface. At that point, Jenny said something about needing to dance this God damn disaster out of her mind. While Jenny's back was still to the door, Angela scrambled from behind the chair and ran.

Not long after, Adam found Angela chatting up some frat boy player down on the beach, and he charged over, grabbing her by the wrist and yanking her to her feet. Wild-eyed and red-faced, he growled through clenched teeth, "Keep your hands off my sister, asshole."

The guy with a Sigma Chi tattoo on his ankle raised his hands in an easy-going sign of surrender, and said, "No harm done here, dude. We were just talking."

Angela could tell that Clay was assessing Adam's surly, rather psychotic attitude, and was likely wondering what her brother was on. Adam glared and ground his teeth, the sound sending ice along Angela's spine and causing Clay to ask, "There some coke floating around the party?" Clay's gaze met Angela's and then traveled to the ruthless grip Adam had on her arm. Slowly, Clay got to his feet and said, "Listen, buddy. Why don't you grab some sand here with your sister and I'll go trolling for a little something to mellow us out. We'll smoke a joint, relax, and watch the waves for a while. What do you say?"

Adam shook his head, snarling as more of an order to Angela, than a reply to Clay's suggestion, "We're leaving. Now!"

Nervously, Angela nodded and Clay dropped back down onto the sand, saying that it had been great to meet her. She knelt just long enough to retrieve her sandals before Adam half pushed, half dragged her away, down the beach, into the heavy-handed darkness of a new moon's midnight.

The loftiest pedestals provide the most destructive falls, and, as Adam plummeted, he didn't want to fall alone. Stopping at the place between the dunes where they had shared their pre-party sips of courage, his breathing rapid, his skin molten, his face contorted as if his skull was inadequate to barricade some building pressure, he staggered to the sand, tugging Angela down with him. A small cry of worry, silenced by the roar and hiss of an unsettled sea, escaped her lips as she tried to make out his features through the blackness. She asked if he was all right, if he was going to be sick, if she should go for help, but he didn't answer.

Angela had witnessed Jenny's shamelessness bring Adam failure's bitter fruit. Alcohol had delivered rage as response. Cocaine had armed him with the authority to react. The twisted trio ripped through his moral fabric, the hole giving jail break to some hideous thing that few could have ever seen looking out from behind Adam Erikson's benign blue eyes. But Angela saw it, and her subconscious rippled with the knowledge that the hideous thing was the spawn of some mutated gene, passed generation after generation, through a masculine-based mythology steeped in stories of man's right to earthly dominion over everything. Both of the Erikson children had been fed spoonfuls of this Biblical thought food since they were old enough to speak, and Angela often pondered how heavy a burden it must be for men to bear to believe that you have been granted power of that magnitude, to believe that woman is but a rib bone by-product, delivered as an afterthought to ease your loneliness, to believe that woman is forever faulted for man's fall from grace. Secretly, Angela had always embraced her gender's connection to Original Sin. At some point, she had decided that she wasn't simply something sprouted from male bone seed. At some point, Angela decided that there were forbidden fruits she wanted to taste, too.

In Adam's black pupils, Angela watched the hideous thing slither out of its sub-conscious swamp, a malignant mantra spewing from its smug lips, becoming Adam's own slurred, chilling words.

"She did this," he repeated over and over, until the "she" that could have started as Jenny seemed to become their mother, Susanne, and then shifted like the sands of a sinkhole, settling upon Angela.

Before Angela could register what was happening, Adam sprang, forcing her onto her back, a snarl of sand spurs biting into her bare shoulder as his ferocious hands tore loose the strap of the sun dress, bruised the flesh of her thigh, and fought to open her, fought to release his rage into her. Angela's mind tumbled into a stagnant labyrinth of thought, as vines of resistance wriggled to choke out more twisted more invasive ideas. What was the greatest sin? Who was the greatest sinner? Did she even care?

Waves rolled and crashed, rolled and crashed, rolled and crashed, their relentlessness scraping at the soft shore, and Angela fought. With teeth and nails and fists, she fought, but the twisted thought, the one that she knew she should not let win, seized control. For a breath, for a heartbeat, for a single grain in the hourglass, she let it seductively coil around her. She gave the thought her hand. Angela let it caress Adam's face. She invited it to press her mouth to his. She let it guide her tongue against Adam's upper lip.

Her sudden unexpected willingness shot a bullet of lucidity into Adam's wild stare and he ceased his onslaught, his fury decaying into disgust.

"You sick," he started, the words punctuated with spittle.

But rather than finish the insult, Adam clenched a fist, cocked it, and started to swing. Angela shoved him hard then, and driving her knuckles into his testicles, she flew to her feet and ran.

She didn't look back. Angela hoped she had hurt him, hurt him badly, hurt him permanently. She hoped and ran, ran and hoped, until she reached the beach house. Breathless, hands shaking, she let herself in, locked the door, and ghosted past the side table where her mother's new racket—a gift from the tennis pro—lay, past the guest room, where her father slept, and up the stairs. She also locked the bedroom door and crawled beneath the quilt, pulling it over her head. Angela curled into a fetal position, her whole body shivering uncontrollably until she fell into a shock-induced sleep.

She awoke to the shrill screams of hungry gulls. No, not gulls, her mother's shrill voice piercing through the dreamless peace, her mother's fists pounding the locked door. Weakly, Angela crawled from bed and opened it. With frantic ferocity, her mother barged in, latched onto her daughter's arm, and shook Angela like a rag doll as she demanded, "Where is your brother? Where the hell is Adam?"

For a half-second, Angela caught her mother taking in the red purple bruises, the torn, dirty dress, and the smell of damp sand and the sour mix of sleep and alcohol clouding Angela's rapid breaths, but Susanne said nothing. Angela was there, in her room, in the house, in the world; Adam was the missing one, and Angela knew, in the depths of that dark place, the dark dank place where all of her dark thoughts and feelings squirmed, that their mother wished for the reverse.

According to her mother, his bed had not been slept in, and their father had discovered the boy's clothing in a pile a quarter mile down the beach. A pair of oily black crows had drawn him towards Adam's belongings as they cawed and pecked at the shiny gold watch band that protruded from a pants pocket. Later, Angela would hear her father say that, in that horrific moment, his eyes had drifted from the clothes to the sea. He had thought of the previous night's intense storms and the perilous rip currents they had created, he had thought of the lessons he had failed to teach his swimmer son concerning them, he had thought of the way in which Adam had never been afraid of water, and, with sureness that iced the marrow of every bone, Angela's father had known his son's fate.

For two days after Adam's disappearance, Angela covered the marks on her body, hid herself away in the screen porch, the jasmine's perfume wrapping around her like a sickeningly sweet, but welcome, shroud, and felt herself becoming less and less visible. Several times a day, Kenneth and Susanne would drift into the screen porch, look through Angela, at the shore beyond, and wordlessly turn and leave.

On the third day, the sea gave back the son, the telltale marks of his sins eaten clean. And Angela, a daughter of Eve, sister to Adam, was taken from the jasmine and posed among the funeral lilies, where she let herself become invisible.

Chapter Five: Certain Agreements

The Las Vegas hotel bedroom's French doors opened with a soft click, rousing Angela from the sofa where she had fallen into a shallow sleep. She expected to see her husband, but Jay Tipton stepped into view instead, deftly closing the door behind him. A suit jacket draped over one arm, the ends of a silk tie dangled loose around his thick neck, he carried his Italian loafers in one hand. Smiling at Angela, he whispered good morning. Sitting up, she swung her feet from the end cushion and offered him a seat. He sat, dropping the shoes onto the floor in front of him.

"Is Lars still asleep?" she asked, as she plucked her phone from the marble coffee table and glanced the time. "You're up early. It's only six."

Jay slid his feet into the shiny espresso-dark loafers, and, without the advantage of a mirror, expertly knotted his tie.

"He's still sleeping. I booked an early flight. My boy has a baseball tournament this afternoon."

Angela rubbed her eyes and yawned, saying," "Would you like some coffee? I'll call room service."

"Thank you, but I have to get going," he said, as he stood, slipped on his jacket and then offered her a hand. "Walk me to the door."

She grabbed his fingers and allowed him to tug her from the settee and towards the door. They paused there and hugged each other. The slight stubble of his cleft chin brushed her cheek and she could detect the familiar wood and amber scent of Lars' cologne.

"Will we see you at the NDSU reunion in August?" she asked as he let go from their embrace and unhooked the privacy lock.

"Yes, but," he started, and then hesitated, the gold band catching the short auburn hair as he ran a hand over his head.

"Gwen is coming with you," Angela finished and laid her hand on his broad shoulder.

Jay nodded, subdued sadness leaking from every fine facial line that secrecy had carved. Taking her hand from his shoulder, she placed her long, slender fingers along his square jaw and said, "Then we'll meet here again soon."

"How, Angela?"

She had known him long enough to understand that the inquiry encompassed a larger question than the logistics of another Vegas visit, but the real answer, the one that only she held, the one that she would never tell, was too complex for this man—or any man, for that matter.

"I love him," she said, her fingertips both warm and cool, but rock-steady against Jay's skin. "And because he loves us both."

Jay nodded, Angela feeling his acceptance of the smaller truth that neatly hid her larger lie, before he left, and she watched him through a narrow space in the open door as he departed down the long empty corridor. It wasn't until Jay Tipton stood inside the elevator and glanced his reflection in the mirrored side walls that he realized the tie he wore didn't belong to him. The mistake added to his edginess, an edginess that had started when she had used the word love.

Securing all the locks back in place, Angela went to where her husband slept, and shrugged off the heavy hotel robe. As she ran a hand along her naked body, she stood at the foot of the expansive playing field of bed for a moment, a field where she once imagined she could find something thrilling, something to ease the chronic numbness, something to remind her that she was the one alive. Lars was on his side, an arm thrown over a pillow, a knee bent towards the side of the mattress Angela had left hours earlier. She moved to the other side and, stretching herself across sheets still imprinted with the marks of Jay's body, sculpted herself to fit Lars' contours.

***

Years before, upon her return to Fargo, when he had called and asked if she would have a drink with him, Angela had believed that honesty would be the most effective repellent.

"I just got out of rehab," she had said.

"We can have coffee," said Lars.

"I have a kid."

"Kids are great. I love kids."

"I'm supposed to be sober for a year before I get into a relationship."

"We'll keep it platonic," he had said, and then added. "At least, until your three hundred and sixty-five days are up, and then you're fair game."

She had declined his offer the first time, the second time, and the third time he called the Eriksons' landline, until, during their fourth conversation, while she lobbed her truth grenades, Lars somehow managing to catch and replace the pins on every one, he launched one of his own.

"I've had sex with eighteen men," she blurted.

There was a brief pause, in which she was sure she had finally thwarted his advances, as Lars brought the receiver closer, and said, "I've only had sex with one."

"One woman?" she asked.

"No," he answered.

They met at a coffeehouse the next afternoon. As soon as they sat down at a quiet corner table, away from chatty college students, newspaper-rustling retirees, and hipster amateur screen writers clicking furiously on wireless keyboards, Angela leaned towards Lars and said point blank, "I want to know something right off, no bullshit. Am I your potential beard?"

Lars grinned at the notion and shook his head.

"No. My current situation doesn't require camouflage. I just asked you out because I find you incredibly attractive. I have for years."

"But you said—"

"Yeah, I know what I said, but it doesn't mean what you think."

"Was it a one-night, post-frat party drunk and curious kind of thing then?" Angela asked while she honed in on his face, searching for hints of an approaching lie.

"No, not a frat party, not just a curiosity. He and I played Bison baseball. That's where it started, and we saw each other, though less frequently, for a couple of years after college."

"Sounds like a legitimate relationship. What happened?"

"Gwen happened."

"Is she his beard?"

"No," Lars said. "That might have made it easier, but it was the real deal. They fell in love. They got married. I was the best man."

Angela picked up a stir stick, popped the lid from the paper cup, and swirled the scalding liquid until the little heap of whipped milk melted. She then tore open three sugar packets and dumped them all in at once. Lars followed her actions, asking why she hadn't just ordered the drink that way. She shrugged.

"Too easy, I guess. Sometimes the sure thing can be boring."

"It can also be safe," he said, as his eyes traveled to the still pink and shiny crescent-shaped scar that shifted into sight when she tilted her head, the blond bangs falling away from her forehead.

"Sure. I guess that's why I'm back here, why I left Minneapolis. Fargo is a safer place for my kid."

He gave an appreciative nod and then said, "For your safety, too, I would hope.

She didn't answer. Fidgeting in her seat, she leaned away from him and began bending the wooden stir stick until it broke in half, then she repeated the ritual with the pieces. Suddenly, she regretted coming, regretted having ever taken his calls, regretted how much control she had relinquished to Kenneth and Susanne in order to be considered responsible. It made her feel so damn cornered, so damn resentful. Was that why she was here in this ridiculous, trendy caffeine junkie joint with this weird, conflicted man whose maladjustment had only made him seem more magnetic? Was she poised to take another plunge into something disastrous? She needed to leave. She needed to call her sponsor. She needed to hand it over to a higher power. She needed a drink.

"Here," Lars said, and offered her another stir stick. "There's more where that came from."

She took it and their fingers touched in the exchange, the pleasurable sensation an unwelcome reminder of how many weeks had passed since she had had sex. Sighing, she set to the ruination of the flimsy wood.

"I'm trying to quit cigarettes, "she admitted. "Rehab brought me up to a pack and a half a day. Take away one vice, double another. Let's not talk about all my bad habits, though. Let's get back to your stuff—it's way more interesting. So does this Gwen person know about you and her husband, or am I the only lucky lady who knows your big gay secret?"

"No," Lars replied, guilt shadowing the admission. "You're the only one."

"Why? You really don't know me that well. Isn't that risky? Wouldn't it have been easier just to keep it to yourself?"

"Would you have preferred the usual mundane first date small talk?"

"No," she said, and gave him a half grin. "But there must be something more middle-of-the-road than this."

"Sure there is, but so far you've told me about rehab, bar fights, and double-digit bed partners, so I figured, what the hell, I'll open my can of worms, let you see everything. You obviously don't have a problem with honesty, so I thought I should meet blunt with blunt."

Angela really looked at him then, and for the first time since she had agreed to meet him, she thought that maybe, just maybe, he could be something more than just a one-time afternoon pass. She liked his faded Levi's, the moss green cable wool sweater over plaid flannel, and the beat-up brown hiking boots. His hair was tousled, styled by wind rather than comb, and he had recently shaved. He looked good, she supposed, by most standards, even handsome. By all accounts, it looked like he knew exactly who he was, accepted it, was comfortable within it, and perhaps actually went so far as to like the man that was Lars Sorenson. Although his unapologetic self-awareness was refreshing, she found the frank approach foreign, hence, frightening. But it felt good, exhilarating, and, entangled with the feeling, a thought swelled forward. She could have sex with him. She would have sex with him. Lars crumpled a coffee-stained napkin into a tight ball and crossed his arms, leaning his elbows on the round oak table, as he stared at her for several silent beats before he said, "You're still here."

Eyebrows raised, Angela said, "Did I pass your little test, then?"

"Hell, Angela, you passed the first time we met, at that country club gig. I thought you were so hot and risky, even though that sexy little nose ring was fake. Yeah, you passed a long time ago. Now I'm trying to pass your test."

I'm in no position to grade on anything but a very wide curve," she replied with a shrug, a long-overdue, but annoying, sense of caution briefly shoving back her sexual urges, warning her not to encourage him too much. "Besides, don't get overly confident. This isn't a date. It's been months since I've been out of view of my parents, a shrink, or some doctor or nurse. You were a ticket out of the house. Kenneth and Susanne think that you're a decent man, as they put it. That's why they were more than happy to watch Jasmine and let me meet you—because I would be in good hands. But honestly, Lars, I don't care who you sleep with because it probably isn't going to be me. But don't worry, I'm not going to out you. I'm not a hater."

He flattened out the napkin, began pulling pieces from it, and asked, "Probably? Did I hear that right?"

"What?"

"I heard you say that you probably wouldn't sleep with me. Not definitely, but probably. That leaves the door open, even if it is just a crack. Probably leaves it open. Definitely would have slammed it shut."

Angela's cheeks went pink and she insisted, "That's crazy. Everything I said and that's all you got out of it?"

He had called her bluff, and something deep within, contrary to what Angela knew she should do, heated to it. For years, she'd been hording bits of negative attention. The bits had become a collection of compacted clutter that never quite filled the void, and although it seemed he might be the man to help her break the habit, she balked at the idea of a clean life. "Good" was just another four-letter word. Angela liked "need" and "take" and the profane queen mother of all four-letter words so much better.

"No, that wasn't the only thing I got," Lars rebutted. "I also detect a strong pissed-off vibe when it comes to your parents. So here's some food for thought: isn't it just a little satisfying to know where the good hands they thought they placed you in today have been and how infuriated they would be if those same hands were ever invited to touch their daughter?"

She let a small smile escape, and then she picked up a chunk of broken stick and chucked it at him. He returned a broader, more confident grin, plucked the debris off his sweater, and stuck it in the pocket of his jeans, as if he had just won her last poker chip.

Lars' secret took root in Angela's thoughts, and the more time they spent together, the more moments she allowed her imagination erotic playtime with Lars and his lost lover, the more encouragement her naïve parents provided, the more the once rebellious girl, now pragmatic woman, viewed Lars as a worthwhile conquest. Before the recommended year had elapsed, Angela brought Lars into her bed. Soon, he had brought her and her daughter into the Sorenson family. Not long after, to the same Las Vegas hotel suite, Angela had brought Lars to see Jay.

"This is our marriage," she had told him. "We make the rules. We make the agreements. I want to give you everything that I can give you, and that includes the things that I cannot."

Guilt played no role in the wake of her decision, except on the infrequent occasions that she was in Gwen Tipton's company, but even then it was mild, and Angela only need remind herself that Gwen was Jay's responsibility and the useless feeling faded. There were only three people whom she was expected to protect: herself, her husband, and her daughter. Through omission, diversion, and careful revision of known transgressions, Lars and Angela had designed a livable place for themselves and Jasmine among the ivory towers and the scrutinizing sect that resided there. It took constant vigilance, complete discretion, and a certain amount of emotional concealment to keep the world into which Jasmine had been born, the world where Angela and Lars met Jay, and the world where the Sorenson family found security in their assigned orbits. To slip, to share too much, to forget the necessity of their segregation, might cause their trajectories to intersect, the worlds to collide, and the upheaval of all their inhabitants.

***

More than a decade's worth of marriage had made Angela an expert in managing the three worlds and her prudency had prevented calamity.

But as the white hot eight o'clock sun sliced its way through a crack in the heavy hotel drapes, Angela opened her eyes to the harsh shaft that intersected her and Lars' naked bodies, and she was blinded by that world's brightness, as the other two worlds drifted ever closer towards one another.

Chapter Six: Borrowed

The drum was in her chest, her heart was inside the drum, and Jasmine Sorenson's eyes were riveted to the rhythmic revolution of regalia passing by below. At the beginning, when the drum circle set the beat, the singers pierced the auditorium air with their high, proud pitch, and the dancers' feet had come alive, she hadn't looked at faces, reluctant to discover dissimilarities to her own. If she focused on the feather bustle, the beadwork, the silver bells, the shiny jingles, the brightly colored shawls, she felt like less of an outsider, less of an outcast, less of an interloper. Her connection to this world had been snipped and tied off, and her mother had taken her from it so soon that Jasmine's memory held nothing of it. Unlike Rosella, whose parents went to every length to offer their daughter exposure to her birth culture, Jasmine's mother tended only to what would grow strongest in the Fargo upper class climate. Unlike Rosella, with her blue black, string-straight bob, high hatchet cheekbones, and a complexion that needed no sun to stay brown, Jasmine's features went only as far as to create questions about what drop of ethnicity had been stirred into a much larger Scandinavian soup. Unlike Rosella, who knelt on the auditorium chair, video recording the action with her phone while she bounced up and down in time to the music, Jasmine sat stock still, feet planted, whole body wooden, except for her heart. It kept perfect stride with the drum.

***

Dave Bordeaux would have never gotten hired to play an Indian in a Hollywood western. His looks probably wouldn't even have landed him the part of the friendly half-breed who warns the white settlers about the renegade war party's plans. Although his mother was Ojibwe and his father had been an indigenous band and clan cocktail of some kind, the French trappers, British soldiers, and German settlers who had leaked into both family's lineage during the last century revealed themselves in most aspects of Dave's physical appearance. It was the catalyst of more fights than he could count and throwing fists—or his tribal enrollment card—at annoying nay-sayers had become Bordeaux's trademark. Down at the local watering hole, this characteristic, tied in with his fragile, volatile personality, had earned him a nickname. For several weeks after its conception, whenever he entered the Silver Spur

Lounge, people yelled out, "Here comes Indian Dave," until he finally knocked the teeth of a mouthy white cowboy type and a couple of more Indian-looking Indians loose. The nickname didn't go away, but it did shift from in Bordeaux's face to behind his back.

On one particular January night, however, Dave entered the Minneapolis American Indian Center New Year's Sobriety Powwow, Angie, a perfect pale backdrop of blonde hair, blue eyes, and bone-white flesh, the mother of his infant daughter, a half step over his left shoulder, and no one, not even the loudest inquisitor of all, the voice in his own head, questioned his right to be there. It was one of the first, and last, times that he and Angie would both be sober. It was the first and last time that he would join with the other members of the urban native community in a dance circle. It would be the first time that, as Dave moved proudly round the gymnasium floor, freed by the drum's urging, with his daughter cradled in his arms, Jasmine smiled. From the bleachers, where she watched, Angie had caught the moment on camera, her child's first expression of happiness reflected in the face of the baby's father.

Like the moment, the picture became lost to spilled beer or spilled blood or to the pervasive discontent that spilled hot and violent from every crack that had eventually split the man, the woman, and the child apart. The photo was long gone, and it had taken the record of all firsts and all lasts with it.

***

Rosella kept recording the action even as she grabbed Jasmine's arm and, shouting so that she could be heard over the drums, said, "I know that guy."

As the boy bobbed past like a pristinely plumed male bird, belled ankle cuffs adding sound to the spectacular sight, Rosella's enthusiasm caused Jasmine to steal a glimpse of the young dancer's face. The first thought that sprang into her mind was that the boy—about fourteen, maybe fifteen years old—was really cute. He had short, wavy brown hair a shade lighter than Jasmine's, round full cheeks that dimpled above his hint of a shy smile, and the solid, muscular build of a junior varsity wrestler. When she found herself unable to look away, a second thought became clear. If he wasn't wearing dance regalia, if he was just eating a slice of pizza at the West Fargo mall food court, if he was just skateboarding or playing video games or hanging with a group of boys from Jasmine's class, she would have mistaken him for any other suburban white kid, would have mistaken him in the way she mistook herself. That was the trouble with the often mismarked packaging of multi-racial people: the exterior color said very little about who lived inside. Despite the boy's rather creamy complexion, somewhere along the line, perhaps when he had reached an age that allowed him to comprehend the concept of race and ethnicity, he had been identified as an American Indian. As he danced from view, Jasmine wondered who had granted it to him. Was it his parents, the native community, or was it a tribal government? Was it recognized by the federal government? Was it all of these criteria? Was it none of them?

More dancers circumnavigated the drum and the complexity of the questions only grew as all the variations on "American Indian" whirled by in a dizzying display of short tight curls and long straight braids, eyes the hue of clear, blue heaven and the color of pure cacao, skin tones that spoke not only of the Americas, but of Africa, Asia, and Europe, too. Only a couple of the exhibition dancers looked like what most of the audience probably expected to see, and, for some, it might have caused enough disruption of their preconceived notions that they would leave disappointed, maybe even somewhat angry, but for Jasmine, her mostly unmet expectations meant something different, something freeing, yet something frightening. Who was she? Did her Ojibwe father's absence from her life make her white by default? Did her up-bringing among the Eriksons and the Sorensons, in the security of their suburb, cancel out anything Indian? Perhaps she was only the sum of her physical features and a Euro-centric childhood. Perhaps that was the only thing anyone would allow her to be. Maybe it was all she should allow herself to be. Jasmine kept her feet firmly on the sticky auditorium floor, her head saying, "You aren't one of them. You're not an Indian." But deep in the center of her chest, another drum echoed from so far in her past she had no memory of it, only a little phantom of feeling that brushed across her lips, causing a smile. The forgotten drum's beat and the present drum's pulse became one, drowning out the head, speaking through the heart, saying, "Yes, you are! Yes, you are! Yes, you are!"

***

"Yes, you are," was all the lawyer had said, his face frozen from indifference and recent Botox injections, as Dave Bordeaux protested that he was Jasmine's father. "However, your name is not listed on the official birth certificate."

He slid the document across the broad expanse of mahogany desk that divided the men, and Dave looked down at the stiff white rectangle of paper, embossed with the Minnesota state seal. His surname was nowhere on it. He had lost this fight before he had ever set foot in this office. It had been lost the moment he heard Angie's car door slam shut, when he no longer could hear Jasmine's hyperventilated screams, when he looked down at the floor where he had just dropped the broken coffee cup and saw Angie's blood smeared across the jagged wedge of ceramic. She might have forgiven him. She had done so before, tethered by having thrown her own punches, having broken his bones, having made him bleed, but that time it was different. Their daughter had gotten tangled up in their drunken dance, and, much newer to the concept of walking than she was to the violence of the adults around her, the toddler caught the swing of someone's leg. Knocked off balance, Jasmine's head hit the crib, her tiny new front teeth biting into her lip as she fell. It wasn't clear which parent had kicked her, but the blood gushing from Angie's forehead accused him, and him alone, for their child's wounds. From the beginning, from their first meeting, from the second she had said that her name was Angela and he raised a corner of his mouth and one thick eyebrow and had told her that he was going to call her Angie, he knew that in the end he would lose. When the great otherness of him that had drawn her became too familiar, became less curative to her upper-class Caucasian woes than she hoped, when Angela recognized that his absent father, boozy mother, overdosed teenage sister were just the flip side of her own tarnished coin, Dave knew he would lose. When Kenneth and Susanne swept in as if returning from a week-long Mediterranean cruise rather than the year that they had spent keeping themselves insulated from their daughter's life and introduced themselves to their newborn granddaughter's father with only stone cold apathetic nods and slipped words he couldn't hear into Angie's ears, an envelope with contents he wouldn't see, into her hand, Dave knew that someday not only would he lose Angie, he would lose Jasmine, too.

"This isn't a dispute that you can win, Mr. Bordeaux," the lawyer said, and laid a gold pen as suggestion on the desk between them. "Mr. Erikson wishes to protect his daughter and granddaughter from any further violence. The appropriate restraining orders have been filed, which preclude you from any contact with Angela or Jasmine Erikson."

Dave's chest felt as if it would explode beneath the constraint of the borrowed dress shirt. His scarred fists closed around the ends of the leather chair's armrests and pulled, as if it might act as a lever to release the pressure pushing in and out from every direction. The outdated borrowed tie ringed his Adam's apple like a dignified noose as he swallowed in preparation for more poison.

"Are you saying that I'm not going to see my kid again?"

"Signing all parental rights over to the Eriksons is in everyone's best interest, especially the best interest of the child. Certainly, you want that, don't you, Mr. Bordeaux? The Erikson family is in the position to offer her a stable home, an excellent education, security and comfort ... a good life."

A back room in his mother's squalid apartment, the knowledge of a kid who had dropped out in the ninth grade, burglar-barred windows and a secondhand mattress, a repeat version of his own unpredictable life: these were all Dave had as a counteroffer. The pen laying on the desk in front of him was worth more money than he'd had in his pocket in a month. No checking account. No car. No job. No power. He looked down at the small tear in the hem of the borrowed dress pants. He had nothing.

"She's my kid. I'm her dad."

The lawyer responded by placing the papers in a neat stack before the crumpled man. This had already taken more time than he had hoped, and he exhaled impatiently when Bordeaux didn't reach for the gold pen. He had appealed to this pathetic person's sense of parental decency; now he took the next most logical tactic when dealing with bottom feeders.

"As you know, Miss Erikson did not press charges. However, a lack of cooperation on your behalf may leave her little choice but to do so. It is my understanding that your criminal record goes back several years. Assault and battery combined with a child abuse charge could put you behind bars."

He paused so that his words had time to absorb, and Dave met the lawyer's self-assured stare with a wave of hatred that washed across the slick desk surface of what had once been Brazilian rain forest, across a pen wrought from something ripped out of the earth, across old growth trees pulped into piles of paper, across generation after generation of robbers and the robbed. The lawyer's expression didn't change, couldn't change, as he leaned back in his high ox blood leather chair.

Dave shoved a hand into a pocket of his brother Jack's thrift store suit coat, and the lawyer's confidence lurched towards apprehension, his own hand moving towards the desk phone, his eye locking on the button for building security. Inside the frayed silk-lined pocket, Dave's fingers bumped up against the unexpected object, and he withdrew it. It was a pen; one of those plastic ones that come ten to a pack. It was missing its cap and someone had chewed the end flat. He took the sad-looking blue ink instrument in his left hand. He would sign their paper—what choice did he have—but he would do it with his own God damn pen, or at least it was probably his brother's God damn pen. He scrawled the signature on a decline, the letters of the surname intersected by the dotted line. The lawyer's self-aggrandizing little smirk kept the pen in Dave's fingers, and, as he spotted the birth certificate half-covered beneath the document he had just signed, he grabbed it. Tossing it on top, Dave slashed a blue line through "Erikson" and printed the name BORDEAUX.

He stood to leave, the chair teetering precariously on two legs for a few beats before settling, but as he turned towards the door, the lawyer spoke.

"Mr. Bordeaux, the Eriksons acknowledge that this is an inconvenience for you."

"An inconvenience?"

They were boiling down the magnitude of their actions, their words minimalizing his loss, turning the documents with which they had cornered him into nothing more than a pink slip, an eviction notice, an auto repossession. The lawyer took a thick business envelope from a drawer.

"They asked that I give you this compensation."

Dave looked at the fat white envelope. He knew there was cash inside, and, as if reading Dave's thoughts, the lawyer lifted the flap, withdrew the hundred-dollar bills, and fanned them out like a hand of poker. Bordeaux pressed his palms on the desktop and towered a few inches above the hair plugs, the men's cologne cloud, the orange spray tan glow, as he said, the scrape of gravel grating his words, "Is that the going rate for an Indian baby these days? A couple of thousand bucks?"

Dave shoved away from the desk and the lawyer shoved the money back in the envelope.

"You tell Erikson to go fuck himself. He ain't buying my kid, he's stealing her."

Dave snatched the defaced birth certificate, and, jamming it into his brother's coat pocket, he stormed from the office. When security assured him that they had seen Bordeaux exit the building, the lawyer straightened the signed papers, deposited them into his briefcase, and slid the envelope of cash into the interior breast pocket of his suit. His old law school friend Kenneth's false presumption would translate nicely into his next bottle of hundred-year-old scotch.

Chapter Seven: Birth Culture

Festival-goers streamed through the enormous chambers of St. Paul's River Center, echoed voices and footfalls flowing into the spaces between the notes of Andean flutists performing off in one direction while a Celtic harp and violin duo played in another. In the section designated as the International Café, myriad sweet, spicy, savory scents wove their way around and around the crowd, until lassoed by chicken curry, chocolate croissant, feta tabouli, fried wonton, and every sausage variety known to humankind, few could wield enough willpower to pass by without at least a small pear-shaped piece of German marzipan or a square of Egyptian-style baklava. At noon, Jasmine and Rosella met up with Rosella's parents and younger siblings, and, as was the usual failed custom of the Bachmans, they attempted to convince their children to take advantage of the multi-cultural dining opportunities.

"I'm not eating that," Cleo said, arms folded, lips pressed into an impenetrable line of derision, as Mr. Bachman set a small paper plate of sesame chicken and white rice before his ten-year-old daughter. "I hate Chinese food. I want pizza."

"Don't bother, Marc," Laura Bachman said with a withered glance at her husband. "She's going through another picky phase. Give it to Daniel. He'll eat it."

Not satisfied with her mother's intervention, Cleo protested further, saying, "Hey, why doesn't he have to eat Russian? Aren't we supposed to be enjoying our birth cultures?"

Daniel pulled paper from a drinking straw, rolled it into a ball and flicked it into Cleo's hair.

"There isn't a Russian booth this year, but if there was I'd eat something from it," Daniel said, digging into the sesame chicken. "I'm not a big whiny turd like you."

Laura tapped her seven-year-old son's shoulder with a firm finger and spoke the admonishment the children heard at least a dozen times a day.

"No disrespectful language, mister. First and final warning."

Never shy of mischief and mouthiness, Rosella poured hot sauce across the lettuce, tomato, yellow cheese, and spicy ground beef of an Indian fry bread taco and then chimed in, "It's a good thing Mom and Dad got you out of Beijing before you had teeth. Just think of all the delicacies you would have had to choke down ... chicken feet, fish eyeballs, pig entrails—"

"That's enough, Rosella," Marc Bachman said, and then addressed his wife. "Perhaps next year we should forego this event. Our children seem immune to our efforts."

Rosella propped up the taco, a trickle of grease creeping down her wrist.

"Look, Daddy. I'm not immune to your efforts," she declared, as she took a huge vulgar bite.

Marc Bachman shook his head and tossed a handful of napkins in her direction.

"Yes, Rosella, you are a model child," Laura said, rolling her eyes as she dug in her purse for Cleo's pizza money. "Can't you see how proud your father and I are right now? It's like all our parental dreams are coming true."

"See where I get my sarcasm?" Rosella said to Jasmine, who responded with an almost imperceptible nod, not wanting to seem disrespectful towards her friend's generous parents.

The loose-reined ride that was the Bachman family often reminded Jasmine of how quiet and uncomplicated her own home life was, how secluded and sometimes lonely it was to be an only child, how much she envied their casual, organized chaos. She quietly listened to their continued boisterous banter as she ate her own first-ever Indian taco, and thought of Rosella, Cleo, and Daniel's good fortune at having parents who allowed them access to any world in which their children wanted to live. Although their interest seemed to ebb and flow, the Bachman children would never be denied their cultural birthrights.

"Are you going to finish that?" Daniel said, his big hazel eyes glued to her lunch.

The boy had spent his first three years of life in a state-run Russian orphanage where fetal alcohol syndrome was ubiquitous and adequate nourishment was not, leaving him with a fear of scarcity that, four years later, had yet to be quelled.

"I probably will finish it," Jasmine told him. "But if I decide not to, it's all yours."

Daniel smiled at her, and then, distracted by a stack of pepperoni that Cleo had tossed on his plate, shoved all the slices into his mouth at once.

After everyone had their lunches eaten—either on their own effort or with the help of Daniel—the group split up. With Cleo and Daniel in tow, Marc prepared to go back to the hotel pool.

"Keep Daniel in the shallow end," Laura said as she kissed her husband's cheek. "He thinks the water wings are for babies, so he won't wear them anymore, but he's not ready for anything over his head."

"Don't worry. I brought trunks. I'll be right in there with them."

Laura gave him a sly little smile, saying, "I'm sorry I'm going to miss the public unveiling of the world's palest, skinniest man legs."

"It's too sexy for you," Marc said, pulling his jeans up so that an inch of moon-white ankle shown above his sock. "But here's a sample anyway. Try to show some restraint … if you can."

"Nice," she said, giving him another quick peck on the lips before Cleo and Daniel tugged him towards the exit.

Laura turned to Rosella and Jasmine.

"So, ladies," she said, "it's just us girls. What would you like to do next? Go check out the bazaar? See a demonstration? It's your call. I'm all yours."

Neither girl had the heart to voice what they really wanted, which was to ditch Laura and cruise the festival, looking for cute members of the opposite sex. Rosella's trolling tastes were general, but Jasmine was hoping beyond hope that she might get another glimpse of the young, dimple-cheeked dancer.

"His name is Sage Koskinen," Rosella had told her when the exhibition had ended and they were leaving the auditorium. "He's Findian."

"Findian? What's that?"

"That's what he and his sister Cedar say. Their dad's from Finland. Their mom's from Leach Lake. Our families met at the Mankato powwow. We went to the same school in Minneapolis. They moved to St. Paul right before we came to Fargo. I haven't seen Sage or Cedar for a long time. He's hot, isn't he?"

Jasmine nodded, and then wondered if Rosella was into him, too.

"He's not for me, though," she said. "He's built and all, but I need a tall one. By the way, you're jittering like you just downed a grandé; I'd say you've got it bad for him."

Jasmine flushed, a mixture of pleasure and extreme nervousness smearing her round face with a rosy glow.

Rosella whooped loud enough to turn a few people's heads.

"It's an Indian thing," she, with a devilish grin, said to a passing gawker, and then grabbed Jasmine's arm, saying, "You've got to meet this boy."

But despite Rosella's best effort and to Jasmine's combination of relief and disappointment, they hadn't found Sage or Cedar or any of the Koskinen family.

Laura Bachman's eagerness lowered a notch when she realized that the girls, newly in their teens and mortified by all things "mother," didn't share her enthusiasm. Laura knew that this gradual separation was natural, was necessary, and she had always promised herself that she wouldn't smother, wouldn't micro-manage like her own mother had done, but when the children had come into her life, Laura could never have imagined how much her need to be needed would compete with that promise. She took in the sight of her tall, cattail of a daughter with all her intelligence and charm and confidence, and smiled a weary smile.

"I'll tell you what. If you come with me to the Chinese calligraphy demonstration, I'll make myself scarce afterwards and you girls can explore on your own until Dad comes back to pick us up. Sound good?"

Before Rosella and Jasmine could respond, a deep, alto voice rang out, "Laura. Laura Bachman. Is that you?"

A short curvy woman, decked out in skin-tight jeans, high-heeled western boots, black spandex top, and enough beaded jewelry to confuse her for some kind of mobile American Indian crafts booth rushed over, her sturdy brown arms thrown open wide. She seized Laura, left neon orange lip prints on her cheek, and then repeated the action when she saw Rosella.

"And who's this pretty little Indian gal?" the woman said with a wink when she saw Jasmine. "I'm Wanda, sweetheart. What's your name?"

Jasmine couldn't help but grin with intense satisfaction at being called "a pretty little Indian gal" and she introduced herself, returning the embrace when Wanda doled out her bilious orange seal of unbridled affection, along with a rib-crushing bear hug. Releasing Jasmine, she took a lock of the girl's wavy brown hair and sighed, "Look at the hair on this one. So gorgeous! Do you know how lucky you are? I do because it's my profession. I own a salon. I've been making the world a more beautiful place one head at a time, for twenty-five years."

Wanda herself wore the big, spikey, permed, colored crown of a 1986 pop star, frozen in time by pungent gel and maximum hold hairspray.

"Don't ever put chemicals on this beautiful mane. You don't want to end up with this," she said, her finger causing a crackling sound as she tapped it against the red shoots of fiery frizz jutting from the side of her head. "Someday, I'm going to step out of the shower and find the whole fried-out mess in the drain. Oh, well, I had to practice on someone. Better me than my clients, right?"

Rosella piped up, "We saw Sage earlier, at the dance exhibition."

Wanda beamed, and said, "I'm so proud of that kid. Cedar was signed on to dance, but she blew a knee out playing varsity basketball. Proud of that one, too. She's a starter this year, has the district's highest free-throw percentage. Well, anyway, when she couldn't do it, Sage stepped up and offered to take his sister's place."

"He looked great out there," Laura said. "I hadn't seen him dance since the U of M powwow two years ago."

"He did really look good, didn't he, Jasmine?" Rosella added, savoring the kid caught with her fingers in the cookie dough look that contorted her friend's face.

Wanda Koskinen glanced her direction, and Jasmine managed to squeeze a chirpy little sound that resembled something in the affirmative. The woman graced the girl's embarrassment with a knowing grin.

"We tried to find him afterwards, but we never caught up with him. I wanted him to meet my girl here."

Jasmine gave Rosella a look, a plea for mercy, a pardon from what was perhaps her most embarrassing moment to date. Wanda patted Rosella's shoulder.

"You're still a pistol, aren't you, little Ro? I'm sure Sage would like to meet your friend. She's a cutie. He went home with his dad to bring some lunch to Cedar. He'll be back soon."

She turned to Laura and shrugged.

"You know teenagers. They don't ever want to face the ultimate embarrassment of being caught in some social situation with their mom. It's especially true when it comes to boys. Sage has taken to walking ten paces behind me in public. I kissed him after a junior high football game last fall, and I didn't quit hearing about it for a month."

Laura nodded her agreement, and said, "Well, when your wonderful teenager arrives, let's you and I get some coffee, catch the calligraphy demo, and cut loose from these charming children for a while."

Sage got there a few minutes later with a buddy, and the mothers happily left the adolescent foursome.

"This is my BFF Jasmine," Rosella said, grinning broadly at Sage as she gave her shy companion a nudge towards him.

Jasmine's "Hi" tripped over his, so they tried again with the same result, and then they both laughed the nervous stutter of inexperience before both sets of eyes sought out the safety of the floor. Sage's dimples were on full display, and, not quite knowing what to do with his hands, he shoved them into the pockets of his black warm-up pants. Girls, particularly ones that were as attractive as Ro's friend, shook Sage's senses like a bottle of soda pop, leaving him afraid that if he opened his mouth an explosion of stupidity might pour out. Rosella was different. They had known each other since they were in diapers, and he had come to think of her as a sister, a cousin, or like one of the guys. After several excruciating empty moments, his friend busted through the awkward strands of silence.

"Keon James, African American Indian," he said, directing the introduction, along with a friendlier-than-just-friends look towards Rosella.

Shielded in calm coolness, she said, "African American Indian, huh? Is that your job title?"

Keon shined a smile on her and said, "No, I just like to let girls know that I'm two great tastes that taste great together."

"Maybe the two cancel each other out." Rosella smirked. "That would make you tasteless."

"You're quick," he said, not dimming the hundred-watt grin. "I like that. I really do! Now, what's your name? I'll want it right when I get the heart tattoo."

Jasmine snickered, and, despite herself, Rosella did, too. Grudgingly, she told him her name.

"Intriguing," Keon said, running a hand over his buzzed hair. "And beautiful."

Rosella raised her brows. She wished he would cease and desist with the puppy dog eyes and the dazzling dental display. It wasn't going to work. Keon, like Sage, stood at least a head shorter than Rosella, and she had decided a long time ago that she didn't want a boy whose sight line was on the same level as her rather flat chest. To his credit, Keon would probably end up with a nasty kink in the neck, but he was keeping his eyes on her face nonetheless.

Spectating their friends' huge, dueling personalities allowed Jasmine and Sage to hang in their quiet comfort zones, stealing furtive, approving glances at one another. He liked the waves in her shiny brown hair. She liked his black hoodie printed with a bright morning star pattern across the chest and the AIM and Free Leonard Peltier buttons pinned next to it. She liked the cowlick that looked like a gust of wind was constantly pushing the hair towards his left temple. He liked the way she kept changing into this incredible cotton candy color every time she caught him looking. Finally, Sage worked up some vicarious courage from Keon, who seemed to have melted Rosella a little, and asked Jasmine, "You're from Fargo?"

The moment the words tumbled out, he felt like he should be crowned the king of the obvious, the king of the idiots, the king of all lame losers everywhere. He dug a quarter from his pocket, rolled it around in his palm, and wished it was a chunk of rat poison. He could swallow it and put himself and this poor girl out of their misery. Jasmine brightened and, fingering her turquoise bracelet as if it was a talisman, said, "Yes, but I was born here. Well, not here exactly."

She paused, her brain gummed with the effort not to come off as any more ridiculous than she had just sounded. She should be crowned the queen of the confused, the queen of the idiots, the queen of all the lamest losers everywhere.

"I was born in Minneapolis," Sage said, and then mentally kicked himself for cutting in.

Jasmine's eyes lit up, as she said, "Me, too. That's what I meant to say."

"That's cool," Sage said. "Do you like Fargo better?"

Can't really say. I was a baby when we left Minneapolis. Fargo's okay, especially since Ro moved there. We saw you dance this morning. It was amazing. Who taught you? Your mom?"

"Actually, my dad taught me, after my Grandpa DeerCloud taught him. Grandpa was a traditional dancer, but he started getting arthritis in his back. Before I was born, he asked Dad to learn so that when I was old enough, I'd have someone to teach me."

Sage's story struck, and a fist-sized stone, smoothed by time, dropped into Jasmine's belly. Flashes of her fifth Christmas twinkled on and off: Lars handing her the oblong box wrapped in gold paper; Angela's exuberance as she said that he had picked it out just for Jasmine without her knowledge, without her help; the joyful expression on Lars' face at his new daughter's thrilled response; Angela's restrained, yet detectable discomfort at what had been hidden beneath the shiny paper. Later, as Jasmine had played beneath the prickly artificial boughs, a plastic forest for her plastic Indian doll, she heard their stormy whispers.

"I know your intentions are good, Lars."

"I just thought—"

"I know what you thought, but you are her father. I am her mother. *This* is going to be her life, not the other."

Not long after the holiday, the Indian doll mysteriously vanished. Jasmine cried inconsolably, and her mother replaced the missing doll with two new ones, both blonde-haired, blue-eyed babies, all white lace and pink ruffles. Graciously, but half-heartedly, Jasmine accepted the dolls, played with them, grew to like them, but the replacements couldn't erase the sad question of where her much-loved Indian doll had gone—and why.

The weight of Jasmine's recollection lifted when Keon announced that he was hungry and asked if he could buy Rosella a lemonade. She gave Jasmine a "you owe me big" look, shrugged, and took off towards the food booths, Keon bounding behind her. Once alone, Sage and Jasmine sunk back into awkward silence, both wanting the conversation to continue but neither knowing where to take it. As before, Sage followed his charismatic friend's lead and said, "Want an ice cream?"

Jasmine nodded and they went off in search of some. Walking beside one another was as nerve-racking as their attempts at conversation, and both wondered about taking the other's hand but neither could work up enough courage to do it. Once, the crowd around them closed in, and their shoulders touched, hands brushing, but both froze, neither utilizing the opportunity. By the time they reached a booth selling gelato, their combined doubts, if tangible, could have filled the massive venue. But somehow their shared ingenuousness, inherent shyness, and an unworldliness uncommon to their generation worked as a slow-action bonding agent.

To Sage's horror, with two cups of chocolate cherry gelato on the counter and a line growing behind them, he clawed through his pocket only to find the single quarter. Once again, as he muttered that he had forgotten his wallet, which happened to be in Wanda's purse, and Jasmine paid, he wished the silver coin was rat poison.

"You can buy next time," Jasmine said, feeling his humiliation. "Will you be at some of the Minnesota and Wisconsin powwows this summer? I'm hoping to go with Ro and her family."

This girl, who was so obviously out of his league, actually wanted to see him again, and the thought brought on the deepest dimples yet. He pulled her chair out and then sat next to her, saying, "I definitely will be at most of them ... in my regalia, and with my wallet."

"I like your badges," Jasmine ventured, as she took a scoop of the frozen confection and Sage glanced down at his chest.

"You know about AIM and Peltier?" he asked. She nodded, and excitedly he said, "These belonged to my grandpa. He was at Wounded Knee in the '70s. My mom went to an AIM survival school when she was a kid, a place called Heart of the Earth. My family, well, I'd guess you'd say we are activists. When the NFL team from Washington plays the Vikings next year, a lot of us from the Native community are going to protest in Minneapolis."

For Jasmine, these were exhilarating, yet unnerving, concepts, and the feelings must have shown on her face, because Sage grew quiet. He started to worry that he had said too much, sounded too full of himself. She took another bite of gelato and then said, "I think that's amazingly cool, Sage."

Her voice speaking his name exploded a Black Cat pack of firecrackers in his brain, the heat rushing to his chest and belly. This girl was the bomb.

Keon and Rosella sauntered up a few minutes later; she with a small raspberry lemonade, he with a bratwurst, a slice of sweet potato pie, fries, and some sort of barbeque meat on a stick. They were deep in an impassioned debate about the blurred lines between pop and hip-hop music, and barely glanced in Sage and Jasmine's direction as they dropped themselves into the vacant seats. When the girls went to the ladies' room, Jasmine said, "Looks like you and Keon are connecting."

"Oh, please," Rosella shrieked. "I'm just doing this so you and Sage can hook up. You know I don't go for Keon's type."

"What type? Hot and charming?"

"Whoa, girl! I thought you were all over-heated about Sage. Now you want Keon, too. Look at you, you big virgin slut. Slow down."

With a playful slap at Ro's shoulder, Jasmine giggled.

"I'm just saying Keon is cool and it's obvious that he's totally into you, Ro. Did you catch the way he keeps looking at you?"

Rosella took her phone from her purse, and said, "Yeah, yeah. He stares like a crazy stalker. You're right, though. He's kind of okay, for a short guy, and not everything that comes out of his mouth is *complete* shit."

Rosella scanned the screen as Jasmine ran a brush through her hair and applied peppermint lip gloss.

"Planning on kissing someone?" Rosella teased, and then scoffed. "Look at that. Keon James wants to be friends on Face book."

She tapped the screen with dramatic force, saying, "Ignore. Ignore. Ignore."

Removing her own phone, Jasmine opened the app and saw a request waiting for her, as well. Sage Koskinen's profile picture poured heat from the top of her head to the tip of her toes, much of it concentrating somewhere in between. She hit the "accept" button, and then, curious, she went to Rosella's page. Rosella Bachman and Keon James are now friends. She grinned. This was turning out to be the perfect day.

They found the boys on their phones when they returned to the table, and Keon waved his at Rosella.

"Check it out," he said, gesturing for her to view the Android's display screen.

Her eyes widened and then immediately fell into indignant slits, her mouth a matching angry line, as she bellowed, "Oh, hell, no."

Jasmine peered at the words "Keon James is in a relationship with Rosella Bachman" and smiled, feeling amused at the charismatic humor, but a little disappointed that Sage hadn't posted something similar—even if it was a flirty joke at this point. Sensing that he had just been thrust into another clumsy position because of Keon's insane, no-holds-barred approach to the opposite sex, Sage bumbled around in his pretty girl-fogged brain, searching for the right move. He didn't know how to play the game as well as Keon. Maybe that was because Sage thought of it as more than just something akin to football or basketball or Xbox. For him, it was like powwow dancing. It was more than just learning the correct steps. It was more than just winning contest prize purses. You had to bring real feeling, real emotion. You brought respect and honor for yourself, for your people. You had to put your heart into it. He tapped his own screen a couple of times and then laid it on the table in front of the prettiest girl who had ever shown him interest, an intoxicating girl who smelled faintly of flowers and sweet peppermint. The post stated that he was at the Festival of Nations with Jasmine Sorenson. The point was clear. Rosella and Keon had not been included. She was special. Wordlessly, she grinned, retrieved her iPhone, pressed the "like" button on Sage's post, and included a comment. Sage picked up his device and saw the line of smiling faces. Rosella was hurriedly responding to Keon's status update by saying that he had forgotten to take his meds, which was followed up with a response that said, "Don't need drugs. Got Rosella Bachman." Four sets of fingers flew; a digital dance of twenty-first century young love, as beyond wide spans of plate glass a chilled May rain began to fall, distorting the outer world into a warped watercolor, the day's earlier warmth quickly washing away. Their silent conversations continued, none of them noticing the weather worsening outside the giant windows or the soggy groups of people rushing through the entrances or the one tall Ojibwe man who stopped to wring rain from his long ponytail and wipe his smeared eye glasses against the hem of his shirt. The occupied teens did not see him slide the silver frames onto his ears, the bows disappearing into the few strands of gray at the man's temples, nor did they catch the spark of recognition light up the man's dark eyes when he spotted them and made his way towards their table.

Jasmine didn't look up when the man's amused voice broke the silence directly behind her.

So this is what passes for verbal communication these days?"

Sage's head popped up, followed by Keon's, both boys wearing sheepish grins. Oblivious, Rosella tapped on, but, tuned into Sage's every move, Jasmine noticed his attention shift to something—or someone—behind her. A rocky landslide of thunder rolled over the River Center as she slowly started to turn, until Sage's words yanked her back, punching the air from her lungs, dropping the device from her hand.

"Mr. Bordeaux. Great to see you."

Chapter Eight: Mothers and Their Daughters

The autonomy given them by the Vegas excursion soon crumbled due to a single, short corrosive phone call. Lars had just tucked the bags in the trunk of the Mercedes and Angela was adjusting the seat belt when the cell sounded from the interior of her purse. Recognizing the ring, Lars slid the key into the ignition, but didn't start the engine.

"Are you going to answer?"

Angela retrieved the phone. He took his hand off the key. They both leaned into the car's cool beige leather.

"Hello, Mother."

Lars watched the rearview mirror as a Ford F150 backed up and its mud-crusted bumper came within inches of the Mercedes before the driver hit the brake.

"We're at the airport … Las Vegas … Lars had a dealers' meeting … yes, another one."

He was eager to exit the parking area, but Angela had the odd quirk of growing nauseated when she was on the phone and the car was in motion, so he waited, crossed his fingers that the conversation would stay within its usual brief timeframe, and observed an elderly woman wobbling towards the Cadillac that was in the slot to the left of the Mercedes. *Come on, Susanne. Get to the point already,* he thought.

"She's in St. Paul … No, with the Bachmans … The Bachmans … Yes, those Bachmans … Yes, adopted … No, Mother, I don't know if they attend church."

Angela began to rub her free temple.

"Listen, we have to get going. Lars is driving a car from the dealership … No, his car is fine. He left it for servicing … Okay … Yes … Yes … Okay, I'll tell him …I won't forget … We really do have to get going."

The elderly woman's even more elderly companion swung open the Cadillac's passenger door and Lars held his breath as the woman relinquished the walker, creaked her way down onto the seat, and the geriatric gentleman placed the folded ambulatory aid in the trunk. Thinking that a door ding had been narrowly averted, Lars exhaled a moment too soon, as the woman fumbled for the arm rest, pushing rather than pulling it. Irritated, he turned his attention to Angela, who had the cornered, on-edge look that always came compliments of Susanne.

"Wednesday won't work. Lars will be out of town … Friday?"

Angela looked to him and mouthed, "Dinner."

Forming a circle with two fingers and plunging in and out of the space with the index finger of the other hand, he smiled. Regardless of whether he had just told his mother-in-law what to go do or those were his Friday evening plans, Angela waved off the suggestion.

"We have plans Friday … Sunday?"

Lars shrugged. Susanne possessed the tenacity of a terrier and would continue to chase down dates until she had one in her grip. The old woman in the Cadillac finally managed to shut the car door and Lars could detect light flecks from the Mercedes paint speckling the midnight blue door edge. The old woman gave him an oblivious smile and, reminding himself that he might reach that ripe, fragile age someday, he smiled back.

"All right, Sunday, then … Yes, we're picking her up after we go to the dealership … No, I don't have concerns. Rosella is okay … I know that's not what you mean … Mother, I don't have time to discuss this right now. We'll see you on Sunday … Yes, one o'clock."

Angela ended the call, pitched the cell into the bag with noticeable force, and exhaled a silent cloud of bitten-back words. Lars started the car and put it in reverse. It seemed like Susanne could sense when Angela's serenity level was at its highest, and would, with a calculated comment or inquiry, gouge tiny slow leaks into that contentment. It probably didn't elevate Susanne's own mood, but it was an effective tool in her continued campaign, a campaign to disallow Angela any amnesia of her sins. As long as the mother was unable to forgive, the daughter would not be allowed to forget. Lars took his wife's hand.

"Sunday dinner at the mausoleum. I knew we were overdue. She hasn't sunk her fangs into us since Easter."

Angela resisted the urge to remind him that it was her blood Susanne wanted, not his. She had to give him credit, though; over the years, he had made a valiant effort to redirect the scorn away from her, onto himself, but the harder he tried, the more it seemed to backfire.

***

The first Thanksgiving Lars joined the Erikson's extended family at Kenneth and Susanne's sumptuous, catered feast, he had launched his first futile, yet memorable, attempt.

Kenneth's parents, Susanne's widowed mother, a collection of aunts, uncles, and cousins from both sides, including Susanne's black sheep younger sister Faye, surrounded the massive antique oak dining table that the Erikson family had possessed since Kenneth's great great grandfather had homesteaded the fertile acres along the Red River in 1886. At the head of the table, Kenneth discussed the ever-shifting prices of the agricultural markets with his father, brother, and nephew, while at the opposite end, Susanne had focused her conversational concentrations on the topic of Angela's family planning. A well-meaning cousin had asked if the Sorenson's would be expanding their family anytime soon—a subject neither Angela nor Lars preferred to discuss over turkey and cranberry sauce. Sensing a weakness, Susanne pounced upon the loose spot, prying beneath, her steely tone a sharp, scraping tool, as she usurped their opportunity to answer, inserting what best served her unrelenting strategy.

"Angela's addiction issues are a concern," she said, and sipped from the crystal wine goblet. "Her sobriety must come before all else. Pregnancy is stressful. We would hate to see her relapse."

Susanne affected an expression, which the cousin mistook for motherly devotion, but was one that Angela had seen countless times before, and knew the façade was carved from pure self-satisfaction.

At that point, Lars laid the fork full of candied yam back on the edge of the Havilland china plate, cleared his throat, and said, "Actually, Susanne, our plans have nothing to do with my lovely wife. She is a wonderful mother."

"Yes," Susanne said grudgingly. "And you are a tremendous man for undertaking the responsibility of both Angela and her daughter, but—"

Lars cut her off, directing his response away from Susanne and towards the other guests, raising his voice so that no one would miss what was to come next.

"Ball cancer."

Across the table, Faye chuckled a low throaty laugh.

"Cancer of the balls," Lars stated again, although the hush that had descended upon the large dining room didn't warrant it. "Though I'm more than willing, I am unable."

Kenneth's assumption that his wife had provoked the digression from polite conversation rewarded him a small smirk as he watched with quiet entertainment her split second recoil and then consequent whiplash-quick recovery. Susanne's mother addressed her granddaughter, the volume adjusted to the older woman's substantial hearing loss, as she yelled into Angela's ear.

"Is there something wrong with his gall bladder?"

Angela shook her head, the elderly woman's cloudy eyes grew quizzical, and Faye glanced at her sister, and then to their befuddled mother, saying with gleeful annunciation, "He said 'ball cancer'. Testicular cancer, Mom, like Uncle Gustave."

Susanne affixed a stony mask. Neither Lars nor her eccentric spinster shrew of a sister was going to rip the reins from her hand. She cast a cold critical glance towards her capricious sibling, absorbing the hateful sight of Faye's purple track suit, the crew cut hair gray as a sway-back mare, sun-ravaged face devoid of make-up, and Susanne took the deep loathing that she had always held for this alien creature that had forever flown free at the fringes of their tightly laced family and turned it into a saccharine semblance, which she aimed at Lars.

"Yes, Mother," Susanne said, although her stare was rooted into her son-in-law. "Lars is a survivor, which we are very proud of. By the grace of God, and this young man's strong will, he overcame cancer. It's a blessing we should all be thankful for … especially our Angela."

"Amen," the old woman professed, as her jeweled, bird-like hand absently stroked the double strand of saltwater pearls hidden beneath the linen napkin she tucked into the ruffled collar of her silk blouse. "The good Lord shines his light upon us."

Angela caught her Aunt Faye's quick eye roll and felt a sudden solidarity with the woman whom she had never really been given a chance to know.

The ground was frosted white, the sky a flat blanket of pale gray when Faye took leave for the acreage north of Fargo. Lars and Angela, in the process of making their own escape, joined the robust woman on the circular drive beside her Jeep.

"It's going to snow. I better get home and feed my animals," she said, squinting above a line of evergreens. "It was good seeing you, Angela, and a real pleasure to meet you, Lars."

She reached for Jasmine, who was in her father's arms, grinning at Faye from under a puffy pink woolen bunny hat. The three year old had bonded with the gruff middle-aged woman the moment Faye had fallen to the carpet on all fours and transformed herself into a spirited pony that Jasmine could hand-feed wedges of smoked gouda from Grandma Erikson's cheese platter, and, in horse/human language, told the enamored child that because she had shared the treat, she could have a ride. Jasmine had giggled the entire time as Faye made a slow, safe crawl around the finished basement's perimeter, the other adults looking on with muted amusement and up-tight discomfort. Faye gave Jasmine's fingers a squeeze through the thick pink mitten.

"You'll have to bring the little one to my farm. I have real horses and dogs and goats and ducks and cats."

"Can we now?" Jasmine said, kicking her legs and bouncing on Lars hip

Angela thanked her aunt for the invitation and said that they would visit soon, to which Faye responded, "Please do. I missed out with you

… and your brother. Maybe we can get to know each other now."

Angela nodded and the women entered a brief awkward embrace. Faye gave Lars a hearty pat on the back and said, "Take good care of my niece. The shiny ones in there—" She jabbed a thumb in the direction of the hulking Tudor-style house. "—they don't value real beauty. Never have, probably never will. I can see that you do, though. That's a rare quality in folks these days; one that I admire. Be well. I'll see you soon."

Beyond that holiday, Susanne would continue her passive, and often outwardly aggressive, assaults and Lars would play defense with similar results, but Faye became a refreshing connection to family that lent a little balance to the situation. Like the details of their Vegas trips, they kept their visits to Faye's acreage covert. Both Lars and Angela knew if Susanne discovered the close ties that had formed between them and her shunned sister, more pettiness would ensue, so the Sorenson's added another secret to their increasing collection.

***

"Maybe we should bring Aunt Faye with us. That would be a nice garlic necklace for your mother, wouldn't it?" Lars said, as he merged onto University Avenue and sped away from Hector International. "I still can't wrap my head around her need to squash anyone who lives outside what *she* deems normal. It seems pathological, like she can't control the impulse to punish everyone simply because they're not her."

Angela, who had been quiet and removed since the call, finally spoke.

"That's how she sees it. Her drinking is social; mine was alcoholism. Her pageants were character-builders. Faye working on the farm, alongside the men, was freakish. She is growing her inheritance because she leased the acres to a fracking company. Faye is squandering hers because she sold the land and is wasting all the cash on stray dogs and rescue horses. That's always been the view from Susanne's tower: "hers are beauty marks; everyone else's … birthmarks."

"You'd think by now, we'd all be immune to her superiority complex."

Although he hadn't meant it to be, the comment felt like an assessment of her mood, and Angela tensed, pulling free from her husband's hand. He couldn't ever have complete understanding about the negative effect that Kenneth's distance and Susanne's scorn had rendered. His parents had supported him through his decision to study business rather than go to medical school, the diagnosis and treatment of his cancer, and the shaky initial quarters of the import car dealership they'd invested money in so that their son could construct for himself a financially sound future. Dr. Sorenson and Dr. Sorenson were warm, receptive grandparents, unpretentious members of a usually pretentious income tax bracket, and accepting of religion, but not participatory in it. In other words, Lars parents were the antithesis of Kenneth and Susanne.

"By the way," Angela said, "Mother wanted me to let you know that she pulled strings, called in favors, and arranged a date for Miss North Dakota to make an appearance for the spring sales event."

It was all about control. Lars had discouraged Susanne when she had mentioned that her influence with pageant executives could make things happen, but his disinterest might as well have been a gilded invite for her to push onward. She loved to have a manicured finger in everyone's pie. He shook his head.

"Isn't the young woman's duties supposed to center around philanthropic

Events? It seems so 1950s to have a girl against a backdrop of cars just to make a buck. I don't like it. It's cheesy—maybe even borderline sleazy."

"To Susanne, feminism is a dirty word. A pretty face is a woman's most valuable commodity and she's almost used hers up, so she likes to trade behind the scenes now, wheeling and dealing in fresh faces. Look on the bright side: your prime demographic is middle-aged rich men, and if perky little Miss North Dakota runs a hand along the hood of a BMW and says that she would love a car like that, I bet the odds of that car selling will sky rocket. Some horny fifty-year-old with a comb-over, a nightstand full of Viagra, and an active imagination, will make an offer. Fantasy fueling finance ... it's the American way."

"Damn. Listen to you. I should hire you to run my advertising department," Lars said, turning into Valley Luxury Motors' lot. "As much as you'd like to deny it, you inherited your mother's savvy."

"No, I didn't," Angela snapped. "I just see things for what they are. A realist doesn't have to like the reality. I was just trying to find some benefit to all her manipulative bullshit."

He parked in front of the show room, turned off the Mercedes, and looked at her. She crossed her arms tightly over her chest and stared at a trio of dull brown sparrows flapping in a muddy puddle of run-off. Vegas had vanished; only Fargo remained.

"It was a joke, Angela; just a piss poor attempt to lighten the mood. You are nothing like Susanne. I shouldn't have made the comparison—not even in jest."

She responded with a slight nod, keeping her attention outside the car, avoiding her husband's face, as troubling thoughts pooled into a headache behind her right eye.

A tall, thin man with close cut black hair, a goatee, and a windbreaker that bore the dealership logo exited the open bay of the service center and waved. Lars pressed the window button, and called, "Hey, Chad. Good to see you, man. Should I pull this one on into the wash rack?"

Chad gave the thumbs up. Lars started the car and drove towards the open bay. Once inside, he suggested that Angela wait until he had transferred their luggage to his Jaguar, which sat, polished to a glossy black sheen, in the next service stall. She stayed put, not wanting to make direct contact with the shop's metallic squeals, clangs, and bangs, acrid air, thick with exhaust fumes, used motor oil, brake fluid, and engine solvents, and the male mechanics who stole lecherous glances at the boss's wife when they thought the boss wasn't looking. She wasn't in the mood to handle any of that; the pounding in her head warned her of it. Actually, she wasn't sure if there was anything beyond the Mercedes' smooth beige leather, the inconspicuousness of its tinted glass, and the protection of its muted, almost noiseless, interior, that she could deal with at that point. German engineering excellence might be able to cocoon and protect her from noise and fumes and intrusive male eyes, but Susanne had already infiltrated, and the shard of thought she had planted spun and spun, around and around, in Angela's mind. She rested an elbow against the door and massaged her right temple, but the sharp, piercing soreness wouldn't subside.

Damn her mother for having asked the question. Damn her ability to sniff out every one of Angela's qualms, every one of her insecurities, every one of her misgivings. Damn Susanne for dredging up the thing that Angela had managed to keep hidden below the surface, while in Vegas, while concentrating on the needs of a marriage, while away from Jasmine. Angela hadn't spoken to anyone, not even Lars, about the uneasy feelings that had crept up in the last year or so, the feeling of discontent and loss that constricted her chest as she watched their daughter grow and change and shift closer and closer to the darker features of her birth father and farther and farther from the face Angela found in her own mirror. How could she admit to the psychological disarray Jasmine's friendship with Rosella had unleashed? How could she tell anyone that she wished to forbid Jasmine from contact with the Bachmans' adopted Ojibwe daughter? She had gone so far as to balk at the plan to include Jasmine on the Bachman's annual trip to the Festival of Nations, had suggested to her that Aunt Faye would love a visit while she and Lars were in Vegas, had made the empty promise that the Sorenson's could go as a family next year, but, in the end, her hasty, reactive suggestions could not dissuade the girl, whose own unspoken desire proved stronger than that of her mother. Lars, certain that his wife's nervousness was just an affliction common amongst parents, especially mothers of only children, reassured Angela that their daughter was responsible, intelligent, and would be under the supervision of adults who had gone through the rigorous examinations of three separate adoption agencies. He had given their daughter some cash and a pre-paid Visa card, and told her to text her mother often so that she wouldn't have separation anxiety. Lars and Jasmine had shared a laugh and a hug, and then the girl had turned to Angela.

"Are you really going to miss me that much, Mom?" Jasmine had said, throwing her arms around Angela's neck and burying her face in the blonde waves of silky hair.

"Of course," she had replied, not quite able to provide enough filler to hide the hollowness where maternal warmth should have resided.

Yes, damn Susanne for intruding into that deep dark cave, torch in fist; damn the imposing light it had shed; and damn the light's revelation, for in it Angela had seen what she had failed to see before. She and Susanne were not so different after all.

Outside the Mercedes, Lars said something, Chad nodded enthusiastically, laughed, and then waved a man in a coverall over from under a hoisted Saab. Lars said something and they all roared raucous baritone laughter. From behind dark, shatter-resistant glass, Angela watched. Like related to like, comfort derived from being among one's own kind, laws of attraction that guided us outside our conscious knowing; this was what she saw, what distressed her about their daughter's future, from what Angela herself had too often over the course of her life felt: separate.

Lars directed Chad over to the driver's side door of the Mercedes, opened it, popped the trunk, and, leaving the door ajar, pointed out the minor damage. The tall man squatted, ran a finger over the panel, and said, "No sweat. We've got touch-up this color. What dinged you?"

A Caddie," Lars said. "Figures, right?"

"Damn domestics."

Both men chuckled. Angela closed her eyes.

Chapter Nine: A Thousand Words Unpainted

The man named Bordeaux bent to retrieve the phone from the floor where the girl had dropped it, set it on the table beside her, and commented that the hot pink protective cover had come in handy. He only glanced at her profile, only caught her name in passing, but neither scratched deep enough into his memory. She wasn't one of his students, nor was the willowy girl who had whipped around to stare as if he were some high-profile headliner rather than a woefully underpaid middle school history teacher. He had even thought for a moment that she had snapped a picture of him, but then she deposited the smart phone into a pocket and the notion suddenly seemed ridiculous. In addition to his duties in the classroom, he was the district's Native American student advisor, and this position brought him contact with many families throughout the Indian community, making it likely that the gawky girl with the glossy bobbed black hair and challenging gaze that, for whatever reason, seemed vaguely accusatory, recognized him from somewhere. He couldn't place her or her shy friend, who kept her back to him during the entire brief exchange, even as she had mumbled, "Thanks." The Koskinen boy had said something about the girls being friends from Fargo. Bordeaux had nodded and said that he would see the young men at school and went on his way.

But hours later, in a Victorian tucked at the corner of two quiet South St. Paul streets, as the man dozed before the fireplace's last glowing embers, and shadows played out stories in the darker corners of the room, the random pieces assembled themselves. Jarred from the edge of sleep by their possible revelation, Bordeaux sat bolt upright and said the shy girl's name aloud.

***

Jasmine discovered that the man's name was Jack.

"Maybe he's an uncle or a cousin," Rosella had whispered while the girls sat cross-legged on the hotel bed and investigated the photo on Ro's tablet. "His last name's Bordeaux. He almost has to be related to you in some way or another. How many different Indian families can there be with that name? He's connected somehow. I just know it."

By the time they had left the festival and reached the Marriott, the crazy collection of food and emotions stirred Jasmine's stomach into an upheaval, and she cowered from her friend's zealous onslaught. Ever since she shared the single shred of information she had on her biological father, she had regretted it. Immediately, Rosella had set forth on a mission to convince her that they should search for him, and despite Jasmine's protestations and her admission that she didn't want to break the promise to Lars, Ro, who would probably never have access to her own origins, kept up the campaign. Jasmine pulled her knees into her chest and pressed her face against them, rubbing her forehead over the soft fabric of the leggings she wore, trying to block out her friend's insistent chatter, trying to keep herself from throwing up. She failed at both, but as Jasmine clung to the cool porcelain, offering tears and everything she had eaten that day, Rosella finally ceased the running monologue about Jack Bordeaux. Laura Bachman checked Jasmine's temperature, brewed a cup of ginger tea with the bags that she always carried, and, when Jasmine said that her stomach felt settled, Laura herded both girls off to bed.

"Maybe you have a mild case of love sickness," Mrs. Bachman said, as she adjusted the blanket around Jasmine's shoulders and gave her arm a gentle pat, to which the girl managed a weak smile.

When her mother had closed the adjoining room's door behind her, Rosella spoke in a low whisper, as not to wake Cleo and Daniel.

"I'm really sorry, Jas. I don't mean to be so insensitive. It was a huge day for you: meeting Sage, and then … well, you know, the whole other thing, which I'm not going to bring up again. If you ever want to talk about it, I'm here, but no pressure, okay? I'm just so sorry. What truly sucks is that I introduced you to, and then made you toss, your first Indian taco."

Jasmine snorted, and then reached for her friend's hand, giving it a light squeeze, appreciative that Rosella's serious side always had a short shelf life.

It's all right, Ro. I get that you're just trying to help, and I love you for that, but it's scary, you know? Part of me wants to look for my connection to being Ojibwe, like if I had names and faces and stuff, it would be more real, but I love my parents, and even though I think Dad would be all right with it, I have a feeling that Mom would totally freak."

There existed another deeper trepidation, one that Jasmine reserved; the one that could hurt Rosella if she voiced it. What if, at the end of her searching, she found a family who did not claim a half-breed girl, a girl they didn't remember, a girl that they didn't have any desire to know? What if Dave Bordeaux didn't want her? What if he had never wanted her? If it had been up to him, would she, like Ro, have been dumped somewhere, a living, breathing freewill donation for strangers in need of children? Rejection was a distinct, depressing possibility that was made all the more probable by the fact that while Jasmine had not been seeking him, Dave Bordeaux had *not* been seeking her, either. The highways, the phone lines, a simple internet search engine were as available to him as they were to anyone else, and yet, all these years, nothing but nothing. His silence, his invisibility, his existence as only the brown of her hair, the tone of her skin, the square shape of her shoulders, seemed to say it all. Dave Bordeaux did not care.

Rosella's voice reached softly into the pause, saying, "Maybe that's why he's never tried to find you."

"What do you mean?"

"Because of your mom. No offense, Jas, but I find her a little intense sometimes."

"*My* mom? Seriously?"

Rolling onto her side, Rosella propped on one elbow.

"Absolutely. She's got that Angelina Jolie vibe: super beautiful and super bad at the same time. I bet she could kick ass with the best of them. I wouldn't want to mess with her."

Jasmine flashed on Angela doing Pilates in their home gym, the most physically active thing Jasmine had ever seen her do, and the thought, along with Ro's assessment, equaled sheer amusement.

"Sure, whatever. Mom's *so* intimidating, he's terrified. And I say, 'Afraid of what?' What would she do? Take off a Jimmy Choo and give him a nasty bruise? Come on."

"I'm just saying your Mom gives me this look sometimes when I'm over at your house, like she thinks I'm up to something, like she doesn't really trust me. Believe me, it's very prickly. I don't know. Maybe it's because I'm Indian."

Jasmine bristled, shifting to face the accusation head on.

That's complete shit, Rosella! I suppose you think I can't see it because I'm not Indian enough, right? My mother only uses her suspicious bitch look for the real deal, like you."

"No! That's *not* what I'm saying. You're her daughter. Of course she's not going to look at you that way. Half of you is her."

Jasmine sweat beneath her over-sized T-shirt, her stomach had begun to tie itself into another knot, and she had the overwhelming urge to shove Rosella off the bed, but she stopped herself. A violent act would probably just fuel Rosella's foolish fire. Words were her only logical weapon.

"So what *are* you saying? That she has something against Indians? Because if that's what you mean, we both know the word for that."

It crackled, white-hot between them, but neither girl touched it. They let their silence hold its danger, its destructiveness, its uninvited illumination, until it became deafening.

"My mother is a good person," Jasmine finally said, anger clipping each syllable into sharp-edged shrapnel.

It was the kind of perfunctory proclamation that rises at the dawn of a waning belief, at the first hint of an ugly truth, but both girls knew its placebo relief, no matter how temporary, was the only mend their relationship had in that moment.

"She is," Rosella replied.

"I want to go to sleep now. My stomach hurts."

"Okay."

They turned their backs towards one another. One girl soon slept. The other did not.

***

"You look tired," Angela said, pivoting in the Jaguar's front seat to glance at her daughter.

Slumped and sullen, Jasmine sat behind Lars, the comment seeming to barely register. "Big weekend, huh, kid?" he said, less finely tuned to the teen girl's mood fluctuations than was his wife. "You'll have to hit the sack early tonight. Isn't tomorrow the start of finals week?"

"Yes."

"Are you all studied up and ready to rock the honor roll?"

"Sure."

Angela caught the girl's exaggerated eye roll, and dipped a tentative finger in, testing the communication climate, asking, "Anything else bothering you?"

Jasmine shrugged, her eyes darting towards her lap, and then towards the window, anywhere but on her mother, as she said, "No, not really. I'm just tired."

"Rosella's mom said that she thought you girls might have had a falling out because the trip home was unusually quiet. Did something happen?"

Even in the early evening's semi-darkness, Angela could see tension working like a puppeteer, tugging Jasmine's shoulders upwards and the corners of her mouth downwards. She could feel the girl shrinking back, avoiding whatever sting the topic wielded, and Angela hesitated for a moment, aware that what she was about to do lacked consideration, lacked character, and, perhaps most of all, lacked courage. The shell had opened, though, its lovely halves separated by some nameless irritant, and within Angela saw a tiny imperfect pearl. The cravenness would mark the victory as small, but she plucked it loose, all the same.

"Rosella and you spend a lot of time together," she started. "Even the best of friends can grow annoyed with one another after a while. I can't remember the last time you girls spent more than a day apart. I'm sure whatever has come between you will resolve itself, but, for now, a little break would probably do you good."

The Jag slowed as they rolled into the sleepy Sunday evening atmosphere of the subdivision, turned down the cul-de-sac, and pulled in front of their four-car garage. Lars pressed the opener, nosing the sleek black car into its space beside Angela's white Mercedes. With the advantage of having a captive ear quickly vanishing, Angela bit down harder, working her teeth, testing the surface.

"Some breathing room, then? Can we agree that you'll take a small vacation from Rosella?"

Jasmine put a hand on the door, shrugged, and said, "I guess so," before hauling herself from the back seat, and moving to the trunk, where she waited.

"Isn't Ro her best friend?" Lars asked his wife, with the understood implication that "best" meant "only." "Are you sure separation is the answer here?"

Angela's look held its own easily-read implication.

"All right," he said, pushing the trunk release, their daughter blocked from view by the raised lid. "Not sure that's the route I'd take, but then I've never been a teenage girl, so my instincts will concede to your experience."

By the time they were out of the car, Jasmine had hoisted their roller bags, along with her own, from the trunk, and parked them beside the door that lead into the mud room. Lars laid an arm over her shoulder as he unlocked the deadbolt. Despite the pampered life they were providing for her, the girl remained thoughtful, empathetic, helpful, and inexplicably unspoiled. Feeling sadness seeping like icy water, shaping his daughter's sloped neck into curved, worn stone, Lars' jaw stiffened. The older Jasmine got, the less effectual he had become, and, sometimes he looked back at the days when a Band-Aid or a cookie or a silly pun about a mushroom claiming that he was a "fun guy" would soothe the hurt, bring a smile, turn tears to laughter. He had the fix then. He was the hero. He was the first line of defense between her and the wild unfairness of the world. Now, although his protectiveness still reared up at the slightest hint of their daughter's dismay, he often found himself feeling uncertain as to how he should apply it, and before he could work it out, Angela stepped in—and Lars stepped back.

Jasmine moved from under his arm, through the open door, Angela close on her heels, and as the girl stopped to untie her running shoes, her mother flowing around her on into the kitchen, Lars was taken up by a strange urgency. From the doorway, before he entered, he said, "I love you, kid."

With a watery half-smile, she glanced up from a knot that had formed, her muted expression clutching him by the throat.

"I love you, too," she said and paused, her fingers digging at the unrelenting lace. Then, as if driven by a necessity that neither he nor she ever forget who they were to one another, she added, "Dad."

Later, as Lars engrossed himself in a sports documentary, Angela carried a stack of folded laundry upstairs to Jasmine's room. She expected to find the girl at the desk, preparing for exams, but instead she found Katniss curled on the chair and Jasmine's laptop open, but in sleep mode. From the en-suite bathroom, Angela heard the shower's vigorous hiss, accompanied by the high, breathy, down-hearted strains of some sweet young alternative songstress, oozing like cough syrup from the Bluetooth speakers. Setting the clothes atop the dresser, Angela looked at the computer again. Total access at any time; that was the stipulation Lars placed upon Jasmine's use of her devices. Anything that gave the girl lines of communication to the entire rest of the planet warranted parental monitoring, and although they had yet to suspect a need for an involuntary cyber search and seizure, they retained the right, often reminding Jasmine of it. Did she have any grounds to exercise the authority now? Wouldn't it simply be an invasion of privacy, spurred by her own corrupted curiosity and insecurity?

The snow-white cat stared at her through slits, the lush tip of her tail twitching. Angela's hearing stretched across the room and, affixing to the sounds that provided her cover, she touched a single key and the laptop awakened. A musical flourish alerted new mail, and she hurriedly maximized the window. A single unread message from rojibwe_bachman@gmail.com waited in the in-box. The subject line read "Awesome Festival Pix." Bypassing the message body, Angela opened the attachments. She didn't expect to unearth anything monumental, just the usual pictorial topics girls of their age photographed, but since she had leaped into these private waters, she felt bound to the mission at hand. Shifting rapidly from one to another, she caught glimpses of Jasmine grinning over an Indian taco; a handsome boy in a black native design hooded sweatshirt; the same boy in dance regalia, blurred by motion; Rosella and Jasmine, arms around each other, heads pressed together, wearing identical huge garish sunglasses shaped liked stars. The farther she went, the worse Angela felt, and she hit the halfway point in the collection, deciding she would cease and desist her feeble foray, but before the decision could reach her finger, she had opened another photo file.

With that, as if in an ominous dream, all the layers of her life peeled apart and flew in the air, landing in a sequence that no longer made sense. The man in the picture belonged to a rawer, deeper layer. He did not belong here and now, in her daughter's room, on her daughter's screen, anywhere in Angela's present life. She blinked, a nervous twitch arrhythmically jerking the corner of her right eye, and she grabbed the back of the desk chair, feeling one world spinning so quickly around another she couldn't recover equilibrium. In profile, mouth slightly open, as if he were speaking to someone outside the snapshot's edge, the photographed man seemed unaware someone was capturing his image. Although he wore glasses, and a thread or two of gray unrolled back from his temples, Angela had recognized Jack Bordeaux at first glance. A decade had only enhanced his striking good looks and honed a self-assuredness into his posture. For more than a year, the younger version of this man had slept on the other side of a thin apartment wall from Angela. The youngest of the brood of Bordeaux children, Jack had always seemed the most likely to break the family's cycle of addiction, violence, and ignorance; a prediction adduced by his enrollment at the University of Minnesota. Angela's support of Jack's actions, and the suggestion that Dave should also apply for a tribal scholarship, had mutated into one of their ugliest fights.

"So you got a thing for college assholes? My high school drop-out dick ain't good enough for you no more?" Dave had spat, and lurched up from the mattress, grabbing her by the arm and dragging her naked from their bed. "You want to wrap those lily white legs around my pissant brother? Joke's on you, bitch."

He shoved her out of the room, into the hall.

"His college boy pecker don't get hard for your type," he laughed, meanness and jealousy choking him as he slammed the door, leaving her to hide in the bathroom for the remainder of the long night, huddled in a dirty towel.

Jack was the one to happen upon Angela, asleep in the grungy tub. He had given her a pair of his sweatpants and a flannel shirt. He had gone to the kitchen and made her coffee and a scrambled egg.

The man in the picture appeared healthy: lean, clear-complexioned, well-groomed, and Angela hoped that this ascertainment translated into a contented life. But regardless of her wishes for him, his pixelated presence was unwelcome here. Who had taken the picture? Was it Jasmine? If not, was she there when it was snapped? Had she already seen it, and, if so, did she know who this man was?

"What are you doing?"

She whirled around, her heart thrashing like a hooked fish. Behind Angela, Jasmine stood towel drying her hair. The girl moved closer and caught sight of the computer screen's content. Trying to read her daughter's reaction, Angela said, "I was looking at some festival pictures. Rosella sent them."

Angela turned calmly back towards Jack Bordeaux's image and asked, "Who is this?"

Jasmine took a brush from the pocket of the robe she wore and began attacking tangles as she threw the screen another glance, shrugged, and said, "I don't know. A boy Ro used to go to school with knew him. I think he's a teacher or an advisor or something."

"I see," Angela said. "Did you take the picture?"

"Ro probably took it. She takes pictures of everything. Did she send the one of Mr. Bachman's super white feet? Pretty gross. She also snapped photos of all the food everybody ate and posted it on Instagram."

Jasmine continued, nerves flooring the accelerator.

"She also does really cool videos and puts them on YouTube. Ro never lays her phone down, never goes anywhere without an iPad or something. She's a million times worse than I am when it comes to device pacifiers. Isn't that what Dad jokes that they are, big kid pacies?"

Angela finally cut in, saying that it was late, that Jasmine needed her rest, and that the girl should be going to bed soon. She closed the computer's open applications and said, "I'll shut this down for you now."

"Sure. Thanks," Jasmine said, fighting to control the tremor she felt throughout her body from effecting her voice as she went back into the bath and, with shaky hands, hung the towel on the rack.

Angela gave her a cool peck on the cheek, left the room and closed the door. The girl collapsed on the bed, the icy sheen of stress causing her to shiver. Beyond the wall, in the darkened hallway, Angela pressed a fingertip to her face, where the corner of her eye continued to spasm.

Chapter Ten: Lesser Evil

Jack Bordeaux plodded into the kitchen, late Sunday morning, still wearing flannel boxers and a plaid fleece robe, belt untied, one end dragging, and rubbed the grit from his eyes. Isaac TwoBears looked up from the round oak table where he had a newspaper section unfurled and was busily clipping and categorizing coupons.

"Good morning, Sunshine," he said, and laid the scissors down to look at his disheveled husband. "You look like the before picture in a sleep aid commercial. Rough night?"

Jack halted his singularly-focused drive towards the coffee pot long enough to plant a kiss on Isaac's cheek.

"You didn't feel me tossing and turning?" he asked as he poured an extra-large Circle of Life Pendleton mug to the brim and took a loud scalding slurp.

"You know me: I'm the after shot of that ad. I sleep like a log that's been carved into a dead baby," he joked and began clearing paper clutter. "What was the source of your shitty night's sleep? Was I snoring? I forgot to buy those nasal strips. Promise I won't forget next time. We now have a coupon for a dollar off."

Jack carried his coffee to the table and sat down, saying, "You were really sawing a chunk of wood. Let's hope it didn't end up as something *that* morbid. It's not why I was awake, though. Heavy thoughts followed by weird dreams, but please do pick up those damn strips."

As was their ritual on Sunday mornings, they abandoned the usual healthy Greek yogurt smoothies they grabbed on the run during the work week and enjoyed a leisurely brunch that mainly consisted of comfort food favorites. It satiated them until the next Sunday ritual rolled around and Jack popped enough corn to fill a gigantic bowl—also known as the Snack Dumpster—and they curled up on the sectional to binge watch The Walking Dead, Shameless, or Game of Thrones.

"So … what's it going to be?" Isaac said as he rose from the table and opened the refrigerator. "Oven French toast with caramel pecan sauce? Sausage gravy and buttermilk biscuits? I could do that frittata you like, the one that has the pancetta and Gouda. They had some beautiful wild asparagus at the farmer's market yesterday. I bought two pounds of it."

Jack yawned, took another gulp of coffee, and said, "Don't care. You choose."

Grabbing the asparagus, Isaac laid the spring green bundle of spears in the sink and went back for the carton of brown eggs, meat, and a half wheel of cheese, saying, "Frittata it is then. Come wash these and I'll interpret your nightmares for you."

Downing more fuel for the requested task, Jack poured the mug full again, and began rinsing the asparagus under cold water while Isaac tossed a pat of butter and some olive oil into a deep cast iron skillet. With Food Network expertise, Isaac broke a half dozen eggs with one hand. While he whisked in a liberal splash of heavy cream, he asked, "What's bothering you? Must be tough if it's messing with both your sleep and your dreams. Is it work? Are you bucking heads with administration again?"

"I'm always bucking heads there, but it's not that. It's family related ... at least I think that it's family related."

Jack slid a chef's knife from a drawer, arranged the spears along the wood cutting board, and sliced the tender tips free.

"What do you mean?" asked Isaac as he adjusted the gas flame beneath the skillet and took a bamboo spoon from a crock beside the stove, swirling the melting butter through the heating oil.

"Yesterday, when I stopped at the festival, I think I ran into a niece."

"Which niece? My side or yours?"

My side."

"Well, that narrows it down," Isaac said, a sarcastic grin appearing. "From about fifty possibilities down to forty-something."

Like Bordeaux's, Isaac TwoBears' expansive family seemed to multiply so easily and so often it was difficult to keep track of everyone, especially the younger additions, and Isaac joked that their families' standard greeting should be, "Guess who's knocked up!" The previous summer, Jack's sister Renee and her oldest daughter were both unexpectedly expecting, which resulted in the not-so-uncommon occurrence of an uncle arriving in the world after his nephew. To add a bit more twist to the already gnarled family tree, the babies' fathers turned out to be half-brothers. Isaac said that their family made the Kardashians look like the Cunninghams, and that some industrious member really should pitch their story as a reality series. Not as tongue-in-cheek about the matter, Jack had always been troubled by how seldom adequate parenting followed the unplanned procreating, and although he secretly envied the position of moral superiority that Isaac took over their heterosexual counterparts, Jack's sense of personal responsibility towards the next generations of children—both in and outside of their family—restricted his sense of humor. His chosen profession brought a sobering daily reminder that the top-heavy, twisted Bordeaux and TwoBears family trees were but two in a vast forest where few found enough nurture, few found any light. It was made of too many shallow roots, dwarfed fruits, stunted saplings; a dark place where you could get horribly lost, where you could fall without anyone present enough to hear you.

Jack offered the cutting board to Isaac and he took it, dumping the asparagus into the pan. Leaning against the marble counter, Jack said, "I think I saw Jasmine."

Isaac's memory clicked through names, trying to attach a face or the right parent or a correct location, but he was at a loss.

"Jasmine. Is that Lionel's kid? Is she the one out in Montana who did time for vehicular manslaughter?"

Jack shook his head and reached for his coffee.

"Do you remember me ever talking about Angie?"

"Vaguely. Did she date one of your brothers?"

"Yeah," Jack said. "She and Dave were together for a while. They lived at Mom's when I started college. They had a kid."

Isaac added shallots, gently mixing the vegetables, as he said, "What happened?"

Jack shared what he knew of Angie's exodus. "As far as I know, she went back to North Dakota. There was a lawyer involved. Dave signed over his parental rights. No big surprise there, right?"

So you think you spotted his daughter yesterday? What did you say?"

"The thing is, when I saw her, I didn't know who she was. Even after I heard her name, it didn't hit me until last night that she might be my niece. The last time I saw her, she was just learning to walk and this Jasmine was with a couple of my students. That would probably make her thirteen, maybe fourteen. You can see why my brain lagged on it."

"Of course," Isaac agreed. "I'm guessing she didn't recognize you, either. I don't think I have any of my own clear memories until I was about four, and those are pretty sketchy. Would there be some way you could find out if she's who you think she is?"

"I doubt it," jack said. "It would be pretty inappropriate for me to question my students about the identity of some underage girl, and since those boys are the only connection I have, well, enough said."

When all ingredients were added, Isaac popped the frittata in the oven and made another pot of coffee, and then warmed cranberry walnut muffins to tide them over while the egg dish baked. He and Jack returned to their places at the table, where Isaac continued the discussion, although Jack's fatigue had begun to deplete his patience with it.

"Are you going to mention it to Dave then?"

"It's probably just a weird hunch anyway, and, on the outside chance I'm right, what would it matter? Dave's already got enough baggage he can't handle. I'm not going to actively seek out more to throw on the pile."

"Too true," Isaac said, both men then lapsing into weighty silence, the thought heavier than what either wanted to carry forward into such a crisp bright May morning, into the warm sanctuary of the Victorian's lemon yellow kitchen, into the stability for which they had labored so hard to create within this life they shared.

They devoured the frittata, Jack cleaned up the kitchen, Isaac took Godiva, their chocolate lab, for a ride to his construction company's current building site so that she could run off energy in the adjacent field, and when they reconvened on the sofa that night, neither man mentioned Dave nor the potential sighting of his daughter again. With another hectic work week bearing down upon them, the only child they could deal with was the flop-eared, four-legged one stretched out between them, begging for popcorn.

Like the delicate scent of the blossom for which the girl was named, the chance encounter lingered faintly in Jack's afterthought, but eventually faded; moving on being the only prudent move.

***

After Sunday, after she had caught Angela spying, after she had developed an unshakeable sense that her mother had reacted with as much dishonesty as she to the photo, Jasmine moved cautiously. She saved the picture that had created Angela's tell-tale eye twitch to a thumb drive, hid the storage device amongst the others in her school bag, deleted it from her phone, and kept the Monday morning breakfast conversation a clean-cut, choreographed exchange that left out more than it included. Although her anger at Rosella hadn't subsided completely and she had agreed to Angela's break proposal, when Jasmine got to school, the girl was the first person she sought out. In the few minutes before last bell rang, Jasmine rattled off the entire incident, to which Rosella nodded and then slipped an arm around her best friend's shoulder.

"That's some wild shit," Rosella said, shoving a coat and a messenger bag inside her locker and slamming the door. "On top of it, you and I are supposed to take a break? That's just cray-cray, Jas. We had a difference of opinion. It wasn't like we ended up in some hair-pulling, kicking, clawing bitch brawl. I hate to point out the ugly and the obvious, but this only supports what I was trying to tell you. Your mother does not like me."

Rosella's assumption no longer seemed arguable under current conditions, and Jasmine's residual antagonism melted away under the heat of apologetic shame.

"I'm here though, aren't I?"

"Yeah," Rosella said, running a hand over her hair to smooth it. "But what about non-school hours?"

"No, but just for a while, I think. Just until ...." Jasmine trailed off as she realized that she didn't have a clue. In the previous night's tossing and turning, she hadn't waded through that thought. All she knew was that Angela's suspicious behavior disturbed her, chipped away at the respect Jasmine was expected to have for her mother, and inched Rosella's allegations closer towards the realm of believability, which lead her to the conclusion that she needed her best friend now more than ever. As Jasmine rushed off to natural sciences and Rosella headed in the opposite direction to world history, Rosella pivoted, back peddled, and shouted, "Don't stress it, Jas. We'll figure it out."

Over lunch, as they both munched on veggie wraps, Rosella said, "So, I'm curious. Did your mom say anything about the pictures of Sage?"

"She didn't mention it. All her weirdness was over the one of you-know-who."

"You-know-who? Paranoid much? She's not lurking behind you."

"I know, but I don't want the name floating out there for anyone to overhear. It's super private to me."

"Okay," Rosella agreed, not wanting to tread over that still-sensitive ground too heavily. "I get that. Why I ask about Sage is that I had a plan that could either prove or disprove my theory about your mom and the whole Indian thing. Let's say, hypothetically, that I'm not one of her faves because of my personality. I've got a really loud laugh; maybe it annoys her. Maybe she thinks I have poor table manners."

To accentuate the point, she flung a guacamole-coated cucumber slice off of her wrap sandwich. It landed in the center of the table and Jasmine laughed.

"Perhaps her freaky response to Bor-—oh, sorry—you-know-who is because he's a man. You know, like some creepy pedophile thing. Maybe she truly doesn't recognize him and she just wants to protect you from skanky oldster guys who might be into underage girls."

Jasmine shook her head, saying, "I told her he was a teacher. She still seemed totally unhinged. You should have seen her, Ro. She gets this eye spasm when she's really about to come undone. Grandma Erikson does it to her sometimes, and I saw it once when she accidently backed Dad's Jag over our neighbor's cat. It doesn't happen over small stuff. The twitch only comes out for something major, and it was the worst one I've ever seen."

"My mom's a heel bouncer. If I see that Sketcher going up and down, I know I better steer clear."

Jasmine slid the lunch tray aside and wiped up the glob of sloppy cucumber.

"So my plan," Rosella said and tossed her balled up sandwich paper onto the tray, "is this. Show her the photos of Sage and tell her you like him, tell her he likes you, and see what she says. Has she invaded your Facebook page yet?"

"She's not on Facebook or Twitter. She says that anyone she wants to have contact with, she already does."

Even as Jasmine said it, the aversion to social media, which hadn't seemed that odd before, took on a sinister new edge, as if her mother's desire to remain anonymous was based in something far more strange. Who was she hiding from? Her father didn't shy away from it. Lars used it for business advertising, as well as to connect with old classmates, teammates, and distant cousins. But not Angela, who maintained a single email account which included only the most necessary of names in the address book. She wouldn't have it at all, she claimed, if it weren't for the need to communicate with Jasmine's school.

"I thought the entire world was on Facebook," Rosella said, clearly astonished by the idea of Angela's absence. "I guess you won't have to worry about her monitoring your every move there. Can't keep tabs on the game if you aren't at the playing field. That's what my mom says, and why she's on all the social sites: so she can dog my every move. Well, for now, that's where we can chat when you're at home under surveillance, until you lay Sage on her."

"I'm not following, Ro. Why do I have to tell her about him?"

Let's call it the lesser of two evils theory. If your platonic Ojibwe girlfriend bothers her, just think what a hot-for-your-bod Indian boyfriend is going to do. Once you've dropped that bomb, wait a day, and then tell her that we've talked out our differences and that you want to hang with me again. By that time, she'll have number one problem, you-know-who; number two, her potential future son-in-law; and moi, who, by comparison, looks like the least hostile Indian. Your mom is crazy smart, so she'll see that guarding you from all of us will come off as more than just a coincidence."

"You're a diabolical mastermind, but what if she doesn't go for it?" said Jasmine. "This could really backfire. I could end up losing you and Sage."

Rosella gave her a gentle nudge. "You aren't ever going to lose me, girl. We're friends for life. We're more than friends. We're sisters. And Sage, well … you may have to keep silent on your devices, but the boy's in my contacts, and you can always use mine. Come to think of it, the whole secret, forbidden love affair thing is kind of steamy, isn't it?"

Suddenly Jasmine saw herself in the front seat of a fast car –maybe a Mustang—Sage at the wheel, racing away from Fargo, windows rolled down, hair flying, music blasting, and then his hand drops from the gear shift, landing possessively on her thigh. Behind them, the Red River rises, a watery wall of silt and debris that barricades all their pursuers. The impromptu fantasy veered off, the path driving towards unvisited territory, until her imaginings brought warmth everywhere: east, west, north, and especially, south.

"Oh, my God, you are totally making out with him in that nasty little mind of yours right now, aren't you?" Rosella teased. "Your bad girl so wants to come out and play. Sage better brace himself; powwow season starts in less than a month, and there's a sex-crazed hottie coming for him!"

Turning a deeper crimson, Jasmine couldn't help but smile as she said, "I've never even kissed a boy. How sex-crazed can I be?"

Tuesday afternoon, Angela was arranging a pot roast, carrots, onions, and potatoes in a pan when Jasmine came into the kitchen, grabbed a diet Coke, and hoisted herself onto a stool at the counter bar, iPhone in hand. As beats of tense silence accumulated and Angela felt her daughter's stare pressing, like two bony fingers, between her shoulder blades, she shifted vegetables, thinking of the most benign topic that could clear the air. The girl took the lead before Angela had a chance to speak.

"Need help, Mom?"

She turned and offered her daughter an appreciative smile and shook her head as she placed the roaster inside the pre-heated oven, and said, "All done. What are you up to?

Angela pulled a seat to the end of the bar and sat down adjacent to Jasmine, her elbows resting beside the image that shone up from the phone screen.

"Nothing. I just wanted to … well, like you know, share something kind of cool with you."

Her daughter's bashful admission lit Angela with a flicker of maternalness, an infrequent dim sensation that had always eluded her, and had been all but absent for some time. It felt odd, but her initial awkwardness abated slightly as she carefully squeezed herself into the uneasy feeling. She touched the girl's hand for implied encouragement and said, "Of course. You can tell me anything."

Screwing then unscrewing the soda bottle cap several times as if winding up more courage, Jasmine eventually abandoned it and reached for her phone. Angela frowned slightly at the sudden shift away from what seemingly might be an important revelation, but she quickly lapsed back into a forced cheerfulness.

"Don't keep me in suspense. Did you ace your algebra final?"

The very mention of Jasmine's least favorite subject, the one that persistently threatened her perfect grade point average, molded a disgruntled expression into the girl's pretty face, and she shook her head.

"I won't know the score until next week. It's something different; something infinitely better than that," she said, her lips curling into a cherubic little grin, her eyes reflecting the phone's brightness as whatever shone upon the screen captured her gaze. "I met a boy. We like each other."

The statement rolled over Angela with the same quiet, inevitable force that had flattened her at other moments. Kenneth releasing his grasp and allowing Jasmine into the deep end of the pool, Lars entering excitedly from the garage to inform her that he had removed the training wheels, the moment a door had closed upon the happy squeals of a birthday party, and Angela driving away from the scene of Jasmine's first sleep-over: each event had arrived, as she expected it would, but it was the horrific feeling of having something torn from her on which she had not counted. If only her child were the one to cause the horrible void, she could speak of it, others would empathize, and she would be considered wonderfully normal, but that was not the case, so she wandered alone in those empty spaces, never naming who had really carved them. She sometimes mused at how ironic it was that something, originally unplanned, had grown into the center of her focus, how her daughter's future had become the destination towards which all Angela's decisions and actions were charted. She hadn't applied for the job of mother, but once in it, she knew that she was expected to succeed. As with previous mile marker moments, she would calm herself, smile, and play her designated role, deliver the right lines, and continue to earn a place on this stage.

"That's thrilling. Who's the lucky boy? Is he a classmate?"

She tapped the screen, laid the phone so that Angela could see it, and said, "No, he's from St. Paul. His name is Sage."

Jasmine watched intently as her mother peered down at the boy festooned in feather, bead, quill, and leather, dancing to the muted music of the video. Dread ripped the script away, Angela's mind retracted, a thousand suns reflecting their blinding light across an endless frozen field of bitter, white cold, and she looked away, her lids shutting in resistance to it. Winter swirled into her blood, penetrating her bones, and violently shook the corner of her closed eye. The tick only worsened as she heard the pinch-lipped sound of her own voice, the disembodied words of some amateur ventriloquist say, "That's very nice. I'm happy for you."

This boy's photo had been with the one of Jack Bordeaux. Hadn't Jasmine said that Jack was the boy's teacher? Too close; everything was too close, and closing in too quickly. She couldn't let her daughter have contact with this boy. What might Jasmine learn? What questions might arise? All the connected links caused Angela's throat to tighten; a long-stifled voice whispered that a bottle from the liquor cabinet could loosen it. Jasmine assessed her mother's response, stole a glance at the video that continued to run silently on between them, and closed it. Out of deference, she wanted to believe that any boy's picture would have caused the same reaction, but the part of Jasmine that drew her to Sage, the part of herself not connected to Angela, the part that her mother so obviously dreaded, so obviously wanted to keep quiet, keep hidden, wailed the truth. Rising from the stool, Jasmine felt her two halves divide, each regarding the other with hostility. She now knew that she could only embrace one. As she passed, Angela's daughter lightly touched her mother's arm, and Dave Bordeaux's daughter departed.

Chapter Eleven: The Death of Angie Erickson

"What are you afraid of losing?"

The question had arisen, time and again, during Angela's sessions with Dr. Adler. The answer never came easily and never was the same one twice; the very reason why Dr. Adler kept asking it. Angela reached for the floral-patterned teacup that sat on the low table in front of her. From the wingback crushed velvet chair across the table, Marian Adler waited with the appropriate level of patience required of her given profession. The antique mantle clock steadily stirred the silence. Angela picked the delicate cup from its saucer, then replaced it without drinking. She didn't care for orange pekoe, although she had politely accepted it.

"Control?" she said, and folded her hands, laying them in her lap.

Marian Adler smiled and said, "You're asking, as if you aren't sure that is the correct response."

Irritated, Angela sighed. The doctor remained impervious, and Angela stole a glance over the woman's shoulder at the tedious clock that pecked unceasingly at her fragile nerves. A mere twenty minutes of their hour had passed. She should have canceled. She should have gone straight home after dropping Jasmine at school, after catching a glimpse in the Mercedes side mirror of something sleek black and crow-quick swooping through the crowd of students towards her daughter. She should have discontinued these round-and-round, solution-less acts of therapeutic futility. She should have quit coming to the contrived calm of this room, created within Dr. Marian Adler's family home, a long time ago. But Angela hadn't, and she wouldn't, because it would only bring more questions for which she hadn't a suitable answer.

"You are free to leave at any time during our hour, Angela," said Dr. Adler. "This time belongs to you."

Of course the hour belonged to her; Lars would be billed, regardless of whether or not Angela stayed.

"There are no wrong answers, so I am unable to validate your response. Only you know if control is the source or the symptom."

Marian Adler had never worn the expected garb of a mental health expert. That day, she wore black bamboo yoga pants, ballet flats, and an oversized silk poet's blouse in ivory. A trio of gold bangles adorned a slender wrist and unobtrusive gold hoops, her ears. She was a young-looking fifty-something, with short reddish-blonde hair, an athletic build, and the quintessential tortoiseshell glasses, which she withdrew and replaced several times during her sessions. Angela had met the woman shortly after her return to Fargo, and Marian Adler was privy to more of the story than most, but had only really scratched the surface; Angela's truths still lay buried miles below where the good doctor had dug. Looking at the woman's unassuming, open, unperturbed demeanor, Angela supposed that she had placed partial trust there before without ill effect. Attempting to wave away the persistent negative funk that clouded her perspective, Angela continued.

"I think control is only an aspect of it. It's more like I'm losing myself."

"Is that how you see Jasmine? As an extension of yourself?"

"Partially I suppose," said Angela, though the words did not ring true to her even as she said them. "I guess I'd say that I feel pleasure when I notice something about her that connects us—especially if it's something good, something positive. It feels like a kind of forgiveness."

The therapist's brows lifted a fraction above the tortoiseshell.

"Forgiveness?"

"Yes," Angela said, and brought her folded hands towards her mouth, as if a prayer might be whispered into them. "Sometimes I feel, if I can raise her as an improved version of me, people will forgive some of the ways I've messed up."

"By people, you mean your parents."

A dry little laugh escaped Angela as she said, "They're always at the center of it, aren't they."

"Do you feel that your role as a daughter is inseparable from your role as a mother?"

Untangling her fingers, Angela rubbed them against her slacks. Dr. Adler slid her glasses off, shined a lens with the corner of her blouse, and then replaced them. They had headed towards this subject at their last appointment, and, as before, Marion felt Angela pulling back from it, which in most cases usually meant it was a direction the client needed to go. As the needlepoint that hung, framed and matted, on the wall behind her so bluntly stated, "Good Therapy Makes Your Ego Sweat."

"If I hadn't gotten pregnant," Angela finally said, her voice diminished to just above a whisper. "I would still be invisible to them. My father adores Jasmine—like he did Adam."

For several minutes, Angela elaborated upon Adam's status with their father, and Marian Adler listened to the familiar information, allowing her client to revisit the already covered ground, while assessing when to gently move the conversation forward.

"And your mother?" she said, when Angela offered an inadvertent pause.

As was her custom with most relationships, Susanne kept Jasmine at arm's length, exhibiting infrequent perfunctory gestures of physical affection when the right people were watching. Often, when opportunity arose, she would sling a racial slur, always making sure that Angela was in earshot, making sure that Lars was not, and never refraining if Jasmine was present. With syrup-coated tone, she would throw out something like "Kay Anderson brought her grandchildren to church last Sunday and they behaved like wild little Indians" or "Senator Smith invited your father to a Redskins game the next time he's in D.C." To call Susanne on the infractions, Angela would have to open herself to Susanne's rant about the absurdity of political correctness, and her well-documented opinion on Dave Bordeaux and his family's social status as welfare-grabbing drunkards with neither ambition nor self-respect. From there, Susanne could remind Angela that, by acting like trash, Angela had attracted trash. Accepting the slurs in silence was simply easier.

"That's far more complicated, but in my mother's odd, hypercritical way, I think she cares about Jasmine. As long as she keeps blinders on about Jasmine's father, she does all right."

The moment Angela heard the statement, she wished she could reel it back, knowing that the intuitive woman would grab hold and run with it.

"I assume you mean your daughter's biological father."

"Yes."

The thought of him spewed a jittery, excessively caffeinated discomfort throughout Angela's body, and she was struck by the sudden urge to flee, to sprint the suburban side streets until her racing heart burst and she was free of this frenzied feeling.

"Does Jasmine have contact?"

"No."

Marian Adler caught the underlying ire in the response.

"Has your daughter shown any interest in it?"

This was the crux of her tension, her anxiety, her resentment, but although she sat within the safe shrine of Dr. Adler's office, in the perfect position to deposit some of what weighed so heavily upon her soul, she glanced the mantle clock, cursed the seven remaining minutes, and shook her head.

"I'm not ready yet."

The admission's double entendre was clear, but Marian Adler knew they hadn't enough time to address the deeper meaning. Liberating the glasses from her serene face once again, she nodded and said, "Perhaps next session then."

Eager to leave, Angela groped for her pocketbook. Leaning forward, elbows on knees, the psychiatrist's voice slowed her escape.

"I'm giving you an assignment, Angela. I want you to choose one person, someone you have a relationship with outside of your family. For example, an old school friend, someone who has no attachment to your parents, your husband, or your daughter; someone who belongs just to you."

"Okay."

Spend time with this person, preferably face to face. If that's not possible, then have a phone conversation. No texts. No emails. No tweets. The human element is very important to the emotional experience. Agreed?"

Angela said that she would do the exercise, both women rose, and Angela took her leather jacket from the brass wall rack.

Once outside, behind the wheel of the white Mercedes, Angela took several deep breaths, trying to establish some inner stillness, trying to gain a composure that would let her face the remainder of the day, trying to think of someone, anyone, who she could call, anyone that belonged only to her. She couldn't think of a single person. She hadn't kept in touch with the two or three girls from high school that she once had considered friends. Even if Angela had stayed in touch, they had never been the kind of relationships that included more than partying together or shopping at the mall; in other words, they had been more friendly acquaintances than true friends. Even if she wanted to get in touch, Angela hadn't a number or an address for any of them. The women in her Pilates class all seemed to know one another and often grabbed a bite to eat or a cocktail afterwards, but after Angela had declined their invitations several times, they quit asking her. Now they only proffered her their chilly greetings at the beginning and end of the exercise session. It was a similar story with the PTA, Booster Club, and Middle School Spring Fling Dance Committee mothers. Although Angela hadn't ever really wanted a place among their petty gossip and their vicious back-biting, forced to consider her list of personal relationships, she felt a horrible isolation settle around her. She shoved the key into the ignition, started the car, and squealed away from the curb.

Thirty minutes later, Angela stood at the Macy's cosmetics counter as a sale associate rang up a pricy pile of eye correction serums, night masks, fine line and wrinkle reducers, moisturizers, and some magic concoction that claimed to abolish the creases where lipstick bled. Angela's vanity table already held most of the items, but need wasn't the point. She had passed a little time, free of much thought, and caught a low-level, yet pleasant, buzz off the acquisitions.

"We're having incredible sales at our fragrance counter," the young woman said, as she tissued the beauty products, arranged them in a Lancôme bag, and offered her the satin handles.

Angela visited the perfume counters next, but not one of the four perfumes she selected was on sale; a fact that magnified the buzz. As an afterthought, she chose the new signature scent of a pop singer she thought girls Jasmine's age liked, and asked to have it gift wrapped. By the time the package was covered in shocking pink paper and gold glitter ribbon, Angela's head began to ache from the multi-layered miasma of scent, sound, and florescent lighting, until the click of her own heels against the tiles became hard, heavy little hammers inside her skull. Back at the Mercedes, the buzz already peaked, her mood crashing fast, she tossed the bags in the trunk, slid into the driver's seat, and took two ibuprofen from the console, downing them with the dredges in her travel coffee mug. Sitting back, she pulled the visor down to shield her eyes from the late morning sun shimmering off the wet asphalt. It was almost lunch time. She was hungry, and the pills were already wreaking digestive havoc. She didn't want to eat alone, but this need only reminded her of the fact that she had no one to fill it. Lars was out of town on business and wouldn't be back until the weekend. Who else was there? Not her mother—Angela wasn't that lonely. She couldn't even imagine sitting at a table for two with her father.

Across the parking lot, a dog barked excitedly as the owner tried to slow the Great Dane's surge towards the pet-friendly animal supply store.

Faye, Angela thought. *That's it; I'll go see Aunt Faye.*

What started as an idea for a lunch date grew into a broader thought. To Angela's way of thinking, Faye, though a family member, was the most individualized attachment Angela had, and although Marian Adler might not agree, Angela would have lunch with her aunt and consider the psychiatrist's little assignment completed. By the time she reached the modest store front clinic of Dr. Faye Gunderson, DVM, Angela felt her spirits, as well as the pressure behind her eyes, lift. Inside, a personable young vet tech greeted Angela and told her that Dr. Gunderson was currently in surgery, but would be finished in approximately fifteen minutes. She thanked him, said she would wait, and took a seat at the end of one of the wood slat benches that flanked the small reception room. She scanned the tidy little area for a magazine, but pamphlets on flea treatments and geriatric pet nutrition were the only available reading materials. Instead, Angela turned her attention to the artwork displayed across from her. The bronze plaque set into the bottom of the heavy wood frame read "Sun Dogs." It was impressionistic, thick strokes of acrylic depicting a juxtaposition of rich greens, browns, and blue against the stark white of a winter landscape.

A dense blue-green pine grove at their backs, two thick-coated dogs—or perhaps, the artist had intended them to be wolves—sat on their haunches, heads lifted to the sky. The subject of their fixation hung in blinding white splendor against a faded blue backdrop. Skirting a sun that lent no warmth to the frigid scape, one at the right, the other at the left, ran the reflective arches of ice crystals known to all familiar to the harshness of Great Plains' winters as sun dogs.

"Why do they call them dogs?" Jasmine had quizzed Lars when he had pointed them out to her one sub-zero morning as he tried to explain to the four-year-old why it was too cold for sledding. "They don't look like dogs."

"They're super far away," said Lars. "If we could take a space ship to the sun, you would see their giant ears, the long tails, and their huge paws."

"Really?" Jasmine said, obviously skeptical, and then turning her attention to Angela. "Is that true, Mommy?"

"That's the way the story goes," Angela affirmed.

Satisfied with a second parental nod, Jasmine asked, "What are they doing?"

"Chasing each other," Lars said.

Jasmine had pondered his answer for a moment before saying, "Do they ever catch each other?"

Angela assessed the broad span of sky beyond the picture window. "It doesn't look as if they will today."

"So they'll just keep running all day long?"

Lars ruffled the girl's hair and said, "They'll rest when the moon comes out."

With an obvious sense of relief, their daughter had stated, "That's good, Daddy. Chasing someone you can't catch makes you too tired."

Angela's thoughts were broken by the clang of the sleigh bell strapped to the clinic's front door, and she looked away from the painting and saw Laura Bachman standing there. She didn't recognize Angela until she had adjusted the collar on a medium-sized, mixture breed dog, and removed her sunglasses, but only managed a small smile of recognition in Angela's direction before the young man came from behind the counter.

"Is Charlie here for his nail trim, Mrs. Bachman?"

"He is," she said. "And none too happy about it. Are you ready for him?"

The tech took the leash and, with impressive canine rapport, managed to convince the reluctant Charlie to follow. Laura took a seat across from Angela and said, "It's nice to see you. Jasmine mentioned that Dr. Gunderson is your aunt. She's a wonderful vet. We were so happy to find her. Charlie is a bit of a handful. She's a dog whisperer. He loves her, so, of course, we do, too."

Angela nodded agreeably, hoping this would be the end of the exchange, but the returning faint pulse at her temple told her it most likely wasn't.

"I wish the weather would make its mind up," Laura said. "Yesterday, I was taking the storm windows down and installing the screens, and today the furnace kicked on."

"That's North Dakota," Angela responded, glancing at the swinging door that lead to the examination rooms, surgical suite, and grooming area. Had Faye finished yet?

Laura folded the sunglasses she was still holding, slid them into the inner breast pocket of her tweed jacket, and began plucking stray dog hairs from the leg of her jeans. Thinking that the compulsory exchange of pleasantries had been accomplished, Angela relaxed slightly, but Laura spoke again.

"By the way, I wanted to say how happy I am that the girls have worked out their differences so quickly. Rosella was a wreck about it. When she came home Monday and told me that she and Jasmine are solid again, I was really relieved."

Monday? Angela thought

The flash of shiny black darting towards her daughter that Angela had witnessed in the Mercedes side mirror that morning suddenly made sense. It had been the back of Rosella's head, more visible above her shorter peers. The realization caused acid to roll through Angela's empty stomach. Although she tried to keep her expression blank while Laura Bachman went on about the wonderful influence Jasmine was for Rosella, and how the girls' racial heritage made their friendship that much more important in a community where few Native Americans resided, Angela felt herself grow pale.

"You and I should have coffee or lunch sometime," Laura suggested, her offer sounding warm, genuine, and utterly horrifying to Angela, who suddenly rose.

"Please excuse me," she said as she fumbled for car keys, almost spilling the contents of her purse. "I just realized I'm late for an appointment."

Laura nodded and remarked that she completely understood the hectic schedule modern mothers must keep, adding as Angela shoved open the clinic door that she would give her a call sometime, to which Angela didn't respond.

The huge house's silence was unwelcoming, and Angela burst into its emptiness and went directly for the bottle of cabernet. It was corked and breathing before she had shed the leather jacket or the ankle boots that were squeezing circulation from her toes. In the kitchen, her hands shook with a hypoglycemic reaction to her not having eaten that day, and she struggled as she ate provolone slices straight from the package. She was coming apart. Piece by piece, what she felt she had left of herself was blowing away, a force too formidable tearing free, scattering everything out of her reach. She no longer knew who or where she was in the grander scheme of things. She no longer knew who Jasmine was; this girl who now kept secrets, this girl who seemed so complicated. Hadn't Angela done enough to thwart all of this? Hadn't she returned to this place of neatly packaged existences, homogenous harmony, a repressive environment where she laced herself tightly into who everyone wanted her to be?

And now, despite all the effort, Jasmine would return to the place where Angela had felt intensely alive, most likely to the man who had been Angela's catalyst for that intensity. She knew she couldn't stop Jasmine. Angela knew she couldn't join her, and, knowing this, along with awareness of her own emotional limitations, knew she couldn't forgive Jasmine.

She took a glass from the cabinet and poured the wine. This, like everything else, had been part of the sacrifice, and she had dutifully followed the single, occasional, special moment rules, but not today. From the moment the girl was born, from the moment Dave had transferred the look once reserved for Angela to their child, from that moment, Angela had known the reckless, raw, passionate life she had with him would have to end. The hot-blooded rage that drove his fists into anyone who dared sample Angela with their eyes, and later drove them both into fits of sexual fury, filled with pleasure and pain so extreme she had once lost consciousness, ended. The feeling that she was his most prized possession ended. The perverse way in which their violence and their resistance to all control, their insatiable craving for everything that had unleashed someone inside of Angela, someone she admired, someone she even feared sometimes, a version so untamed, she could not name it, was the second afterbirth of their daughter's delivery. Angie died when Jasmine was born, leaving only Angela to raise, to stand in the shadow of, and resist resentment for, the girl. If not for her, Angie would live, Angie would thrive in the chaos, Angie would still flail and fight and fuck in the exhilaration of pure survival. Angie would still love Dave Bordeaux.

Purchased for the purpose of a marinade, the wine was a lesser quality, inexpensive label, and it became a warm, liquid memory of him. Angela swallowed in large, unrefined, mouthfuls, until the first glass was gone.

"He was mine," she said, Jasmine solidifying before her mind's eye, and then stopped, as if someone might hear her most twisted, most taboo secret.

Jasmine had taken him from Angela, the girl had taken Angela from herself, Angela had taken Jasmine from him, and Angela would be damned if she was going to let Jasmine and Dave take each other back. She reached for the bottle, poised to pour a second glass, when her phone rang. The day, thus far, had driven her to drink, and, seemingly married to the purpose of her complete undoing, it was Susanne who now called. Angela felt the red wine wiggling through her veins, loosening her tongue. She pressed the accept button, a dramatic soap opera edge soaking her words as she said, "Hello, Mother! What wonderful news do you have for me today?"

She listened, poured more wine, and then paused, disinterest abruptly shoved aside by her mother's unfurling information. Abandoning the glass, Angela suddenly left the kitchen. Thoughts raced into the near future as she settled on the leather sofa, nodded with newfound eagerness, as Susanne laid out a proposition.

Chapter Twelve: Worlds Apart

The pork loin was overcooked, the table conversation stilted, and the soft monotonous tinkling of adult contemporary piano lulled everyone towards a coma. The usual tedious elements of an Erikson Sunday dinner were in place, but as soon as Lars and Jasmine had stepped through the front door, they both sensed a disturbing variable. Susanne had greeted them with her typical little gestures of something resembling affection, but then she had taken Angela by the arm and, in a chummy tone, suggested they go to the sunroom and chat. Without the backward glance of distress Lars would have expected, Angela hurried off, leaving him shaken by her sudden abandonment of their safety in numbers policy. When the women rejoined the group in the family room twenty minutes later, they both wore a strangely similar smile, and Jasmine shot a raised-browed glance at her father, who returned his own disbelieving look. Lars and Jasmine continued to harbor uneasiness and, over coffee and strawberry rhubarb pie a la mode, their instincts were validated.

"You have a birthday coming up, don't you Jasmine?" Susanne stated with a solicitous smile.

Her grandmother's acknowledgement seemed premature—Jasmine wouldn't turn fourteen until August—but the girl nodded anyway. She was looking forward to it. Lars promised he would take her to test for a learner's permit and begin giving her driving lessons. Lars' love of cars and the freedoms they provided had rubbed off on his daughter, and she was already campaigning for the model she hoped to have down the road, when she turned sixteen.

"Well," Susanne gushed, "your grandfather and I have a surprise for you. It's an early gift."

Jasmine looked at Kenneth and his eyes lit up with the deep excitement and love that only his granddaughter could elicit as he said, "Yes, my sweetest girl, we do."

At that point, Lars tried to make eye contact with Angela, who had become extremely interested in her dessert and didn't meet his inquisitive gaze. From nowhere, he was struck by an inexplicable bolt of paternal protectiveness, and he laid his arm across the back of the dining chair and rested a hand on Jasmine's shoulder.

"We are going on a Scandinavian tour and *you* are coming with us," Susanne announced, it sounding more edict than presentation. "We will leave as soon as school breaks for summer and will return in August."

A pause, made all the more obvious by an ill-timed piano crescendo, ensued as the adults in the room awaited the girl's reaction. Jasmine felt her father's fingers tighten on her shoulder and she avoided Susanne's eyes, first looking at her mother, and then her grandfather. Angela appeared nervous, but was nodding her encouragement. Kenneth beamed, finally breaking the silence.

"Norway, Finland, and our ancestral homeland, Sweden," he said. "It will be wonderful to show you where your great, great grandfather was born, wonderful to have an entire summer with my favorite granddaughter."

It was their little joke, and, as expected Jasmine offered the usual response, saying, "Of course I'm your favorite, Papa. I'm your *only* granddaughter."

Unable to remain beneath the bus under which he felt he'd been thrown, Lars cleared his throat.

"This really is a surprise. A very generous one, but a huge surprise nonetheless."

Angela refused to look at him, and Susanne moved in with a cool smoothness indicative of a high-price defense attorney.

"The opportunity arose quite quickly, and since you were away this week, Angela and I worked out the arrangements. We didn't want to disrupt your business trip with details of our little pleasure trip."

What is this we shit? Lars thought, still staring at his wife, first willing, then challenging her to face him.

"So, what do you think, Jasmine? Are you looking forward to traveling the world with your granddad? We're going to have an incredible adventure together," Kenneth said, his enthusiasm immune to the mounting tension.

She offered her grandfather a weak smile. Behind him, beyond the wall of glass that overlooked the now empty covered rectangle, sunlight shone around him, promising that it might soon be warm enough for them to fill the place where Kenneth had taught her to love the water, to love their swims, to love *him*. Before Jasmine had arrived in Kenneth's life, after Adam's drowning, the pool had been drained and left dry, but the bright-eyed child had come, bringing with her the power to fill spaces Kenneth never thought could again be filled. She had taken to the water, filtering out Kenneth's woes, showing him playfulness and joy that had never attached itself to the competitive races and focused intensity once waged there.

The gravity of Kenneth's love suddenly felt like a great stone she had been given to carry, and Jasmine realized who was responsible for the burden she couldn't lay down without breaking his heart. Angela had won this round. She had orchestrated a plan that would eliminate

Rosella, Sage, and an entire summer's worth of powwows with something as seemingly innocent as a generous birthday gift. She must have known how thrilled Kenneth would be, how much more difficult that would make it for Jasmine to decline, how ironic it was that the trip took the girl safely out of reach of her Ojibwe culture while simultaneously introducing her to the origins of their Scandinavian heritage. It was as fluidly executed as a word processing program's find and replace function.

Yes, Angela had won this round, but there would be many more.

"That sounds amazing, Papa," Jasmine said with as much zeal as the underlying anger at her betrayer would allow. "Thank you."

With fervor uncharacteristic to his usual staunchness, Kenneth tossed the linen napkin atop his pie, sprang out of the host chair, and hugged his granddaughter. With similar actions, but quite opposite emotion, Lars excused himself from the table.

No one spoke during the short car ride home, and as soon as they were inside the house, Jasmine stated that she would be in her room, and then looking defiantly at Angela, said, "To Skype Rosella ... and Sage."

She stormed up the stairs, leaving her red-faced mother and brooding father to the argument Jasmine knew was about to erupt. As soon as the girl had slammed her bedroom door, Angela went on the offensive.

"I wasn't going to deny our daughter the chance to experience her family's culture firsthand, Lars. They are generous to offer it, and I would have been a fool to turn it down."

He looked at her, trying to detect something that would link this woman to the one he respected. The shift had come on slowly, but he had been aware for quite a while that there was a bitterness rising to her surface. In recent months, he had caught her in moments of tense contemplation, in some distant place he didn't recognize and couldn't seem to reach, where the lows seemed lower and longer, her highs fewer, further between, and fettered by a growing discontent that he sensed, but to which she would not admit. An edge now made frequent appearances in Angela's voice, her movements, and her reactions that hinted at hidden resentment and although Lars felt its cutting sharpness, he couldn't comprehend its catalyst.

Without warmth or apology, Angela crossed her arms, met his gaze and held it. The coldness, ice upon concrete, cracked his resolve and the fury he had been restraining, leaked out. He grappled to keep himself from shouting, but he lost the battle after two or three words.

"Then Jasmine isn't *our* daughter, because usually when a decision that large is made concerning *our* daughter, you consult me. You're packing her off halfway around the world, for Christ's sake. You couldn't give me a God damn phone call? A text? Anything? Since when do you and Susanne cook up things together? When I left for Seattle on Wednesday, she was still the enemy. Now today—surprise! She's taking Jasmine out of the country for the entire summer with your blessing."

"My father will be on the trip, too."

"Really, Angela?" scoffed Lars. "Is that the best you can do? Kenneth is the anti-venom? By the way, he seemed genuinely shocked that I didn't know anything. Do you know what he said to me? He apologized and then said that I shouldn't feel too bad because Susanne usually excludes him from planning, too."

Angela didn't respond. Lars rose from where he sat and paced to the window, then turned, dropped back onto the couch, and ran both hands through his thinning blond hair.

"Is that the kind of marriage you want? Like your parents? You want to pull all the strings, make all the choices, and I just nod and smile, and am okay with an inactive role in my daughter's life?"

Inwardly, Angela winced at the comparisons, but she stayed calm, stayed true to what she had set into motion.

"She doesn't want to go," he said, disturbed by the blankness in his wife's eyes, the lack of remorse and compassion he saw there. "You do know that much, right? Did you see how conflicted she was, Angela? I think she's even more confused than I am and I suspect even angrier. You betrayed me, but worse, you betrayed Jasmine."

Abruptly, Angela shot to her feet, her shadow swooping down on him. Balling her fists, she yelled, "Yes, you're both such victims, aren't you? It's a damn birthday present. It's a vacation, not two months in a teen boot camp. Besides, you were there when she told her grandfather how excited she is."

Who the hell is this woman? The manipulative nature reeked of Susanne, but was clearly all Angela. The part of him that loved her, the part that was indestructible, receded nonetheless, as, for the first time in their marriage, repulsion rushed in. Yes, he would always love her, but, in this moment, he did not like her.

"She loves Kenneth. There's no denying that. I know that's why she said what she did—to appease him. That doesn't mean she actually wants to go. It seems like emotional blackmail, if you ask me. Oh, wait, that's right, you didn't ask me, Or her. So I guess I'm wondering what's at the bottom of this giant shit heap. What's the motive? With all the behind-the-back plotting you and your mother did, there has to be a motive."

Stepping back, Angela sunk back into the leather recliner, her face set in stone as she resumed control, saying, "You're over reacting. My parents wanted to give this to her, the tickets are non-refundable, and I thought that I would have your support."

Who's the victim now? Lars thought.

"Apparently, I was wrong," finished Angela, rising and leaving, a trail of self-righteous indignation marked by every heavy footfall.

Lars stood and followed her into the kitchen. She wasn't going to dodge answering the most relevant question. Ignoring his pursuit, she pulled a bottle of Riesling from the refrigerator, a glass from the hanging rack inside one of the frosted glass front cabinets, uncorked the bottle, and poured herself a generous amount, not offering any to him. He stared at her alarming, yet somehow predictable, actions. As he watched, she drained the glass, but he didn't give her the satisfaction of showing any concern.

"Why, Angela?"

She held up the empty wine glass. He shook his head.

"You know what I mean. Don't play games. It's beneath both of us," he said, although he thought she was now operating at a level much lower than he would allow himself to sink. "You and I have never avoided the truth, no matter how ugly. Let's not start now."

"The truth is I've said all that I'm going to say. There's no secret motive. Your need to control everything is what's really in question here."

The untruth came so easily it almost pleased Angela, as her conscience settled into the modified reality she was creating for its comfort. Having told herself that she had done nothing wrong so many times since Susanne's fateful call that the affirmation hummed behind her thoughts like a mantra, she had fallen beyond a tipping point. For her, belief and lie were now synonymous.

His jaw dropped and then tensed as he yelled, "Me? I'm the one with control issues? Are you serious?"

"Yes. You're the one who's pissed off. You're the one who's forcing the issue. You're the one who won't leave me alone, who followed me in here so that you could blow up."

The twist of her words was too tight, and, wiggling free of the noose, he backed away. Whatever warped thing Angela was trying to distort this scene into, Lars wanted no part of it.

"All right. I apologize. I shouldn't have raised my voice," he said.

He turned and glanced at the door to the garage, an exit from what he would say, what would be used against him. He would take the Jag out into the country, let it run the back roads, let his anger run its course. She wasn't going to give him answers. She had deflected everything, throwing it all back on him, but despite these tactics, he refused to believe the lie. There was a hidden reason, and, as with most ulterior motives, Lars suspected there would be unfortunate consequences. He scooped the key ring from the cloisonné bowl on the table at the door and grabbed a windbreaker off the boot bench.

"I'm going to get some air," he said with a steady calm he didn't feel, but before he had his hand on the doorknob, he heard the shatter of glass, and spun back towards the kitchen.

Angela stood behind a sinister crescent of crystal shards glittering atop the ceramic tile floor. There was no shock, no surprise, no common immediate response to the accident on her part, and it struck him that the destruction was intentional. Her calm, her perfect stillness, etched more creeping frost beneath his skin.

"Do you need help?"

"No," she said.

"Okay. I'll go then."

She nodded and looked down at the mess, but didn't tend to it.

He went to the door, opened it, and left. Through her fingers, he felt their whole world slipping, falling, crashing. Angela was hiding behind the broken pieces, somehow thinking she was untouchable, somehow thinking that the truth could not be dug from beneath the wreckage. Lars gunned the Jag out of the driveway, but guilt hit as he reached the end of the cul-de-sac and he stopped, grabbed his cell and sent a text to his daughter.

Hey kid taking a drive want to go?

Lars had just enough time to wave to the orthopedic surgeon who lived in the ultra-modern glass and cedar number, two doors down, before a ding sounded from the cell.

No thanx dad bikes w/ro.

A face with heart-shaped eyes punctuated the end. The tiny image brought him an unexpected smile. He was pleased to know that her friendship with the Bachman girl was intact again, too. It wasn't a mystery why Kenneth wanted to spend the summer with his granddaughter. What remained a mystery was why Angela did not, and how Lars would cope with the absence of Jasmine's sweetness. He had once thought that Angela Erikson was the great love of his life, until he met the beautiful brown haired, big-eyed child who the courts had soon allowed to become his daughter. His bond to her was as strong, if not stronger, than biology, and in the innumerable moments of pure joy and love they had shared, Lars had silently wondered how Dave Bordeaux kept himself away. At times, he even felt pity for the man of whom he knew so little. Although Angela had revealed details of her past that many women would have chosen to exclude, over the years, Lars became more aware of who—and what—were consistently omitted . At first, with the wounds fresh, the incident that had fueled her exit too close, Lars understood Angela's reasoning, but years and then a decade piled up between, and he began to wonder how so much time, so much stability, so much therapy, hadn't insulated her enough to at least mention the man with whom she had a child.

Lars drove through their subdivision into another, and then another; the houses, yards, speed bumps, and number of street lights shrinking, until he reached the edge of Fargo's city limits. But rather than steer the Jaguar west, out into the country, he took the nearest entrance ramp onto I-94. Traffic was light and the speedometer quickly reached a hundred as he flew down the highway, drawn by direction but without destination. The late afternoon sun glinted off the Red River's gunmetal gray current, although thin fingers of cloud reached towards the light. As he crossed the bridge, slowing to eighty, the fingers clasped together, holding back the descending day as if it belonged only to them. Over the boundary, out of North Dakota, into Minnesota, out of angry, into apathetic, he drove, until nothing but oceans of overturned, fresh black topsoil rolled out from both sides of the mostly empty four-lane and available exits became fewer, farther between. The tug-of-war of going on or turning around came with every sign, every mile marker, every slow-to-die speck of a farm town that the Jag raced towards, but Lars sped on, the calming purr of the engine winning out over prudency. Distance and time melted his thoughts and flowed them through his mind in a cool stream of consciousness that brought him to clearer places where memory, knowledge, intuition, and suspicion ran towards truth. So close he could almost feel the answers forming like drops, almost wetting his tongue with the words that would give them meaning.

But everything muddied when the Jag skipped a stride, Lars decreased speed, and the car began pulling to the left. Before he had it maneuvered to the shoulder, he knew that something had punctured a front tire. He zipped up his jacket and got out of the car. Wind ripped off the empty flat land, tearing at his clothes and throwing grit against his back as he crouched and searched for damage. Nothing was visible, but the tire had lost too much pressure. He climbed back into the Jag and pushed the on-board roadside assistance button. The middle of nowhere on a Sunday wasn't where he had imagined himself, but he was there nonetheless. When the tow truck arrived an hour later, the operator, a short, barrel of a woman in cowboy boots and a brown Carhartt jacket with the business's logo embroidered on the chest, hopped out and offered up a wide gap-toothed grin. Wind whipped rogue strands of graying brown hair from a messy bun at the nape of her neck. After introducing herself as the actual Toni of Toni's Tow, she expertly hooked up the Jag to the truck, and she and Lars exchanged small talk.

"So, if you don't mind me asking," she said when the car was hoisted into position, "how does the owner of a dealership manage not to have a spare in the trunk?"

Lars shrugged and gave the hard-edged but likeable woman a sheepish grin, saying, "I rely too heavily on the shop to keep things in check."

"Some sorry son-of-a-bitch going to get fired for this?" She chuckled and climbed into the cab.

Lars got in beside her.

"No. This one's all mine."

Toni steered back onto the highway, chatting on about her business, her daughter Tyrene's atrocious bookkeeping skills, and her on-going battle with the IRS. By the time they reached their turnoff, Lars knew much more than he wanted to, including that all her daughters' names started with T, she loved classic country music, and that their destination was only an hour west of Minneapolis. The last bit of information was a sponge that drained all the moisture from his mouth. He had driven for two hours, oblivious to the passage of time, oblivious to what lay ahead of him, and yet, the entire trip, something had operated beneath the surface, guiding him by the gut. Where had it been taking him? Were there answers there?

Were you heading into the Cities?" Toni asked in between divulging the summary of her life story.

Lars swallowed. Had he been? For what? She slowed up behind a tractor crawling along the two-lane blacktop in front of them and didn't wait for a reply, but began elaborating on how she had met husband number three at an Indian casino south of St. Paul. Lars nodded here and there, as if he were listening, but his thoughts had carried pieces of her story into a separate tributary, and they were bobbing along with the discarded debris of some other, more familiar history. Again, he sensed himself drawing nearer to clarity. He felt that, at any moment, all the pieces could swirl into place, forming something crystalline.

"Trudy, my youngest, did a year at Minneapolis Community College. Wild little thing found trouble enough for ten girls. I brought her butt home. Told her I wasn't paying for her party anymore. But I guess the city didn't make her that way; she was born with a broad streak of it. My other two ain't angels, but Trudy, well, she takes it to a whole different level. Crazy flakes for breakfast, lunch, and dinner. It's what she thrives on."

Lars mind became a torrent and everything spun through the white water. The woman chattered on, his thoughts rolled on, until his thinking cascaded into feeling, the head pouring into the gut, returning to what had guided him there in the first place.

"You got any kids?"

"Yes, I have a daughter," Lars said, feelings of love and pride and uneasiness welling.

Jasmine was still his, wasn't she? He scowled. He wouldn't let doubt become the by-product of his wife's enigmatic behavior, and yet ... Lars had questions. Jasmine had questions. Angela denied them the answers. Now his gut felt empty.

They reached Toni's shop and Lars bought a Dr. Pepper and some corn chips from the machines and ducked into the cramped waiting area, where he slumped onto a metal folding chair. An oscillating fan, bolted to the wall near the ceiling, stirred the smell of imitation pineapple from a tree-shaped car freshener dangling from the blade cage. That, along with the salt, the saturated fat, and the carbonated corn syrup he was washing it down with further deflated his already-sagging mood, and loneliness settled over him. He wanted to call someone. If he was being honest with himself, he wanted to call Angela, but he knew he would get her voicemail again, as he had earlier. She had sent a brief text after, curtness heavily implied in its brevity, in its singularity. He had heard nothing since. He looked at the photo that served as the phone's wallpaper: Jasmine cheek to cheek with him, the silky white cat beneath their chins, all perfectly posed for the selfie. The corners of Lars lips twitched and he tapped the number. She picked up on the second ring.

"Hey, Dad, what's up? Where are you?"

Angela obviously hadn't bothered to tell her.

"Waiting for the tire to get fixed. Had a flat."

"That completely sucks. When will you be home?"

"Not for a couple more hours. How was your ride with Ro?"

"Fine. We biked the trails. Ro said she saw a coyote, but I think it was a dog."

"Did you have your pepper spray? I don't want you girls going anywhere without it, What about your phone and your helmet and—"

"I know, I know. And my knee pads and the water bottle, and—"

"Okay, I get it. You did have all those things, though, right?"

He grinned, sensing her dramatic eye roll, as she said, "I might have dropped the pepper spray when we stopped to take candy from that guy in the van, but I had everything else."

"Ha-ha. Very funny, kid. So, by the way, who's Sage?"

"Dad!"

"Well, I heard you say you were going to video chat with Ro and someone named Sage. So I'm curious."

"I think you mean suspicious."

Lars leaned back, crossed his ankles and exhaled. "So Sage is a boy then, right?"

There was the sound of her shifting the phone, taking a drink of something, followed by a blown out breath.

"This is totally embarrassing. You're my dad."

The words took him in their arms, lifted his heart, spread a mist over his eyes.

"Yeah, I am, so I need to know what kind of kid is chatting up my beautiful daughter. Is he cool, or should I load the shotgun?"

Her light laughter tinkled like tiny silver bells that soothed his disquieted mind.

"He's really nice, Dad. He's a friend of Ro's."

"So Mr. Sage is just your buddy, or do I need to revisit the shotgun idea?"

Was it possible? Was she really old enough to have interest in boys? Lars supposed time had delivered them here and, as much as denial appealed to him, he would face the facts.

"He's a little more than that … I think. But he lives all the way in St. Paul, so relax. It would be great if at least one of my parents was sane about it."

Again, Lars felt himself looking in from outside the circle. How much more had Angela withheld? His neck muscles tightened and he forced the tension out of his voice.

"I'm sure your mom is just feeling protective like I am. Boys are a huge leap forward."

Out of the corner of his eye, Lars saw the hoist with the Jag on it being lowered, and Toni strutting towards the office, an invoice in hand.

"Listen, Jas, the car is done. I want to talk more about this, okay? Don't worry; I was only slightly serious about the gun. I trust your judgment when it comes to friends, and that includes the boy variety. If he's a friend of Rosella's, I'm sure he's a decent kid. Seems to me the Bachmans have raised her to make good choices. She chose to be your best friend—that says it all right there."

"Thanks, Dad. I really appreciate you not freaking out about Sage. He's completely amazing, trust me. You'd like him. I'll show you a picture when you get home."

Lars laid a credit card on the counter and Toni ran it.

"Send it. Let me get a look at him," he joked as he slid the American Express back in the wallet and signed the receipt. "You know, like a police line-up or a mug shot album, so I can commit him to memory."

"Seriously not funny, Dad," she chided, but he could hear the smile that shone past her annoyance. "I'll only send pictures if you promise not to tease me anymore."

Lars said that he promised, told Jasmine that he loved her, and said that he would see her when he got home. He thanked Toni, who told him again that a spare or, at the very least, a can of tire fix-it, would be a wise idea for a man with a fancy car dealership, and then he was back in the Jag, a fingernail of sun still showing on the horizon. The phone's text alert caused him to brake at the edge of the shop's gravel lot. With the county road stretching out empty in both directions, Lars opened the first photo. He looked at the young man closely: the open expressive face, the shock of dark brown hair, the Twins jersey, and the broad shoulders. Lars wondered if the kid played baseball. He was a nice-looking boy. Had the build of a potential batter. Tapping on the video, he watched the boy execute the dance moves. *Really athletic,* Lars thought.

If Sage wasn't out for baseball, Lars bet he excelled in some other sport. It wasn't difficult to understand Jasmine's crush. At first glance, the kid looked all right; Lars just hoped he wouldn't break Jasmine's heart, although he knew first loves usually ended badly. It seemed to be a foregone conclusion when it came to that first real head-over-heel, grab-you-by-the-gut person that entered your young life and taught you how miserable a case of love sickness could be. His had been Angela, and crush was an apt definition—then *and* now. He had handed over his heart and his biggest secret, giving her the power to destroy one with the divulgence of the other. Lars suddenly wondered if he would soon come to regret having given her either one.

The boy's regalia moved with his every sharp, clean-edged motion, the cut-glass beads of his moccasins glittering like tiny bright spotlights into Lars's recent memory, and in his mind's eye, Lars saw his own first love captured behind her jagged glass shards. The young man knew who he was, embraced his identity, wore it with dignity, with pride. Had that brazen girl in the country club golf cart, with her temporary nose ring, her temporary hair tint, and temporary loathing for Lars known who she was? Did she know now? If she did understand, did she accept it? Was she moving closer to or further from the real Angela, and where would the transition leave Lars? Where would it leave Jasmine? Head held high and with a smile that held genuine happiness, the boy named Sage spun across the small screen again.

"Don't hurt our daughter," he said under his breath.

The pit of his gut answered. She would hurt them all.

Chapter Thirteen: Perfect Imperfections

For Lars and Angela, brief exchanges about lawn care, dinner menus, and dry-cleaning tickets suffused the first few weeks of Jasmine's absence, neither wanting to venture anywhere that might end in an argument. Prior to the trip, the girl had acted as a buffer for Lars, and he for her, as the final days counted down to the departure date and Angela's mere appearance in a room put their teeth on edge, but when their nest emptied, Lars and Angela clicked into a kind of survival mode indifference. Moving cautiously around one another, they exerted just enough energy to deal with life's perfunctory details, and everything they did, everything they said, was coated in a thin layer of politeness. Lars put in extra hours at the dealership and in his home office. Angela crept off to their room early, never tapping on the closed office door to tell him, and by the time he came to bed, she was, or pretended to be, asleep. In the string of nights, as summer spread out like a hot sodden blanket, they lay at their opposite edges, backs turned, the space between them growing colder, more silent, until Lars could no longer take the chill.

"I'm going to bed," she said, one late July evening as she passed through the living room where he sat reading a magazine. He tossed it on the coffee table and rose to his feet.

"I'll join you."

She hesitated, one foot on the bottom step, and Lars knew he had taken her off guard, but he wasn't going to retreat. She shrugged, then continued up the stairs. When they reached their room, Angela said that she was going to relax in the tub for a while, and offered him the bathroom as she plucked a silk nightgown from a drawer. Lars brushed his teeth, washed his face, stripped down to boxers, and crawled beneath the duvet. If she thought he would be asleep when she returned, she was wrong. Propping himself on three pillows, Lars clicked the television on and turned the volume low. She could soak for an hour if she chose. He wasn't tired, only ready; ready to confront whatever had twisted their relationship from lovers into acquaintances, whatever had turned her towards Susanne and away from Jasmine. Nearly an hour passed before he heard water draining from the tub, and he clicked off the news. Expecting Lars to be asleep, Angela gave a startled gasp at the sound of his voice as she stepped out of the bathroom into the dimness of the bedroom.

"Did you enjoy your bath?"

She crossed the room and sat at the dressing table with her back to him and began to brush her hair, saying coolly, "I did. It was very relaxing."

Through the black silk, the taut line of her shoulders said otherwise.

"Good," he said, and swung out of bed. "Because we need to talk."

Spinning around to face him, she slammed the silver brush down on the table, toppling the bottle of jasmine oil, and, as Lars drew closer, he could smell the spilled fragrance, could smell the alcohol on her breath.

"Talk about what? What a horrible person I am? What a shitty mother? Because if you're on another witch hunt, I'm not in the mood."

Lars leaned against the foot of the bed and crossed his arms over his bare chest. He had expected her reluctance, but not the level of animosity. It seemed over-reactive, considering he hadn't even touched on the intended topic—although it did include her attitude towards Jasmine. Since the trip began, Angela had only had contact with the girl once in the form of a minute-long phone exchange. In contrast, Lars had spoken to their daughter almost every day.

"No, I just feel like there's been a change in you and I want to try to understand where you're coming from. It feels like you're distancing yourself from me ... and from Jasmine. What's going on? Is there something that you need to tell me? Have I done something?"

Angela got up and came within inches of his face, the smell of what might have been red wine swelling between them, her lips so close he could have kissed her, if he had wanted to, as she said, "Oh, no, Lars. You haven't done a thing. You're perfect; the perfect husband, the perfect father, the perfect man. And do you know how I know you're the perfect man?"

He felt himself involuntarily pulling away from her, but she leaned closer and pressed her breasts against his chest, her groin against his.

"Because everyone tells me that's the way it is. Who am I to argue with the entire rest of the God damn world?"

Straightening, Lars gently laid his hands on her shoulders and tried to move her away, but she grabbed his wrists and bit her nails into his skin.

"You're being unreasonable," he said, and shifted his weight to break her hold.

She squeezed tighter and laughed a disgusted, sarcastic laugh, saying, "That's right. I'm unreasonable. Angela's unreasonable. She doesn't know what's good for her."

Lifting his hands from her shoulders, he broke her grip and began to slip from where she had him pinned against the foot of the bed. At that moment, everything about her caused a surge to his nervous system. He had only wanted a civil conversation, open lines of communication, an opportunity to fix what was crumbling around them, but her raw rage, the mad glint in her eyes, the aggressive way in which she seemed to want to insert her physical authority extinguished his need for answers. Her presence radiated peril; a home invader waiting for him to unlock the door, and, for the length of a breath, fear ran an icy finger across Lars' neck.

"Listen," he said, "this obviously can't go anywhere constructive. I wanted to talk like two sane adults, but I can see that's not where you want to be right now, so I'm done here."

"The hell you are," she spat.

It took a second for his brain to register what hit him in the ribs, until he looked down and saw Angela's balled fist cocked back, preparing to strike another blow. He caught the next punch with his forearm as he raised it to deflect her, grabbing her around the waist with his other arm, the momentum bringing them down onto the bed, Angela on top of him, kicking and slapping.

"What the hell are you doing?" he yelled. "Are you crazy?"

Her attack went on, his words swallowed up in her animalistic grunts and growls, until he was able to capture both her arms, throw her onto her back, and trap her writhing body beneath him. Still fighting, she broke her hands free and delivered his cheek a hard blow before he could gain another hold—this time using his hand to cuff her wrists above her head. In their struggle, the black silk tore, and he could feel her hard, bare nipple pressing into his flesh. Their breathing was heavy and, slickened with sweat, their bodies slid against one another.

"Fuck you!"

She screamed it again and again, until "you" became "me" and Lars felt her mouth viciously clamp onto his. Tasting wine and salty copper, he didn't know if her teeth had drawn his blood or her own, and, although his mind resisted, when she opened her legs and wrapped them around him, he grew hard as the silk rode up over her hips and he felt her fiery wetness.

He began to let go of her wrists, but she demanded that he keep them pinned. Mentally, it felt so terribly wrong, but he couldn't stop the physical response, didn't want to stop it. For too long she had kept herself from him. His free hand pulled the waistband of the boxers down to his thighs, and, with her toes, Angela hooked the fabric, tugging the underwear to his ankles and then kicking it to the floor. As he slid inside her, she ripped a hand loose and locked her fingers into the hair at the side of his head. As he plunged, harder and faster, at Angela's commands, she yanked his head towards her mouth, and, in a rabid pant, snarled, "I'm Angie. Call me Angie."

He opened his eyes for a moment, and the woman beneath him wasn't someone he knew. No one called her Angie, but he knew that was exactly who he was looking at, who he was screwing, who was screwing him. He said the name. He said it again. He said it with every forceful thrust of his hips, of her hips, until she uncoiled her fingers from his wet hair and screamed, "Hit me. I want you to hit me. Slap me. Now. Hit me."

Suddenly, her hand flashed out, delivering a blinding strike across his cheek and temple.

"Hit me," she cried. "I want you to smack me. Come on, you pussy!"

Again, her palm cracked hard against his face as she fought to provoke what she desired. Lars felt himself, still inside her, grow flaccid, physical quickly mutating into mental torment, as his mind took control once more, and, in ragged gasps, he said, "I can't, Angela. I just can't."

The next morning, he left before she woke up. In a state of lingering disillusionment, Angela pulled herself from bed, wandered downstairs, and numbly sat sipping black coffee, watching sprinklers whip the back lawn towards its greenest green, and she wondered where she could go from here. She had drawn Lars' eye to a tiny peephole, had shown him the woman she had once been, the woman she wanted to be again, a woman whose soul could not be filled with marriage, with motherhood, with the mundane entrapments of stability structured from social norms and servitude. She wanted no praise for selflessness, no nods of approval for her nurturing, no harnessed passion under the guise of respect for being the mother of some man's child. She knew now that she didn't even want love. It gentled lust and slowed the blood to a calm complacency that only seemed to draw death closer with more quickness. Yes, she had lured him to look and, for an instant, she believed that he might not blink.

Angela glanced around, taking inventory of what living a lie had gained her: designer furniture, gas fireplace, granite counter tops, twenty-foot vaulted ceilings, all the comfort a rich man who loved her child more than her could buy. She wanted none of it. She wanted, she needed, what Dave Bordeaux could give her, the stimulant drug, the pulsing wildfire possessiveness that could heat someone to boiling or burn them alive.

"She's mine."

The words had always flowed from his lips like tainted honey, sweet nourishment to her ego, poison to the men who approached "his Angie" in Dave's view. His violent jealousy was an aphrodisiac and the chaos that it swirled through their blood brought them both something that only the other could give. Could she and Dave have that again? Now that Jasmine was almost grown, now that Lars would always take care of the girl, could she circle back? If she could shed the role of wife, throw off the yoke of motherhood, would Dave re-claim that woman?

Because it would have made things easier, part of Angela wished that Lars hadn't failed her test, wished he hadn't flinched at what she revealed, wished that love was enough, but a larger part, the part she knew would win, hated him. Perfection was subjective. Lars, Jasmine, this house, this lifestyle, this acceptability, none of it could provide her brand of crazy, cataclysmic perfect. Angela had only ever known one source, and if she were to fight the numbness before it became constant, she would have to search for it, seize it. She would have to hunt for Dave Bordeaux.

Chapter Fourteen: Man in the Moon

"I booked a flight to Las Vegas."

The announcement was stunning. They hadn't spoken since their disturbing bedroom encounter days earlier. Considering the glacial divide that now seemed to separate Lars from Angela, her arranging for them to meet with Jay was the last thing Lars would have expected. He hadn't been able to find the words to close the gap, melt the disappointment, the confusion, and although her gesture could be construed as a non-verbal attempt at reconciliation, Lars was wary. The timing felt wrong, as if their bankrupt relationship had purchased something it couldn't afford. From across one of the bistro's best tables, untethered to any emotion, Angela flashed a quick, tight smile, and continued picking at an endive salad. Glancing away, he exchanged a friendly nod with one of the dealership's best customers, a local bank president. The much-younger woman on the influential man's arm wasn't the wife—a much older, much stouter woman—who had purchased a silver Mercedes from Lars a week ago. Rumor had it the banker often escorted euphemistic nieces and female second cousins around town. Fargo qualified as a city, but operated much like its small rural counterparts, and indiscretions rarely went unnoticed, rarely went unchastised. Was this the reason Angela had insisted they dine out this evening? Why she chose a location where people who shared their income tax bracket, their neighborhood, their church, and their school district would be? The intimate dining experience placed tables in close proximity to one another and kept patrons' conversations quiet and publicly appropriate. None of the upper crust wanted to go to the tennis club the next day only to discover that other blue bloods, while sipping cocktails and savoring poached salmon, had overheard their previous evening's marital spat.

"You did?" Lars said and took a drink of his vodka martini. "That sounds nice. When do we go?"

Angela studied his face as she said, "I'll leave Friday morning. You're scheduled on the evening flight."

They had never made the trip separately and Lars raised a quizzical brow, but Angela saw the question rising to his lips and gave another chilled smile, saying "I'm going to do some shopping in the afternoon. We can meet at the hotel."

"Fine. I look forward to it. Will our old friend be in town?"

Vegas plans usually implied Jay's presence, but the subtle variations

Angela already had in place caused him to wonder if her intent was to change up more than just their travel schedules. Perhaps she preferred that their time be spent without the third party, without anyone to distract or diffuse. Perhaps Angela wanted him all to herself. The thought lifted Lars' spirits. It had been a while since he had seen Jay, but, when it came down to it, Angela, their marriage, and their family were Lars's highest priority. If Jay's exclusion was what was needed in order to smooth all the rough spots that had cropped up, Lars accepted it completely, even happily, if it meant regaining a few inches of ground with his wife.

"He'll be there," she said. "I've arranged for drinks and a late dinner."

Lars nodded. Jay hadn't ever felt like a wedge—until now. Masking his disappointment, he filled Angela's wine glass and asked, "Are you sure? We could get together with him some other time, keep the weekend about us, if you'd like."

Emptying half the glass in two large swallows, she set her wine down and shook her head. Her hair was pulled back in a severe knot, and Lars could just make out the crescent moon scar showing through the mineral makeup. Ordinarily, she styled the blonde waves and applied the cosmetics in a way that hid it, but tonight it seemed as if she flaunted the old injury like a medal, like a challenge, like the lewd sexually suggestive message she had once penned between her breasts when they were still teenagers.

Although, to him, nothing in their lives seemed it, Lars said, "All right," and dropped his eyes to the shrimp scampi the waiter placed in front of him.

Angela touched the young man's arm and ordered another bottle of pinot noir.

"Jasmine will be home next Friday," she said, as if the shortened trip was but a casual tidbit that hadn't warranted mention until that point.

Lars paused and stared at her. Vegas plans were first on her agenda? That was higher on the list of priorities than their daughter returning two weeks early?

"Apparently, my father ate something that upset his sensitive stomach. He's been sick a few days. He wants to see his—as mother put it—real doctor. They don't trust socialized medicine, so they're cutting the trip short."

Bothered by her flippancy towards Kenneth's health, Lars replied, "That must be upsetting to Jasmine. She loves him so much. Seeing him ill could really scare her."

Shrugging, Angela pushed the salad plate aside and said, "Yes, I'm sure she's worried."

"You didn't talk to her?"

Angela sat more erectly, leaning away, setting her jaw, as she said, "No, she was asleep when mother called. They told her that it's just food poisoning and that he'll be fine—which, in mother's opinion, is a safe assumption."

Not so far in the past, Lars would have joked that Susanne was probably the one who slipped him the poison, Angela would have nodded, laughed, but none of it was amusing to Lars anymore now that his own wife shared in the kind of toxicity her mother dealt.

"I'm sorry for Kenneth's bad fortune," Lars said, as the waiter delivered the second bottle of wine and filled Angela's empty glass, "but I'll be glad to have our girl back home."

Taking a sip, she made a little meaningless sound in response. Again, he found himself zeroed in on the scar, and, for the first time in their marriage, he wondered about the truth of how it had come to be there. After all, he had only ever heard her version of the story.

***

Behind the bars of a rickety crib, their toddler gnawed on a rubber teething toy, listened fretfully to her parents' voices build into shouts, and when her gums ached too much that she could no longer stand it and the noise began to trouble her, she added her own wails to the fray.

"Admit it," Angie had roared, shoving Dave in the chest. "She's the only thing that you give a shit about. You don't care about me. You don't give a fuck about what I want, what I need."

"Take her out of that damn crib. She hates it in there. She's crying. Are you just going to leave her in there bawling while you bitch at me?"

Dave pushed Angie out of the way and lifted his daughter from the soiled mattress where she sat rubbing her red eyes with grubby fists.

"You aren't listening to a word I'm saying. It's like I don't even exist anymore. It's all about *your* kid," she slurred, shifting into a sarcastic tone, as Jasmine calmed and then began to squirm in her father's arms. "Angie, did you remember *my* kid's diapers? Angie, feed *my* kid; she's hungry. Angie, you shouldn't drink so much around *my kid*. You're such a hypocrite! Hell, you're drunk right now, aren't you, Dave."

He sneered at her, set Jasmine on her feet, the toddler grabbing the crib rail for better balance, and said, "Not as drunk as you. Not so drunk that I can't see what a selfish cunt you are. You know, Ang, I thought my ma was messed up, thought she was the self-centered sauce whore, but with all your bullshit, you almost make her look good. You're actually whining your sorry ass off because I love my kid? Because I pay attention to her? Because I ain't paying enough attention to you? Listen,

Princess, the world don't revolve around you anymore. I might not be the smartest guy, and I may not have had any kind of example to show me how to be a dad, but I know one thing, and that's your kid's supposed to come first."

His judgement whipped Angie into a greater fury and she grabbed a mug, with a half inch of apple juice at its bottom, from the milk crate, and threw it at Dave's head. It missed, smashed against the wall above the crib, and landed in sticky chunks of broken ceramic on the spot that, a moment earlier, had been occupied by their daughter. Dave glared before turning his back on her and picking the sharp pieces out of the child's reach as Jasmine tried to stretch her little hand towards a shiny wedge painted with a tiny red bird. The cup had been her favorite and when Dave helped her drink from it, he would ask, "What does the baby bird say when she wants some juice?" Jasmine would tweet like he'd taught her and Dave would smile. Clutching the broken cup handle, Dave saw her fingers inching towards the sharp object just as Angie jumped on his back and began choking him. In one labored breath, he swung his leg out to push his daughter away from danger, swung a hand, the jagged handle still in it, behind him to fend off the assault, and swung everything in Angie's favor.

Beneath the alcohol's fog, Angie's mind had still been able to quickly process what the blood dripping from her head and the blood dripping from the child's mouth could mean. The kid had ruined everything. Angie had wanted to terminate the pregnancy. Dave had talked her out of it, and, thinking that it would solidify her position with him for good, she had finally agreed to have the baby. But now Angie was second, had always been second, would always be second, and all the aspects of Dave's life that she had tolerated before—the cramped apartment, the lack of money, his volatile, ignorant family—no longer felt worth the sacrifice. With no payoff for this vile existence, why should she stay? Although he wanted the child and she did not, Angie would take her because, back in Fargo, back where the family money waited to proffer her the comfort to which she was better suited, back where family values were the credo to which all must pay lip service, Jasmine was the key. To return a fallen woman who abandoned her child would not be prudent, would not be profitable. In fact, Angie, thinking every second more and more like Angela, it wouldn't be possible. From the day Susanne and Kenneth had come to the hospital and slipped a card which conspicuously read "For Jasmine" and contained cash, along with the promise that their only grandchild would always be taken care of, Angela understood that the Erikson wealth that her own choices had dried up to a trickle could flow freely through Jasmine.

Perpetrator turned victim, Angie had snatched up her squalling ticket back to North Dakota and, counting the prolonged anguish it would cause Dave Bordeaux as bonus, had driven into the night.

***

"You haven't seen her tonight?" Lars said, after he set down the carry-on and Jay had asked, "Where's Angela?"

Jay looked confused, shook his head, and said, "I got a text earlier. She said she was taking the later flight with you."

"No, she came in this afternoon. Said she was going to do some retail therapy. Are you sure that's what she texted?"

Sliding the Android off the bar, Jay shrugged.

"Pretty sure. Yeah, here it is. She sent it seven thirty-five p.m."

Something hooked itself into Lars' core and tugged. The message had been sent while the flight was in progress, while all devices were supposed to be powered off or in airplane mode. Retrieving his own phone from the outer pocket of the bag, he powered on and checked the messages. The barb sunk deeper, yanked harder, as he glanced her text. At 7:47 p.m., she informed him that she wouldn't be in Vegas. She wasn't feeling well. He need not call. She was fine.

"Would you like a drink?" Jay asked when he saw the sober way in which Lars was staring at the phone. "Everything okay?"

Lars wasn't sure if he wanted to invite Jay into the weirdness of what had been going on with Angela, but he took the scotch and slumped onto the couch. Certain facts couldn't be avoided, however.

"She's not here. She's not coming."

The men hadn't spent time alone in more than a decade, and the revelation released an unforeseen wave of discomfort for them both. Angela's absence suddenly shifted what had previously felt like something that could be condoned into something for which, both men realized, they could be condemned. Too many secrets kept from too many people for too many years. Jay poured a drink for himself and sat in an armchair across the oval glass coffee table.

"I don't want to start anything here, but you know this doesn't add up, right?"

Lars ran his fingers through his hair, slumped deeper into the sofa cushions, and sighed.

"There's been a lot of that lately. Angela and I … well, let's just say that she's gotten pretty good at pulling the rug out from under me."

Jay nodded, but Lars could tell by the nervous bounce in the other man's knee that he wasn't up for hearing further details; besides, Lars was still trying to convince himself that Angela's odd actions equaled a phase, a temporary glitch. She could become who Lars had once thought she was again. She could be happy, he could be happy, they could be happy again, couldn't they? There was no need to drag Jay into it. By the next Vegas trip, everything might be back to normal, and Lars would feel like an ass for having laid his marital woes out for someone who, despite the sex they occasionally shared, was now more an old acquaintance than a trusted confidant. Undoubtedly, Tipton had some marital strife of his own. Didn't everyone?

"Women can do that, can't they?" Jay said with a tentative half-smile, tactfully redirecting the conversation. "Gwen delivered a shocker a couple of days ago."

Prepared to commiserate, Lars chuckled, saying, "Gwen, too, huh? Must be something in the water. How's yours making life difficult?"

Jay shook his head, feeling somewhat guilty for having created a presumed connection between their situations. The misinformation Angela had fed Lars, as well as to him, had "affair" written all over it, and, in truth, wasn't it the same tactic with which he had been suspending Gwen's belief for years? Who was he to shine a spot light on anyone else's questionable actions? It was better to back away from it and focus on why he'd come here in the first place.

"Shocking, not difficult. Actually, I couldn't be happier. Gwen's pregnant."

Since the birth of their son ten years earlier, the Tiptons had been trying and had all but given up on expanding their family, so, although the news further twisted Lars already-knotted stomach, he jumped up, laughed, slapped Jay on the back and said, "That's beautiful, man. Congratulations."

"Things will get crazy. You know Gwen's last pregnancy was a tough one. And having a baby in the house again, the shitty diapers, the middle-of-the-night feedings, the crying, the endless ear-piercing crying, it's going to be wild." He laughed, and then added, "But it's going to be wonderful."

Awkward silence fell between the two men for a moment. Lars spoke first, sensing what was woven into the announcement, reading what was in Jay's eyes as they darted away from him to the large windows overlooking the brightly-lit City of Sin.

"You're going to be a busy man," Lars said, the contrived levity wrung dry from his tone.

"Yes, I will. A lot is going to have to change. I want to do it right this time."

Jay hadn't thought it would be easy, but he had relied on the assumption that Angela's presence would soften it and allow for a more graceful exit.

Lars shrugged and took a long pull of scotch.

"You're a good man, Jay. You've got your shit together, your head on straight. You've got your priorities in the right order."

"Same goes for you. That's why I know you understand. It's not your fault. I just feel too divided, too guilty, and I know, as my family gets bigger, it's only going to get worse. I'm sorry."

Lars winced at the compliment, at the admission, most of all at the apology, recovering enough to cast Jay an empty smile. Pulled rugs: women could do it to you. Men could, too. He wanted to blame Angela's disappearing act for it, but he knew things would have unfolded like this anyway. He raised his glass in mock toast, Jay reluctantly followed suit.

"To the sacrifices of fatherhood."

"I'm sorry," Jay repeated, drawing back his glass before Lars's glass could touch it.

Lars shook his head, withdrew his own drink from the failed toast, and drained it. For the second time in Lars's life, Jay Tipton had chosen Gwen. Maybe it should have hurt more than it did, but Jay was right. He did understand, and it was this understanding that turned his thoughts to Jasmine. He could lose Jay. Perhaps—although the idea was a sharp-clawed animal in his heart—he could even lose Angela. Lars could survive these losses. But, without doubt, the loss of his beloved Jasmine was inconceivable. That loss would kill him.

The edge smoothed out of his voice as he said, "Don't apologize. Your children are lucky."

Tension drained from Jay's shoulders. "Thanks. So is yours. And no matter how many rugs she's been pulling lately, Angela is lucky, too."

"Sure," Lars said, shoving his phone into a pocket and placing the empty glass on the table; the spacious suite suddenly causing him to feel claustrophobic. "What would you say to heading downstairs, grabbing some dinner, and losing some cash?"

Suddenly, in the back of Lars's mind, Angela's actual words repeated themselves. "I booked a flight to Vegas ... a single flight. I'll leave Friday morning." She didn't specify that she would leave for Nevada. If he called her right now, he knew she wouldn't pick up. If he caught the next flight home, he knew he wouldn't find her there.

"Sounds good," Jay said, doing little to conceal his eagerness to escape the intimacy of the suite.

When they were in the hall, a door closed between what had been and what would now bee, Lars turned to Jay and asked, "Does Angela know about Gwen's news."

Jay shook his head, saying, "Actually, I never talked to her. We just texted back and forth. I wanted to tell you both together. Angela usually calls. I was kind of surprised when I got the messages. She's always been more …."

"Discrete?"

"Yes, discrete, more thoughtful."

Thoughtful Lars silently contemplated. Since Angela's suggestion, since her first invitation, since her seeming acceptance, she had brought the men back together with a great deal of thought, but had it ever been born of thoughtfulness, of her love for him, of her dedication to their relationship, or was Angela's discretion, her careful private planning that seemed to protect everyone linked to something selfish, even sinister? At the risk of handing himself over to undue paranoia, Lars suddenly thought of his wife's cold new capabilities and the descending elevator car in which the men now stood became a mirror-lined cage, reflecting back the image of what she had captured. Jay had fallen in love with Gwen and Lars had accepted it, moved on from it, even found comfort in seeing his friend and former lover happy, but Angela had brought them back. Why?

"You'll never be truly content," she had told Lars, even when he argued that she fulfilled what he wanted, what he needed. "How can you be? I'm a woman. He's a man. Why deny yourself? You can have both. I want to give you that. Let me give you that."

At Angela's urgings, at her convincing him that it was what was best, he had let her draw Jay in, too. After a long arduous pregnancy that had inflicted a great deal of financial, emotional, and psychological strain upon the Tiptons' marriage, a weakness had developed, and Angela stepped right through, selling Jay on the idea that his needs were as important as Gwen's and that his satisfaction was the key to reinforcing a shaky marriage. She had played them both. Without Angela's intercession, the men would have gone on in the comfortable position of old lovers turned distant friends. They would have regretted nothing, knowing that their time together had been a lesson in temporary love that would prepare them for the lifelong ones that they would later find. For Tipton, that had been Gwenn. For Lars … he was no longer as certain as he had been the day he slipped his grandmother's diamond on Angela's finger. His father's assessment had been accurate, to say the least. Angela was indeed complicated, and something more. The forever crescent moon of past pain that crowned her seemed to best symbolize it. She was treacherous.

On the casino floor, Lars let the din, the lights, the frenzied energy of loss and gain swallow him whole. He was just another stranger among strangers, all seeking respite from their realities by deluding themselves with a heavy dose of fantasy. He moved from table to table, soon losing track of Jay and the number of chips won or lost, until he was staring at a queen of diamonds and a three of hearts.

"Hit me," he heard himself say, Angela's sexually-charged voice an echo twisting through his brain. "Hit me!"

The dealer turned over the card. The queen of spades. To Lars' right, someone groaned; behind him, maniacal laughter erupted, and, abandoning the remaining chips and ignoring the phone that had begun to vibrate in his pocket, Lars walked away.

Outside the hotel, Jay Tipton slipped his phone back in his bag and hailed a cab.

Somewhere, on a dark Minneapolis side street, Angela pulled the moon-white Mercedes to the curb, threw her hands to her face, and screamed.

Chapter Fifteen: Watcher

Nostalgia is a powerful tool, a weapon incognito, a drug to reach for when displeasures of the present and fears of the future amalgamate, making the past seem a perfect pill. Nostalgia sells product, puts politicians in office, and drives old lovers back into each other's arms. As she tossed a garment bag and a cosmetics case into the Mercedes trunk that Friday morning and roared out of the subdivision, Angela thought of how well it had served her. At first, she had believed her own sexual appetite, the one repressed by unwanted motherhood, could find satiation in a Jay and Lars reunion, and, in the beginning, the newness of watching them together almost ignited what had once burned so hot for Angela with Dave. Jay had been easy; Gwen's complicated pregnancy had dried up their sex life. Lars, on the other hand, had held out longer, claiming contentment, until, one day, Angela discovered him holding the key.

"Is that him?" she had asked, peering over Lars's shoulder at the photo in his hand. She had walked in on him as he stood over the open drawer of a file cabinet, the light from the home office window illuminating the sentimentality that sculpted Lars face into joy and longing.

"That's us." He nodded at the two young men, black smudges beneath their eyes, in grass- and dirt-stained Bison baseball uniforms, proud grins bright white in the camera's flash. "1999. Jay had just pitched a no-hitter and that future hall of famer"—He tapped the younger image of himself, more wistfulness sweeping over him—"Eighth inning. Bases loaded. I smacked a high line drive just left of center. Tipped off the guy's glove and goodnight … over the fence, baby."

That final game of the season had drawn RedHawks and Twins scouts, every player wishing it was his talent that had brought them, but every player knowing it was Tipton and Sorenson, no player knowing that by the next spring, Tipton would be recouping rotator cuff surgery and Sorenson would be undergoing chemo and radiation.

"You just never know," Lars said, gravel grinding through his voice as he slid the picture back into the drawer and closed it.

The signed baseball on the desk, the NDSU Bison cap on top of the file cabinet, the framed picture of him as a boy standing beside Kirby Puckett, the excitement he couldn't hide when spring training rolled around or when a RedHawk player bought a car from the dealership, the memorabilia, the urgency, the longing: Angela added it up and suddenly she had the tool, the weapon, the drug she needed.

Smiling, she sped onto I-94. It hadn't really been Jay that Lars wanted. It was the window of time out of which Jay had been such a large part, a time in which Lars had viewed himself a future star, a baseball bat-wielding god, an invincible body bound for glory. It was the time before cancer, before all dreams drained away, replaced with a desk at a car dealership, long before nostalgia would have had the power to sway him.

At some point, while Angela was still deriving what she craved, Lars had begun to lose enthusiasm for the trio's Vegas rendezvouses, and she worried he might refuse to participate any longer, so she procured a Bison uniform.

"Put it on. Surprise him," Angela had encouraged when she handed the pants, jersey, and cleats to Tipton. "Lars will love it."

As she had wagered, the stunt worked, time-traveling Lars back and moving her plans forward. For years, she pushed the men's buttons, pulled their strings, whispered suggestions, dropped comments, until what she had contrived for her own gratification began to slowly lose its luster. As she became less satisfied, she became more critical, until she found herself silently critiquing, deconstructing, despising the acts, the movements, the gestures, the male bodies, singularly and entangled, that she had once voyeuristically consumed as sweet, sweaty visual candy. For a while, it had curbed her former appetites, but only for a while, and eventually her sexual methadone could no longer stop Angela from wanting her heroin.

But none of that mattered now, Lars and his boyish baseball fantasy, Tipton's ridiculous sham marriage, their tired old Vegas routine. No wonder Gwen was more interested in being a mommy than a wife. No wonder Angela had lost interest in Lars. Regardless of how or with whom you coupled them, the men were tedious, a double scoop of plain, old vanilla every time.

"Done with that," Angela said aloud, took the Mercedes thirty miles per hour over the limit, and tapped shuffle on her '90s playlist.

***

It wasn't until Jack Bordeaux was out of his Camry, arms loaded with books, laptop, and balancing a tall vanilla latté while walking backwards, hitting the lock button on the key fob, that he noticed the white Mercedes parked a few slots away. The woman who climbed out of it looked as out of place in the South St. Paul Middle School's parking lot as the car, and, at first glance, Jack didn't recognize her.

Definitely not a teacher, not driving that, he thought and turned towards the building's main entrance.

Fall semester didn't begin for a month. He was one of the few faculty members who began home room preparations this early, and most of the staff were still at lunch, so when the woman waved for his attention and began walking towards him, he groaned inwardly, hoping it wasn't the disgruntled parent of some former student upon whom Jack had bestowed a low grade. "I'll get that for you," she called, and rushed forward to open the door.

"Thanks," he said, stepping into the vestibule, his eyes, behind shades, struggling to adjust from the August noon sunshine to the low-lit interior.

"Jack," she said, entering behind him.

In this locale, in these situations, he grown accustomed to being called Mr. Bordeaux, and that, with the familiar way in which she said his name, halted him just beyond the second set of doors.

A simple internet search had turned up next to nothing on Dave Bordeaux, but his brother Jack, on the other hand, seemed to occupy any page devoted to American Indian education, teaching excellence, Native youth programs, or community organizing. She'd only had to follow the relatively few dots to find him here. She slid off her sunglasses and flashed him her warmest, most sincere smile.

"You don't remember me."

Her tone implied that Jack should feel a tinge of guilt about that fact, and, laying down what he carried on a nearby table, he removed his own glasses to get a better look at the thirty-something blonde in designer high-heeled sandals and a flowing sundress, cut low at the neck and high at the hem. Very put together. Very polished. Very pretty.

"Angie?" he stammered, as all the past and present pieces fell in place.

"Yes," she said, moving forward and throwing her arms around him before he could sidestep the advance. "It's so good to see you."

Extricating himself from the awkward embrace with as much courtesy as possible, he said, "It's good to see you, too … but what are you doing here?"

"I'm sorry. I should have called first."

In truth, she had spoken to a helpful young administrative secretary an hour earlier, who had conveniently offered up that Mr. Bordeaux had gone for lunch, but would be back shortly, if Angela wanted to leave a message, which, of course, she had not.

"I didn't have your number," she said as she looked down at her hands and bit her lower lip a bit, as if slightly embarrassed. "I didn't want to bother you at your workplace, but I hadn't another way to reach you."

"That's all right. Really. I'm just surprised to see you. It's been a long time. You're looking well."

Mentally overlapping his face with the picture Angela had discovered on Jasmine's computer, she donned a modest smile, and returned the compliment. She needed to grab for her objective quickly, before he had too much time to think, to formulate questions, to shake off his shock at her impromptu appearance.

"Listen, Jack. I realize that this may be an inconvenient time for me to drop by like this, but I was in town, taking my parents to the airport, and I hoped—although I thought it would be a real longshot—of finding you here. I wouldn't bother you if it weren't for Jasmine."

Dutiful daughter, devoted mother, she could see by Jack's softening expression that she had chosen correctly.

"Do you remember Jasmine?" she asked, again framing it in just enough accusation to trigger any potential misplaced culpability, and then adding to it for full effect, "Your niece."

Jack's memory flipped back to May, to the Festival of Nations, to the girl named Jasmine, to his suspicion about her identity, to his decision not to pursue it, and he nodded, casting his gaze over her shoulder rather than meet her eyes, which, in their intensity, were a cold contrast to the rest of her warm, friendly demeanor.

"She's fourteen, a lovely girl, smart, inquisitive, a joy to me and my husband."

Jack was pleased at the thought that Angie had found someone and that Jasmine was being raised with a father figure.

"We've given her the best of everything, but the older she gets, the more questions she has. My husband Lars has been wonderful, but ...."Angela felt her nails digging into her palms as she continued to paint the Sorenson family portrait, all the time weighing Jack's response, wondering if he was buying the story.

"For Jasmine's sake, for her sense of wholeness, we think it's important that she have the opportunity to get to know Dave. I've tried to find him, but I haven't had any luck. I'm hoping that you can help me."

Something tightened in Jack's throat, in his chest, in his core, as his brother's anger pulsed through his brain.

"That's a done deal. Some shit, you've just got to let go of and move on. I'm warning you. Leave it alone. It's none of your damn business," Dave had said a few years earlier when Jack had asked if he ever wondered about the child that Dave hadn't seen in over a decade.

It wasn't his business, not really, but having grown up without a father, Jack couldn't help but relate to Jasmine's need. As her uncle, maybe it was his business, maybe it was his obligation, and maybe it was the reason the universe had directed Angie here first. She seemed sincere in her efforts, even a bit desperate, and Jack wanted to help, but was unsure of how much he wanted to get involved. In his pocket, in his phone, in his contacts, he had a number. Over two months had passed since he'd talked to his brother, though, and usually when Jack did call, Dave didn't respond. Should Jack just give it to her? Dave didn't need his protection, did he?

"I understand," Jack said. "I have a number, but I'm not sure whether—""I don't want to infringe upon anyone's privacy," Angela anxiously inserted, knowing a number wouldn't get her what she had come for. "I've thought about how I would feel if I were to receive a call like that. I was thinking of something more gradual. A phone call might be too large a first step. I would hate for this to go wrong. Jasmine could get hurt if we don't do this right."

Jack's face reddened, suddenly feeling foolish for not having thought it through as much as Angie obviously had, and he said, "You're right. I'm sorry. What do you think would be best?"

Inwardly, Angela reveled at the closeness of the prize, a reward for all her careful planning, and, choosing her conscientious, level-headed mother voice, the one she pulled out for PTA meetings and parent-teacher conferences, she said, "A letter. I thought she could start by writing Dave a letter."

Already knowing what his response would be, she prepared to appear somewhat shocked. "He doesn't have an email address, as far as I know."

Angela didn't breathe, her nails biting the flesh of her palm once again, as she waited, willing him to continue, willing him to offer the crowbar that could free her from her locked life. Behind the pretty pink smile, she silently screamed, "Say it. God damn you, say it!" A bead of sweat ran between her shoulder blades, down her spine, to the tip of her tailbone, its descent chilling her inch by inch. Perhaps she had played this wrong. Maybe he could see through her cover, see through the sheer material of the dress to where her heart threatened to beat from her chest, see through her feigned motherly concern to what was beneath it.

Juggling the pros and cons of what he thought he was about to do, Jack considered Dave's privacy and the effect this could have on their relationship if Dave linked him to a breech in it. He thought of the sweet, innocent face he'd only glimpsed at the festival and how the girl's future might form if she were to never know his brother, her father. He recalled how, secretly, he had cheered Angie's choice to leave Minneapolis and, despite Dave's rants about it, Jack had retained the opinion that she had always had their child's best interests in mind. Even now, as Angie's hands trembled slightly and the corner of her left eye twitched, Jack couldn't help but believe that her intentions were noble. She had gone to the effort, driven out of the way, with no guarantee that she would even catch him here, her daughter her only motivation. Would Jack's mother ever have gone that far for him, for Dave, for any of her nine children?

Knowing, he ran ahead, hurtling across the empty holes in his own childhood, and said, "I have a street address."

After she was gone, Jack wondered if he should have given her more than that. Should he have filled in at least some of the blanks, to warn her, to prepare her, to, perhaps, dissuade her? In the end, he told himself that some stories, especially those like Dave Bordeaux's, were simply not his to tell.

***

By early Friday evening, Angela had left St. Paul, reached Minneapolis, located the Bryant Avenue duplex, knocked on the south unit's door—with vicious barking the only response—drove up to Lake Street, found a liquor store, and returned to Bordeaux's house. With the pint of vodka on the seat beside her, she parked across the street and waited. Her loosely-knit plan hadn't included a stakeout, and the few pedestrians passing through the neighborhood alerted her to how conspicuous the Mercedes was. Although the heavy tint on the windows gave her some cover, the looks the car attracted jangled her nerves. She broke the seal and took a drink. Thirty minutes passed, then forty-five. At the hour mark, the bottle was half empty, and she caught movement at the front of the duplex. A morbidly obese woman came out of the north unit on a motorized cart.

That explains the ramp, Angela thought, watching the woman slowly roll down from the raised slab of concrete patio that the two units shared.

Like the other passers-by, she gawked at the Mercedes for a moment before motoring on. Glaring, Angela said under her breath, "That's right, bitch, keep moving. There's another donut out there with your name on it."

Twisting the cap off the vodka, she wondered how a person like that let themselves become such a mess. Didn't the woman have any self-respect? The sun dipped below the rooftops and the elm and maple trees that lined the street, casting things in deep shadow. The bottle was two-thirds gone, when she slipped into memories edited by fantasy. Angela is twenty, Dave two or three years past it; the parking lot where they first meet, he, a six-pack in hand, she, a bag of apples, a pack of cigarettes; the hood of the Mercedes; he lifting her onto the hot metal, ripping the costly dress from her flesh, she raking her nails deep into his biceps, neither caring who sees, who knows, who objects. They are snarling wordless sounds. His arms bleed, the muscles of his legs are taut, punishing, bruising the inside of her thighs. Her teeth lock into his shoulder, tongue tasting sweat, tasting blood. She is aware that someone watches. It is someone who shouldn't want to see this and that is why she wants them to keep watching. The watcher comes closer. She can see who it is now, and she smiles, pleasure and pain flooding her, flooding Bordeaux, flooding Adam, as his cold blue eyes meet his sister's stare.

A vehicle approached behind her and Angela's lids flickered open in time to see a van pull into the duplex's driveway. The angle didn't allow her to see who was at the wheel, but when the driver's door opened, a woman climbed out. She was wearing a black tank top, cargo shorts, and sneakers. Her dark hair was cut very short, and when she unlatched the back door of the van, Angela caught a glimpse of a sticker supporting the troops and another that said something about veterans. From the other side of the van, a boy, around five or six years old, appeared and held out a hand. The woman, who Angela presumed was his mother, gave him a bag of groceries, and the boy raced up the ramp to the door of the south unit. With muscular arms straining under the weight of several more packages, the woman left the van open and followed the child up the ramp, unlocked the door, a brown and white pit bull shooting out to the yard to lift a leg against an evergreen bush, and then woman, boy, and dog went inside.

Angela's stomach fluttered. Who were they? A wife? A son? A sister? A nephew? Because she preferred it, Angela's mind recalled how the Bordeaux family used to tend to congregate under one roof—parents, grandparents, sisters, brothers, nieces, nephews; basically any member who needed a place to flop, to get their feet back on the ground—and she told herself that they probably were a single niece and her son. Angela wondered why she had left the van open like that, and, after a few minutes, when it didn't seem as if the woman was going to return, Angela silently chastised such irresponsible behavior. Someone could come along and steal something.

The boy came back outside and stood at the top of the ramp, bouncing from foot to foot, looking expectantly towards the driveway. Along the avenue, streetlights began to blink on; some of the light pooling at the van's open rear door, and Angela's eyes moved from the child to where the halogen shed its glow.

A breath just taken lodged itself in her chest as reality came into view from the side of the van and stopped at the open rear door. She couldn't breathe. She couldn't drag her eyes off of it. She couldn't pry her mind from it or believe who was trapped in it.

The boy jumped the length of the ramp and ran to meet him. The man pulled out more grocery bags and the boy took them. The last sack, the man placed on his lap and slammed the van door. Steering to face the street for a moment, he squinted at the Mercedes, and Angela choked as she forced herself to look at the twelve inches of stump that remained where the man's legs had once been.

The boy jack rabbit hopped up the ramp and, with a shake of his head and a grin, Dave Bordeaux secured the bag on his lap with one hand, using the other to push the wheelchair's control stick forward. By the time the pair reached their front door, Angela was gone. Somewhere in Las Vegas, Lars Sorenson walked away and left his remaining chips on the table. Somewhere, on a dark Minneapolis side street far from Bryant Avenue, Angela pulled the moon-white Mercedes to the curb, threw her hands to her face, and screamed.

Chapter Sixteen: Evidence Tampering

Faye Gunderson bookmarked the Cornwell paperback, wondering, as she often did, why she chose to read about sociopathic serial killers and gruesome crime scenes before bed, and was reaching for the night table to flip off the lamp, when the dogs began to bark. Her heart raced as she glanced at the iPhone and realized that it was after midnight, and, momentarily considering the handgun in the antique dresser's bottom drawer, she crawled from beneath the covers, pulled a robe on, and peeked out from behind the curtains at the farm yard below. Through the pitch darkness of the grove, headlights, set on bright, were approaching up the long gravel lane at a rapid rate. Like Faye, the dogs were unaccustomed to late night visitors, and they let go a frenzied chorus of growls, whines, howls, and yips, but she wasn't going to quiet them or leave the room that held the firearm until she figured out who the hell was tearing onto her property like the law or the devil was in hot pursuit. The car reached the wide area of gravel that lay between the barn and the house, and the driver did a braking turn that sent sprays of pea rock and dust flying across the adjacent flower bed. Shifting from anxious to angry, Faye muttered, "You better have not hurt my geraniums, you son of a bitch."

With the high beams now pointed at the lane, the yard light revealed Angela's white Mercedes, and Faye's annoyance melted a little, the apprehension returning, as she went downstairs. She calmed the dogs the best she could and stood by the door, but several minutes passed and Angela, or whoever was driving her car, didn't show.

"Maxwell. Come here, boy."

The German Shepard hurried over and stood beside Faye's leg, pressing, waiting, protecting. The smaller dogs protested, wanting in on the action, but she commanded them to stay, opened the front door, and she and the largest dog stepped onto the porch. The car's headlights still slashed through the dark towards the gravel road beyond, and just above the sleepy song of crickets and the soft rustle of cottonwood leaves, Faye could hear the faint rhythmic warning ding of an ignition bell and the sound of someone retching.

"Let's go see, boy."

The huge dog shot off the porch, and Faye grudgingly followed, dreading what she thought she was about to find. That girl was too young to be out drinking and joy riding. Surely, Lars and Angela had more control over her than that, but, then again, Jasmine was Angela's daughter, and Faye supposed Angela's troubled youth might be the girl's unfortunate inheritance. Did the kid think that her good old aunt was going to bail her out of this? God, she was glad that the only youngsters she had ever raised had paws, hooves, and wings.

She found Max standing beside the open Mercedes door, frantically wagging his tail, while some pathetic creature groaned, "Get away," and then deposited more puke onto the gravel.

"Damn stupid kid. It serves you right," Faye said under her breath as she stomped over to the Mercedes, prepared to find Jasmine and probably a teen accomplice or two.

Once more, feeling satisfied with the decision to have gone into veterinary medicine rather than motherhood, she asked the obedient shepherd to step aside, as she seized the handle and yanked the car door wide open. With a pitiful moan, Angela lost balance and fell out sideways onto the vomit-soaked gravel.

Despite the fact that Faye's profession regularly involved wrestling with large dogs and livestock, her drunken niece posed more than her share of difficulty on the way out of the car, up the porch stairs, through the house, and to the tub, where Faye unceremoniously dumped her, still clothed, and turned on the shower.

"This is a three hundred-dollar Lilly Pulitzer," Angela shrieked, the words slurred together like the water spots, vomit, and mud stains marring the fabric from bodice to hem.

"That's the least of your troubles, sweetheart," Faye said, and aimed the shower head at Angela's filthy arms, then her hands, finishing at her grimy bare legs and feet. "Thank God we left those nasty shoes on the porch. Now skin off that overpriced dress. It's ruined."

As if her aunt's statements were more offensive than her own middle-of-the-night intrusion, the younger woman scowled, leaned against the tile wall, crossed her arms, and made no effort to remove the sodden garment. Faye raised a brow and, with the gentleness of an electric nail gun, said, "Do you think this is a game? I'm not playing. You don't get to bring this into my house and then act like a spoiled brat. You fouled my driveway, you got my dogs upset, you took out part of my flower bed, and, worst of all, you risked your life and the lives of anyone who was on the road between here and Fargo. That pisses me off, Angela, so if you don't want to piss me off further –and believe me, you do not—you're going to wipe that bitchy look off your face and listen to me, or the sheriff is just a phone call away."

Crumpling beneath the threat, Angela pulled her knees into her chest and began to shake violently, low sobs rising, gaining horrific strength until they became wails of such soul-ripping sadness the hair on Faye's neck rose. As if uncertain of their existence, Angela kept running her hands up and down her lower legs, pausing at her feet, examining each toe before she slid her fingers back towards her knees, until the sobs choked off into a ragged whimper. Faye sighed and then, with gentle firmness, helped her niece out of the wet, stained wreckage of her clothes, while Angela shuddered and mewled like a wounded animal.

When Faye had her clean, dry, and wrapped up in a soft terry robe, she said, "I'm going to call Lars."

Angela's eyes widened and she shook her head with more insistence than Faye would have guessed she still had energy for at that point, saying, "No, don't. He's in Vegas."

Faye frowned, running fingers through her short gray hair, as she recollected the number of times in the last few years that he and Angela had gone there. He was in Nevada now and she was home alone, drinking her way towards alcohol poisoning. Gambling addiction? Money troubles? Angela's choice of attire gave Faye pause, though. Who shimmied into a sexy little sundress, a lacy bra and thong, and high heeled shoes for a night at home with a bottle of booze?

"Okay," she said and put a glass of water in her niece's hand. "Drink it all. You'll thank me in the morning."

Angela shoved strands of wet hair from her face and drank. The shower had sobered her up a little, but she looked haggard, on the verge of collapse. Her eyes were a dull blue pane of scratched glass and spidery lines crept out from their corners. The crescent scar shone pink at her hairline, drawing Faye's attention, adding to the trickle of sympathy she had begun to feel, despite the lingering irritation. For better or for worse, Angela was family, and the fact that Susanne was her mother was enough to warrant at least some sympathy. Susanne took all her practical knowledge of how to relate to a daughter from her and Faye's mother, and Faye knew firsthand the icy pragmatism of it.

She slid an arm around Angela and guided the unsteady woman to the guest room. They could work things out tomorrow in the light of day, when coffee had been brewed and aspirin swallowed. She helped Angela into bed and pulled a quilt over her as the younger woman's lids drooped towards sleep.

"We'll talk in the morning," Faye said, patted her niece's shoulder, turned off the light, and closed the door.

Once upstairs, after she had cleaned up and was in a fresh nightgown and beneath the cool comfort of her own sheets, Faye could not extinguish the thoughts firing through her brain. She lived a quiet life, an uncomplicated life, a life that, by design, kept her content and out of the kinds of human drama that she had always detested. There had been those who couldn't understand her choices—most notably and vocally, her mother—but Faye lived by a kind of inner guidance system, and her system had never been wrong. It had selected her career. Her status as a single woman resulted from it. Even the quiet, remote acreage where she lived was its approved destination. Often people had the nerve to presume how lonely Faye must be without a husband, without children, so far from town. They would shake their heads and comment that they could not imagine it for themselves. But she didn't share their opinions or embrace the names she knew that they used behind her back because Dr. Faye Gunderson, spinster hermit, had peace, fulfillment, success, the devotion and companionship of the animals she rescued, and, over the years, as the need arose, a lover here and there. In fact, she wondered sometimes if their unwarranted pity was really just envy in disguise. But Angela's after-hours arrival tossed too much salt in the soup, and the questions floating to the surface wouldn't let Faye sleep.

Finally, she propped the pillows behind her, turned on the lamp, and opened the crime novel. Three chapters later, as another corpse was discovered and the medical examiner snapped on latex gloves, she finally dozed off.

Despite the previous night's excitement, Faye rose with the sun as she usually did. She checked on Angela, who was still dead asleep, and made coffee before she headed out the kitchen door. With the dogs close at her heels, she set off to do morning chores. The damage to the flower bed was more evident in daylight and she knelt to see what could be salvaged and which ones were a loss. Her love of plants was second only to her love of animals, and she whispered an apology as she sadly deposited the ruined marigolds and bachelor buttons onto the compost pile. Next, she connected the garden hose to the well pump and dealt with the fly-covered mess beside the Mercedes. Angela owed her answers, as well as an apology.

After the horses, ducks, and chickens were fed and watered and she had mucked out the stalls and thrown down a couple of fresh hay bales from the loft, Faye stood at the door of the barn, wiped sweat from her forehead, and considered the white Mercedes for a minute. Her niece most definitely had some explaining to do, but, having watched Susanne dodge reality for most of their lives, Faye wondered if her sister's daughter had ever learned how to come clean. Somehow, she doubted it. Angela wouldn't be rising any time soon and, if she did, the window of the guest room was on the opposite side of the house. Sometimes, you had to collect on what was owed. One way or another. Faye looked down at her leather work gloves and smirked. *No fingerprints* she thought, as she sauntered towards the car and opened the door.

It didn't take much of a detective to follow the evidence trail. Two empty Smirnoff bottles lay on the floor of the passenger side. Wadded up sales receipts littered the seat, along with a half pack of Marlboros. Flattening out the register tape, Faye blinked, her heart lodging in her throat. She checked the date and time twice, and then a third time, unable to accept what it meant, and how much more serious the situation had just become with the revelation. She found Angela's purse in the back seat, and lugged it into the front. It held a hair brush, lipstick, prescription sedatives, and all the other usual contents of the average woman's handbag. Reaching into a smaller front pocket, she pulled out a folded slip of paper. On one side, it was imprinted with the requested information needed for a student hall pass, but the spaces were blank. On the opposite side, in neat handwritten script, was a Minneapolis street address. Somehow knowing what she would find, Faye took Angela's smart phone from the cup holder and accessed the GPS history. Briefly, she wondered if she was going too far, prodding too deep into Angela's private life, but, for whatever reason, her niece had chosen to recklessly deliver herself and the uglier aspects of that life into Faye's hands and, if there was one thing everyone knew about Faye Gunderson, it was that she didn't deal in deception and drama. If you were going to stir the pot, you better be ready to admit to why you picked up the spoon. Suddenly, she caught movement out of the corner of her eye, and she froze, prepared to justify her actions, but when she turned to look, Max and Vince, her Springer Spaniel, were trotting optimistically towards the car. She exhaled and took the keys from the ignition, climbed out, and said, "Sorry, guys. We'll go for a ride in our truck later, okay?"

Seemingly satisfied, the dogs sat on their haunches and watched as she popped the trunk. The overnight bag's assortment of sex toys and condoms only tossed another line into Faye's quagmire of suspicions. Jammed next to the wheel well, crushed beneath the baggage, there was a glossy paper shopping bag. Faye opened it to find a collection of high-priced cosmetics and a gift-wrapped box that looked like it could be perfume. The glittery neon ribbons made her think that it might be for a teenager—perhaps Jasmine. The bag's receipt indicated that the purchases had occurred in May. It was just another odd piece in an already-strange puzzle. How could Angela have forgotten nearly two hundred dollars' worth of merchandise, including a present for her daughter, in the trunk of her car for three months? With its bent sparkle bow and crushed corner, the abandoned gift sent a flicker of sadness through Faye. More than just this had been damaged and forgotten. She placed the cosmetics beside the overnight bag, but she set the brightly wrapped gift on top before carefully shutting the trunk lid.

"So what are you going to tell her?" Angela asked the washed-out, puffy-eyed face in the bathroom mirror.

She could hear Faye in the kitchen pouring kibble into stainless steel dog bowls, the ping of hard bits against metal suddenly shoving a vacant wheelchair, blindingly shiny, through Angela's thoughts. Though empty, her stomach lurched and she gripped the sink. Faye would demand answers and Angela couldn't bear the ugliness of the truth. She couldn't confess to the now unattainable fantasy, or how the loss of it made her wish that she could dig her nails into her mind and rip out the repulsive reality that had robbed her of it. How could she look the woman in the eye and say, "If I return to that house, that man, that child, I might lose my sanity"?

When she had left Fargo the day before, her intention had been to return after reuniting with Dave, after greedily grabbing as much of what he had once given her as she could, and after they had arranged future clandestine meetings. She had constructed a scenario which saw to all her needs, both sexual and financial, because, upon closer consideration, she had recognized that she really would miss the upper class lifestyle to which she had grown accustomed. She would simply apply the model she had fabricated with Lars and Jay to her unique situation. It had all seemed so workable. In a few years, Jasmine would be leaving home and the bulk of Angela's mothering would be done. With her blessing, but without her participation, Lars could carry on with the Vegas trips. If it became too complicated or if Dave asked, she would leave Lars and take her half. Yes, it had seemed so simple. The plan had fueled her forward, and she had imagined that it would pump enough life into her that she could go back, but now she was back and she was still empty, without hope of ever again feeling full.

Through her thoughts, the faces of Angela's disappointments began a slow slideshow. Kenneth, Susanne, Adam, Lars, Jasmine, Dave: they came laden with lists of reasons why she resented them. Each shadowy image delivered the details of her downfall. They were the cinder blocks, steel bars, cold concrete of her prison, and she felt them pressing, pressing, pressing in on her until she wanted to scream, but the words only fell into the sink as soft, gritty powder.

"I hate you."

She said it to each, she said it to all, until they faded, and the cell that held her crumbled. She looked in the mirror again. There was a new hardness to the line of her jaw, in her stony stare, set into the horizontal uniformity of her mouth. She could tell that most of the softness had been chiseled away, and she liked it.

"Run, Angie."

She would, but this time, she would not just impetuously flee as she had done when she was young and impervious and ignorant to what *really* turned the world on its axis. This time, she would prepare; a marathon runner training for an organized event. This time, she wouldn't leave empty-handed.

Though her head ached, the hot laser-cut of it carved her thoughts into more clearly concise ideas, pressure, the propulsion driving her forward, and she pushed a finger hard against the most tender spot at the temple, thrilling for an instant at the sensation. The knock at the bathroom door startled her and she jerked the finger away, Faye's voice reaching in.

"There's a cup of coffee for you on the kitchen table."

Tuning to something that sounded slightly weak, a little remorseful, and appropriately gracious, Angela responded.

"Thank you, Aunt Faye. I'll be out in a minute."

Funny how she had ended up here last night, when the thought of being alone had twisted her inside out, and how, in this moment, as sunlight stabbed between the window blinds, beautiful slashes of soreness sweeping her head clean, she only wanted, only needed to be with herself, with Angie. But now was not the time to begin the run. Now was the time to train, to lay the ground work, to test the capacity of someone who might defend her move, to make everything appear organized, look reasonable, perhaps even look admirable. Another sharp needle nose pinch behind the eye brought everything more brilliantly into view: the course, the finish line, and the pace she would have to keep to reach it. For a little longer, Angie, the escapee, must hide herself between the protective folds of Angela's life.

Coffee and dry toast consumed, and Faye's admission to everything she had found in the Mercedes setting the pieces she had to work with before her, Angela assembled a story. Its beginning established a tone of apology and recognition of wrongdoing, Angela pausing often to cast a look downwards, bowing and shaking her head slightly, as if shame and disbelief were in control.

"I wasn't thinking clearly. I found something, it completely rocked me, and I just reacted. At first, I was hurt, and then I got mad. It took over."

Across the table, Faye pushed her bowl of yogurt aside, leaned forward, resting her elbows on the woven fiber mat, and said, "Would you like to tell me what it is that you found? I assume it's monumental enough to have destroyed your sobriety."

Angela sat back a bit and meekly nodded, as if the topic frightened her, but as if she acknowledged and appreciated her aunt's willingness to discuss it. The commitment was there; now all Angela had to do was seize it. She paused, caught her bottom lip in her teeth for a moment, assumed a distraught expression, and delivered the main conflict of the tale she was twisting together out of fact and fiction.

"It's Lars. I think he's having an affair."

Faye sighed, but didn't appear overly shocked, instead darkening under the memory of her own dalliances with a traveling pharmaceutical rep who she later discovered had a wife and three kids back in Bismarck.

Angela worked a tear to the surface. "We were supposed to spend the weekend together in Vegas. He flew out early on business and I was going to meet him late yesterday afternoon. I don't know why, but things have been really strained between us lately, and I've tried to talk to him but he never wants to discuss it. He just seems more and more withdrawn. I thought ... well, you know, that we could relax, maybe get the spark back."

Faye remembered the contents of the overnight bag, cringed slightly, and then nodded. Angela mentally marked that indelicate detail as covered and continued.

"I've been suspicious for a few months, ever since he took off one Sunday afternoon and wound up with a flat tire just outside of Minneapolis. He never told me why he was going there, and when I pressed, he got angry and accused me of not trusting him. So I let it drop, but it kept eating at me. Yesterday, I called him before I left for the airport, just to check in, tell him that I was looking forward to our time together."

Angela hesitated, squeezed her eyes closed for a moment, as if holding back tears.

"He was already at the hotel and he wasn't alone. I could hear someone in the background laughing, saying his name. I asked who was with him and he told me that no one was there, but I know what I heard. He lied."

She must tread carefully now. If she slipped and said, or even insinuated that Lars was cheating with another woman, it would be difficult to backtrack later on if the leverage the truth could provide ever became necessary.

"I lost it then. I tore through everything: his desk, his drawers, his closet, file cabinets, everything. That's when I found a flash drive with pictures and the address. I know it's crazy because I knew I wasn't going to find anyone there, but I had already had a couple of drinks and I kept looking at the address like it had all the answers. I thought if I went there, saw the house or the apartment or whatever I was going to see, it would make sense. It would make it clear to me why ... how Lars could do this to me, to Jasmine, to our family."

The righteous indignation needed to bring the story to its conclusion came easily. All she had to do was think of Dave Bordeaux's ruined body, the way the sight of it had made her want to escape, vomit, and violently attack him, all at the same time, how that pathetic, useless, crippled son-of-a-bitch had blown her hopes to bits while he looked at that little boy and smiled, as if, in that mangled body, in that wrecked life, Dave Bordeaux had the audacity to actually be happy, to be happier than her. Holding that one scene, she created another as she repositioned people, places, and events, put her thoughts into someone else's head, shoved her own recently-spoken words into Lars' mouth, and dismantled, then reconstructed, everything to suit her objective.

When she was finished, Angela looked at her aunt. Faye sadly shook her head, stared out the kitchen window at the hot, hazy Saturday melting into shape, and said, "I'm sorry to hear this, Angela. I really am. It doesn't excuse you, but I guess it better explains it."

"What happened last night, the drinking, the way I showed up here, the way I acted ... it won't happen again. Thank you for everything, Aunt Faye, especially for being someone I can confide in," she said, trickling a thin line of embarrassment into it. "I haven't decided how I will handle things with Lars, but I would appreciate it if you—"

"Of course," Faye quickly intervened. "You shared this with me. Only me. I won't break that trust."

For a heartbeat, Angela felt a barely distinguishable tic. It might have been regret, or maybe even guilt, but it passed quickly, stilled by something stronger, a craving that had neither tolerance nor time for compunction. Angela lived for Angie now; everyone else, including Faye, were just dots on a map that she must pass through to get where she wanted to go. Angela didn't feel beholden to the woman, but she did admire the comfortable, unapologetic way she had always lived in her own skin. Angie liked that about her, too. Maybe someday, when the run was over and the dust settled, the two would meet.

Later, as Faye walked her niece to the Mercedes, Angela wearing one of her aunt's Humane Society T-shirts and drawstring knit shorts, along with her own hosed-off glitzy designer sandals, Faye took long looks at the odd ensemble and tried to understand why, even after Angela had fit all the strangely shaped pieces together, the larger picture didn't seem quite clear, quite plausible, quite true. She couldn't put a finger on what kept her from believing it, but as Angela told the story and Faye sensed much of it to be a lie, something also told her it would be risky to voice that disbelief.

Angela froze for a split second as she opened the trunk to put the plastic bag that held her ruined dress inside and glimpsed the bright gift that Faye hadn't mentioned earlier perched on top of her luggage. In that instant, before she threw the bag in and slammed the lid, Faye caught the lightning flash of deep disgust that crossed the woman's icy blue eyes. Faye Gunderson knew that look well; her mother had struck Faye with it a million times, Susanne a million more.

When the Mercedes drove away and disappeared from her view, Faye called her dogs; they gathered around her, and, in need of something to thaw what gripped her heart, she dropped to her knees and opened her arms to their eager warmth.

Chapter Seventeen: Invested

The woman Lars worried he wouldn't find when he returned home from Las Vegas wasn't there, but the one he did discover waiting somehow disturbed him more. With calm, collectedness, and a level of consideration previously foreign to her, Angela greeted him, arms open, assurances on her lips. First, she apologized for her no-show status, saying that she was feeling much better, and that she hoped the men had enjoyed themselves without her. Angela's sallow complexion and the puffy discoloration crowning her cheekbones quickly erased Lars' theory that the illness claim was a ruse, and guilt trickled through him every time he caught a glimpse of the angry red spider veins creeping across the whites of Angela's eyes. At the news of Gwen's pregnancy and Jay's exit, she was again conciliatory, but quickly added that she was happy for the Tiptons, a tight smile of satisfaction curling her mouth as Lars looked away. When he brought his attention back her direction, the smile vanished, she patted the loveseat and asked him to join her, and, for a moment, her invitation of physical closeness made him wary, despite how much he had missed it.

"Let's talk," she said in a voice so pacifying it hinted at incapacitation, and it set off warning bells that if he were not careful, he would be pulled under its narcotic power. But, unable to resist, Lars sat. She took his hand and ran a manicured finger along the platinum wedding band. "We need a fresh start."

Angela felt him tense beneath her touch, and she knew what he must be thinking. She paused, letting enough time pass for his fright to form a thin sheen of perspiration across his forehead, and she considered how vulnerable, how easy, the loyal and the committed made themselves. Lars finally opened his mouth to speak, but before he could, she said, "I believe Jay has the right idea."

He stayed soundlessly agape for another moment, and then sealed his shock behind a stony pale grimace. A fist in his chest and a voice in his head told him that the thought that had gnawed away at him the entire return trip was on the brink of becoming reality. Angela was going to leave him. Bracing, he turned to meet her eyes and with surprising composure, said, "What do you mean, he has it right?"

She smiled, her hand slipping down and cuffing his wrist with a startling amount of strength, causing the Rolex she had purchased with their money to pinch uncomfortably into the pulse point. She watched the shift of his Adam's apple as he tried to swallow the thing he thought she was feeding him.

"I want us to re-invest in our family."

He felt his whole body crumble inside the rumpled suit jacket, and he blinked back tears of relief as she spoke of her emotional absence, her wish to return, and her remorse for having been gone so long. Well-schooled in the terminology of counselors and the counseled, she said all the right things—intimacy, quality time, shared responsibility—and he listened, nodded his enthusiasm, seemingly unaware that she never once used the word love. Only later, as she reached for him in their bed and he felt the steady, single-gear movements that gave her apathy away did he doubt whether he had really been given what he thought he wanted. But when he hesitated, she again chose words that a committed, loyal husband could not resist, and Lars let himself fall forward into Angela's emptiness. As he climaxed, he buried his face in the curve of her neck and breathed in, searching for the familiar sweet scent of flowers. But he didn't find it. In its place, he detected something stronger, and its almost overpowering dark spiciness seized him, causing him to cough and roll away from its source.

***

Lars watched Jasmine unwrap the gift from Angela, briefly wondering why it was in such shabby shape. The glitter bow was bent, the corner crushed, and it hadn't included a birthday card. He told himself that it didn't really matter, that he had become hyper-observant of all Angela's actions since their fresh start, and that the beautifully decorated bakery cake and her acceptance of Rosella since Jasmine's return from Europe outweighed the present's odd outer shell.

"Perfume," Jasmine said, staring at the box's image of the pop music star who attached her name to the product. "Thanks, Mom."

"Nice!" Rosella added, as she lightly kicked Jasmine under the table and reached for it to get a better look at the brunt of so many of their jokes. "She's such an amazing dancer. I'm sure her fragrance is epic."

Remembering Rosella's favorite farcical imitation of the star's moves, which basically added up to Ro pretending to hump everything in range, Jasmine started to snicker, and then she caught her mother's unreadable expression, stopped, and took the last bite of chocolate cake. Angela wanly smiled. She could tell that the girl didn't like the perfume.

"You're welcome, Jasmine," she said, keeping the tone perfectly balanced between warmth and coolness. "I'm glad that you like it." An awkward pause followed, all of the occupants at the Sorenson's dining table feeling the silence's compression, until Rosella grabbed a shiny turquoise gift bag and set it in front of Jasmine.

"Mine next," she said excitedly. "I so hope you love it.

"Jasmine took the tissue-padded object from the bag, unfolded the paper, and, gasping, turned a bright shade of pink on both sides of her huge grin. She cradled the heart-shaped beadwork keychain and stared at the picture framed in its center. There stood Sage Koskinen, in full dance regalia, looking directly into the camera, looking directly at her. Not letting go of the beautiful handmade keepsake, she threw her arms around Rosella, saying, "I really, really adore it!"

"Yes," Lars teased when he glimpsed it. "And I bet she likes the key chain, too."

"You're going to need it when you get your learning permit and your dad gives you driving lessons." Rosella grinned at her friend and then at Lars. "Right, Mr. S?"

"Sure," Lars said with mock seriousness. "That's the first question the DMV will ask. Miss Sorenson, do you have a cool keychain? Because if you don't, we can't issue a permit.

"From her safe distance, Angela watched, as if observing everything from behind a two-way mirror, and as the Bachman girl let loose another burst of laughter, Lars played the role of World's Greatest Dad, and the gift that couldn't scream "Indian" any louder if it tried, dangled off his daughter's finger, Angela prided herself on the way all of it no longer caused her care. The marathon training was going well, and the thought of her accomplishments brought a smile just as Lars glanced her direction. His eyes brightened and he moved a hand towards Angela, as if expecting her to grasp it. "Would anyone like another slice of cake?" she asked, ignoring his gesture and rising from her chair, and although none of them said they did, she disappeared into the kitchen, and Lars moved the hand to wad up a chocolate-smudged party napkin. *She is re-investing in our family*, he thought, and for the second time that week, the notion was followed up with his mind flashing a scene from *The Stepford Wives*.

After the party, when Jasmine and Rosella had hidden themselves away in the girl's room and Lars and Angela were at the opposite end of the house in their own forms of seclusion, Rosella sniffed at the open bottle of perfume.

"This shit doesn't stink as bad as I thought it would," she said and held it under Jasmine's nose. "Not too awful. It's unfortunate it has that skank's name on it though."

Jamming the lid back on, Rosella set the bottle on the desk and dropped into the chair.

Jasmine sighed loudly, and stroked the purring cat curled on her lap as she asked, "Ro, have you ever thought that one of your parents was acting really weird?"

"Yeah, like every other day. Why?"

"I don't mean like the normal weird way adults act. I mean like those movies where an alien pod moves into someone's body and the person starts acting too perfect because the totally creepy thing inside of them doesn't want anyone to know until its ready to take over the world."

"You like the sci-fi horror stuff, Jas? That's so geeky chic."

"I'm being serious here. Have you ever thought that about your mom?" Jasmine said, and then added, "Or your dad?"

"No. I guess they're mostly just freaky in all the usual ways. Are you saying that while you were in Europe, Mister and Missus S drank some UFO Kool-Aid? Because if that's what you're saying, I'm going to think *you're* the one who's gone mentally missing.

"Jasmine hurled a throw pillow at Rosella, and said with more irritation than she actually felt, "I didn't mean it literally."

"I know. I know," Rosella responded, tossing the pillow onto the bed beside Jasmine. "Just making sure that perfume didn't damage any brain cells."

Jasmine gave her another wilting look.

"I'm sorry. I'll be serious. So are you talking about your mom?

"Jasmine nodded. Since she and her grandparents had come home, Angela had done some unusual turnarounds concerning Jasmine's contact with both Sage and Rosella, and although she no longer felt her mother's reluctance, the feeling definitely couldn't be confused with acceptance. She didn't discourage, but she didn't encourage, either; it was as if Angela simply didn't care. But, then again, she treated everything that way these days. She cooked nice dinners, made pleasant, neutral conversation, did all the mundane mom things she had done forever, but all of it had a there-but-not-there quality that Jasmine mistrusted.

Rosella kicked off her flip-flops, propped her feet on the edge of the bed, examined the silver peace signs painted on her big toes, and said, "Maybe your dad helped change her mind. He's pretty chill when it comes to me and Sage."

Jasmine shrugged. "I suppose."

"Maybe your mom started taking antidepressants or something, you know, to even things out. Taylor Not-So Swift's mom is on them now. She had a complete meltdown at a softball game this summer, screaming, dropping the F-bomb everywhere, crying. I saw the whole thing. It was YouTube-worthy, but Dad wouldn't let me video it. Supposedly, it's her whacked out old woman hormones—you know, menopause."

"Did Taylor lose it? I would love to have seen that."

"Oh, yeah, she was totally humiliated, but she threw her own shitshow. She swung a bat at the assistant coach and slapped Lindsey Moore in the face with her glove. Classic Taylor stuff. So what about Missus S? Is her lady juice drying up?"

"That's so gross! I can't even think about my mom like that."

Rosella laughed, rolling her eyes. "Oh my God! I'm not talking about sex. Nobody can stand to think about their parents and *that*. Is she going through menopause?"

"No," Jasmine said defensively. "She's too young—at least, I think she's too young. She's only in her thirties. Is that even old enough?"

"I don't know," Rosella replied with an indifferent shrug. "I just started my period last year. Why should I care about it now? It's like a million years away. I'll worry the granny stuff when I get there."

To the girls' surprise, Jasmine's iPad suddenly alerted an incoming video chat, and she jumped up, knocking her friend's feet off as she rushed into the bathroom grabbed a brush and began hurriedly fluffing her flat hair."

Oh, birthday girl, it's Sage looking for a virtual bootie call."

The alert sounded again. Jasmine quickly smoothed on some lip gloss and glanced into the mirror, unconvinced that she looked pretty enough.

"I'm going to answer," Ro teased, "and tell him you're in the bathroom, squeezing out some second-hand cake."

"OMG, I'd totally kill you," Jasmine shrieked as she rushed over and seized the tablet from Rosella's hands.

A third alert sent her into a greater fluster. "Where should I sit? At the desk? On the bed?"

"Does it matter?" Ro giggled. "Sit on the bed."

Jasmine sat, smoothing the quilt to either side of her, readying the stage.

"Unless ...," Ro added with a demonic grin.

"Unless what?"

"Unless you don't want him to think you're a big slut. Just kidding. Just kidding. Stay on the bed. I'm done being annoying."

"Good. You're flipping me out," Jasmine yelled, as another melodic alert rang. "You better answer. You're going to miss him. Don't worry. You look really hot."

"Sweaty? I look sweaty?"

Rosella shook her head and said, "No, Jas. You look gorgeous."

As a sweet smile spread across her best friend's face, Rosella reached over and tapped the accept icon, and Sage appeared on the screen.

Grabbing some fashion mags from the floor, Rosella went into the bathroom. The teen couple cuteness was just too much for her sometimes. Besides, Jasmine was making small surreptitious kicks in her general direction, which could only mean she wanted privacy. Twenty minutes later, when she could no longer hear nervous giggling, and was thoroughly educated on the topic of which jean is best for which body type, Rosella peered through a crack in the door.

"Is it safe? Can I come out?"

"Yes."

Jasmine was lying on her back, her feet still planted on the floor, with the iPad hugged to her chest. Rosella sat down next to her, saying, "Wow. I think this look could only be called totally love-wasted."

"He's just so …."

"Uh-huh."

"It's like he's totally …."

"Uh-huh."

"I …."

"He feels all that stuff for you, too, Jas."

"He does?"

"Absolutely," Rosella said. "The guy has completely lost his mind for you. I told you how he spent the entire powwow season going, 'Ro, do you think she really likes me? Ro, should I text her again? Ro, you don't think she's going to meet some Swedish guy while she's gone, do you?' I will not even go into how long it took for him to approve of a picture for that keychain. Ridiculous."

"For real?"

"I swear. He's as messed up for you as you are for him."

Squealing, Jasmine flapped her hands, flung her legs in the air, and did a wild bicycling motion. Rosella sighed, shook her head with amusement, and said, "Love really makes some people crazy."

Chapter Eighteen: Prolonged Silence

Another St. Paul school year began, autumn rushed headlong into winter, but Jack Bordeaux's fear that the other foot was about to fall never faded until his husband suggested that Jack should either address it and deal with it or force it from his mind for good.

"Don't you think Dave would have chewed your ass by now?" Isaac TwoBears said when Jack brought up Angie's odd visit for what seemed like the hundredth time. "And if not him, you know Cassie would have run you down about it. She's too protective to let something like that slide. If a long-lost daughter and half-sister showed up in her guys' lives, we'd know about it. Either call Dave or call Cassie and stick your hand directly into the meat grinder, or let it go."

Jack pushed the grocery cart forward and Isaac laid a twenty-pound frozen turkey in the bottom rack.

"But it is weird, isn't it? I started regretting the decision the second Angie walked away with their address, and I've been preparing my defense ever since, sure that some very heavy shit was going to roll downhill, but it's like the whole bizarre scene with Angie never happened, like I hallucinated it."

Isaac took the list from Jack's hand, and gave him a stern shake of the head, saying, "It *is* weird. That's why we should leave well-enough alone. Quit obsessing. Besides, Dave, Cassie, and the Miracle Child will be with us for Thanksgiving, so if there's drama brewing, we can do what most families do: ruin a perfectly delicious holiday meal with it."

For the last five years, Dave, Cassie, and their son, Dave Jr., known to all as Davy, had spent their holidays in Arizona with Cassie's Navajo relatives, and Jack's knuckles whitened as his grip tightened on the cart handle at the thought of their presence in his and Isaac's home. Cassie was all right, and Jack liked Davy, despite the boy's wild behavior, of which Isaac was far less tolerant. It was Dave who usually put Jack's teeth on edge. Although closest in age of the Bordeaux siblings, Jack and Dave had never been close. Throughout their childhoods, if Dave wasn't beating Jack down with fists, he was doing it with words, which grew more vicious when Dave found out his youngest brother was gay. Cassie had filed off the sharp edges of Dave's homophobic swipes, making it clear to him that traditional Native cultures were not only accepting of Two Spirited men and women, gay and lesbian members of some tribes were ceremonially honored and held in high regard, but Dave still tossed an inappropriate comment or crude joke Jack's direction when Cassie was out of earshot. Jack knew it wasn't really because he was gay. In fact, Dave got along well with Isaac. Jack's sexual orientation was the easiest soft target for Dave's personal attacks. If Jack were straight, Dave would find something else about him through which he could vent resentment.

"How long were you going to wait to drop that on me?" Jack asked, pitching a pound of butter into the cart with more force than necessary and gouging a chunk out of the stalk of celery.

"Well," Isaac said, his tone soaked in sarcasm, "I planned on waiting until Thursday when the doorbell rang, but since *you* brought the subject of your brother up—again—I figured, what the hell. Really, Jack?" Isaac pointed at the marred vegetable. "Really?"

"Sorry," Jack said. "Dave just gets under my skin. Has ever since we were kids. And now … well, you know."

"You can't punch a legless war hero in the face," Isaac finished, and caught a disgusted glance from a passerby and a guarded smile from Jack.

"I couldn't punch him in the face before. The bastard could always run faster than me."

"Maybe that's why you gave Dave's ex his address."

"What?" Jack asked, steering the cart into the baking aisle.

"You want to finally see someone catch him."

***

"Dad," Davy shouted, jumping from the kitchen chair and waving glue-crusted scraps of paper in his father's face as Dave Bordeaux rolled towards the dinner table. "Look what I made!"

"Chill, kid. I can't get a look at it with you hopping around like a jack rabbit."

The boy sprang back onto his chair and slapped the object of his excitement onto the table in front of his father. Dave grinned at the uneven cut-out of his son's handprint. The boy had chosen conventional brown construction paper, but had gone with neon green, orange, and blue for the glued-on feathers.

"It's a turkey," Davy announced as Cassie turned from the stove, winked at Dave, and said under her breath, "Crossed with a parrot."

"I see that," Dave told the boy. "Very cool. Should we hang this awesome bird on the fridge?"

Snatching the Kindergarten art project away with one hand while wiping chocolate milk off his mouth with the other, Davy stubbornly shook his head and said, "Nope! I'm taking it to Uncle Jack and Uncle Isaac's house for Thanksgiving'."

Really," Dave said, but he wasn't smiling or looking at his son any longer.

Cassie felt her husband's glare pinned into her and, without acknowledging it, continued to dish up scalloped potatoes and ham.

"I thought we were staying here," he said as she brought the food to the table.

Cassie sat, took a bite, shrugged, and said—using just the right blend of casual non-commitment and former Army officer firmness—"Change of plans."

With a grunt, Dave attacked his ham as if it was alive and posing threats. Money was tight. Arizona hadn't been an option this time, but he had strongly suggested that they have the holiday dinner at home. Keep it small. Keep it simple. He didn't think he could stomach an entire day with Jack's teaching awards and Jack's designer furniture and Jack's fancy-ass china and Jack's fancy-ass house with its fancy-ass landscaped yard, so that Jack's fancy-ass dog had some place fancy-ass enough to take a shit.

As if reading Dave's mind, Josie, their pit bull, entered the kitchen and sat beside him, looking expectantly from man to boy and back again.

"Don't feed JoJo at the table" Cassie warned when she saw Davy tearing a piece of ham off with his fingers.

Dave shot Cassie a defiant look, cut a large chunk free, and tossed it to Josie. *His* dog wasn't fancy-ass.

Calmly, Cassie shook her head and said, "We're going, Dave."

"Why?"

From the moment she accepted the invitation, Cassie knew her husband would balk at the idea, but to her, family was important, and, at this point, Dave's petty resentments were not. Unconsciously, she touched the side of her head. Beneath her cropped black hair, there was a four-inch-long scar. Beneath the scar, there was a titanium plate. Beneath that metal, there was a mind that no longer contained snatches of memory. Those memories had blown apart and disintegrated, along with the Apache helicopter and five fellow soldiers.

Her answer was armored in ice. "Because they're family, because it's a holiday, and because I average a fifty-hour work week and I'm not cooking the whole meal by myself just because you've got a hair up crosswise. Any more questions?"

Davy waved a hand in the air, as if asking permission to speak, but didn't wait for approval before blurting, "What's Dad got a hair up? Why's it crossed? What's that mean?"

Dave's ego stung, Cassie told their son to never mind and to eat his dinner, and, for a moment, the meal carried on in tense silence.

"I can pick up more hours when the semester ends," Dave finally said. "Give you a short break."

Cassie threw him a sideway glance. Dave worked part time selling car insurance and was studying for a degree in accounting, which, for now, placed Cassie in the role of primary bread-winner, a situation that she did not mind and encouraged from the beginning. It wasn't really about her overtime at the V.A. hospital, where she worked as a physical therapist, and Dave damn well knew it.

"Great," she said with about as much enthusiasm as when he told her the trash had been taken out. "But we're still going."

Dave launched another attack on his dinner, saying, "I feel a headache coming on. Probably be huge by Thursday."

"Headache?" Cassie replied. "Good thing I got a book to keep me busy in bed 'til Friday."

Davy chimed in, "I finished. Can I have dessert?"

Dave looked at his son's empty plate and at the odd, obvious hump in the vinyl placemat.

"I'm not going to find broccoli under here, am I?" Dave asked, reaching for the mat.

The boy frowned and said, "I was going to eat it last, so I put it under there."

"And?" Dave said.

"And I put it under there," Davy squirmed, and, finally coming up with an idea, said, "so it wouldn't get cold."

"Okay," Dave said, plucking three room-temperature florets' up and dropping them on the plate. "They're ready for you then. Eat up."

Slumping back, lower lip in full pout, Davy complained, "I hate broccoli. It smells like a fart."

Dave snatched a glance at his own untouched green pile. He wouldn't argue that observation, but he stabbed a piece with his fork and took a bite anyway, saying, "You know who eats a lot of broccoli? Spider Man."

"Does not."

"Does to. In fact, that's how he shoots webs."

Davy gave him a skeptical look, but he reluctantly lifted his own fork and began prodding at one flattened floret. He almost had a tiny piece to his mouth when he stopped.

"I ate broccoli last week. I can't shoot webs."

Grinning, Dave shoved more in, chewed, swallowed, and said, "You're just a kid. Spider Man is a grown-up. You don't get to shoot webs until you're an adult."

"Then why do I got to eat it now?"

"It doesn't work like that. You've got to start eating it when you're a kid. That's how Spider Man did it."

"Did you have to eat it when you were a kid?"

Dave's childhood hadn't included many vegetables—or anything very nutritious, for that matter. He could remember many nights when his mother had gone to the bar, leaving Dave and his siblings with nothing but a canister of uncooked oatmeal or a bag of microwave popcorn or a single package of Ramen noodles.

"Nope. I wasn't lucky like you are. Nobody ever made sure I got my broccoli, and see," Dave said, setting his face into a look of hard concentration and pointing a hand at his son as if to launch a web, "no super powers. Now eat up."

The boy still seemed dubious, but as he watched his father grudgingly choke down the vegetables, he did, too. For a moment, warmed by loving approval of how well Dave read their son, Cassie's face softened, until she caught Dave looking her way with a self-satisfied grin. Her softness solidified back into slate, as she mouthed the words, "We *are* still going."

***

The early morning dusting of snow had begun to melt as the noon sunshine cut through the last tatters of gray sky and Cassie pulled the van into the space Jack and Isaac had left open in their driveway. Davy leaped out and ran towards the old Victorian's back door. Eight years ago, after an explosion along a desolate stretch of Afghani road and Dave returned with a military medal and a wheel chair, Isaac had built a ramp that allowed Dave access to his and Jack's home. For a rocky ten months following Dave's return to the States, it had been his transitional home, too. Although it was one of the few places among their family members that Dave could enter independently, the irony was never lost on him that it was the last place he wanted to visit. Today was no exception, and as he rolled his way upwards towards the inviting smell of roasted turkey, his stomach knotted at the sight of his younger brother standing at the landing, holding the kitchen door open in welcome. Davy was already inside, tormenting Isaac with the garish construction paper art project.

"Can we put it on the table, Uncle Isaac? Can we? So everybody can see it?"

Jack and Dave exchanged cool pleasantries, Cassie hugged Jack, handing him a casserole of scalloped corn, and the three entered in time to hear Isaac suggest, "Why don't we set your turkey in a place of honor, here in the center of the kid's table? That way, you can keep an eye on him."

Isaac had gone to great lengths to create a chic, tasteful arrangement for the dining room table: a hand-crafted birch bark cornucopia filled with colorful corn, dried gourds, autumn wild flowers, and carefully arranged pheasant feathers, set between twin gold candle sticks topped with deep forest green tapers to match the identical shade in the embroidered linen table runner. Davy crossed his arms, stomped a foot, stuck out his bottom lip, and said, "No, I want him on the big people table."

Isaac gave Jack a withering look, and Jack intervened, saying, "Did this turkey come home from Kindergarten with you, Davy? He sure is a fine-looking young bird."

Nodding, the boy offered Jack the now rumpled current bane of Isaac's sense of good taste, and with great earnestness, Jack inspected the tail feathers.

"This *is* a very young turkey. Do you know how I can tell? See all these colorful feathers here? Those definitely belong to a bird under the age of five. Wouldn't you say? Your bird isn't older than you, is he?"

Frowning a bit, Davy considered it. He didn't know about turkeys, but he knew he didn't like older kids very much. They could be mean, could be bullies, could make the other kids laugh by throwing a soccer ball at your head at recess, like that second grader did last week. Davy was certain his turkey could never be that big of a jerk.

"He and me is the same age," the boy finally said, as he accepted the bird from Jack.

"Well, then, he's a kid. Kids sit at the kid table," Jack said, then added when he saw his nephew's crestfallen expression. "But before we eat, I think you should take him around and let everyone meet him. What's his name?"

Brightening, Davy paused, searched for a name, and then, with a gleam in his deep brown eyes, said, "Isaac!"

"How truly original," Isaac said under his breath as the boy raced out of the kitchen. Jack playfully elbowed his husband in the ribs. Without another word to his brother, Dave gave the men a sour look and joined the rest of the family in the living room, muttering to himself about fancy assholes.

The meal went smoothly, everyone stuffing themselves full of comfort food favorites, with Jack and Dave strategically seated at opposite ends of the room, out of sparring range of one another. From her vantage point mid-table, Cassie did catch several uneasy glances from Jack during dinner, and she wondered if Dave had managed to sling a couple of offensive zingers while she had been in the kitchen helping Isaac make the gravy. The furtive looks unsettled her. It wasn't Jack's usual reaction to Dave's bad behavior. Cassie's easy acceptance and ability to rein Dave in had sealed a comfortable alliance between her and Jack, who, in the past, hadn't ever seemed to hold her responsible for Dave's outbursts. Over pumpkin pie, Cassie felt Jack's twitchy stare again, so she met his eyes, gave him a small smile, and raised her brows as if to ask, "What's up?" Immediately, he reddened, and looked away. Was he embarrassed about something? Ashamed?

When the dishes were washed, all the kid cousins were busy playing board games, and most of the adults, including Dave, dozed in and out of food comas around the big screen, where the Packers were about to deliver a humiliating loss to one of their northern division rivals, curiosity about Jack's uncharacteristic behavior caused Cassie to search him out. Landing a light friendly punch to his bicep, she smiled at him and said, "I'm going to get some fresh air, walk off that second helping of cream cheese mashed potatoes. Join me."

Jack hesitated, and Cassie's tone shifted to what he knew must be the "no bullshit, no prisoner-taking, no whining" attitude she used with her stubborn V.A. patients.

"Okay," he relinquished, when she crossed her arms and didn't budge. "Let me run upstairs and grab a coat."

Hoping all the while that maybe someone else might want to go with him and Cassie, Jack sighed when he reached the bottom step to find Cassie holding Godiva's leash, the dog vibrating with anticipation. If things turned ugly, Jack was fairly sure that Godiva's only defense of her owner might be an attempt at licking Cassie to death. She handed the dog off to Jack and they exited into the late afternoon chill.

The sky was now completely shrouded in gray and a biting north wind chewed at their backs as they walked briskly south, neither Cassie nor Jack venturing to speak for several blocks. As they crossed into a walkway that wound through a park, passing empty benches, empty picnic tables, and an empty playground, the silence finally got to Jack. He slowed, looped the leash around his wrist, and jammed gloved hands deep into coat pockets, seeking extra warmth, extra courage, a split second of extra time, before he shoved them into the metaphorical meat grinder.

"Listen, Cass. There's something I need to ask you. Or actually, it's something I need to tell you."

Slowing to meet Jack's pace, a chunk of ice fell into Cassie's belly at the gravity threaded through his voice, a seriousness she knew couldn't be stirred simply by one of Dave's tired old taunts. Frigid gusts slapped at her face and she choked a little as she said, "All right. What is it?"

Jack stopped then, sagged onto a bench, and thrust his hand into the grinder. He told her about Angie's pop-up visit to his workplace, Jasmine's need to know Dave, Jack's unsubstantiated feeling that he had met the girl at the Festival of Nations, and, finally, he admitted that he had given Angie their home address. When he was finished, he looked up. Cassie was no longer standing, but had dropped onto the bench beside him, her face frost-pale, eyes locked on a row of vacant swings twisting, banging, and tangling against one another as the wind relentlessly threw punches. Jack waited uncomfortably in her silence, unable to read Cassie's thoughts, judge what she was feeling, or predict her next reaction. The combination of quiet and calm tweaked Jack's nerves like Russian roulette, the minutes clicking past one, two, three bullet-free chambers, until he thought he might pull the trigger himself.

And then she spoke, holstering the pistol, replacing it with something more unsettling.

"We weren't supposed to have kids—at least that's what Dave's doctors said. After the crash, with my head and body all screwed up, they weren't very hopeful about me, either. Dave never talked about it, so I always figured that he just accepted it. Though I'm not sure that I would have ever fully accepted it myself. I'll never know because, despite everything, we got pregnant. So we ended up not having to live with more war losses than just pieces of my memory and Dave's legs. When I found out we were going to have a baby, I was so God damn happy. I raced home from the doctor, ran in the house, and I remember your brother looked at me and said, "Did you win the Lotto jackpot?" I was laughing and shouting that it was something better, way better, and then I told him."

Godiva laid her head on Cassie's thigh and Cassie stroked the dog's velvety ears as she continued.

"Dave just looked at me. He didn't smile. He didn't laugh. He just looked at me. And then he said, 'I can't do it again.' I asked, 'Do what again?' So he told me. We had been married for a year, together for two, and the son of a bitch chose that moment to tell me. He spilled his guts about Angie, their daughter, her rich prick family, how they threatened him, tried to pay him off, how he walked away, what a coward he felt like for not fighting it, how he thought he could go to the recruitment center, sign up, fight away the anger. He didn't think his life was worth much at that point anyway. Why not hand it over to Uncle Sam? Every word that came out of his mouth whittled another little piece off my happiness, the joy I felt at the idea that I was going to be a mom, that he was going to be a dad, that we had beat the shit out of the odds, that two parts-missing people were about to bring something whole and new and amazing into the world, until finally he just quit whittling and stabbed me right in the heart. He told me again that He couldn't do it and then …."

Jack hadn't ever seen Cassie cry and even then, it seemed as if the muscles of her face contorted to prevent it. But a tear broke loose anyway, and she angrily swatted it from her cheek with a leather gloved finger.

"He wanted me to have an abortion. That's what they did to him, Jack. Angie, her family. That's what they did. They robbed him of fatherhood once, almost twice. They almost robbed me, almost robbed our son, if I wouldn't have stood up and said that I was having our baby, with or without him, if I hadn't held your brother while he sobbed out every drop of poison they convinced him to drink, and all the horror of everything that came after. If I wouldn't have held on tight, promised him that I could, that I *would* be strong enough for both of us, that I would never, could never, do what that heartless bitch and her cold, soulless family did to him, they might have gotten away with it."

Tentatively, Jack put a hand on Cassie's shoulder. To his surprise, she didn't push it away, so he ventured forward, saying, "I didn't know, Cass. I'm so sorry. I just didn't know. Dave loves you. And he loves Davy. I've never seen my brother care about anyone the way he cares about you and your son."

"I love Dave, too," she said, steel sharpening each word. "And our boy. I'd do anything to protect them. Anything."

Letting go of Cassie's shoulder, Jack thought he already knew the answer, but he asked, "Has there been any contact?"

"No," Cassie said, piercing Jack with her stare. "And I'm not going to tell Dave that it's a possibility."

She dug her fingers hard enough into Jack's arm that he could feel through the thick coat sleeve the punctuation of what she was about to say.

"You're not going to tell him, either."

Jack nodded, knowing that, after everything Cassie had shared, omission was best, but he couldn't help but wonder why Dave hadn't heard anything from Jasmine. Angie had made the girl's need to know Dave seem urgent, seem sincere. In Jack's opinion, Angie had gone to some length to track him down, obtain what the girl needed, and assist in possibly re-building a long-ago burnt bridge. So why hadn't Jasmine reached out? Jack knew the ever-changing interest levels of young teenagers and how today's singularly focused obsession is quickly became tomorrow's "whatever." Maybe Jasmine's desire to know more about her father had been replaced with a junior high crush or wanting to take up a musical instrument or just the day-to-day effort of wading through a middle school's complex social scene. Jack wanted to believe any of those possibilities, all of those possibilities, but something, a tiny pinch in the pit of his chest, an uncomfortable twinge of intuition, wouldn't let him.

Cassie rose from the bench and began to retrace their path. He followed. For the time being, it seemed as if the past would stay silent, stay hidden, but that discomforting, persistent little pinch told Jack that, despite his and Cassie's pact, it couldn't last.

This was eye-of-the-storm silence, jury deliberation silence, the pause in the horror film before the slasher's butcher knife flashes silver and red, the silence that feeds the imagination fists full of darkness with which to sculpt images of one's greatest nightmares. Jack had been there, in that silence, for a while. Now Cassie Bordeaux, wife and mother, was there, too. Under its weight, they tugged their coat collars higher, bent their heads to the first icy flurries of the day's second snowfall, and walked back.

Chapter Nineteen: Family Getaway

Christmas swept through the Sorenson home in its typical excessive, contrived, overly polite fashion. The family gathered to admire the ten-foot Douglas fir, the adults sipped eggnog spiked with enough brandy to keep conversation civil, and between parents, grandparents, and Aunt Faye, Jasmine's huge pile of gifts bordered upon obscene. But despite the many holiday norms, an alien undercurrent swirled beneath the shiny surface. It subtly shifted tried and true traditional family tensions in new and inexplicable directions. The icy glares Susanne usually bestowed upon Faye seemed duller, less punishing, while Faye's easygoing demeanor tensed into clipped, awkward responses whenever she was forced to speak to Lars. Angela didn't flinch at the few backhanded comments Susanne bothered to fling at her, instead seeming to collect and calculate her Aunt Faye's every interaction, action, and reaction. Except for Lars and Jasmine, no one seemed to notice or care about Kenneth's introspective quiet, the dark half-moons beneath his eyes, the way his trousers and sport coat hung a bit looser, or the way he pushed his uneaten dinner around the plate. When Lars brought Kenneth his drink-of-choice, three fingers of scotch, and Kenneth declined it, he admitted that his stomach ulcers had flared up again, then excused himself before Lars could respond or ask questions. At one point, Jasmine thought she overheard her mother and Faye having a disagreement in hushed voices, but when Jasmine stepped into the kitchen, both women grew quiet; her mother looking perturbed, Aunt Faye looking sad. Struck with a strong urge to avoid whatever she had accidently walked into, Jasmine turned to leave, but Faye reached out and caught the girl in a hug. With a hint of desperation fringing her words, she said, "There's my girl. Are you having a happy Christmas, honey? I hope so. You're such a good kid, Jasmine. Such a good, good kid."

"Sure," Jasmine said inside the tight embrace. "The best. Thanks for all the great gifts, Aunt Faye."

Faye let the girl loose, but kept a hand on Jasmine's arm, saying, "When are you going to come out to the acreage and see me? The dogs miss you. So do the horses. Now that you have your permit, you should drive out with your mom and visit."

Angela had turned her back on the exchange and was fully engaging herself with the violent scrubbing of a ham glaze-coated pan. She had far underestimated Faye's ability to surpass boundaries. Actually,

Angela had thought that Faye would be pleased with her decision to "forgive" Lars' alleged indiscretion. She had somehow imagined Faye applauding her for keeping the family intact for the sake of the child. Instead, Faye had the audacity to confront Angela, tell her that, after having time to think, she did not agree with Angela's choices. She even went so far as to compare Angela to Susanne, a woman, according to Faye, who would coldly dismiss the fact that her husband dipped into other women as long as she could continue dipping into the bank accounts.

"It's the example our mother set for Susanne and me. It's what Susanne's been doing for years. I thought maybe you would be the one, Angela, to break the cycle, show your daughter how to live a life of self-respect."

Angela turned the water hotter, scrubbed more viciously. She was nothing like Susanne. Nothing. The water scalded her hands, but, inside, Angela smiled a bitter, excited smile. Faye would soon see the errors in her perception. They all would.

"Actually, Dad is teaching me to drive," Angela heard Jasmine say. "Mom says it would make her too nervous. She doesn't even ride along, but I'm sure Dad wouldn't mind if we drove out to your place sometime. He's training me to handle winter roads and I haven't tackled any rural stuff yet."

Although she would have liked to, Faye couldn't deny the spark of pure love that shone in Jasmine's eyes when she spoke of Lars. The man had raised her, cherished her, and adored her, for the greater portion of the girl's young life. Perhaps Lars's extramarital activity was a single, isolated incident. Maybe, just maybe, Angela's decision to remain in the marriage was based on what was right for her daughter. Faye combed her fingers affectionately through Jasmine's thick brown ponytail.

"All right then. You and your dad motor out to see me real soon."

"How about next week, while I'm still on winter break, and Mom's gone?"

Angela felt Faye's unwanted attention suddenly shift onto her and she tried to appear nonchalant as she turned and dried her hands on a dish towel and said, "Yes, I'm going out of town for a few days," and then added before Faye could ask the question Angela knew would follow, "Florida. Siesta Key. I'm going to the house."

Faye's mouth tightened into a thin pale line, the color leaking from her face. She had understood why, after Adam's death, Susanne and Kenneth hadn't returned to the beach house, and, to a lesser degree, understood the choice not to sell it, but Faye could never fathom what they had finally done with the property. On Lars and Angela's wedding day, Kenneth had presented Angela the deed; a generous gift to those who did not know the history, a morbid handing-off of painful memories from Faye's point of view. As far as Faye recollected, Lars, Angela, and Jasmine had only visited the house once since taking ownership, and Faye had always assumed that they must have quietly placed it on the market while the Florida real estate boom was still in full swing. Faye didn't know why the idea that they still possessed the house churned up her stomach acid, or why the thought of Angela going there alone caused Faye's tongue to go dry, but she couldn't silence the unsettled inner voice that kept ranting, "Wrong. Wrong. Wrong."

An awkward pause ensued before Faye made an abrupt, untimely exit, leaving mother and daughter shrouded in another kind of discomforting silence. Beyond the fifteen-foot glass panes of the breakfast room that sat adjacent to the kitchen, Jasmine's eye caught the shimmering outlines of sundogs skirting the mid-afternoon sun. Once, she had believed her father's story of huge canines chasing each other around and around, but that was a long time ago. She was too old for the story, and an elementary science class had stolen its magic years before anyway. The little girl who had believed in the fanciful frozen animals would have excitedly pointed them out to Angela, would have tried to draw her mother into the childish wonderment of the discovery, but Jasmine wasn't that girl anymore, and the dogs were only ice crystals. Angela kept her back to her daughter, until, like Faye, Jasmine retreated.

***

It felt so right: the cool sand under her bare feet, the January sun caressing her shoulders, the salt air swirling in off the Gulf of Mexico, teasing the hem of Angela's gauze skirt, filling her lungs, filling her head with forbidden memory. She walked the beach, the same twisting route she and Adam had taken home the night of Angela's awakening and Adam's death.

The old Lazlo house now stood empty and, as Angela stopped beside the sea oats that scratched against the weather-worn boards of the house's deck, she briefly wondered where wild Jenny Lazlo was and what had happened to her. The thought thrust images of the naked, reckless girl coiled around Adam forward, and Angela felt her nipples harden against the thin gauze. Pleasurable, pulsing heat swept through her, until the tiny flames licked between her thighs and her knees weakened. Angela stole to the steps of the deck and, hidden amongst the natural dune plants and over-grown oleanders, she sank to the wooden planks. Beneath the skirt and the silk panties, her fingers found the slick, swollen bump of flesh, and with fast, furious strokes, she finished what the vivid visual memory had started. When her breath finally slowed and her heart followed, she rose, straightened the sundress, and returned down the beach.

Twilight threw thin spears between the mesh of dormant jasmine vine, arranging knotted veins of shadow across the floor of the screened lanai, the chaise lounge where Angela reclined, a glass of red wine in her hand, and across her brooding face. She sipped and then set the glass on a low wicker table. To the best of her knowledge, Jasmine had been conceived here—or if not in the very room itself, somewhere just beyond, in the white sand or in the tepid, rolling surf. Angela closed her eyes, tried to remember.

"Road trip to Florida?" Dave Bordeaux had asked, his words fast yet a little slurred around the edges. "That's crazy, Angie—even for you."

Angie had taken the bottle of tequila from him and took a drink, laughed, pointed to some loose pills scattered on the bed between them.

"We've got uppers," she said, and then waved the liquor bottle at Dave. "We've got something to even us out. We've got my car. Mommy and Daddy Erikson have a beach house they aren't ever going to use again. Let's go."

Dave had still resisted, but Angie had dropped to her knees, unzipped his fly, her mouth changed his mind, and twenty-seven hours later, the glassy-eyed couple had landed on Siesta Key, where the night-blooming jasmine was in full bloom.

Angela opened her eyes, reached for the wine, and savored the memory of Dave Bordeaux's deeply tanned skin, well-muscled arms, his sculpted chest, abs, those strong, masculine legs kicking through the salt water, walking towards her, bending down, wet and cool, between Angela's own paler, sun-warmed thighs. If only ....

The wine suddenly tasted bitter on Angela's tongue. It seemed like a thousand if onlys haunted her past. Ahead was the only direction to look, the only direction to think, the only direction Angela's carefully routed marathon could take her if she were to be happy. Or if not happy, content. Or if not content, at least, at the very least, free.

All of Lars' strings were tied to Jasmine and his steadfast determination to provide the girl the family experience he believed she deserved, making Angela's job of pulling those strings almost effortless.

"She's growing up so fast," Angela had mused, Lars agreeing, a melancholy shadow shifting a grayish tint into the blue of his eyes. "We don't have much more time. It seems that she's quickly moving to that point where we're going to get squeezed out of her social life. We should plan some fun trips together, as a family. Go somewhere a girl like Jasmine would enjoy. Someplace where she could work on her tan, check out boys, swim."

Lars wrinkled his brow at the mention of boys, but he knew realistically that Jasmine's days of viewing all members of the opposite sex as motley, loud, overly-soiled, pestilent alien creatures were already behind her. The girl never went anywhere without that heart-shaped keychain, and Lars gently teased, but it didn't stop her from staring moon-eyed at the photo of that boy, Sage, framed inside it. Yes, boys were now going to be a permanent aspect of their daughter's life. Lars just hoped he had set a decent enough example of how a man should treat a woman.

"What about spending some time down at Siesta Key?" he had suggested, and Angela had smiled, pleased at the swiftness with which Lars had followed the trail of crumbs.

"I love that idea. Jasmine would love it, too," Angela gushed enthusiastically, then hesitated, catching her lower lip with her teeth for added effect. "It's just that ...."

Caught in the current of his desire to please both Jasmine and Angela, Lars urged an explanation, and Angela had been more than happy to oblige.

"The house isn't in good shape. The property manager contacted me recently. The central air conditioning unit was damaged during the last tropical storm. It's running, but not efficiently. The roof is over twenty years old, the fixtures and furnishings are from 1985. I'm sure the wiring, the plumbing, the security system all need up dating. If we're serious about using it as a second family home, I think we should invest some money in its renovation. We could make it beautiful, a paradise where Jasmine would love to stay, spend time with us, make memories. And who knows, Lars, maybe someday, when Jasmine's grown, you and I could spend our empty-nest years there together. You have to admit, it *is* romantic."

Soon after, Lars had established an account in Angela's name and deposited $100,000, to which Angela remarked, "That will be a good start."

Upon Angela's first trip to Siesta Key to meet with, hire, and oversee the people who would transform "outdated" into "outstanding," she took a quick day trip to Grand Cayman, where she opened an account and siphoned $75,000 from the Fargo-based home improvement fund. The same evening, she phoned Lars and told him that, unfortunately, everything was going to cost much more than they anticipated. Lars had simply given a little acquiescent laugh and agreed that their family was worth every penny.

Angela sighed with satisfaction, rose from the chaise lounge, and carried the empty wine glass inside. She took the bottle from the bar, uncorked it, and refilled the glass. Another afternoon, another empty bottle. She tossed it in the bin with the others. Angela's gaze swept lazily over the rooms. Some improvements had been made, of course: coats of paint, some new flooring, and a few pieces of high-end furniture. Lars was a busy man. The dealership, the business trips, the pursuit of Father-of-the-Year every year, it kept him occupied and had kept Angela in charge of their Fargo and Florida properties. Most of the time, Lars possessed little awareness or recollection of conversations he and Angela had about property upkeep and repair. Because she had always done it so well, he simply trusted, without question, Angela's ability to handle those financial details. That trust had made it easy to fabricate a damaged air conditioning unit, an aged roof that actually had been replace two years earlier, and plumbing and wiring that was regularly inspected and in excellent condition. The security system had always been the best money could buy and upgraded as technology advanced, but just that morning, Angela had had the codes and locks changed.

Angela's marathon was moving forward as planned. The Cayman account was fat, soon to grow fatter. The fictional plumber had found a fictional leak which would require a lot of fictional digging, which mandated a lot more real money. Lars would understand, especially when Angela explained that the additional injection of cash might allow for a family trip as early as March, just in time for spring break.

Angela crossed the room to a new ox blood leather sofa, still covered in plastic, where earlier she had tossed her shoulder bag. Buzzing with a rocket surge of exhilaration, she shoved a hand in the bag, groped for her cell phone, intending to call Lars with the story, and instead brushed up against her latest purchase. Angela withdrew it, a sensual smile tugging at the corner of her lips. The grip felt erotic as she pointed the barrel at the empty club chair across the room and pulled the trigger. The hollow click echoed, she tingled, exploded into laughter, and then lowered the unloaded Smith and Wesson to rest between her legs.

Dear old Aunt Faye had planted the seed last summer as Angela cowered on the tub floor, soaked in vomit and ice cold shower spray, and Faye railed.

"You're lucky I recognized your car, lucky I didn't grab for my gun. It's the middle of the night. I'm alone out here. You're just lucky I've got the gun, but no enthusiasm for using it."

Yes, Faye had unknowingly planted that .38 caliber seed and it had taken root, growing, flourishing, filling the fertile hothouse of Angela's thoughts. No enthusiasm? Faye was a fool. Once again, Angela stroked the handle, ran a finger along the cold metal, felt the weight of the sleek, beautiful weapon. Enthusiasm wasn't strong enough a word.

Chapter Twenty: Filling Spaces

Cassie Bordeaux's nightmares didn't care that it was three o'clock in the morning or that she had to be at work in five hours. They weren't keeping a count of their too-frequent invasions of her peaceful sleep. They just rolled mercilessly through her head, night after night, jarring her awake, racing her heart, dampening the sheets with her sweat. Tonight was no different. With a scream lodged in her throat, Cassie kicked and punched at another shadowy dream intruder tearing at another faceless child who cowered beside her. Eventually, she clawed her way back into a wakened state. Next to her, Dave slept on undisturbed. After a few mindful breaths, her pulse slowed, she rose and left their bed. As she had done each time since the nightmares began, she hurried across the hall to Davy's room, again to find him there, safe and sound. She placed a light kiss on her sleeping child's forehead and wished she could lift him in her arms, cradle him close, take him back to her and Dave's bed, as she had done when he was still a baby. Maybe, if she could have the boy curled between her and Dave, if she could feel the light warm weight of their child, if she could drift to sleep with her son's even breaths as her lullaby, then maybe, just maybe, the nightmares wouldn't come. But Davy had outgrown—except on the rare occasion of one of his own bad dreams—the need to crawl into their bed and Cassie was proud of the boy's ever-increasing ability to self-soothe. With that in mind and a resigned sigh, Cassie left Davy asleep bathed in the Bat signal nightlight's low glow. She moved stealthily into the kitchen and, in the semi-darkness illuminated only by a mixture of moonlight and a nearby street lamp, she heated a cup of almond milk. It wouldn't return her to sleep, but she felt chilled, and the pound of Oreos she had stashed behind the protein bars on top of the fridge required something in which to get dunked. Disturbing dreams followed up with secretive binge eating had become the nightly ritual and, consequently, dark circles beneath the eyes, additional inches to her once trim waistline, and a short-fused temper had become part of Cassie's existence, too.

Slumping into a chair, she mindlessly dipped and chewed, dipped and chewed, until one entire double-stuffed row had disappeared and her brain buzzed bright, the sugar rush crackling through all her circuitry. Alert, uncomfortably full, and pissed off, Cassie grabbed her tablet from its charger, logged on, and, although she knew it would only feed the current rotten feeling, gave into the other unhealthy habit she had developed since Jack had told her about Angie's return and request. Cassie tapped her way through the pages and photos she had searched and saved, the captions and faces all too familiar now. Kenneth and Susanne Erikson, attendees and platinum-level donors at a Fargo charity event, an announcement of the couple's thirtieth wedding anniversary with mention of daughter and son-in-law, Angela and Lars Sorenson, a candid group shot of a NDSU reunion that included a broadly-smiling Lars and a straight-faced Angela: they were the images Cassie had expected to find; social graces and false faces in all the right places. Acid rose into her throat, hatred causing Cassie to close what she had come to think of as the Rich White Trash files with a vicious thump of her forefinger. She took a breath, another cookie, and a glance at the time. She might as well continue her little ritual of self-torture; sleep was a lost cause. She opened the Facebook app.

The girl was pretty, and, as Cassie had done with all the previous views of Jasmine's photos, she categorized the girl's features: those that resembled Angie or Angela or, as Cassie called her, Bitch, and those attributes Cassie could connect to Dave. The more she looked at the girl, the more times she scrutinized the hair, the eyes, the shape of her face, the angle of her shoulders, the more nights Cassie Bordeaux lingered on the girl's sweet, shy smile, her seeming innocence and subtle naivety of a late-bloomer, the less maternal influence Cassie saw, and before she could stop herself, she had formed a third category. Jasmine had Dave's chin. So did Davy. Like Dave, Jasmine tended to cross her right arm over her chest and grasp the left shoulder. Davy often assumed the same position, especially when he was nervous. Dave, Jasmine, and Davy had the same thick beautifully shaped eyebrows, squarish, blunt hands, and long-lobed ears.

This girl wasn't just her husband's daughter; Jasmine was her son's sister. And the more this fact whittled away at Cassie's sleep-deprived resolve, the more she found herself wanting to reach out, to facilitate a reunion, an introduction, perhaps even a reconciliation of sorts. At the onset of her cyber searches, Cassie had told herself that whatever she found would only assist her in keeping the secret, only reinforce her decision to do so, only allow her to know the enemy, but all of her reasoning soon crumbled. With every photo of Jasmine decked out in beaded earrings, her arm slung around a best friend whose racial heritage was undeniable, with every post about Standing with Standing Rock, with every mention of a young man name Sage Koskinen, who turned out to be among the native students in one of Jack Bordeaux's Facebook groups, Cassie realized how much Jasmine longed for what her wealthy, white Fargo family could not, or perhaps would not, give her.

Along with this realization came another: the degrees of separation between Jasmine and Dave were far more narrow than the girl probably knew. Cassie supposed much was dependent upon what Angie/Angela/Bitch had told Jasmine. The girl's last name, Sorenson, implied that the husband had adopted her. Was Jasmine aware that her biological father's name was Bordeaux? If so, it would seem simple for the girl to have done her own searches, connected the minimal dots. Granted, Dave had no web presence to speak of, but there were a ton of Bordeauxs on Facebook alone, starting with Jack, who was a single click away from one of the Koskinen boy's pages, and Jasmine's latest post announced that she was "in a relationship" with the young dimpled powwow dancer. It was clear to Cassie, despite the unknown variables, that inevitably all their paths were going to intersect, and some might not walk away from the unavoidable crashes unscathed.

She leaned her elbows on the table, stared at the tablet, and wrestled with her conscience. Should she finally come clean with Dave? Should she bring these photos up, show him the images of his fourteen-year-old daughter, let him see for himself the girl's obvious attachment to what culturally belonged to his side of her lineage, and encourage him to make the first move? Then what was next? Should she and Dave try to make a connection, try to make a place for Jasmine in their lives? Or was waiting the best option for everyone involved?

Beneath the weight of the many unanswered questions, her eyelids slid shut for a moment, and her thoughts travel back to her own girlhood. So much had been lost, so many memories left among the wreckage of the military helicopter crash. Bits and pieces, that's all Cassie's damaged mind could find, could recognize, could treasure. She remembered a lightning-quick Appaloosa horse named Star, but not the barrel racing competitions they had won together. She could still clearly see her family's modest ranch and stark, yet beautiful, high desert vistas that surrounded it, but she had had to re-learn its location and how to get there. Some familiar family faces had no names, while some familiar names detached themselves from any recognizable faces. With each hole she discovered, Cassie filled it back in with the information and memories of others, but filling in the holes never felt truly like remembering. The content could slowly be returned, but the feelings that had formed the first time around could not. For Cassie, her life before the crash sometimes felt like a box of souvenirs that someone else had collected.

Cassie wondered what memories, if any, Jasmine had of Dave, or whether the girl's blanks had been written in by her mother. Was Jasmine Sorenson carrying around a box of someone else's mementos, too?

I could change that for her, Cassie thought. *I have the power to change it. I can't change it for myself, but I could change it for that girl— my husband's daughter, my son's sister.*

There was a soothing, healing quality to the thought that mended the raw edges and slipped Cassie towards sleep.

"Mom, who's that?"

Davy's voice ripped Cassie awake, her head jerking from its slumped position, causing a knife-like point to momentarily stab her neck. Her eyelids slammed open and she saw what her son was looking at. Before she could react, Davy pressed a finger to the picture of Jasmine lighting up the surface of his mother's electronic tablet and asked again, adding, "Is she gonna sit for me Saturday?"

Catching his mother's confused look, Davy continued, "You know, for when you and Dad have date night, when you go and do dumb grown-up stuff and I have to stay home with a sitter. So is that her? I know you didn't like Mandy 'cause she let me watch real ghost stories on TV, and let me be awake really late, and let me eat the whole rest of the Captain Crunch without milk or anything. I just eated it right out of the box, on the couch, while the ghost show was on. Mandy was cool. Is *she* cool?"

Davy shot a suspicious glance at the photo of Jasmine and then stared at his mother, the boy's and the girl on the screen's similar deep brown eyes pinning Cassie down, as if demanding a truth Cassie didn't think she had the courage to offer—at least, not yet, not tonight. Davy had given her the perfect out, a convenient lie that could easily be explained away later, but Cassie couldn't allow herself to do that to either child.

"No," she said simply, and closed the app, locked the screen, and set the tablet aside. "Not your new sitter. What are you doing up, kiddo? You've got school in just a few hours. Let's have a drink of water and go back to bed."

"Can I have one of those?" said Davy, reaching for the cookie package.

"No," Cassie said, then softened under the boy's disappointed expression and her own guilt. "Oh, crap. This makes me a bad mom, but okay. Just one."

She rose from the table, got a glass of water, and gave it to her son.

"Drink this. Swish some around your mouth, get the sugar off your teeth."

Davy gave her a chocolate cookie crumb-flecked grin and said, "Love you, Mom."

***

"So where's your mom?" Rosella said as she and Jasmine entered the empty Sorenson house and tossed their book bags on the floor near the kitchen bar. "Still in Florida?"

Jasmine took flavored waters from the fridge and tossed one to her friend. Ever since Ro said that even the diet stuff could cause belly bloat and the brain to crave sugar, she and Jasmine had been off soda. Ro had become way more conscious of important tips like that since she finally broke down and admitted that she was crushing on Sage's best buddy, Keon, a confession to which Jasmine had sworn secrecy. Ro didn't want Keon to think that he had won, which Jasmine thought was a strange strategy, but kind of plucky, too; in other words, in true Ro-form. Jasmine could hide Rosella's crush, but not the delight she felt that her BFF and her boyfriend's BFF were a secret couple. It just all seemed so perfect. The important people in Jasmine's life were fitting together into an amazing puzzle picture. Well, most of the important people, anyway.

"Yes, she's still in Florida, or maybe she just went back. I lost track," Jasmine said and took a sip of cucumber melon water. "Dad said something about us going down for spring break, but that was like a month ago, so I don't know. If we do, you should totally come with us."

Rosella grabbed the can of jalapeno almonds Jasmine took from the pantry, popped them open, and hopped onto a bar stool. Healthy fats were good for the skin.

"That would be sick. The beach, working on our tans, the most brilliant bikinis, something to showcase my excellent new rack," blurted Ro with mounting excitement and playfully stuck out her almost-noticeable breasts. "Okay, so they got a ways to go, but remember just like a year ago? Absolutely nothing. Totally tit-free! Now look at me. Small, but mighty."

Rosella flexed her arms and shoulders like a body builder and Jasmine laughed, saying, "Impressive. So if we go, you and your fabulous boobs have to go, too."

Jasmine munched some almonds and then, eyes widening, she added, "Wouldn't it be the ultimate, best ever, to the moon and back amazing if Sage and Keon could spring break with us in Florida, on Siesta Key, at our beach house?" Jasmine paused, clutched Ro's hand, and with a devilish grin, added, "And no parental supervision!"

At that, Rosella lapsed into a romantic, PG-13-bordering-on-R fantasy description of such a scenario, until she had Jasmine blushing and giggling with nervous excitement and a tinge of trepidation.

"Geez, Ro! Don't you think that you should at least tell Keon that you like him before you seriously make out like that?"

Smirking, Rosella ran her fingers through her shiny, blue black hair.

"He knows. I kissed him."

"What? Oh, my God! When? Where was I? Why didn't you tell me? Does Sage know? I'm completely freaking out!"

"Well, it was when Mom and Dad took us to the Cities Christmas shopping, and we were at the Koskinens' house for dinner."

"*That* night?"

Rosella shrugged, saying, "I didn't want to steal your thunder. We all knew you and Sage were going to do the whole first kiss thing. Me and Keon, it was just totally spontaneous. You and Sage had snuck off and left us down in the media room to watch that Avengers movie and suddenly I'm looking at him and thinking that he is really cute, and that he is taller than me now, and he's got that lower, older hot guy voice. Finally, he catches me stealing glances and then, in this super sexy way, he asks if he can kiss me, even though he says he thinks I will say no, he thought he would take a chance. And ... well ... I just leaned over and kissed him first, on the lips, no tongue. Just once, only once, even though it was absolutely amazing. Then I kind of had a tiny meltdown."

"What? A meltdown? Why?"

"I didn't want him to make a gigantic deal about it, didn't want him to think that I'm into him."

"But you *are*!"

"I know that! But I didn't want him to know that—not then. Besides, it was supposed to be about you and Sage and your big moment."

Jasmine still felt warm and watery every time she remembered the way Sage's mouth found hers in the quarter moonlight as they shivered together and held each other in the deep shadows of the Koskinens' snow-covered back patio. He had brushed his hand over her hair while they kissed, and for a moment, just one incredible, fabulous second, their tongues met, tangled, and the December cold burst into hot steam. Then adult voices filtered down from the floor above, Sage's gloveless hand clasped her numb fingers, they both let go of pent up nervous laughter, and stole back inside.

"I told Keon not to make a bunch of noise about it because it didn't mean anything, and if he said one word to Sage, he would be a shitty friend. He agreed that it was supposed to be you guys' night and that he would keep quiet, but ...."

"But what?" Did he tell Sage? Am I the last one to know all this?" Jasmine said and waved her hands in agitation.

"No, no! He hasn't told Sage anything, which just makes me like him more. No, what he said—these were his words, not mine—was that he would keep the secret of my tasty, gorgeous lips to himself as long as I would share them with him again. So please don't be mad, Jas. I really was trying to do right by you."

Jasmine shook her head, saying, "I'm not mad. I get why you did it and it's super thoughtful. Actually, I think it's even more incredible now that I know that you and I had our first kiss experiences on the same night. Besides, you didn't steal thunder—I got tongue and you didn't!"

"Next time," Rosella said assuredly. "Definitely next time. You know what is so unfair? Here we are, every day after school, at your house, with *no* parents, and our boyfriends are three and a half fricking hours away. The universe has a really twisted sense of humor."

"Absolutely," Jasmine nodded, and glanced at the screen of her smart phone before going to the freezer and taking out a disposable aluminum pan sealed tightly in foil.

"So what has your Aunt Faye cooked up for you and your dad this week? Last week's beef stroganoff was killer."

Glancing at the neatly printed label, Jasmine set the pan on the counter, and answered, "Teriyaki chicken, vegetable, and rice hot dish. Thaw one hour. Bake at three-fifty for forty-five minutes."

Since Angela's more frequent and more prolonged absences, Aunt Faye had taken it upon herself to keep Lars and Jasmine well stocked with her homemade frozen dinners. Although Lars was perfectly capable in the kitchen and had taught Jasmine the basics, they appreciated Faye's considerate gestures, even though Faye seemed to tense up, get quiet, and rush off whenever Lars was around. Jasmine thought it weird, but then so much of what adults said and did these days seemed weird, so why waste time trying to figure them out. As Jasmine peeled the instruction label from the food, she tried to recall the last time her mother had been there for dinner. When was the last time she had called or texted? Jasmine couldn't recollect having had more than a few words with Angela in … a month, maybe? Jasmine supposed that was kind of a long stretch for a mother and a daughter; she couldn't imagine Laura Bachman going more than twenty-four hours without reaching out to Ro. But that was different. Rosella and her mom had this thing, this closeness, this kind of inseparability, that Jasmine didn't have with Angela—or, to be more exact, that Angela didn't have with her. Although, on some level, Jasmine had been aware of this ever since she and Rosella had started hanging out together, lately—if Jasmine were to be completely honest, for the last year—the contrast between the two mother-daughter relationships seemed far more vivid. At first, it was little things: the sparkle of pride in Laura's eye whenever Rosella excelled; Laura's frequent pats, cheek kisses, and little squeezes that caused Ro to roll her eyes, although she always returned the affection; the way Ro's mom cared enough to get angry when Ro screwed up and Ro cared enough about what her mother thought to argue or yell or sometimes cry. As these witnessed moments built up in Jasmine's thoughts, she realized more and more what was absent in Angela's eyes, how rarely she showed Jasmine physical tenderness, and how emotionally contained Angela always seemed to be in their interactions. Looking further back, Jasmine also realized that Angela's reserved portrayal of motherhood wasn't much different than the way Grandma Susanne behaved: selecting the correct gesture, the correct response, the correct smile, at the correct moment. It was as if Laura Bachman was a mother and Angela and Susanne were acting out a standardized role. These days, it no longer was just absent feelings, absent emotions. Angela was just plain absent. And although Jasmine thought that maybe it should bother her, make her miss the woman she called mother, or feel a kind of sorrowful void, Jasmine couldn't find those feelings, no matter how hard she tried. In fact, the time spent with Rosella and her mom, Aunt Faye, and, most of all, her dad, was more than enough to fill the space left by Angela. In some ways, Jasmine thought that life currently seemed more real, more comfortable, easier, happier, and although the thought made her feel a bit guilty, she wished it could stay this way.

Jasmine was about to ask Ro if she wanted to stay for dinner when the classical cello piece that was Mrs. Bachman's ringtone blared from inside Rosella's book bag. Grabbing the phone, Ro tapped the screen and sang out, "Hello, Mumsie. What's up?"

A brief exchange followed, Rosella's "okays" and "uh-huhs" quickly taking on a more serious tone, her eyes several times flitting towards and then away from her best friend. When the call ended, Jasmine assessed Rosella's expression and asked worriedly, "Your mom usually texts. What's wrong?"

"She's coming to pick me up. She'll be here in five minutes."

"What's going on? Should I come with you?"

"No," Ro replied, as she busied herself with replacing the phone back in the bag, unable to meet Jasmine's questioning stare. "Mom said—"

Before she could finish, Jasmine's phone came to life and silenced Rosella. both girls jumped at the sound and Jasmine swallowed hard as she reached for it. It was Lars' ringtone. Not the usual, everyday little stuff tone of his incoming texts, but the old-school ringtone, and Jasmine felt franticness trickle cold and gritty into her veins as she answered.

"Dad? What's wrong?"

Chapter Twenty-one: Papers

The day began in Lars and Jasmine's new norm since Angela's trips had become longer and more frequent: Lars and Jasmine chatted over her yogurt parfait and his whole wheat toast about an upcoming history exam, the Aunt Faye frozen special they would dine on for dinner, and the progress Jasmine was making behind the wheel, which lead to the inevitable question of whether Lars could take her driving later. The answer was always "yes," and as Lars dropped his daughter off at school, gave her cheek a kiss, and told her he'd see her at six thirty, Lars had every reason to believe that the happiness, the contentment, the hopefulness that Jasmine's parting smile cloaked him in, would carry him through the day. But at exactly 4:52 p.m.—Lars happened to be glancing at the Rolex Angela had given him—a mountain of a man showed up outside Lars's office. The mammoth stranger blocked the light from entering the open door, and asked if he was Lars Sorenson. Lars nodded, half smiled, and inquired what he could do for the expressionless visitor who remained hulking in the doorway.

"Mr. Sorenson," the man said, a slow, sliding boulder rolling forward, eclipsing more light, as he tossed a thick envelope onto the desk, "you've been served."

Even now, more than an hour later, the words "You've been served" swarmed Lars's head, buzzing, stinging, welts upon welts, torture on top of torture, but still he could not quite fully accept their meaning. At first, he simply couldn't understand. Served? With what? By whom? The content of the fat envelope soon provided the caustic cure for Lars' bafflement. The Law Offices of Somebody, Somebody, and Somebody had filed divorce proceedings on behalf of their client, one Angela Edwina Sorenson. Captured in a state of disbelief, unable to process the document's significance, Lars's initial thought was how much Angela hated the use of her middle name, homage to a dead grandmother she had never met. Lars held onto this tiny, brittle twig of a thought for as long as he could. He desperately fought not to drown as the document's deeper, wider, faster raging river of shit rolled over him, twisting and tossing him in the filthy fists of its true purpose. At some point, Lars realized he wasn't breathing, exhaled raggedly, inhaled quickly, before he felt himself getting pulled back under. This breathing, then not breathing, lasted as he read each and every word, once, twice, a third time, and then he replaced the papers in the envelope. He balled his hands into fists, pressed them against closed eyes, tried to keep the quaking sensation rising from his core from reaching the surface. How much he wanted to lie to himself, tell himself this wasn't happening, hand himself that old worn out line about how it must be some kind of mistake, but on his second thought, Lars seized upon something more powerful and far more pragmatic. Angela had lied to him. He didn't know for how long or about how many things, but she had lied and Lars would be damned if he was going to pick up where she now intended to leave off. No, this was reality, and his intestines churned, his temples throbbed, and his heart raced violently as all the possibilities that could be a part of it rushed to mind, and Lars felt the inner tremors he had been trying to harness seize every muscle. He had to go home. He had to get to Jasmine.

The twenty minute drive from the dealership was a blur, the envelope riding shotgun like a homicidal hitchhiker, Lars taking spooked, corner-of-the-eye glances at it, as he pushed the Jaguar to dangerous speeds. When he reached the house, he roared up the drive, slammed the garage door opener, the Jag's roof missing a vicious scrape by a hair's width, and lurched into park. To Lars' right, Angela's moon-white Mercedes sat in the space it always filled, and, for a fleeting moment, Lars let himself linger in the normalcy of it, the memory of the thousands of other moments he had come home to the reassurance of its presence, her presence. And with Angela, came Jasmine. And without Angela? The envelope, nearly the same color as Angela's Mercedes, still lay against the Jag's charcoal leather, its conspicuous threat causing Lars' fury to bubble to the surface. Pounding a fist down upon it, again and then, again, he snarled through clenched teeth.

"Not my daughter! You will not take my daughter!"

Lars left the bent, misshapen papers where they were and, pulling himself together best he could, slowly got out of the Jag. Jasmine was waiting for him just inside the door, her face creased with worry, confusion, and dread. When he had phoned, he only said that he was coming home and that he needed to talk to her. He had tried to keep bleakness from seeping into his voice, but by the way Jasmine's hands now shook, he knew he had failed. She threw her arms around him, the tears choking her voice.

"What's wrong, Dad? Is it Grandpa Kenneth?"

Lars kept hugging her as he answered that this wasn't about her grandfather. Although Kenneth had been diagnosed with esophageal cancer shortly after Christmas, he was responding well to treatment and had been given an optimistic prognosis. Frantically, Jasmine ran through the rest of the family, starting with Lars and, strangely, excluding Angela, until Lars framed Jasmine's tear-streaked face with his hands and met her solemn brown eyes.

"Everyone is fine. No one else is sick and Grandpa Kenneth is doing better every day. You know that, right? He loves you, Jas, almost as much as I do, and he's going to fight like hell to get as many years with you as he can."

Jasmine nodded and her lip quivered, her voice dried petal fragile as she asked, "Then what is it? Something's wrong. I can tell. What is it? What's going on?

In his haste to reach her, Lars hadn't established how he was going to tell Jasmine about this. How did you tell your kid that her mother didn't want to be married to you anymore? Where did one find words to express that you don't want this, that you don't have a clue why this is happening, that you don't want to let it happen, but that you're not sure that you can stop it?

Lars slipped an arm around his daughter and walked her into the family room. Guiding her towards the couch, he sat down beside her.

"Listen, Jasmine. I need to know if you've talked to your mom in the last few days."

Shoulders hunching, Jasmine shook her head, frowned, and said, "I sent a text yesterday, but she didn't answer. Is she okay?"

"I think so, it's just that, well, today I received a letter."

"From Mom? What about?"

"In a manner of speaking, it was from your mother. I don't think it would be appropriate if I gave you the details, but I think there is somethings that she and I need to talk through. Why I chose to share what I have with you is because I'm going to have to leave for Florida."

"Why didn't she just call you, or talk to you when she gets home?"

Lars thought of the dozen or so voicemails and text messages that he had sent since being served, none of which had been answered, and he fielded the questions with an awkward hesitancy that made Jasmine stare him down with a suspicion-filled narrowing of her eyes, a trait she had inherited from Angela.

The girl's delving gaze took in everything her father's face could not hide: the paler-than-usual appearance of his skin, nervous perspiration barely visible on his upper lip, the deep sadness swimming through the blue of his kind eyes. What had her mother done? Suddenly, Jasmine's stomach clenched, her body two clicks ahead of her brain, but when the thought formed, her own face contorted with horror, and she blurted, "Divorce? Is this about a divorce?"

In the too-long pause it took for Lars to process how his daughter had so rapidly surmised what he wasn't disclosing, Jasmine knew and Lars recognized her knowing, but he attempted to answer anyway.

"Your mom and I need to talk, need to sit down face-to-face. We are a family," he said, and, with his finger, wiped a tear from Jasmine's cheek. "I love you, Jas, and your mom loves you. No matter what happens, you have to remember that you are loved."

Jasmine stared, unable to respond to what she knew was the standard placation parents had been uttering since the invention of divorce, the same placation every adult rolled out just before they turned a kid's world upside down, a placation Jasmine knew to be true when it came to her father, but her mother? In that moment, as Lars' pleading eyes searched hers for some sign of understanding, Jasmine felt an unsettling wave of intense pity—not for herself, but for him. Dad had been the one who had brought her the news of her grandfather's cancer. Angela hadn't even bothered to mention it to Jasmine since Kenneth's diagnosis. Dad was the one who held her hand, told her that Grandpa Kenneth would be all right, told her that he had the best doctors, the best treatments, the best chances of a full recovery. Her dad was the one who brought the bad news, but he also was the one who brought the hope. Jasmine leaned her head against Lars' shoulder and searched for the hope she knew he wanted her to have, but, unlike Grandpa Kenneth's intense desire to remain in her life, Jasmine simply did not feel the same desire from her mother. Somehow, Jasmine knew Angela's absence was permanent this time, even if Lars did not. The greater part of herself wanted to cling to her father, beg him not to go, beg him just to leave her mother in Florida, but Jasmine knew her father wouldn't give up that easily.

"I've loved your mom since we were teenagers, and even though the feeling definitely was not mutual back then, once I started falling for her, I never stopped," Lars had told his daughter on more occasions than Jasmine could count.

No, Jasmine couldn't hope for her father to share in her hopelessness because his fall wasn't over yet.

Jasmine felt her father's lips press against the crown of her head as he told her that he would fly out the next morning. She grasped his hand and nodded when he said that he'd ask Aunt Faye to stay at the house with her and that Rosella could stay, too, if it was all right with her parents. Jasmine kept nodding, kept squeezing his hand, kept silent, as he reminded her about the emergency pre-paid credit card he had given her, as he told her he didn't know how long he'd be gone, but that he would come home as soon as possible. He said that he would bring her mother back, that everything would work out, that they would be all right.

The more his daughter nodded, the more tightly her hand closed in his hand, the more strength Lars felt, the more courage he collected, the more hope he harvested, until, by the time the early March sun had fully set and he said that probably neither one of them was very hungry, but that they should try to eat a little dinner, and Jasmine again nodded in that way that seemed so much like quiet acceptance, Lars had moved towards something just next door to calm. Soon though, as Jasmine's silence persisted and he watched her push pieces of chicken and vegetable around the plate without lifting the fork to her mouth, Lars's nervousness returned.

"What are you thinking, Jas?"

"I don't know," she answered, her voice suddenly sounding much younger, much less secure. "I think I'm trying not to think. It's kind of too much, you know what I mean?"

Lars knew what she meant. He lifted a napkin to his face, while offering a slow nod, but he could feel the crush of their unspoken thoughts as they hovered around them, crowded out any comfort, and sucked up all the breathable air from the room. There wasn't anything that could be said that would lift them out of this limbo, no exchange of words that would change whatever future Angela had in store for them.

"Well, if you do have a thought or a question, I'm here. Okay?"

"I know, Dad. Thanks."

They continued to share the stifling silence for a few more minutes, and then Lars cleared his throat.

"Listen," he said, and pushed his chair back from the table. "I need to make some phone calls. I'll be in my office for a few. Could you put the plates in the dishwasher?"

Jasmine tried to keep the relief out of her tone as she agreed to clean up and Lars left the kitchen.

In the privacy of his home office, Lars dialed Laura Bachman. With as little detail as he could include, he explained the situation. When he had finished, Laura spoke.

"I understand the sensitive nature of this, Lars, and I assure you I will make Rosella understand it as well."

Lars leaned back in the desk chair, heaved a sigh, and continued, "Thank you for picking Ro up earlier. I know my first call today was heavy on panic and light on info. I figure Jasmine is going to turn to her best friend for support while Angela and I are working this out, so I wanted to keep you in the loop. I've told Jas that Ro is welcome to stay here with your permission. I'll be asking Faye to keep an eye on things while I'm gone."

"Yes," Laura said. "That's fine. Doctor Gunderson is great. Ro has been raving about Aunt Faye's casseroles lately. You know, Lars, I would love to invite Jasmine to come here, but both our younger kids have the flu. It's a small miracle Rosella has managed to stay healthy. Will Doctor Gunderson be at the clinic tomorrow?"

Puzzled, Lars scratched his head, and then said, "I suppose she will be. It's a Friday and, as far as I know, she's there every day except Saturday afternoon and Sunday. Why? Is your dog okay?"

"Our dog is fine. It's just that the girls won't have school tomorrow because of the teacher in-service."

"That's right," Lars said. "That slipped my mind. I'm not concerned about Jasmine being here during the day. I mostly just want Faye around for the overnight hours. Although, right now, it might be better if Jasmine had some companionship. She's putting on a brave face about all this, but, well …."

Laura offered to drop Rosella off in the morning and finished by saying, "They'll be fine. More than likely, those two will spend the entire day texting their long-distance boyfriends. Not much trouble in that, I guess. Listen, Lars, I want you to call anytime if you need anything. We love Jas like she's one of our own. I wish you the best."

Lars thanked her for her kindness, ended the call, and tapped Faye's contact number. With only slightly more information than he had given Laura Bachman and with the hint of unexplained coolness Lars had come to expect, he secured Faye's agreement that she would come to the Sorenson home as soon as she was done at the clinic the next evening. For a brief second, Lars considered calling his parents, and then, taking into account the lukewarm neutrality they had always had towards Angela, decided against it. He definitely wouldn't want to put the stress on Kenneth right now and Susanne would surely unleash every cutting comment in her repertoire, so the Eriksons were also excluded from his need-to-know list. Out of the corner of his eye, Lars caught the framed photo atop the oak file cabinet. Jay Tipton's and Lars' younger selves, both in their Bison uniforms, looked back at him, and reminded Lars of other unhappy endings. Why had he left that photo there? Wasn't it time to let go of all the shit he wasn't ever going to get back?

Suddenly, wrath launched him out of the chair and towards the cabinet. He grabbed the photograph and spun around, searching the best, most destructive place to pitch it, but then he stopped. From two doors down, Lars could hear the faint sounds of soft music and Jasmine's voice, just loud enough to be heard above the song's slow rhythm, but not loud enough for him to make out her words. Lars dropped the framed photo on the leather loveseat, dropped himself beside it, and, elbows on knees, pressed his face to his hands, squelching the primal scream that threatened to explode through the granite line of his lips. As he struggled to regain composure, he could still hear the rapid cadence of Jasmine's voice, and Lars imagined that she was talking to Rosella. The thought caused his scream to recede until it became just a single dry, stifled choking sound. He took two deep breaths. Jasmine had someone to talk to about this. That was good. He took another, deeper breath, let out more weight from his chest. God, he loved that kid with every cell in his being, with his every breath. She was his daughter, his reason for everything. For a second, Lars thought he caught the sound of her laughter, but then wondered if it had really belonged to Jasmine or was just a product of wishful thinking. He strained to hear it again, but didn't.

Down the hall, Jasmine ended her call with Ro, curled up on the bed around the soft warmth of the sleeping cat, and tried to pick through her thoughts as they flew hot and fast as lightning. Rosella had been super supportive, just like Jasmine knew that she would be, but their talk had given rise to some troubling possibilities, and now Jasmine could not stop her mind from clutching to the worst-case scenarios. Although Jasmine knew her father would want her to go to him with the questions that were causing her stomach to reject the small bit of dinner she'd eaten, she talked herself out of it. If she did get up, force her unsteady legs to venture down the hall, knock on his office door, what would he say? In his quest to remain positive, to save their family, bring her mother home, would he tell Jasmine not to worry, not to get ahead of the situation, not to imagine a bad ending? And maybe, despite what her instincts said, he was right; their family would remain intact, all Jasmine's fears about the future would go unfounded, and the mother Jasmine knew Angela to be would surprisingly turn out to be the one Lars' delusions told him Angela was.

Jasmine rolled away from the comfort of the snoring cat and grabbed her phone. With shaking hands, she texted her mother.

"What is going on?"

Jasmine's teeth clenched like a vice as she saw that the text had been delivered and then that it had been read. Without breathing, she clutched the phone and waited, one heartbeat, two, three, her blood rushing hot, then cold, then hot. Another moment passed, she breathed, kept her grip on the phone and anticipated exactly what happened. Angela did not reply.

Sometime later, Jasmine heard her father's office door open, and his footsteps tread heavily down the stairs. She wrapped herself more tightly around the fluffy white cat who finally awoke, purred softly, and stretched a paw to touch Jasmine's hand. Jasmine started to cry again. Everything that held her together was going to tear apart.

Chapter Twenty-two: Delayed

The window Lars thought the weather might leave open slammed shut and, along with his fellow passengers, he groaned as the O'Hare information screen added their flight to a long list of delays. Several people labored to their feet, off in search of something to do with the two hours they now had in Chicago, leaving Lars alone in the cluster of chairs nearest the gate. He looked across the wide hall at the freezing rain pelting the plate glass. The flight from Fargo could easily make his top five worst airplane experiences, and although the delay was going to give him more time to think than he wanted, he couldn't argue with the airline's decision to avoid the rapidly deteriorating weather conditions. He dug his phone from a pocket and tapped the weather app. Earlier predictions of a quick-moving, narrow band of moisture had updated to reflect the current monstrous swath of low pressure system cluster-fuckery; snow showers in North and South Dakota, Minnesota, and blizzard watches and warnings as far into Iowa as Des Moines before it turned into the treacherous icy soup that now plagued the Windy City.

Lars shook his head. He might be lucky if he got out of here at all. Some previous delays had already changed over to cancellations in the few moments he had checked his phone. Although he wasn't a particularly religious man, he whispered under his breath, "What are you trying to tell me, God?"

He adjusted the small roller bag in front of him, leaned back, and propped his feet atop the luggage before writing a text to Jasmine.

Hey, Sweetest Girl. Safe in Chicago. 2 hr delay on connecting flight."

Because Lars knew it made his daughter smile and roll her eyes when he accidently used them improperly, he chose the emoji of rain drops, snowflakes, and the slightly unhappy face. For a second his finger hovered over the red heart, and then switched back to the letter keyboard.

"I love you."

He hit send. When a response didn't come right away, Lars extinguished the tiny flare of frayed nerves he suddenly experienced by telling himself that Jasmine and Rosella were probably binge watching something with the surround-sound cranked. They were safe at home in Fargo, He was safe here in this ass-numbing airport chair. Everything was fine.

***

Rosella picked up Jasmine's phone, read the text aloud, and then squealed in a most un-Ro-like way, "What are we going to do?"

Jasmine stared straight ahead, her focus locked on the task at hand, her expression cold, hard determination. The calm steel edge of her voice cutting off Rosella's skittish stream of questions.

"Answer him."

Rosella began to protest, saying, "He'll know it's not from you. He's going to know something's up."

"He's not going to know *anything*! Just write a damn text," Jasmine snapped. "I'm a little busy here, in case you haven't noticed."

Rosella had not wanted to go through with any of this, but when she tried to talk Jasmine out of it, Jasmine got angry and told Rosella that she was doing it—with or without her. At that point, Ro knew Jasmine wasn't backing down and, as her best friend, couldn't let Jasmine take this crazy, complicated, and, yes, even criminal, step alone.

"Sorry, Ro," Jasmine said. "I'm not really myself right now. I didn't mean to get bitchy."

Turning for a moment, Rosella tossed her a half-smile, and said, "Totally understandable. Now, before I send it, how does this sound?"

***

A few more tedious airport minutes passed, and then Lars grinned at the sound of Jasmine's text tone. A thumbs-up, a snowflake, and a face blowing a kiss said it all, and Lars let a little more tension leak from his neck and shoulders. Now he could continue to mentally prepare for the rest of the journey and, more importantly, what his plan would be when he faced Angela.

***

Earlier that day, after Rosella had waved goodbye to her mother, considered the few flakes of falling snow before entering the Sorenson's garage entrance, and Jasmine seized her arm, urgently dragging her inside, she had soon discovered that the plans she and Jasmine had discussed in the wee hours of the morning had mutated into more of a plot than a plan.

"That's insane, Jas," Rosella had railed. "Do you have any idea the kind of trouble we're talking about here? I understand why you want to find your birth father, especially now, but I thought the plan was pretty clear."

The girls had agreed to comb the search engines hard, get info and, if they hit dead ends, they would contact Jack Bordeaux. Sage had given them Jack's number the previous night, when Jasmine explained everything to him.

"Why, all of a sudden, are you taking this to extremes?"

In response, Jasmine had looked at Rosella with such a tortured expression Rosella had started to cry. Jasmine said, "Because if I don't do this now, if I don't find him—and I don't just mean find him on the web, but *really find* him—I will lose my chance. If my mother divorces Dad, and she forces me to go live in Florida …."

She and Rosella had imagined many of Jasmine's fears for the future the night before: As birth parent, Angela might try to take full custody of Jasmine, excluding Lars from Jasmine's life; Jasmine would end up thousands of miles from Rosella, Sage, her grandparents—all friends, family, and fathers, removed from Jasmine's life.

Jasmine's voice shook violently as she forced out the remaining jumbled thoughts, "Dad adopted me. What rights does he have? She could take him away, just like she did my first dad. I was too little to remember anything. I don't remember *anything*, Ro. Nothing. If Dave Bordeaux walked in right now, I wouldn't even recognize him."

Tears warbled the words, but Jasmine ranted on, yelling, "I won't forget Dad. He's loved me and I've loved him for too long, so she can't make me forget *him*, and he will fight for me. I know he will. But Dave, my other father, that's different."

Not wanting to dump more hurt on her distraught friend, Rosella didn't point out that Dave Bordeaux *hadn't* fought for her, *hadn't* ever attempted to find her, and might not even be available to be found. He could be in prison. He could be on the other side of the world. He could be dead. Instead, she hugged Jasmine tightly and let her cry herself dry.

"Okay," Rosella stated firmly, her usual sardonic humor breaking through the seriousness. "I will go with you, but I better get to see Keon, because after this, my parents are going to lock me in my bedroom until I'm eighteen—that is if you and I aren't already behind bars."

Now, as Rosella pressed her tense body against the Mercedes' creamy beige leather, she took a long look at Jasmine. Lars' driving lessons had taught his daughter well, and she handled the sedan confidently through the light early afternoon interstate traffic and the snow, which was still falling, but starting to slow. Although the car windows were heavily tinted and the girls' ages might not have been noticed, they had tried to appear more mature. Jasmine had wound her long hair into a bun at the nape of her neck and Rosella had used a curling iron and loads of hair spray to alter her youthful cut. Both girls had lifted some items from Angela's belongings: Jasmine wore a long black leather coat and a pair of matching driving gloves, and Rosella peered through the abandoned reading glasses Jasmine discovered on Angela's nightstand. Both had made up their faces with amounts and shades they called "mom masks". Small gold hoops adorned Jasmine's ears, the quarter-carat diamond studs Kenneth had given Jasmine for her thirteenth birthday sparkled against Rosella's lobes. They might not look that much older, but they definitely gave off the comfortably wealthy vibe, which could just be enough of a societal pass to get them where they wanted to go. All of a sudden, it struck Rosella as absurdly funny and she said, "So here we are, just a couple of Real Housewives of Fargo, on our way to a champagne luncheon."

Jasmine allowed herself a small smile, saying, "I love you, Ro. I don't know how I'm ever going to be able to pay you back for something so big, but I'll try. This goes beyond friendship into sisterhood."

Rosella shook her head. "No payback necessary, and, by the way, this is better than sister stuff. I would never do this for Cleo, and she would for sure never do it for me. She'd just be all like, 'Mom, Rosella is planning to steal a car! Mom, Rosella is going to drive it to Minneapolis! Mom, Rosella is looking for her birth parents without your permission!' She's my sister, so I have to love her, but—"

Her words were cut off by what she spotted in the side mirror.

"Uh, Jas. I don't want you to freak, but you should check out the rearview."

About four car-lengths behind them, approaching rapidly in the right lane, was a vehicle with lights atop its roof.

***

A plane had skidded sideways on a runway, and though no one was hurt, O'Hare now had another delay/cancellation headache on its hands. Standing at the wide windows, working on his second double espresso, Lars watched the emergency flashing lights in the distance. The icy rain still bulleted the asphalt; miraculously, his Tampa flight had not been cancelled yet. He might still reach Siesta Key before nightfall. He walked back to his little base of operation just in time to watch the information board add another two hours to his flight's delay.

"Damn it!" he whispered.

For some reason, the thought of confronting Angela after dark made his skin prickle. He really shouldn't have gone for a second coffee. The caffeine was beginning to do a number on his nervous system. He got back up and tossed the remainder in a trash receptacle. Returning to his seat, he picked up the paperback he'd bought out of boredom. The gift shop book selections were pretty picked over, and all Lars had to choose from were romance novels, non-fiction political fodder, or a couple of crime fiction titles. He dug through the outer pocket of the roller bag, extracting the travel-size package of almonds Jasmine had given him that morning. She was such a considerate girl; always concerning herself with other's feelings, their needs, their happiness. Thinking of his daughter lessened the weird heebie-jeebies he kept having. Distraction would probably help, too, so he cracked open the murder mystery, landing on the dedication page.

For my wife, who, during the long and arduous journey that has been my writing career, has rarely considered committing my murder. Thank you for your love and patience, honey.

At some earlier, happier, more secure time, the intimate little snapshot the words created, would have offered Lars Sorenson a chuckle. Today, it just reactivated that nasty prickle.

Chapter Twenty-three: Arrival and Departure

It wasn't *if* Lars was going to show up at what Angie had come to think of as her fortress, but *when*. She was certain it would be today; after all, her lawyer had called yesterday, the papers were served, and now all she need do was wait for Lars's predictable reaction to her silence. Ambling to the bar, Angie considered her collection of spirits, finally deciding that the vodka would best assist in passing the time. Tumbler in hand, she walked, barefoot and clad only in last night's torn red silk chemise, into the lanai and slumped onto the chaise lounge. She hadn't looked at a clock since she awoke twenty or so minutes ago, but the sun's intrusive rays were stabbing through the room's west screened wall, as they did most late afternoons. She reached for the bamboo shade and lowered it. As she did, she saw the faint bruises on her wrist and, checking, found almost identical marks encircling the other arm. Angie smiled.

***

The half-smile drained from Jasmine's face as the Minnesota State Highway Patrol creeped ever closer. Her eyes flew to the speedometer, although she already knew she wasn't speeding. This could be it. She and Ro could be on their way to jail.

"Keep cool," Rosella said through her teeth. "The lights aren't on. He's about to pass us."

Jasmine's legs began to tremble uncontrollably and she lifted her foot off the gas a little.

"Don't slow down," said Rosella in a hushed scream, and gripped the edge of the seat as if they were about to crash. "It looks suspicious!"

Still jittering, Jasmine managed to force her foot to cooperate, and they regained the small amount of lost speed. For fifteen heart-pounding, throat-closing, pants-pissing seconds, the patrol car drew up next to the Mercedes and the vehicles ate up I-94 in tandem. What seemed like a lifetime later, the patrol car pulled ahead, sped up, and merged into the left lane in front of them. At that point, Jasmine signaled, shifted into the right lane, and took the first available exit. A quarter mile off of it, she pulled into what looked like an abandoned farm yard, threw open the car door, and unceremoniously tossed her cookies.

"Eeuu! Sorry, Jas," Rosella said, as she touched her friend's back. "Are you okay?"

Without turning around, Jasmine reached a hand behind her, saying, "Give me those anti-bacterial wipes—now!"

A few minutes later, after Jasmine had rinsed her mouth out with some strawberry cucumber water and cleaned barf off the toe of her shoe, Rosella tentatively said, "Do you want to go home?"

Popping two breath mints, Jasmine replied, "Why? Do you?"

Rosella wiped her sweaty palms on her pants, and shook her head, then added, "But if you do ...."

Jasmine rolled her eyes and gave Ro's shoulder a soft punch.

"I'm not going to let an isolated case of panic puking mess this up. Besides, Ro, we're almost there," she pointed out, showing their location on the phone's map app. "See, less than an hour. Just one thing."

"Anything," Rosella answered.

Jasmine nodded at the steering wheel and said, "I think you should drive the rest of the way. I know your mom took you driving the last time you were in the Cities, so you can be more confident with that kind of heavy traffic. All my training has been around Fargo. If I handle the GPS, I know you can get us to Sage's house."

Without argument, Rosella climbed out of the passenger seat and came around the car, but stopped short, wrinkled her nose, and stated firmly, "Back up, I'm not jumping across that!"

Relieved, Jasmine started the car, put it in reverse, and when the Mercedes was beyond range of the mess she had deposited, she put it in park, hopped out, and fist-bumped Rosella, saying, "It's all yours.

***

"Is this yours?" the man, known only to Angie as Carlos, had said the night before, when she unlocked the door of the beach house and led him upstairs to Adam's old bedroom.

Intuitively, Angie had known he was the right one from the moment she spotted him, from his presence at the up-scale cocktail lounge Kenneth Erikson had once frequented after golf rounds, and the arrogant, misogynistic manner in which he ordered the waitress around, to his heavy gold and diamond ring, deeply tanned, yet smooth face and pricey designer suit. When they were in her brother's room and she grabbed his silk tie, yanked him on top of her across Adam's bed, and told the almost-perfect stranger that she wanted it rough, Angie learned that her intuition had been accurate.

It had been her reward, her reminder, her re-introduction into her past, and when Angie was done with the darkly decadent party she had thrown for herself, she simply told Carlos to get out. He didn't argue—after all, men like that never wanted to stay the night, and even if he had objected to her abrupt dismissal, she wouldn't have worried. That was the purpose of the gun Angie had slipped beneath Adam's bed prior to her hunt.

Remembering it now, she thought perhaps she should retrieve it from its hiding place, just in case. Lazily, she got to her feet. When she entered Adam's room, the smell of sex still clung to the mangled bed sheets, and Angie breathed deeply as she dropped to her knees and groped for the .38. As her fingers brushed the cool metal, a rush like the mounting tension of an approaching orgasm clutched her. Its power, her power, so thrilling, so intoxicating, and she wanted the gun near her, on her, touching her skin.

She searched around the room that she had slept in every night since her return to the house, and found a pair of black denim shorts she had left on a chair. Leaving the ruined chemise on, and without panties, Angie slipped the shorts on and stuck the barrel of the gun between the waist band and her naked flesh. Satisfied, she went downstairs for more vodka. It wouldn't be long now.

***

"Not much farther," Jasmine said, scanning the GPS. "Siri says our exit is coming up in a quarter mile. Hang tough, Ro. You're killing this."

White-knuckled, Rosella let loose a maniacal laugh and a storm of profanity, and then added, "After this, I may never want to drive again."

Ever since they had reached the western edge of Minneapolis, the traffic had grown heavier and heavier, and that, paired with her limited driving experience, had Rosella's nerves in a twist she wasn't sure could be unraveled anytime soon. She heaved a gigantic sigh when the exit sign came into view and she signaled right. As they moved away from the more congested roadways into the quieter residential streets of South St. Paul, Rosella's stress lowered a notch and Jasmine's raised by ten. At her core, a tight fist of franticness had formed, and even as Rosella brought the Mercedes safely to a halt at their first destination and Sage and Keon jogged out of the Koskinen's front door and assured them that Sage's mother was not home, the fist squeezed tighter and tighter. This was it. They were here. Jasmine couldn't curl up and hide in the car, she couldn't go back, and she sure as hell couldn't throw up again—not in front of Sage.

Rosella was already out of the car and Keon was fully animated as he raved about the Mercedes, Rosella's badass driving skills, and how crazy this all was. Sage came over and opened Jasmine's door.

"You okay?" he said, squatting beside the car and grabbing her hand.

Carefully, so as not to start crying, she nodded, and let him tug her up and out of the car and into a welcome embrace. After a moment, Sage whispered, "I think maybe we should put the Mercedes in the garage. It's kind of showy for this neighborhood, if you know what I mean."

"Will you do it? Ro and I have had more driving than we can handle, at least for now."

Sage popped a quick kiss on her lips before releasing himself from their hug, circled to the opposite side of the car, climbed in, and told Keon to go open the garage door. Keon grabbed Rosella's hand and they disappeared through the side entrance. Jasmine got back into the car beside Sage.

"You're the absolute best," she said.

Sage's expression stayed serious at the compliment, and he answered, "I'm going to help you find your dad. I promise."

In that moment, Jasmine remembered the daydream she had once entertained of her and Sage escaping together in a hot, fast car, how he would touch her, how it would set everything ablaze. What if they did run away? What if she forgot about all of the adults who had too little care, too much care, too many complications? Teen couples ran away together all the time, didn't they?

But before she could solidify the courage to voice these questions, Sage started the engine and steered the Mercedes into the second stall, and all Jasmine's fragile soap bubble fantasies burst.

Sage killed the engine. Jasmine reached out her hand to him, and he started to pull the keys from the ignition, but she shook her head.

"No, just give me your hand for a sec."

She felt tears threatening to spill again, so she swallowed hard and grasped his offered hand. He swallowed, too, not knowing just what to say at first, then, seeing the sadness she was trying, but failing to hide, he went with the hot, explosive next thought that bulleted into his head.

"Adults can be really screwed up sometimes, Jas."

Sage knew this to be true; not from his own experience—the Koskinens were oddly average and mostly functional—but from the drama that seemed to constantly be unfolding in Keon's household. Only two weeks ago, Keon and his sister had moved in with their grandmother after their mother's boyfriend had put a bullet hole through the living room ceiling. Keon had shrugged, huffed out a sardonic half-laugh, and said that at least nobody had been home upstairs. That was Keon's jam, drown the horrifying with the humorous, but Sage could tell that Jasmine hadn't quite discovered her coping weapon yet, and he began to rewind the comment, saying, "I mean … you know …."

"No, you're right. They *are* screwed up. They're the ones we are supposed to respect, supposed to listen to, and they're all messed up."

Sage thought of his parents, thought of his grandparents, thought of his wrestling coach, his chemistry instructor, and Sage and Keon's favorite teacher, Jack Bordeaux, and he interlocked his fingers with Jasmine's.

"I know some of them are completely whacked, but some aren't, and some are actually pretty chill. I guess if we're going to grow up with any chance of being all right, we have to find the cool ones."

Keon knocked on the car window, breaking apart the seriousness of the moment, and said, "Are you two just going to sit in that sweet ride all day and make out, or what?"

"Let's go," Jasmine said, a bit of the malaise gone from her voice, as she leaned over and kissed Sage's cheek. "I think I'm ready."

***

With the vodka softening some edges and sharpening others, Angie looked in the mirror, the gun's cold metal against her skin, and smiled.

"There you are, Angie," she cooed, forming her hand into a weapon and pressing the index finger barrel to her head, then lining it up with the quarter moon scar. "Ready?"

She pulled the imaginary trigger.

"Ready."

Chapter Twenty-four: On the Doorstep

The doorbell rang once, twice, a third time. Godiva jumped up from where she slept at Jack's feet, flew down the stairs, barking wildly, and Jack rubbed the spot along his jaw where earlier that day he had had a botched root canal molar extracted. Although he had taken a personal day, he still had a few student emails to browse before he could feel comfortable with closing the laptop, popping a prescription-strength pill, and taking a nap, and his mouth throbbed with each additional intrusive ding-dong. Apparently, this interruption wasn't going to be ignored, so Jack pulled himself out of the chair, tossed his reading glasses on the desk, and headed for the top of the stairs. At the first landing, he paused, squatted, and tried to see if he could get a glimpse of his unwelcome guest from that vantage point, but Isaac had recently decided to update their window treatments and had added something called a valance to the top of the front door's window, which now obstructed Jack's view.

"Shit," he mumbled under his breath as the doorbell ceased, urgent knocking started, and the chocolate lab lost her mind in a fit of jumping, howling, and woodwork scratching.

Jack made his way down the final flight of stairs and froze. On the porch stood Sage Koskinen and his buddy Keon. Two other young people stood hidden behind them. The little group couldn't see him through the mirrored glass and, for a second, Jack considered creeping back upstairs, but obviously the kids and, therefore, the dog, were not going to leave him in peace. Jack sighed, looked down at his fleece-lined moccasin slippers, faded-out sweat pants, and Timberwolves T-shirt, and pressed a finger to his swollen cheek. As well-meaning as his students might be, he would explain his situation and politely, but quickly, dismiss them. Grabbing Godiva's collar, Jack unlocked the door.

***

Faye Gunderson locked the clinic door and walked to her truck. The last two appointments had cancelled, allowing her and the staff an early start to their Friday evening plans. Maybe she would take Jasmine and Rosella out for pizza and a movie. The thought cheered her as she tapped Jasmine's cell number. No answer. Unworried, Faye left a happy-go-lucky voicemail, ended the call, and turned the truck towards the Sorenson house. In route, she changed her mind. She would put together a homecooked meal; some comfort food. Maybe a shepherd's pie, some hearty beef stew, or perhaps a meatloaf. Faye turned the truck around. She had all the ingredients at the farm and she could check on the dogs. The girls wouldn't be expecting her for another couple of hours anyway. When she reached the gravel road to her house, Faye frowned, suddenly struck with the recollection of Angela's rude reckless after hours visit the previous summer.

For Faye, there were still too many things that didn't add up about Angela's story. Sure, on the most basic level, the details of it jelled together, made it possible, but Faye's gut, the longer she had tried to digest it as truth, said that it wasn't plausible. For one thing, Lars' devotion to Angela, and especially, to Jasmine, had, to this day, seemed indestructible. And wouldn't a man with Lars' integrity exhibit some signs of post-affair guilt? Despite the private nature of it, wouldn't he have addressed directly or, at the very least, alluded to Faye's knowledge of Angela's discovery? Lars was a straight shooter, open and honest about his most intimate of shortcomings. Wouldn't the guy who announced at the Thanksgiving dinner table that he was infertile because of "ball cancer," say *something*? But after Angela's story and her apparent forgiveness of Lars's indiscretion, he had behaved in Faye's company as he always had: friendly, warm, loving, and welcoming, like a man who had nothing for which to feel uncomfortable. Either Lars's ability as an actor trumped Faye's bullshit detector, or Angela, in order to cover her own crooked tracks, had lied.

***

Jack Bordeaux couldn't lie. As much as he wanted to in order to avoid the landslide that would surely follow the truth, he couldn't lie. There she stood, on his front porch, her knuckles white as she clutched the Koskinen kid's hand for dear life and visibly shook. There she was, the girl from the festival, the girl named Jasmine, the girl who looked so much like Jack's brother that her paternity was absolutely undeniable.

Godiva was on the porch now, licking Keon's hand, while the taller girl—Jack also recognized her—scratched the dog's ears, and the straightforward, no-nonsense, let's-get-down-to-business question that Sage had blurted the moment Jack had opened the door still hung in the charged air, unanswered.

"Do you, Mr. Bordeaux?" Sage urged. "Do you know Dave Bordeaux?"

Jasmine's eyes found Jack's and, in that moment, all her silent pleading, all her unfulfilled need, all her trepidation and uncertainty and fragile hope, traveled the distance between them and pierced Jack's heart like an arrow. Without taking his eyes from her, Jack nodded and said, "Yes, he's my brother."

***

The loss of her brother, maybe that was the greatest factor that had contributed to Angela's unruly behavior over the years. As Faye let the dogs out and gathered dinner ingredients, she could not avoid the single question that kept weaving its way into her thoughts. What was Angela up to now?

***

Suddenly not knowing which end was up, Jack paced the kitchen and tried to buy some time. The kids were now in his living room and he had ducked out—ran away, actually—claiming that he would get something for them all to drink, but now that he had five glasses full of ice and cola on a tray, he couldn't force himself to pick it up and return to face the questions he wasn't sure he should be the one to tackle. Call Cassie; yes, that was what he should do next. Call Cassie and tell her what was going on. But where was his phone? He jammed his hands in the sweatpants pockets and came up empty. Upstairs, on his desk, of course. Hastily, Jack grabbed the tray, slopping soda as he hurried into the living room, set the drinks on the coffee table and, excusing himself once again, darted up the stairs, only to find that he had forgotten to charge the precious piece of communication technology that might have been his lifeline, and it was dead. After mentally screaming about a dozen profane words, Jack took a deep breath and paused to collect himself. Ironically, he had always expected Jasmine to eventually show up on Dave and Cassie's door step, but, for some ridiculous reason, the universe had placed the girl on Jack's front porch. Buffer? Mediator? Whatever the reason, Jack had a girl who had been courageous enough to search out something hugely uncertain and steeped in potentially emotionally crippling disappointment downstairs in his living room. Jack wasn't sure whether or not he could deliver on the dad thing, but he could at least give Jasmine an uncle.

Four sets of teenage eyes scrutinized him as he entered the living room and took a seat in the wing back across from Jasmine. She was still clinging tightly to Sage's hand, and the notion finally struck Jack that the two were a couple, of which, already feeling protective towards his niece, Jack approved. Resting elbows on knees, he leaned forward towards Jasmine and said, "I think I know why you're looking for Dave, but I don't want to make a mistake. All right?"

"Yes," Jasmine replied, her voice as sweet and soft as her name. "I understand, Mr. Bordeaux."

"Is your mother's name Angie? Angie Erikson?"

Jasmine's face went blank for a moment. She had never heard anyone call her mother "Angie," but she nodded and added, "But everyone calls her Angela. Our last name is Sorenson."

"From Fargo?" Jack asked, to which she responded in the affirmative, before he continued. "So my brother Dave is—"

"My birth father," Jasmine finished and the tears she had kept at bay all day spilled down her cheeks. "And you are ...."

Jack took the girl's free hand in his and said, "Your uncle. I'm your uncle."

With an iron grip on Jack's hand, Jasmine smiled at him through her tears and said, "Uncle Jack, do you know where I can find my dad?"

Before he could formulate a reply to that overly-complicated question, in strolled Isaac TwoBears who, as if he came home to find a quartet of kids in their living room every day, said with a jovial casual tone, "Hey, Jack! You forgot to tell me we were having a party."

Isaac thought he vaguely recognized the two boys. Was it Gage and Leon? He truly didn't know how Jack kept track of the names of all his students. Jack flashed him a serious look, saying, "You're early. I didn't hear you come in. You remember Sage and Keon."

Isaac fist-bumped the nearest boy—which one, he didn't know—and said, "Sure! Good to see you guys."

"And this," Jack cut in, "is Jasmine and ...?"

Embarrassed, Jack realized that he hadn't asked the other girl's name.

"Rosella," Jasmine timidly provided. "My best friend."

"Okay," Isaac said cheerfully, still unaware of the situation, and started to leave the room in search of an ice cold Guinness. "Great to see you all."

"Hold up," Jack said, as if he were drowning and Isaac was taking the only life preserver with him. "This is *Jasmine*. Dave's daughter."

Isaac's eyes widened, he released a long, dramatic "Oh," and dropped onto their recently-upholstered sofa, plaster-speckled work jeans and all.

Jack shook his head, directing his comment as much at Isaac as to the girls, "The man over there depositing construction site debris all over our new couch is my husband, Isaac TwoBears."

Both girls offered their hands and Isaac shook them, while assessing their "long-lost" niece, and she shyly stole glances back at him. Finally, she looked at Jack and said, her cheeks taking on a pretty pink, "I woke up this morning and I didn't have any uncles, and now …."

Jack could sense what Jasmine was searching for in the pause and shot a look at his husband. Isaac read its meaning and said, "And now, girl, you've got two."

Jasmine's face brightened at the words, and Isaac wondered if the kid would be completely overwhelmed when she realized how sprawling the Bordeaux clan was, which lead to the next thought. Where the hell were Dave and Cassie and the Miracle Child?

***

An hour later, in two states, in two garages, two harried women, terror scraping their voices, said to themselves out loud, "Where are those kids?"

Faye Gunderson stared at the empty spot where a white Mercedes should have been parked, Wanda Koskinen stared at the occupied spot where a white Mercedes should not have been parked, and, with cold terror running through them, both women grabbed their phones.

Chapter Twenty-five: Again, We Meet

Siesta Key was bathed in shades of purple twilight when Lars slowed the rental car to a stop at the beach house and, for a moment, took in the beautiful surroundings. He slid the window down and inhaled the balmy salt air laced with floral. Jasmine? He drew deeper, thought of his daughter.

"I didn't name her," Angela had told Lars once when he had asked. "That was Bordeaux's doing, not mine."

Up to that point, Lars had assumed that Angela had made the choice based on her love of the flowering vine. When he inquired what Angela would have chosen to call her, a shadow had fallen across Angela's mood, vague irritation clipping her words.

"I don't know, but not *that*."

There were lights on in the beach house, both up and downstairs, and as Lars got out of the car, forgetting that his phone was still in the pocket of the discarded coat on the back seat, he followed the inviting scents of evening towards the potential ugliness of the unknown.

***

There were some unknown details about the teenagers' ambush family reunion, and although it seemed as if Jack had not thought of them, Isaac's suspicious nature started an avalanche of questions crashing into his mind. Weren't these girls from Fargo? What was their connection to these St. Paul boys? Where were their parents? Did anyone know they were here? He didn't want to throw a bucket of ice water over all the nice warm feelings, but he was damn certain that he and Jack could be wading around in deep legal sewage if any one of these minors was a runaway. Treading lightly, Isaac said, "So, how do you guys and gals know each other?"

All the young glances roamed frantically back and forth between one another, until Rosella said, "My family and Sage's family have known each other since he and I were babies."

Sage hurriedly added, "Yeah, Ro and I go way back, and her parents come from Fargo to hang with mine all the time. That's how I met Jasmine."

Isaac smiled, nodded, and remembered as a teenager how good he had been at presenting just the right facts in order to cover the larger lie. Prior to coming out, Isaac's mother had been convinced that he was dating a classmate, Joanna Miller. How many times had Isaac rushed out, while his mother washed dishes at the kitchen sink, telling her that he was going to the Millers to see Joe? Every time, Victoria TwoBears had nodded, smiled and said to say hello to Mrs. Miller, never knowing that Isaac was secretly meeting Joanna's older brother, Joseph.

That silent E had served Isaac well, and he bet Jasmine and her compatriots had their own silent letters.

***

Despite its over-illumination, the beach house radiated a weird silence, and Lars halted a few steps from the door as the voice of raw reality suddenly shouted in his head. By now, Angela would have changed the security code, and if he knocked, she wasn't going to give him entry. The woman who had delivered divorce papers into Lars' life like a drive-by shooting couldn't be expected to behave rationally. Lars walked to the property's edge and glanced towards the beach. The dunes between the house and the water were a dense wall of overgrowth and appeared fairly impenetrable, but he noticed that the house next door had a realtor's sign, and he walked past it and found a narrow path on its north side. Was this trespassing? If anyone discovered him, he could simply say that he was interested in the property. He hoped his hunch was correct, but Angela had become such an enigma, he might be wrong.

Years earlier, when they had brought Jasmine here, Angela had spent almost every sunset reclined in her father's old wooden Adirondack chair, staring out over the gulf, her eyes following the sun until the last light sliver disappeared, and then continuing to search for something among the folds of darkness. Lars had tried to join the ritual, but Angela had said that it was her "alone" time, and he had respected her wishes. Would she be there now?

A shaving of sun still hung above the rough surf and sooty clouds pregnant with rain, wind, and lightning inched onto shore to the south. Lars could feel the atmosphere shift as he held back slouched bunches of sea oats and continued forward, the ever-nearing storm starting to land gusty punches. Somewhere, far up the beach, a dog barked.

***

Godiva lifted her head, issued one low bark, and sprang to her feet. Isaac raised an eyebrow at the dog.

"Outside?" he asked, but the Labrador's nails could already be heard on the kitchen tile, followed by the creak of the dog door swinging open and closed, which Isaac found odd.

Since installing it a month ago, he and Jack hadn't seen her use it without large amounts of encouragement—which usually translated into dog biscuit bribery. Just as Isaac was about to mention this peculiarity, one of the kid's phones began to vibrate, followed by a second, and then a third. Uneasy looks began to fly between all four young people as, from the backyard, Godiva's excited bursts of barking added more tension to the moment. Jack and Isaac exchanged a glance. What teen didn't grab for his or her cell when it was making noise? Isaac jabbed a thumb towards the back of the house.

"I'll go check *that* out."

Outside, on the rear landing, Isaac called to Godiva, She appeared from the side yard, still whining and stealing looks at the gate that lead to the driveway. At the mention of a treat, the dog abandoned whatever had riled her and scurried up the ramp. As Isaac started to close the mud room door, he thought he heard voices. Someone must have been walking past. He offered Godiva a biscuit, she took it and headed for the dining room, to her favorite rug on which to deposit crumbs, and Isaac started to leave the kitchen when he heard the mud room door open. In the split second it took him to register the hell that was about to break loose, the Miracle Child shot through the mud room, into the kitchen, and towards the living room, something in a plastic grocery sack swinging from one grubby fist. Close behind, Cassie darted in, scolding as she moved.

"Davy! I told you to knock. Jack might be resting. Get your butt back here!"

Before Isaac could utter a word of warning, Cassie, accustomed to chasing down a hyper-active five year-old, threw a "Hi, Isaac" and an apologetic glance over her shoulder as she rushed by a dumbstruck TwoBears.

"Uncle Jack, I brought you pudding cups," Davy hollered happily as he dashed into the living room and hopped up and down in front of Jack, twirling the gift above his head like a custard-filled mace. "Mom said you got a *big* tooth pulled out. Did it hurt? Did you get to keep it? Can I see it?"

Jack went pale and shoved himself up by the chair arms, almost toppling the piece of furniture. Cassie showed up not far behind Davy. Instinctively, Jack moved to block her view of Jasmine. Like Isaac, Cassie didn't immediately interpret the scene, until Davy crawled into Jack's vacated chair, peered at the pretty girl sitting across from him and said, "I'm Davy. Who are you?"

***

Through half-mast lids, Angie detected blurry movement about fifty yards to her right, and slowly rotated her lolling head away from the violent march of waves and towards the north swath of sand. She squinted at the figure as it emerged from the dunes, and mumbled, "Who are you?"

As she leaned on the right arm of the Adirondack to get a closer look, her bare foot knocked over the vodka bottle tilted in the sugary sand beside the thick wooden chair leg, but there wasn't enough left for Angie to notice the liquor that splashed over her toes. The figure began to move towards her and mind clouded, night falling quickly, storm clouds nearing, She watched, wrapped in weird fascination as the figure became Kenneth, moved closer, became Lars, melted back into Kenneth, before becoming her brother. Angie staggered to her feet, swayed, and took a few unsteady steps towards him.

"Adam?" she whispered.

Of course it was Adam. Only two nights earlier, she had seen him down the beach emerge from the sea. He had looked towards the old Lazlo house, looked back at Angie, and then vanished. That didn't matter now, because he had returned. Adam was here.

Wind picked up sand, mixed it with fat raindrops and hurled it against Angie's bare skin, as she lurched into a clumsy run. They would be together. It was okay. There was no one to stop them now.

When only a handful of feet remained between them, rain and tears smearing her vision, a shard of shell sliced into Angie's heel and, with a shocked cry, her knees buckled, and she sprawled onto the ground. A deafening thunder clap muffled the voice attached to the strong hands that firmly clutched her forearms, leveraged her onto her knees and back onto her feet. The hands wiped the sand from her face, the torrential rain washing it off her closed eyelids, so that she could open them, so that she could look at him, so that she could see Adam.

"Angela," the voice boomed, reaching above the storm's din and ripping through her delusion.

Angie's eyes flew open and horror distorted her face.

***

It was nothing less than horror that gripped Cassie Bordeaux when she finally got a view of the girl.

"Davy, that's a nice name. I'm Jasmine."

For a half second, the girl gazed up at Cassie, then back at Davy, and recognized the connection. Cassie's breathing quickened, her hands shook, and Jack took her by the arm. Cassie allowed him to guide her into an empty chair, where she peered up at Jack and mouthed, "What the hell is going on?"

Leaning to Cassie's ear, he quickly whispered, "Just showed up. Only here twenty minutes. Looking for Dave."

"Why you crying, Jasmine?" Cassie heard her son say, and turned her attention from Jack.

Cassie found the girl's wet brown eyes searching towards her for something on which to steady herself, but Cassie, feeling lost as to where to go next, said, "Davy, could you go with Uncle Isaac? I bet he'd take you upstairs."

Isaac, who now stood in the doorway, rubbing the bridge of his nose, a habit Jack recognized as nervous release, gave a beleaguered smile, slapped his hands together, and said, "Come on, kid! Uncle Jack's got some excellent games on his computer. I bet you three chocolate chip cookies you can't beat me at *any* of them."

Jack threw his husband a grateful look as Davy dropped the sack of pudding, jumped out of the wingback, and raced upstairs, Isaac dragging behind him. Another volley of cell phone vibes began and this time Sage looked at his screen. Rosella glanced at hers, too, but Jasmine continued to ignore the buzzing in her purse. She knew they were busted, but she could feel it in all its terrifying glory. Jasmine was on the brink of meeting her father.

"Tell your mom that you didn't know we were coming, Ro and I just showed up," Jasmine softly urged Sage, her sudden calm composure strange even to her as she looked up at Rosella and gestured for her best friend to move closer.

Call your mom. Let her know you're all right. It's all my fault. She and Aunt Faye will come for us, but that still gives me some time," Jasmine whispered into Rosella's ear.

Both Rosella and Sage hesitated, but Jasmine released Sage's hand, gave him a little push, and said, "Go."

Sage unfastened the "Honor the Earth" badge from his windbreaker and placed it reverently in her palm. Like the others, it had belonged to his grandfather.

"Be brave," he whispered.

Jack offered to show Sage, Rosella, and Keon into the library, a room that still housed walls of books, but also contained a jumbo flat screen. Jack slid the pocket door closed behind the teenagers and returned to sit beside Jasmine. Cassie was the first to speak, her voice low and gritty with her effort not to relinquish it to emotion.

"There probably were better ways for this to happen, but—"

"I'm sorry," Jasmine interrupted, staring into her lap at the badge in her sweaty hand before sliding it into a coat pocket for safe keeping. "I really am. It's just …."

Cassie shook her head, saying, "No. You're not the one who should feel sorry. You're still a kid. We're adults. Yes, this is sudden and surprising and scary, but that doesn't make it something you need to apologize for."

In support of protecting Jasmine amidst her profound vulnerability Jack said, "She's right, and you might already have figured it out, but this is Davy's mother, Cassie."

Jasmine nodded and attempted a small smile. To her, Cassie looked like someone of whom you would never want to get on the bad side, and the chokehold on Jasmine's insides loosened ever so slightly when Cassie returned a guarded, but genuine, flash of a grin. Suddenly a thought struck Jasmine hard. Her forehead creased, and she asked Cassie, "How do you know who *I* am?"

As Jack and Cassie stole a look at each other, in search of missing pieces, both wondering what exactly the girl knew and didn't know, it seemed obvious that Angie had never given Jasmine the address Jack had provided, or else they might all be sitting in Cassie's living room right now. But why had Angie gone to the effort all those months ago if she wasn't doing it for her daughter?

"It's complicated," Jack offered, disliking the way the phrase kicked the problematic truth down the road, but he sensed that each fragile layer of this required delicate handling and other layers were higher priority.

Cassie heaved a heavy sigh. All those sleepless nights as she stared at Jasmine's picture, agonized about who to tell, what to do, how to cope, one thing had persisted: if Dave's daughter reappeared and wanted access to her father, Cassie would do everything in her power to facilitate it. With that access, Cassie felt that Jasmine also had a right to the truth, no matter how complicated. Unwaveringly, she looked Jasmine in the eye and spoke.

"Dave told me about you. Five years ago, when I was pregnant with Davy, he told me about the relationship he had had with your mother, how it ended, and how she had taken you back to Fargo."

Cassie stopped, helped herself to one of the untouched soft drinks still sitting on the coffee table, and took a sip. She still struggled with the bitterness that arose when she thought of Dave's revelation and the unthinkable request it had festered. Another sickening suspicion now lingered around Angie and her dark motives. Had she sought out Jack and sweettalked Dave's address out of him not for Jasmine, but for herself? Did that bitch want Cassie's husband?

Jasmine's lower lip trembled and tears fell into her still-open palms. As if to bury the manifestation of her anguish, she tightly closed her fingers and wiped her eyes with the back of a hand. Cassie imagined the question that must be clawing its way out of the girl, and she sure as hell wasn't going to make the poor kid ask it.

Legal papers were drawn up," Cassie started, and then paused.

How could she frame this without vilifying Angie and her parents? No matter how much animosity Cassie felt towards the Erikson family, it wouldn't be right to exhibit those feelings in front of Jasmine. She was innocent.

"Legal papers that gave your mother and your grandparents sole custody of you," Jack said, to which Cassie mentally threw arms around her brother-in-law in appreciative relief.

Jasmine wasn't naïve; she had grown up observing the subtle—and not-so subtle—ways in which her grandparents' name and the money and power behind it influenced, orchestrated, and restricted others' behavior. Grandpa Kenneth was a judge. It must have been easy for him to insure who and who wouldn't raise his only grandchild. With this information, Jasmine tried hard to convince herself that her grandfather must have had her best interest at heart, but she fell short of complete acceptance of that idea.

"Did he want to sign those papers?" Jasmine asked.

In unison, Jack and Cassie blurted, "No."

Jasmine brightened ever so slightly at the conviction in their voices. Dave hadn't wanted to give her up. He hadn't had a better choice. Expectantly, she looked at Jack and then at Cassie, saying, "Where is he? Can I meet him?"

All of a sudden, Cassie's eyes went saucer-wide. In incidences of high stress, the unreliable portions of her less-than-whole mind tended to toss out short-term details. On the first day of Davy's Kindergarten, she dropped him at school and, for a solid minute, hadn't remembered the route to work. A tense morning could find her in the shower still in her underwear, or holding a slice of bread, trying to recollect where they kept the toaster. On this fateful, angst-saturated afternoon, Cassie had forgotten about Dave.

***

What the hell was taking them so long? Dave scratched his smoothly shaven chin, tugged at the tie his wife had convinced him to wear to the veteran's job fair, and stared at the house. He had wanted to go straight home, but Cassie had planted the suggestion of a good deed in their son's head, and Davy was dead set on delivering pudding to Jack. Finally, Dave gave in—after all, the poor son-of-a-bitch had undergone oral surgery. Dave glanced at the radio's digital clock. They had been in there fifteen minutes. Maybe something was wrong. Was Jack okay?

Although their relationship was strained at best, the guy was family, and suddenly Dave found himself opening the van door and lowering the ramp. Even if Jack was perfectly fine, Dave thought he might snag one of Isaac's fancy-ass beers. It had been a good day; the jobs fair had landed him a couple of great prospects for future employment, Davy had gone an entire week without a behavioral alert from the Kindergarten teacher, and Cassie said that he looked hot in the tie and jacket, which, after they got the kid to bed tonight, he thought he just might use to his advantage. He was still smiling about it as he entered the mud room, went through the kitchen, and followed voices towards the living room.

"There are somethings you should know about Dave," he heard Cassie say.

Yeah," Dave said to himself before he reached the doorway. "Like I look crazy sexy in a tie."

But then Dave turned into the living room, still in good-humor, saying, "What should you know about me?"

In an instant, Jack and Cassie jumped to their feet, Jack stepping in front of the third person in the room, and Cassie rushing in Dave's direction, but neither reacting quite fast enough. In that half-breath, Dave Bordeaux saw his daughter, Jasmine Sorenson saw her father, and the world turned upside down.

Chapter Twenty-six: Because

Angie gave Lars a brutal shove, backed away clumsily, and howled, "Leave me alone!"

"Angela, stop. We need to talk. We need to make sense of things."

The demands Angie had, for months, been meticulously planning to make upon Lars, now swirled in the frenzied churn of her alcohol-driven rage, and as she retreated and he pursued, loose threads of incomplete thoughts penetrated the storm, astride her hateful screams.

"Everybody's going to know. Do you think I care? Do you think I ever gave a shit? I'm going to win. *I'm* going to win this time"

She turned, started to run towards the beach house, but then slid to a stop, pivoting back towards Lars. They were both drenched, but he could feel heat rolling off her as she got inches from his face, and spat, "You are the loser. I will win. You will lose."

Crackling veins bled through the darkness, back-lighting her snarl of hair, smearing her face with shadow, accentuating madness, but Lars didn't stand down. He shook his head, shouting over the monsoon rains, "This isn't about winning and losing. This is about us, our family, Jasmine!"

At the mention of their daughter's name, Angie exploded into fits of frigid, bitter laughter that stabbed Lars's ears, pierced deep into his brain, and transformed the water on his skin into a million skittering insects. From the onset of Angie's plan, she had known that the kid would be a key piece of leverage—that and Lars's best-kept secret. Angie fisted the collar of his soaked shirt and yanked. He could smell the vodka now, as she growled, "Yes, let's talk about your precious Jasmine. Let's talk about 'Uncle Jay'. Let's talk about what she might think if she found out Perfect Daddy Lars and Uncle Jay used to bang each other. Yes, that's what I want to talk about, you screwing Jay Tipton. And you know what, Lars? I bet I'm not the only one. I bet your parents would love to hear about it. I bet your employees, your customers, your advertisers would all want to know. I really think it's high time for *everyone* to know, and I'm going to tell them, starting with precious Jasmine"

She let go, pushed Lars again, and started to turn her back to him. Before Lars could stop himself, his hand shot out, seized her arm, and spun her back to face him.

"You cannot do this, Angela. It's one thing if you hate me, want to hurt me, want to destroy me—though we both know I've never given you reason—but how in the hell could you even think of doing that to your own daughter? What is it you want? What is it you're trying to prove? I don't understand."

The storm weakened, but the grip he had on her arm did not.

"Tell me, Angela. Why are you doing this?

She glowered at the man. It didn't matter whether it was Lars. It could have been Kenneth. It could have been Dave. It even could have been Adam. They all had dismissed, disappointed, judged, put her last, made her vanish, took her, twisted her into what they wanted, not what *she* wanted, not what Angie wanted. She ripped her wet arm away from his grasp, from all their grasps, and felt the barrel of the gun still pressed to her hip. Lars stood dumbfounded, his gut roiling at her cruel threats. He absolutely could not—would not—lose Jasmine to this woman, who, right under his radar, had demolished the foundation of their family while apparently, losing her mind. This wasn't Angela. This wasn't anyone Lars knew. But wait. Maybe he did know her. Hadn't he met this violent, sadistic bully of a creature months earlier, in their bedroom? That woman had demanded he call her Angie. As she limped backwards on her cut foot, never taking her hate-filled, murky blue eyes off Lars, he held up his hands, as if in surrender and said, "Please tell me why."

She continued her strange, staggered, backward retreat, until he spoke again.

"I need to know why, Angie."

She halted, twenty feet or more now between them, and, for a single second, Lars watched her expression shift from loathing to disbelief, and then to something that resembled confusion, before warping back into a hideous mask of pure rage. The vicious predator's shriek that tore from her lips froze Lars's marrow; instinct had him stepping back several feet, stretching more distance between them.

"You want to know why?" her voice roared through the final drizzles of storm. "You really want to know why?"

Hatred and a revulsion so thick and ugly she ground her teeth against it caused every earlier thought of fat alimony payments extorted and ransomed for secrets and the child that Angie had never wanted to incinerate in the vengeance- and vodka-fueled fire. Angie reached beneath the filthy hem of her chemise and drew the gun. Her wet hand shook around the rain-slicked handle. She pulled the trigger.

"Because I hate every last fucking one of you!"

She fired again. Lars toppled onto the sticky sand after a second hot explosion tore through his thigh, briefly overshadowing the blinding pain in his upper chest. Vision blurring, wounds bleeding profusely, Lars pressed one fist to the bullet hole above his heart and, with the other, gripped the earth. As life flowed, tinting the white sand red, Lars thought of Jasmine. She had loved this place. Fighting to stay conscious, he closed his eyes, saw her as a happy salt- and sun-kissed six-year-old again. She splashed in the surf that rolled across the backs of his lids, spilled from the corners, and trickled into his ear. She was smiling now, waving for him to join her, but Lars couldn't move. And the night's deepening darkness suddenly grew darker.

Chapter Twenty-seven: Returning

For Jasmine, upon first seeing her father, it wasn't the wheelchair or the obvious reason that necessitated it that gave her pause, but the fact that Dave was wearing a suit jacket, dress pants—altered and folded over to conceal his stumps—and a rather bright, cheerful necktie. Of all different ways her imagination had configured him, none had included Dave in something that resembled Lars's usual work ensemble. For several seconds, she kept her eyes pinned to the tie, afraid to allow herself a view of his face, and when she finally mustered courage, exhaled, and let it happen, Jasmine immediately wished she had stayed focused on the swatch of patterned silk.

The moment he saw her, Dave had little to no doubt about her identity, and he felt the symptoms, felt himself slipping towards a state he had managed to fight his way out of for over four years. His mind disconnected from the present and hurling into the past, he felt all his senses following to that most dreaded destination: the one in rural Afghanistan. He white-knuckled the wheelchair's armrests, his breathing grew rapid as it chased his pulse, beads of sweat sprang to the surface of his ever-reddening face, black inky spots dotted his vision, and a high, choked sound, like the tie was slowly being pulled tighter around his windpipe, escaped him as his entire body started to shake.

Although one hadn't occurred since shortly after their son's birth, Cassie recognized the signs of her husband's pending full-blown departure from reality into a PTSD-related panic attack, and she rushed to kneel beside him. Covering Dave's clenched fists with her hands, Cassie firmly said his name, demanded that he look at her, kept telling him that he was safe, that he was home, but he only winced under her touch as if it were torture, and Dave's exit continued until his wild eyes rolled back in his skull and he was gone. That was when his screams began.

***

"Keep driving, Bordeaux," the squad leader screamed over the Humvee's roaring engine, but Dave continued to brake.

The girl was sprawled across the dusty road, directly in the vehicle's path. Although dressed in the loose trousers and shirt of a young Afghani boy, when the child had darted out and fallen in front of them,

Dave had glimpsed a face that belied the clothing. The truck slowed and the squad leader snarled, "Move the hell forward, soldier. That's an order!"

Like all U.S. troops serving in this region, PFC Bordeaux had been warned of the various methods the Taliban used to distract, divert, detain, and destroy, but despite the real possibility that the girl was a decoy, he could not bring himself to run her over in cold blood. The unarmored vehicle whined to a halt. The child didn't move.

"Back up and go around him," the squad leader bellowed, "before you get our asses in a jam!"

There wasn't enough space at either side of the prone girl for the large vehicle to clear, and, again, Dave refused the superior's underlying proposal.

"The kid's hurt," Dave said. "You want me to run down an injured Afghani citizen? A kid?"

"Jesus Christ, Bordeaux. When did you turn into such a bleeding-heart pussy? Well, you put us in this jam, you get us out. Drag that little bastard off the road, or I'm taking the wheel and we're going, whether he moves or not. You got it?"

"Yes, sir," Dave said, procuring his weapon and exiting the truck.

Off to the left, about a hundred yards away, Dave could make out a collection of small, drab buildings, with what might have been goats grazing nearby, but he detected no signs of human activity. He closed the fifteen feet between himself and the girl, who had now pulled her skinny legs to her chest, wrapped equally-thin arms around bony knees, and tried desperately to hide her face. With each crunch of gravel beneath his boot, she trembled more, until his shadow fell over her in the late afternoon light and she froze. Dave opened his mouth to speak a question he thought she probably wouldn't understand, but before the useless words materialized, the girl looked up at him, their eyes met and, for a breath, Dave found himself whisked away into a thought, a thought of his own daughter, a daughter he felt cynically sure that he would never have a chance to know. Wouldn't Jasmine be about this girl's age by now? Eight? Maybe nine? Did this girl have a father, or had he been killed in this war, or the last war, or the one before that? The breath ended, a tear mixed with the dust on the girl's cheek and left a thin muddy trail, and hidden beneath a brother's clothing, an indispensable son their father would never sacrifice, the explosives detonated.

"Where's the girl?"

It became Dave Bordeaux's death chant. He screamed it as he lay heaped at the roadside, coated in her flesh and blood, his own blood pooling around the mangled mess of what remained of his legs. He wailed it beneath the deafening blades of a Medivac helicopter. He mumbled it to army nurses, chaplains, the liaison that told him that no other members of his platoon had been seriously injured. He asked the gray walls of a Kabul military hospital, the stark interior of a C17 as it departed from Bagram airbase, and the gurney that wheeled him into another military facility in Germany. He asked the full urinal at his bedside. He asked bleached white sheets gripped in his shaky hands. He tossed the silent sheets aside and asked the phantom limbs, but their only answer came as an itch and then a burn. He asked the faceless occupants of his nightmares. When awake, he asked the vacant faces of other wounded warriors, but they had plenty of questions of their own that no one could or would answer.

"Where is the girl?"

Dave carried the question back to the States, back to Minnesota, back to the only place he could go, but by that time he had quit asking it aloud, it surfacing as screams in the wee hours of rare, disturbed sleep.

Isaac had built a ramp, Jack had put together a makeshift bedroom in their library. Isaac had installed lift bars and a shower chair in the downstairs bath. They helped Dave get on the waiting list for low-income housing for the disabled. They did what they could, often biting back petty responses to Dave's mean-spirited jabs at Jack, but neither Jack nor Isaac knew what to do when Dave wailed the same question in almost all of his fitful sleeps.

When Dave and Cassie met and eventually became more than just friends who shot pool together in the V.A. recreation hall, Dave's disturbing nocturnal inquiries prompted Cassie to bring up the subject of post-traumatic stress.

"So you think I'm crazy then?" Dave had said defensively. "You want me to go get on a thousand-mile-long waiting list to talk to the vet head shrinker so he can give me another bottle of pills? They've already got me on so much shit I can't tell my ass from a hole in the ground."

Cassie had understood where he was coming from. She had been through all the V.A.'s broken PTSD fixes and had, after an attempt at suicide and the onset of kidney damage, finally discarded the multiple bottles of antidepressants, tranquilizers, opioids, and sleeping pills and discovered a better answer.

***

Cassie reached inside the inner breast pocket of Dave's jacket and felt relief rush through her when her fingers wrapped around the vape pen. Withdrawing it, she clicked it on, pressed the button, guided the mouthpiece to Dave's lips, and told him to inhale. When she thought he had drawn an adequate dose of cannabis, she slipped the pen back into his pocket, and held her fingers to his wrist. Soon his pulse went from a run to a gallop, and finally to a normal trot. The shaking ceased, the alarming redness drained from his face, and his breathing became slow and steady again. Fishing a tissue from her coat, Cassie gently dabbed the perspiration from Dave's face, loosened the necktie, and waited for him to fully return. Another minute slipped by before he reached for her hand, clasped it lovingly, opened his eyes, looked at his wife, and then glanced over her shoulder. Dave's voice was calm, but still infused with fragile emotion when he finally spoke.

"Where is my girl?"

Cassie turned and scanned the living room. Jasmine was gone.

Chapter Twenty-eight: You and Me

Jack was gone, too, but when Cassie went to look for them, neither he nor Jasmine had ventured far. She found them in the back yard, seated on the steps of the gazebo, Jack's arm around the girl's shoulder as she hunched over her knees, depositing ragged sobs into her hands, and, realizing that they all were still outsiders to the distraught teenager, Cassie approached with as much softness as her rough-around-the-edges personality permitted. Jack raised his brows questioningly, pointed at the house with his chin, and mouthed, "Dave?" Cassie nodded, gave the okay sign, and took a seat on the wooden step next to Jasmine. For a half dozen seconds, Cassie worked the damp earth with the toe of her athletic shoe while she focused on an old oak's twisted bare branches. She wasn't good with girls, never had been—even when she *was* a girl. Growing up, she had preferred the companionship of her older brothers over her younger sisters. Later on, she had admittedly experienced profound relief when her second trimester sonogram had revealed a boy, feeling that she would be the right mother to a son, but now there was no rolling back the fact that this girl, with all the emotional complexities Cassie had spent most of her life avoiding, was going to be a part of the family. Tentatively, Cassie patted Jasmine's knee twice and then quickly retracted her hand into her lap, saying, "Listen, Jasmine. Dave's going to be all right. He was just surprised to see you."

That was the understatement of the century, but Cassie didn't want the girl to feel overly responsible for Dave's disturbing reaction, either. After all, Jasmine would have had no way of guessing what she was going to find in her search. The risk was huge, and still the teenager had taken it.

"Dave—I mean, your dad—he's a veteran. He did two tours, one in Iraq, and the last in Afghanistan. That's where he lost his legs. His injuries weren't just physical. There are times, when he's in situations where he feels things in an extremely concentrated way, either good or bad, he has difficulties dealing with it. People who have experienced war carry invisible wounds, too.

More composed than she had been at Cassie's arrival, Jasmine wiped her face on her sleeve and asked, "Is it like PTSD?"

"Yes, exactly," Cassie answered, mildly impressed, and somewhat encouraged at the teenager's intuitiveness. "But it's important that you understand. What happened in there is not a regular occurrence. Your dad has overcome incredible challenges and is capable of amazing things. It's just that …."

Jasmine had begun nodding gravely at the unfinished remark, and as a breeze more soaked in winter than spring encircled them, she shivered, her teeth chattering a little in her attempt to complete Cassie's thought.

"I was the last person he thought he would see today. He wasn't ready. Maybe he won't ever be ready. I'm sorry. I should leave."

She started to struggle up from the gazebo stairs, but both Jack and Cassie placed a hand on a shoulder and gently eased her back down.

"No," Cassie stated with enough authority that the teenager froze in place. "You should stay. He wants to see you and to talk to you. It seems to me you want that, too. What you've done, showing up, taking such a big chance, putting yourself on the line, it's all pretty bold. It would be a shame to turn back now, don't you think?"

Jasmine's mouth curled slightly at the corners. Maybe it was too soon, but she liked Cassie, appreciated her honest approach, admired the sincerity and toughness that dominated the woman's voice when she spoke of Dave, and, unexpectedly, Jasmine got a little burst of gratification from Cassie's comment about courage. Perhaps someday, if the hodge-podge of mismatched pieces were given a space to fit together and a relationship grew, she could consider Cassie her stepmother, but right now that sort of wishful thinking was crazily premature, maybe even delusional.

As Jasmine wiped the rest of the tears from her face, Cassie stood and held out a hand, saying, "Come on. This big adventure of yours isn't supposed to end with you chickening out. Your dad is one of the bravest people I know and you're his kid, so hoist your butt off that gazebo and go get what you came here for."

"She's absolutely right," Jack affirmed and pushed himself up to stand by his sister-in-law.

Somewhat calmed by their encouragement, Jasmine let Cassie pull her to her feet. To Cassie's mild dismay, the girl kept ahold of her hand until, with Jack in tow, they were back in the kitchen and Cassie gently let go. In silent agreement, she and Jack stayed behind, Cassie waving Jasmine on to continue. Nervously, the girl gave them a final glance for reassurance, and they both gave her a thumbs-up. Jasmine heaved a huge outward breath, mentally replayed Cassie's voice saying "bold", and returned to where Dave still sat, waiting for his daughter.

Once back in the living room, Jasmine stopped, unsure of what to do or say. The conversation that she had worked on in her head for the last few days didn't seem appropriate anymore, and even if she could find the right words, she wasn't quite sure her mouth could handle them right now. She opened and closed her hands, trying to keep them from shaking so much. She thought she must look like a complete unhinged mess.

Late afternoon sunlight filtered through the front windows, tinting the girl's edges in gold, and as Dave looked up, her beauty squeezed its warm, gentle fingers around his heart. Although more than a decade stretched between this moment and the final one when Angie ripped their child from his life, Dave could still make out the sweetness of that baby in the lines of the older girl's face, and the rush of love that suddenly flooded him began to crumble and carry away the years of absence. Her smile was shy as she crossed her right arm over her chest and clasped her left shoulder. After another beat or two, she snatched a glimpse of Dave, whose right arm had assumed an identical cross-body pose. Her expression brightened and in a voice like wind-shaken, new spring leaves, she said, "Hi. I'm Jasmine."

Immediately, her lovely cheeks flushed pink, but before her eyes fluttered away from him, Dave offered her a similarly self-conscious smile.

"Hi. I'm Dave. I'm your dad."

They both laughed anxiously at their obviousness, but quickly fell silent. He saw her knees start to tremble and he motioned to an adjacent wing back. Jasmine took the few steps required to reach the chair and, feeling as if she had just run a sprint, sat next to him.

"I'm real sorry about how I acted earlier," Dave began, but Jasmine shook her head and he quit speaking.

He should have known that the subject would scare her, and he threw a mental punch at himself for having launched into something too heavy, too soon.

"It's okay. Cassie explained everything," Jasmine clarified when she saw the lines of his forehead deepen and his expression darken.

Dave looked down at the remainders of his legs, at the wheel chair, and then at Jasmine, saying, "Everything?"

"Yes."

He searched his daughter's face, wondering if he would find fear, revulsion, or, worst of all, pity, but he could only find nervous curiosity and a warm openness that helped to quiet some of his false assumptions. Still, he thought that he *must* be disappointing to her.

"I'm probably not the kind of guy you thought you would find, am I?"

Before her jumble of thoughts and feelings would allow her to filter the response, Jasmine said, "No. I didn't think you would be wearing a tie."

Relieved that it was something as changeable as clothing, Dave chuckled hoarsely, tugged the unexpected neckwear a little looser, and said, "Trust me, this is not my everyday look."

Jasmine shaded a deeper pink.

"It's a nice tie. It looks good," she stammered, wishing she hadn't mentioned it at all, and then added, "I'm very nervous."

Dave swallowed hard. He wished he could put her more at ease. She seemed so delicate, so fragile. Part of him wanted to take her hand, but another part told him it was too soon. She was no longer the giggly toddler who used to wrap her tiny fist around Dave's index finger. She was a young woman now, and he didn't want to further frazzle her nerves by doing something a teenager would interpret as awkward parent behavior. He hadn't earned that privilege yet. After a few more ticks of uncertainty-laden time, he went with his gut, ran a palm over the spiky terrain of his dark brown and gray sprinkled hair, and gave tried and true no-frills honesty a try.

"I'm nervous, too. I think we're supposed to be. It's been a long time since we've seen each other. We've both changed a whole lot."

The more he looked at her, the more he remembered the precious infant that had been the beginnings of this stunning girl. He recalled her fascination with birds and the stuffed parrot toy that always brought her belly laughs when he flapped its wings and squawked her name. He still could recall the way her first budding tooth felt against his finger. Her hair was darker now, almost the same shade as his own, but a clear image of an after-bath time baby Mohawk he had brushed into her wet hair still lit the corners of his mind. Her first wobbly steps, the first time he heard her say "Da," the first sloppy, drool-coated pucker she had planted on his cheek: it all flew past his mind's eye like shiny-winged dragonflies. But what memories did she have of him? At their separation, she had only been two. What could he recall about his earliest years? Nothing. Not a single thing.

To him, Jasmine was a long-lost child, returned to receive the love he had not been able to give in more than a decade, but he understood that, to Jasmine, he was someone she had just met, little more than a stranger. If only time travel was possible, he could take her back, invite her into his vivid memories, so that she might feel some of what he was feeling, but whimsical thinking wasn't going to move them forward. They were at square one. Dave held his breath, chewed the inside of his cheek. Square one, all the way back at square one. For a drawn-out moment of debilitating disappointment, Dave felt penned within that square, until, like some sacred geometrical intervention, the first quartet of ninety-degree angles led him to think about another parallelogram, the one inside his pocket.

"I want to show you something," he said as he took a wallet from inside his jacket.

Once Dave had thought it long gone, lost, ruined, taken, but when their mother died, his brothers and sisters had cleaned the apartment where the late Mrs. Bordeaux and, at one time, Jack, Dave, Angie, and baby Jasmine, had lived, and found the precious square of paper tucked between the pages of a battered romance novel. Upon Dave's honorable military discharge, a box of random articles from his past life awaited him.

"Throw it away," he had snapped when Jack came into Dave's temporary library bedroom and set the box on the coffee table. "Why would I want any of that old crap?"

Jack had ignored his brother's angry order, and the box had stayed on the table for three more days, until boredom drove him to rummage through it. As he had suspected, he didn't want most of what he found, but at the very bottom, hidden under a raggedy AIM T-shirt, was a sacred object. For the days, weeks, months, then years that followed, Dave had carried it, hidden, close to his heart. He shared it with no one, not even Cassie, only looking at it when alone and safe and prepared to accept whatever it provoked within him. Somedays, it was a bullet to the heart, others, only a bee sting. On the best days, it was sugar and sunshine and a thin slice of salvation that kept the demons at bay.

Right now, it was medicine, it was magic, it was their time machine. He slid the photo from its concealed compartment and handed it to his daughter.

"That's you," she said, the deep brown of her eyes becoming shiny melted chocolate.

"That's us," Dave replied. "You and me, Jasmine. That's you and me."

"Where were we?" Jasmine asked, something inside of her already knowing. "What were we doing?"

Pride, longing, regret, and love shook his vocal chords, as he said, "We were in the circle, at a powwow. We were dancing."

Jasmine was crying as she said, "You loved me."

Dave fought back his own tears and nodded.

"I loved you, and I've never stopped."

Jasmine felt a tugging in her chest. She wanted the feeling to be there, so that she could say the words back to him, but it wasn't there, not yet. And as she inwardly searched for some memory of her affection for him, her thoughts carried her back to Fargo, home to countless times and countless ways Lars Sorenson had expressed his love for her and the immense love she had for him. Suddenly, guilt caused a troubling sense that she was betraying the only father she had ever truly known to crash heavily into her conscience. She stared at the photograph in her hand, and tried to steel against the discomforting wishbone pull between the past and the present, between one father and the other. Could she love them both? Would they let her, or, at some later, horrible point, would she have to make a choice?

"I've missed you. Every day, I've missed you, Jasmine," Dave said, rubbing his wet eyes with a knuckle.

The admission inched his leg of the wishbone closer to its breaking point, and she noticed now the way she was smiling at him in the photograph. But she had been a baby. Did infants have the capability to love? Was that what she was looking at, or simply a smile mimicking a smile? Reluctantly, Jasmine lifted her gaze from the picture and looked at Dave.

He could see conflict playing itself out in each shifting expression of her face. She held the picture out to him and he took it.

"Thank you for finding me. It's a brave thing you've done. I admire that, and I sure hope we can get to know each other better because I bet there are a lot of things about you that I would find very cool. You might find a couple of things about me you like, too. Who knows? I just know that I would like us to have that chance. Okay?"

Jasmine's face softened, some of the strife erased, and she nodded.

"Yes, I'd like that, too. Can I ask you some questions?"

"Yes, that's a good place to start."

Question after question, regardless the difficulty of the subject, Jasmine asked, Dave answered, until she paused and said, "Tell me about Davy."

Intently, Jasmine listened to the story of her half-brother and, when it was done, she took a deep breath, crossed her fingers that the wishbone would stay unbroken, and began the telling of her own story.

"There's someone who is really important to *me*. I think you need to know about him. His name is Lars. He's my dad."

Chapter Twenty-nine: Motives and Promises

"Any word from Lars?" Laura Bachman inquired when Faye Gunderson slid back into the passenger seat and secured a large coffee into a cup holder.

Faye fastened the seat belt, cracked open a bottle of water, and shook her head, saying, "No, not yet. I tried calling again, but it's still going straight to voicemail."

Laura hurried the minivan away from the convenience store and back towards the interstate. Although up until this point, the women's only connection was the Bachman's dog, their forced three-plus hour road trip was proving them easy, agreeable travel companions. The initial miles of their excursion had included a back-and-forth rant of worry, disbelief, and aggravation at the wayward teen girls, but when those overly-charged ions settled, their conversation had deepened. Careful to provide relevant facts that might better explain Jasmine's behavior, without the taint of too much personal opinion, Faye had offered some insight into Lars and Angela's pasts. Laura had listened, keeping her own prevailing thoughts silent. Although she had always found her interactions with Lars warm and friendly, Laura had long wondered why Angela consistently responded to her with dismissive coldness.

"The timing of this is unfortunate, considering the reason for Lars' absence," Laura had tentatively ventured, to which Faye had responded, "It's all pieces of the same mess, and that mess started long before Jasmine was born."

Faye had stopped herself then, and Laura hadn't pushed, but later, feeling an ever-growing trust in Laura, Faye added to it.

"I didn't bother contacting Angela. Lars told me last night that she hasn't responded to any of his calls or texts. I tried several times after he and I spoke, with the same results. Worse than that, according to Lars, she hasn't replied to any of Jasmine's attempts in more than a week."

The idea chilled Laura. She couldn't imagine disconnection from her children, especially Rosella. Only death could break communication between them, and that thought had stabbed the ice that crept across Laura Bachman's skin, deep into her bones.

"Thanks for the coffee," Laura said, as she set the van's cruise control as many miles above the posted limit as she thought prudent, and reached for the hot beverage. "I suspect I'm going to need the extra energy."

***

"Got a text from Mom," Rosella whispered to Jasmine. "They just stopped for coffee. Will be here in about an hour.

Jasmine looked around at the others seated at Jack and Isaac's dining room table. Cassie had ordered pizza, and everyone, including Sage and Keon, and the recently-arrived Wanda Koskinen, dined quietly on some thick crust extra cheese supreme. To her left, Davy, who had insisted that he should sit next to his "new big sister" kept stealing furtive glances at her, flashing goofy grins, and asking if she wanted the vegetables off of his demolished slice of pizza. At opposite ends of the oak rectangle, Isaac and Jack exchanged occasional serious looks. Jack had foregone the pizza, instead dining on Davy's much-appreciated pudding cup gift and some noodle soup Isaac had heated for him. Across the pizza-laden divide, Dave and Cassie eagle-eyed their offsprings' interactions with a shared sense of cautious pride. In the past, Davy hadn't ever issued any complaint about his only-child status, so his reaction to Jasmine was a surprise, and Jasmine's easy, patient response to the inquisitive five-year-old seemed to come quite naturally, but despite how well it was going, each arriving moment felt like a leap with no guarantee of safe landing. Polite awkwardness was the best way Jasmine could describe it, and Rosella's update caused her already-tense neck and shoulders to grow rockier at the thought of Aunt Faye's approach. Dave, Cassie, Jack, and Isaac were now fully informed about the how, what, when, where, and who of Jasmine and Rosella's journey, and Wanda had delivered them the additional news of Laura and Faye's plan to retrieve the girls. The entire group was on edge—except for Davy, whose unexpected joy at discovering a sibling in his uncles' living room was akin to the day they had brought home the pit bull puppy.

Jasmine cleared her throat, laid her napkin next to the plate, and said, "I think I should talk to my aunt—before she gets here. Please excuse me for a minute."

In unison, the adults at the table eagerly agreed, and Jasmine stood, made Davy promise he wouldn't eat the green peppers off of her pizza, which made him laugh, and left the dining room. Once in the library, she held her breath, chewed her lower lip, and tapped the call icon.

"It's Jasmine," Faye responded, tapped the accept icon and, without greeting, asked, "Are you all right?"

"I'm fine, Aunt Faye," Jasmine quickly said in a windy release of held breath. "And I'm really sorry. This isn't anybody's fault except mine. I'm the only one that should be in trouble for this."

Faye knew she should probably take a firm stance about the girl's actions, but the integrity behind her niece's adamant confession softened her reply.

"Yes, Mrs. Bachman shared what Rosella told her with me and, trust me, Jasmine, I do understand what you were trying to do, but it was dangerous, and there will be consequences. However, that's not my department. Punishment falls in the parental category. I'm retrieving you, the car, and getting both home in one piece. That's my job."

Jasmine paused, bit her thumb nail, and then asked, "Does Dad know?"

"No, I haven't been able to reach him."

An insect-like sensation skittered up Jasmine's spine. It wasn't like him to forget to take his phone off airplane mode, especially now, since Angela had cut off communication.

"Okay, Aunt Faye," Jasmine said apologetically. "I'm sorry. Thank you for making this trip. I'll see you when you get here. I love you."

"I love you, too. We're family—always. I'll see you soon."

Call ended, Faye turned to Laura. Behind them, the sun squatted low on the horizon, its light dimmed by the lingering gray cloud blanket.

"Obviously, I'm better with dogs and cats than I am with kids."

Laura smiled and said reassuringly, "You did great. Jasmine and Rosella are, despite this ill-planned misadventure, very good girls, and, you're right, there *will* be consequences, but, in Jasmine's case, it's difficult to focus on the behavior without her motive overshadowing it. I can't help but feel sympathy for her. If Rosella ever reaches a point where she wants to seek more information about her birth parents, I'll help her run down any lead available, not that I think much would be found. Her birth mother dropped her at a fire station a day after Rosella was born. I did some searching when Ro was small, but came up with nothing. More than likely it was a home birth because none of the local hospitals had any record. Even though she has never asked, I feel badly that it's something we can't give her. I'm sure that's why Ro didn't take much convincing when Jasmine wanted her help. She wanted to give her best friend something that, for Ro, is out of reach."

Faye took a drink of water, hoping to dislodge the lump that had formed in her throat. Too often, she had arrived at the clinic to find a cardboard box of abandoned kittens or puppies on the back door step. Sometimes, the more caring individuals left a note apologizing for their inability to keep the animals, thanking the clinic for its help. With each abandonment, Faye had to reel in her disgust for the irresponsible human beings who tossed their poor choices in the forms of the innocent into someone else's hands, but more often than not, the animals were placed in loving homes, and her faith was restored. Rewarding their compassion, Dr. Gunderson extended discounted check-ups and appointments to all families that rescued the clinic's box babies. For Faye, those who were willing to step into the void left by others were higher spiritual examples of humanity.

Rosella is a great kid," Faye said. "It's pretty clear that you and your husband have been excellent parents. I see Lars as having done much the same for Jasmine."

"I agree. Lars is super. Jasmine lights up whenever she talks about him."

"That's what puzzles me a little. As close as Jasmine is to him, it seems strange that she's chosen to search out this Dave Bordeaux."

Laura shook her head knowingly.

"Not so strange. There's some upheaval going on in their family right now and teenagers tend to act out in far more exaggerated ways than usual when there's extraordinary circumstances as a backdrop. Plus, this isn't just about looking for her birth father, Faye. Jasmine is looking for the culture she believes will come along with that parent. Has she ever talked to you about being Ojibwe, about being Native American?"

Faye bristled at the question, but said that the girl hadn't ever discussed it.

"What if she had? What could you tell her about it?" Laura said gently.

Faye shrugged. "Honestly, I don't know that much about that kind of thing, but I wouldn't have ever dissuaded her from talking to me about it."

"Of course not. You would be a great listener, but perhaps she needs more than that. When we adopted Rosella, I read everything I could get my hands on about American Indian history, culture, spirituality, art. You name it, I read it, but at the end of the day, I realized that we needed to offer her more than just facts. We needed to give her opportunities to meet and spend time with other native children and adults. That's when I met Wanda Koskinen. At that point, our families embraced and merged and we've all been better for it. I've seen it, Faye. The way Jasmine responds to anything tied to her and Rosella's birth culture. She's hungry for it. I may be out of line, but without the original tie to it, which is Dave Bordeaux, Jasmine may not ever feel completely whole. It's one thing if that connection is an impossibility, like Rosella's origins, but it's something quite different, I would go as far as to say worse, if that original birth culture bond is denied."

Bothered by Laura's implied suggestion, Faye prepared to defend, but then her sister Susanne's voice grated across her memory. The disparaging comments about the girl's darkened summer complexion, the overt opinions on Jasmine's friendship with "that Bachman Indian girl," the incessant reminders about the importance of a Christian upbringing to override any "pagan tendencies." Susanne's worn-out hit list—hit seeming to mean strike every bit as much as preferred—punched Faye's conscience, taking the teeth right out of her defensiveness.

"Yes," was finally all she could manage as a response, but then, with the raw further reminder of the entitled, heavy-handed way in which Faye knew Kenneth and Susanne had legally barricaded Jasmine from her paternal birth family ripping away any lingering need Faye might have had to explain their actions, said, "No one should have their right to feel whole taken away."

Faye paused and focused on the distant glowing skyline of the Twin Cities that had begun to erupt into view. It was what Faye had struggled against her entire life: her recognition of the elements that she knew would strengthen her spirit, make her soul complete, pitted against the Gunderson and Erikson families' rigid mold of what a woman should be. Yes, Faye understood perfectly well how hard it was to have to fight for self-identity and wholeness, but she also knew how gratifying it was when one continued to grind against the grain until you attained them. It took courage and determination and, often, a deaf ear and a blind eye to detractors who believed that their unsolicited advice, condescending commentary, disapproving frowns and eye rolls somehow would minimize the discontentment of their own lives. Inwardly, Faye felt a small smile bow around her heart, travel as pleasurable warmth upwards through her chest, and find its destination upon her lips as a barely perceptible, yet gratified grin.

"You could say that what Jasmine and Rosella did is half-cocked and compulsive, and even a tinge crazy, but there's no arguing that their stunt took a lot of courage."

Laura gave a sardonic laugh, and said, "No, those two—especially in tandem—have no shortage of confidence. They are some strong-willed young women."

"Good," Faye said firmly. "We wouldn't want them any other way."

"Amen to that," Laura agreed.

Not so long ago, Faye might have inaccurately categorized some of Angela's youthful actions as a courageous attempt to establish her own identity, to break with family and societal norms, and to search out her true version of self, but now, evaluating the much broader picture, including this latest Florida drama, Faye saw it differently. Self-serving, dishonest, unstable; Faye didn't want to think the things that she did about her niece, but none of Angela's behavior disproved the thoughts. And still no word from Lars—another thought that had begun to scrape a sore spot. He should have arrived in Florida by now. She unlocked her phone and searched for Lars's flight information. The plane had landed over an hour ago. Faye sent another text, made another call, left another voicemail.

"Take a deep breath," Faye silently told herself. "Do not catastrophize this. Everything will be fine."

***

Jasmine told herself that everything was going to be fine, pocketed her phone, and went to join the others.

Let's give this family some more private time together before your mom and Jasmine's auntie get here," Wanda had said as she herded Rosella, Keon, and Sage out of the dining room a few moments before Jasmine returned.

When Jasmine was back in her seat, she smiled weakly at the remaining people at the table. All at once, it felt as if a timer was counting down at a lightning-fast pace, and she wondered if these quickly disappearing seconds would be the only ones she would get with her father, her brother, her uncles, Cassie. As if she could read what the girl was thinking, Cassie said, "We know that you'll be going back to Fargo tonight, but we will see each other again. You have your dad's number, you have my number, and you have Jack's number, so, whenever you want, you contact us. Okay?"

Jasmine nodded, and looked at Dave.

"Absolutely," he said. "You found me, and, I promise, we aren't ever going to lose each other again."

A heavy mist of emotion surrounded everyone, the words penetrating each person to a different depth. Jack looked at his older brother, who hadn't taken his intense gaze off his daughter. For the first time in their lives, Jack saw the tenderness and the vulnerability that had been buried beneath all of Dave's anger, the soft meat of a nut freed from its hardened shell, a shining shard of crystal quartz washed from an underground cave, the rarest of winged creatures, entombed for eons in amber, now liberated, lustrous, and air-light. Cassie saw it, too, and laid a hand on Dave's shoulder.

"We *will* see each other again, Jasmine, all of us," Dave said, sweeping a glance across each person in the room. "I'll make sure of it. Whatever I have to do, we will give you your place in this family."

Everyone nodded their agreement, and, although he didn't fully understand, a strange wiggly tummy feeling made Davy jump up, wrap his skinny arms around Jasmine's neck and, lip quivering, hide his face against her shoulder. The little boy smelled of chocolate chip cookies, pepperoni, and the unmistakable scent of dog. Tilting her cheek to rest against his mess of spiky hair, Jasmine hugged back, closed her eyes, and made a wish that their father's promise could be kept.

Chapter Thirty: The Next Battle

The Sarasota police lieutenant had the victim's North Dakota driver's license matched up with further databank stats by the time her partner made it back down the dune.

"They taking him to SMC?" she asked, still scanning the small screen for marital status, locating it, and then committing the spouse's info to memory.

It wasn't a homicide—yet. Lars Sorenson still had a flutter of a pulse when a nearby resident and his dog found him. The resident had reported thinking that he had heard gunshots earlier, but then written it off as cracks of thunder. Understandable, as the wealthy beach community rarely experienced the jolting sound of firearms being discharged. In the lieutenant's opinion, the persistence of a schnauzer and the fact that his owner was a retired physician were the two crucial elements that had prevented Mr. Sorenson's death. One only needed to glimpse the sand inside the crime scene tape to assess how much blood he lost.

"Yes, and he's still got a heartbeat," the detective said. "Also, that key in his pocket unlocks a blue four-door parked in front of the next house over. The place is lit up like the fourth of July. Odds are, someone's home."

"Did you run the plates and the address?"

"Car's a rental. The vic's travel bag, a jacket, and a phone were inside. The house belongs to an Angela E. Sorenson. She and Lars Sorenson share a permanent address."

"Okay. We have some footprints, bare, what looks like a little blood mixed in one. Lead up to the rear of that particular property. Also grabbed this."

The lieutenant held up an evidence bag that contained an empty vodka bottle.

"This is looking fairly domestic, but we don't have a weapon or the wife yet. Let's get the procedural stuff in place."

The detective nodded, called for the issuing of a warrant, and police backup. If the wife was hunkered down in her lit-up vacation home, she might have weapons, and she might not be alone.

***

Angie crouched halfway up the stairwell. Earlier, she had heard what sounded like the wailing approach of police cars and an ambulance. Someone had found him. Moments ago, the vehicles, sirens blaring, departed. They wouldn't turn them on if he was dead, would they? She didn't think so, but her thinking wasn't exactly clear. Her head throbbed, the vodka and the adrenalin still hobnailed boot marching on her cranial capillaries, as she worked to organize her scattered thoughts.

What had she done with the gun? She needed to get rid of it. The ocean would be the easiest place to dump it. Yes, that's what she would do; she would wait until after midnight, when the beach was empty and very dark, and then she would take the gun, walk far away from the house, and throw it, as hard as she could, into the ocean. First, she needed to remember where she had left it.

"Is it in the lanai?" Angela wondered, and then a hazy recollection of the Smith and Wesson sliding from her wet fingers and into a rattan chair floated sketchily forward.

Angie bolted up, swooned, grabbed the railing, and steadied herself. She paused. The bones and muscles in her legs didn't feel completely solid, and her blurry vision fell on, and followed, the bloodied sand trail down five steps to the Italian tiles of the vestibule. She blinked. The doorbell rang. She froze. It rang again, and then a third time, followed by a heavy, persistent pounding fist, and a loud, authority-armored female voice.

"Mrs. Sorenson. This is Lieutenant Falwell of the Sarasota Police Department. Open the door. We need to speak with you."

"Angie," she growled under her breath. "Not Mrs. Sorenson."

She brushed a hand over the waistband of the soaked shorts. If the gun had still been tucked there, Angela would have put the barrel in her mouth and pulled the trigger. But not Angie, never Angie.

***

"I hope like hell they got whoever pulled the trigger," the on-call surgeon said in a quiet, focused, calm voice, as he honed-in on the slug buried just below Lars Sorenson's left clavicle. "A few centimeters south and this guy would be in the morgue right now."

Heaving a long outward breath, the surgeon dropped the slug and the instrument with which he had removed it on a metal tray, while the assisting surgical team quickly clamped, cauterized, and cleaned up.

"Between this and his leg, it's going to take a lot of physical therapy hours," a nurse said as he carefully sutured the final stitches.

The surgeon turned his attention to the heart monitor and replied confidently, "He's up to it."

***

Faye woke with a start, her heart loud and fast in her ears. As the wild palpitating ceased, she became aware of the ringing phone, and groped around in the unfamiliar surroundings of the Sorenson's guest room for it. When she finally located it, she realized that it wasn't hers. Before leaving St. Paul, Laura had revoked privileges and taken Rosella's cell, whereupon, without Faye's instruction, Jasmine had handed over her own device. Still worried by her dad's non-responsiveness, she had asked that Faye tell her immediately if Lars called on it. Faye slipped on her glasses, and looked at Jasmine's screen. By that time, the ringing had stopped, but the name on the back-lit iPhone read, "Grandma Sorenson."

Swinging her legs off the side of the bed, Faye pulled herself into a fully seated position. Why would Lars's mother call her granddaughter at one o'clock in the morning?

"Nothing good ever happens after midnight," Faye mumbled the favorite adage of her own grandmother, as she coughed the sleep gravel from her throat and returned the call.

***

Lieutenant Falwell took into account Angela Sorenson's torn, damp lingerie, the vodka on her breath, the bloody sand on her feet, the bruises on her wrists, and the reddened, glassy eyes that wouldn't make contact, cleared her throat and asked, "Did your husband threaten you in any way?"

"I didn't want him here. He tried to get in," Angie snapped. "I already told you that."

The Sorenson woman's story kept shifting, but Lieutenant Falwell remained cool, saying, "Actually, I don't believe you mentioned that before, Mrs. Sorenson. Your husband attempted to gain entry without your permission? At that point, did you try to contact the police?"

"I'm Angie," she huffed impatiently. "He was at the door, I got scared, and I couldn't locate my phone."

"All right ... Angie," Falwell said with the obvious feigned patience she reserved for those who danced around the truth. "I understand. At which entrance did Mr. Sorenson arrive?"

The lieutenant and her detective exchanged a quick glance and a subtle nod.

"Detective Torres, please retrieve prints from both the front and rear entrances."

Angie had waived her right to an attorney, but now, as she realized the physical evidence wouldn't line up with her claim, she shook her head nervously and said, "I've changed my mind. I want to call my lawyer."

***

"We've hired a lawyer, son."

Lars nodded wearily at his father's words and gently extracted his right hand from his mother's grip, but recognizing the look of maternal edginess that rose in her eyes, scratched the stubble on his chin, and placed it back on hers, giving his mother's fingers a light squeeze. She offered him a thin smile, the kind he defined as her "the doctor in me predicts full recovery, but the mother in me remains terrified" look. It was an expression Lars hadn't seen since the cancer, since the day his oncologist had given him the all-clear.

He shifted his weight. Sharp fireworks exploded from the center of the thigh wound, shooting hot sparks along the nerves in all directions. Grimacing, he dropped his mother's hand and groped for the button connected to his IV.

"Thanks, Dad. I appreciate it," he said, and pressed a thumb against what he hoped would be quick relief.

Forty-eight hours had passed since the shooting, and despite the near-death experience, the emergency surgery, the police questioning him as he regained consciousness in post-op, and the frantic arrival of his parents, Drs. Michael and Alicia Sorenson, Lars found himself feeling like an outsider peering in at a situation so bizarre he could not imagine himself a participant in it. If it were not for the physical reminders currently lighting his leg and chest ablaze, he might think it all the result of watching too many episodes of *Law and Order* before bed, their content trickling in and becoming bad dream ingredients.

"Did you talk to Jasmine today?" he asked.

"Yes," his mother assured. "She's fine, but, of course, still very worried about you. Your Dad and I both have promised her that you will be all right, but she's not going to be fully satisfied until she can see for herself."

When Michael and Alicia had arrived at the medical center and reined in the emotional response of parents enough to assess the situation with the pragmatic attitude of medical specialists, and after his mother had conversed with Faye, Lars had spoken to Jasmine for a few minutes so that he could hear her voice, so that she could hear his, so that he could try to quell the intense terror he knew his daughter was experiencing. At the time of that first call, Lars begged his parents and Faye not to tell Jasmine what the source of his injuries was, but to keep it vaguely veiled as an accident until some of the legal ends could be dealt with and he could deliver something conclusive along with the truth.

"Jasmine asked if, when you're feeling up to it, you could call her on FaceTime. Faye says that she's chomping at the bit to get down here and doesn't understand why they just can't hop on a plane. I suppose Jasmine feels that if she can't be right in the room with you, video chatting is the next best thing."

"I know, Mom." Lars sighed. "But look at me. I don't need a mirror to know that I look pretty rough. Besides, she's too smart. She's going to stare me in the eyes and know I'm not telling her everything. What am I going to say when she asks about Angela, or what kind of accident it was, or why she can't be here?"

Michael Sorenson's face hardened as he said, "That's why we need to get the lawyer here as soon as possible, and you need to decide whether or not to press charges."

Less than a week ago, Lars had believed he and Angela's marriage was on solid ground again, that they would be spending their daughter's spring break vacation as a family, in the newly-renovated beach house, and that last year's rough patches had all been smoothed out, but those beliefs had been blown to bits, and now Lars needed to pick through the rubble and choose what he was going to carry forward. First and foremost, Jasmine topped the list, and as the sweet relief of morphine wrapped the jagged edges in cool satin, between the receding physical discomfort and the inevitable drug-induced sleep, his mind discovered a window. Through it, Lars viewed the pieces and the players, and the possible moves, and, with perfect clarity, he realized exactly what he must do. Angela had weaponized herself with his secrets. With the next battle on the horizon, he had to disarm her before he could pick up his own weapon. Maybe the morphine would help with that, too. Lars looked at his mother and then back at his father.

"Call the firm. See if they'd be willing to meet with me here in the morning."

"All right, I'll do that. This is a good decision, Lars. Your mother and I will support you every step of the way."

"I appreciate that support," Lars responded, his voice taking on a lightly sedated slur. "Because as we start this process, I need to come clean about something."

Michael and Alicia exchanged a glance, seeming to brace themselves for whatever was going to come next, and then encouraged their son to continue.

"Do you remember my old friend, Jay Tipton?"

"Yes," his mother said hesitantly. "Bison baseball. He was such a nice young man. He came to the house to visit and he always brought those fast food burgers you craved after your treatments."

"Good guy. Great friend," Michael picked up the praise where Alicia had left off. "What about him, son?"

"Sit down, Dad," Lars said and, still holding his mother's hand, he told them the truth.

Chapter Thirty-one: No Easy Way

At the end of Lars's confession, Michael Sorenson scanned his wife's face, searching for direction, but she hadn't stopped looking at their son since his story began. Suddenly overwhelmed with all the revelations of the past few days, Lars's father said that he needed some air and excused himself.

Alicia saw their son's features crumple at Michael's abrupt exit, and she said, "It's all right. He'll be back."

Deep down, Lars knew his father's actions weren't rooted in moral judgement. Michael Sorenson was more a man of science than a man of God, and although he acknowledged the power of prayer, he had largely refused to embrace any particular religious doctrine, leaning towards a more Libertarian world view. Alicia gave her son an affectionate pat.

"It's his way, Lars. He requires space and time to convene his thoughts. No one, not even me, has ever gotten a verbal response out of him until he's ready to address something logically. For better or for worse, your father is exacting in his methods. For him, thought always precedes response. Perhaps that's why his specialty is the brain."

"And yours is the heart," Lars replied, to which Alicia smiled. "You're not off thinking this through, Mom. Are you okay? You seem fairly calm for having just heard the details of your son's sexual secrets."

"Honestly, Lars, there was a time, about a year before your cancer diagnosis, when I was certain there was something more than friendship between you and Jay."

Lars drug-droopy eyes suddenly widened, his slackened jaw fell a bit more, and all he could manage was, "What? How?"

"I had stopped by your apartment one morning. Jay was there and you were cooking breakfast. You both seemed taken off guard by my drop-in visit. Jay said that he was there to pick you up for the gym. None of it appeared out of the ordinary to me, until I stepped into the kitchen to put a lasagna in the freezer and I noticed Jay's feet."

"His feet?"

"Yes, he was sitting at the table, drinking orange juice, ankles crossed, and his feet were bare. At the time, I remember thinking that it was February and if he had just arrived to take you to the gym, why would he have taken off his shoes and socks. Also, his hair was wet, which seemed odd. Why would a guy shower before a workout? Then I asked if I could use your bathroom quick before I headed for the hospital, and you swapped the most peculiar look with Jay before you said that I could. When I went in, something else jumped out at me. Your toothbrush was in the rack. I knew it was yours, because at that point, you were nineteen, and I was still buying you a new one every three months, still doing that careful mothering routine, trying to see to the details I thought you might overlook. I always bought blue, like you preferred."

Lars cast a lopsided sardonic grin, saying, "Still get blue, every time."

"The blue brush was in the rack, but there was a green one, wet and a little pasty, left on the edge of the sink. My mind started to slide those pieces together, but then I told myself, 'No, Alicia, you're being ridiculous.' But when I left the bathroom, I could hear you and Jay talking in low voices, and I knew. Right then and there, I knew."

"What were we saying?"

Alicia's countenance turned soft and knowing. "It wasn't your words, son. It was your tone. I heard that particular note in both of your voices. It's only present when there's a certain type of intimacy between two people. I remember looking through the open bedroom door, and I saw Jay's shoes and socks piled beside your bed. As a child, you were always a neat sleeper, barely wrinkling the comforter. In the morning, I only ever had to fold the sheets and blanket over. When you were old enough to do it yourself, you made your bed every morning. That day, however, I couldn't help but notice that the bed was an unmade mess—both sides."

"Jay was never very tidy," Lars reflected, and then asked, "If you knew, Mom, why didn't you say anything?"

"I was waiting for you. It was yours to tell—well, yours and Jay's. A year or two later, he was engaged, and you hadn't said anything, so I began to think that I had misinterpreted what I had seen. On the day you married Angela, I looked at Jay, standing beside you as your best man, and I briefly entertained the thought of you and Jay together rather than you and Angela. It was a silly fantasy that helped me get through a wedding your dad and I had plenty of misgivings about. Even though Jay was there with his wife, I imagined I saw something when he looked at you. I never saw that look in Angela. I wanted to, but I never did."

Lars blew out a long breath. "So you wanted me to be gay more than you wanted me to be with Angela."

"I wanted you to be happy, Lars. I knew she wasn't it, but I also knew that precious little girl that came with her lit every corner of your soul."

Lars grew misty at the mention of Jasmine, murmuring, "She certainly does."

Alicia stood, bent forward and kissed her son. "Get some rest, honey. I'm going to find a decent cup of coffee and your dad, in that order."

"I love you, mom," Lars professed, drowsiness running the words together.

"I love you right back—forever."

The following day, with one challenge behind him, and so many more ahead, Lars suddenly felt an urgency to proceed. The next most critical conversation had to be face-to-face, and so, following a taxing three-way conference with his long-time Fargo attorney and, at Lars' bedside, one of southwest Florida's top-notch lawyers, Lars asked his mother to book Jasmine and Faye's flight.

"Are you sure, son? A few more days of recuperation would do you good. I worry that taking on all of this at once may be too much."

"No, Mom. This has to be done. I refuse to inflict more change on Jasmine without her input. I'm not Angela."

It was the first barely-barbed comment Lars had uttered about his wife, and his conscience automatically tried to jump in.

But as he started to apologize, Alicia stopped him. "No, you certainly are not her, in any way, shape, or form," she said, her voice cold, hard, full of motherly venom. "You've recognized Angela for who and what she is, and you need never apologize for that—not to me, not to your father, not to anyone who loves you."

It's such a God damn mess." Lars sighed, testing small movements in the leg and shoulder to see what he could tolerate. "My disbelief is over and now I'm fully pissed off, but I can't bring the resentment I have towards Angela into the conversation I have to have with Jasmine. The facts are brutal enough as is."

His mother's handsome features twisted into a scowl. "Of course you wouldn't do that to your daughter—neither would I—but I want you to know, if you need to scream and rage and say any vile thing that you want about that hideous woman, I'll not only listen and agree, I'll join you. She tried to kill you, Lars. She tried to kill *my* son and, because the law prevents me from ripping her apart with my bare hands, the next best thing would be to see her rot in prison. In the meantime, we will vent to one another as often as we need, no apologies."

She shook as she wiped angry tears and rose from the chair at the foot of her son's hospital bed.

"I'll book their flight," she said, shifting quickly back into her usual state of composed confidence. "I want this to end—for all of us."

***

Alicia's text said that they were at the airport. Lars set the phone on the table. In order for proper healing of his chest, shoulder, and fractured clavicle, he was required to wear a sling, and mono-handed texting was challenging, so he chose a single red heart and tapped send. That morning, the physical therapist had begun gently exercising the injured areas, and Lars was glad now to have the dully aching appendage stabilized again. His leg was no picnic either, but the small amount of introductory PT made it clear that the chest wound was going to be the steeper hill to climb. Nervous anticipation of his daughter's arrival caused his fingers to tap fast-paced beats against the chair arm. Despite the nerves, bathing, dressing in the lounge pants and T-shirt his mother had purchased, and the therapists short, yet concentrated visit, had left him fatigued, and although the bed suddenly looked irresistibly inviting, Lars would be damned if he was going to let Jasmine find him sprawled out in it. He laid his head back against the recliner and closed his eyes for a moment to collect his thoughts.

It was Jasmine's voice that drew Lars out of the light doze. Like melodic birdsong, it drifted down the corridor and into the room, floating ever closer. A second later, she was there. Rushing forward, Jasmine wept and laughed and tried to figure out how to hug Lars around the propped leg and sling-cradled arm.

"Dad," she said again and again, her cheek pressed tightly to his, his good limb encircling her shoulder. "Are you all right? I'm not hurting you, am I? I'm just so glad to see you."

Lars chuckled through his tears, "I love you, kid. I'm all right. I'm really happy to see you, too."

Faye Gunderson and the Sorensons reached the room and kept a respectful distance from the joyous reunion. As he and Lars had planned, Michael announced that Faye, Alicia, and he would be in the family lounge down the hall. Lars and Faye exchanged fast, yet cordial greetings before the three took their leave. Michael and Alicia would now take on the complicated task of telling Faye what had transpired between her niece and their son. While on the plane from Fargo, Faye and Jasmine had put together their own plan of action.

With quarters being as tight as they were, Jasmine stayed as close to Lars as she could by perching on the edge of the bed. From there, she could still reach out and touch his free arm. When she had taken a better, more considerate look, and saw where and how he was bandaged, she wasted no time in asking, "What happened, Dad? Grandma and Grandpa and Aunt Faye keep telling me it was an accident, but no one will say what kind."

"We'll talk about that in a minute, but first I need to know something."

Jasmine tensed. Did he somehow already sense the news she had to divulge about Dave Bordeaux? But how could he know? She and Faye had agreed Faye would tell her grandparents, while she told Lars the story of her and Rosella's misdeeds and the meeting with the Bordeaux family.

"Okay, Dad, what is it?"

As he had done prior to departing for Florida, Lars asked if she had spoken to Angela. With what seemed like relief, the girl reported that they hadn't had any communication. Lars exhaled. According to his lawyers, any contact initiated by Angela post-shooting could indicate her plan to still use Jasmine as leverage.

"All right," Lars said, and reached for his daughter's hand. "There is absolutely no easy way to tell you what I'm about to tell you, so I'm just going to give you the facts, from the beginning."

He repeated verbatim what his parents had heard the day before, and then paused for Jasmine's reaction. Lars could see his daughter's embarrassment, her discomfort, but, regardless, she was still holding his hand, clutching it more tightly.

"Are you upset? Are you angry with me?"

Jasmine slowly shook her head, and said, "No, not angry. It's just that … well, it's weird."

Lars tensed at the unexpected response. Would she have used the word weird if the relationship had been with a woman? When Lars had chosen who to place on the short list of need-to-know, he had imagined his parents as the less receptive ones, but now, watching Jasmine squirm, her gaze darting anywhere in avoidance of his face, Lars sensed he had overestimated his teenage daughter's ability to accept the unfamiliar. As the seconds ticked by, he became more disturbed at what seemed like Jasmine's intolerance and finally, feeling it was his duty as a socially responsible parent, he broached the subject.

"Weird is a pretty harsh word," he ventured carefully. "Is it because Jay is a man?"

Immediately, Jasmine's flighty stare came to rest on Lars. "Oh, no, Dad, it's not that! I have classmates who have two moms or two dads, and I know kids whose brothers and sisters have come out. Some people make it hard on them, like bullying, but I'm completely not like that. Everybody should be allowed to be who they really are. It doesn't make a difference to me if someone is gay or bi or trans or straight; it only matters to me when people are mean. Believe me, Dad, it's not weird for me because it was Jay. It's weird for me because it's about sex."

A lightbulb flashed on for Lars, and a wave of relief came with it, as he responded, "It's weird because I am your dad, and what kid wants to think of a parent having a sex life of any kind."

"Yes! Exactly," Jasmine said excitedly, but then her excitement vanished as she seized upon another line of thought. "Do Grandma and Grandpa know? Does this have to do with your accident? Did someone hurt you because of it?"

"I told your grandparents. They have been great about everything," Lars assured. "And this wasn't exactly an accident, though it's not connected to Jay or our past relationship."

The difficulty with which Lars had told his daughter about Angela's request for a divorce paled against what he must now tell Jasmine, but, knowing he didn't have a choice, he pushed forward. When he was finished, Jasmine was visibly trembling, her face a mask of unadulterated terror, her eyes wild. A full minute slipped by, until, in a strangled, frantic whisper, she spoke.

"She could have killed you!"

Lars wished that he could hold her, console her, somehow carry her beyond this point of acute panic, but he could only squeeze her fingers and stroke a thumb across her knuckles.

Tone tough as concrete, he said, "I'm here, Jasmine. I'm alive. I'm here. I'm not going anywhere."

Great waves of grief that eventually curled into anger roared through the girl in wretched sobs, until the tidal wave broke, her emotions ebbed, and her irises darkened to a brown so deep, they were almost black. Jaw clenched, Jasmine looked straight at him.

"What's going to happen now?"

Chapter Thirty-two: Almost Everything

It wasn't difficult to find legal representation when you were the daughter of a judge, despite the fact that the judge in question knew nothing of said daughter's crime. One call to her Fargo attorney's office—and a reminder of Kenneth Erikson's position on the district court—had delivered Angie what she had needed in Florida. She hadn't spoken to Susanne or Kenneth since December, and she knew that, eventually, news of her predicament would leak back to them, but Angie had no intention of contacting them herself. As complicated as it all seemed, she hadn't lost confidence that she could walk away with everything she wanted, which included estrangement from her parents.

Deidre Garrett, Angie's new lawyer, didn't share her client's confidence. Across the cool, gleaming expanse of gray marble conference table, Bennet Dirk offered Deidre a perfunctory nod before turning his laser gaze on Angie.

"Mrs. Sorenson, I have been retained by your husband, Lars Sorenson so that we may address the matters at hand. As you may know, Mr. Sorenson is unable to join us today at the current advisement of his attending surgeons and physicians."

Angie's expression stayed steely, even as her lawyer gave a brief look of real sympathy. Bennett opened a leather binder and removed a set of papers.

"At this time, my client has yet to bring charges against you."

Angie's hard lines softened ever so slightly, and Bennett thought he caught a flash of self-satisfaction. With each additional second he was in this woman's presence, Bennet Dirk's dislike for her grew.

Deidre Garrett interjected, "'Yet' meaning your client may still press charges at some later date?"

Angie, her hair swept back in a severe tightly clipped tail that exposed the quarter-moon scar, turned to glare with open hostility at her lawyer.

Resolutely, Bennett Dirk picked up the papers, offered them to Ms. Garrett, and stated matter-of-factly, "That depends upon Mrs. Sorenson's willingness to come to these specific agreements. Optimally, I know we all would prefer to keep this outside the criminal court system."

The corner of Angie's frosty blue eye started twitching spasmodically. The events leading up to and directly following Lars and her confrontation remained hazy in Angie's memory, but regardless,

Angie hadn't, not for a single second, lost her sense of justification for her actions. She had protected herself against the theft of her identity. Lars had come to the beach that night to abduct Angie, drag her back into the life she detested, and wring the wild out, until all that was left was Angela. In Angie's opinion, she had done nothing more than stand her ground.

Bennett Dirk rose from the conference room chair, saying, "I'll give you and your client some privacy to go over the intricacies of this document, though I believe you will agree upon reading it that it is very straightforward. Shall we say thirty minutes?"

Thumbing through the pages, Deidra Garrett nodded, "Yes that should be an adequate amount of time. Thank you, Mr. Dirk."

***

"What's going to happen now?" Jasmine had asked, to which Lars had responded, "I'm going to give your mother the divorce she wanted, but *not* in the way she wants it."

As Lars expected, Jasmine's emotions swelled again, her pretty face turning ashen as she stammered, "What about me?"

Lars's memory replayed Angela's cruel, bitter rants, the unstable tirade that had concluded with "I hate every fucking last one of you" and bullets ripping into his body, and he said as soothingly as he could, "You are *my* daughter, and I love you more than words can express. Nothing will ever change that. I want to be in your life, and I definitely have a preference as to how that looks, but here's the thing, kid, we're all at a crossroads, and you, despite how it may seem, have choices. You have rights."

***

A half an hour later, Bennett Dirk returned to the conference room. Deidra Garrett looked harried and her client was fuming. Angie tore off the linen jacket she was wearing and glared at Bennett, as if ready for a street brawl.

"Mrs. Sorenson has some concerns," Garrett began, before Angie's raised voice interrupted with, "Where's the spousal support? I get a property that legally already belongs to me, and he walks away with everything else?"

Bennett sat down. Not out of character that this woman was worried about spousal support first and foremost. The daughter didn't make the top of her list, but Dirk knew that once he said what he was about to, Angela Sorenson's next strategy would include the child.

"According to Mr. Sorenson's financial records, he has transferred several sizeable sums to your accounts since the beginning of this year. My client, as do I, wonder why you continued to request these large sums, even after your initial contact with the law firm that drew up the divorce papers discovered in Mr. Sorenson's rental car the night of the shooting. My client feels as if he has provided enough spousal support to carry you comfortably through the transition of this divorce."

Angie's face took on an unsettling combination of fire and ice. "I used that money to make improvements on our beach house."

Bennett laid his palms on the cool marble, offered Deidra Garrett a pitying glance, and said, "Don't you mean 'my' beach house? You stated a moment ago, which we know to be factual, that the Siesta Key property is in your name and only your name."

"Well, yes," Angie retreated a bit. "But the renovations were for the benefit of the entire family."

Dirk proffered a thin dismissive smile. "Perhaps my client would reconsider if he were able to view receipts from the months of home improvement projects you oversaw, Mrs. Sorenson."

Furious, Angie didn't answer, her hands clenched into tight fists, waves of hate radiating from her every pore. Intuiting where her client would next head, Deidra Garrett halfheartedly attempted to compose her, without success.

"What about child support?" Angie demanded.

***

Joint custody, sole custody, visitation, supervised and unsupervised; Lars and Jasmine waded through the quagmire of her choices. As monumental as the decision was, it did not take long for Jasmine to make it. She placed her hand atop Lars, lacing her fingers between his, the darkness that had shadowed her eyes earlier, now replaced with the usual warm chocolate brown.

"I want to live with you, Dad, *only* you."

Visible relief flooded Lars, knowing that Jasmine's decision saved her from the likelihood of her mother's rejection. On the outside chance that Angela went so far as to attempt to receive child support by using their daughter as a meal ticket, Lars and his new lawyer had a card Angela could not beat. If she were low enough to go *that* far, Lars had given Bennett Dirk permission to slap that winning card down on the table and end Angela's game playing for good.

***

Bennett Dirk stared down Angela Sorenson. She was everything her soon-to-be ex-husband said she was, and all the things Dirk had warned Lars Sorenson a person like Angela might become when facing an imminent loss.

"I have a daughter. What about child support?" Angie again posed.

Without reply, Bennett kept staring. There was an ugliness to this woman that the sum total of all her undeniably beautiful physical features could not mask. If there was any spirit behind those frigid blue eyes, it was purely mean. Dirk took a slow breath, let it out, as if he had all the time in the world, and then said," Mrs. Sorenson, the documents state quite succinctly that Mr. Sorenson, as well as your daughter, wish full custody to be granted to Mr. Sorenson. As also stated, my client isn't seeking child support."

Angie's voice rose an octave as she snapped, "Of course not! That's not what I mean, and you know it! She is *my* daughter. I gave birth to her. He's not even her real father! He adopted her."

"The family courts consider an adoptive parent a *real* parent, Mrs. Sorenson, and need I remind you which end of the gun you were on?"

Deidra Garrett cleared her throat, and said, without much conviction, "Mr. Dirk, I find that comment inappropriate."

Angie pounced again, all claws and fangs and righteous indignation. "I was protecting myself. He came to my house, uninvited. He shouldn't have been there. He came to my property, I felt threatened, and I protected myself. Besides, it was raining, and I wasn't even sure who it was. I just felt unsafe. If we went to court, I would win!"

Bennett sat back and calmly listened as Angela Sorenson dug her own legal grave.

When Lars Sorenson had conveyed his story to Bennett Dirk, Lars had admitted gaining access to the beach by following a trail beside the vacant property next to Angela Sorenson's house. Upon further questioning, the lawyer discovered a strange, yet valuable, coincidence. This discovery had led Bennett Dirk to follow up on the suspicion born of that coincidence. As if the legal gods were grinning down upon him and his client, the suspicion panned out.

Straight faced, despite the little rush of pleasure he felt, Bennett addressed Deidra Garrett and her seething client.

"I'm going to share a story with you. When Mr. Sorenson retained me as his lawyer and we began to discuss the incident at Siesta Key, it didn't take us long to realize the peculiar smallness of the world. See, Ms. Garrett, the property that sits to the north of your client's house belongs to my father and mother in-law. It's currently on the market because they downsized and simplified and now live in a nice condo community that caters to the senior set. Their Siesta Key home hasn't moved quite as quickly as expected, and they were a bit nervous about it sitting empty. There is a security system in place, of course, but my father-in-law was particularly concerned about one area. Finally, I suggested that we install cameras in the spot that he thought would be most vulnerable to a break in."

Dirk watched the twitch in the corner of Angela Sorenson's eye return. Scowling, she crossed her arms tightly across her chest.

"I installed those cameras myself. Tech gadgets are a bit of a hobby of mine. Their range covers a wide swatch of the beach. In fact, it covers all the way from the north edge of the property to the south edge. That edge, of course, meets up with your property line, Mrs. Sorenson."

Deidra Garrett was far too intelligent not to see where this was going, and she thought about intervening, but Angela Sorenson had been a nightmare client thus far, and Deidra Garrett didn't feel as if she owed this woman a pass.

So I was curious," Bennett Dirk continued. "Had my amateur security system captured anything on the night of my client's *accidental* shooting? It turns out, it did—every gruesome second of it."

Fury rising, Angie clutched herself more tightly until her fingers dug into her ribs, and the screams inside her head couldn't reach her mouth, although her lips twisted into an unnerving snarl. She imagined lunging across the conference table and raking her nails deep into Bennett Dirk's smug face. Noting her expression, Dirk moved in for the kill.

"Mrs. Sorenson, you have the opportunity to move forward, to go on with your life, and to allow Mr. Sorenson and his daughter the same opportunity. You can sign the divorce papers, relinquish all parental rights to my client, and agree to the details of the settlement, or you can pursue your day in court. But understand this: if that day comes, I will most certainly be present with the digital evidence that clearly shows that the shooting was neither in self-defense nor an accident."

Deidra Garrett gave Bennett a slight nod and requested some additional time alone with her client. When Dirk had closed the door behind him, Garrett turned to Angie.

"It seems as if you haven't been completely honest with me, Angela."

Angie didn't bother to answer the useless bitch lawyer, instead fantasizing what it would feel like to tear every last wretched red hair from the woman's scalp. Deidra arranged the papers so that the empty signature lines were visible.

"All things considered, Angela, I believe this is the best you could have hoped for."

Garrett handed her a pen and slid the first page in front of her.

"Let's start with the most difficult one first," Deidra said compassionately.

Without a shred of the sorrow or hesitation Deidra might have expected from a mother signing over a child, Angie seized the pen and scrawled her name across the line. When finished, she tossed the paper back towards Garrett, motioning for her to present the next page. It wasn't until Angie saw the financial sections of the settlement that any emotion surfaced. Livid blood stained Angie's cheeks, her hand shook, and for a long moment the pen hovered above the signature line. She had gotten *almost* everything she wanted, but the one thing Angie would be denied was the thing that caused her to feel nothing but cheated. Jamming the pen point into the paper, she wished, as she had done on countless occasions since pulling that lovely trigger, that Lars would have bled to death, alone on the sand.

Deep and black, the ink bled Angela Sorenson's name onto the final page of the document. Without another word, Angie hurled the writing instrument at her attorney. The woman formerly known as Angela Edwina Erikson Sorenson stormed out of the room, out of the law firm, and out of reach of all redemption.

Chapter Thirty-three: A Click Nearer, a Click Off

As earth-shatteringly monumental as the reunion with the Bordeauxs and the events leading up to it had once seemed to Jasmine, her father's near-fatal injuries, the removal of her mother from their lives, and the peak and valley bag of emotions that came with it all kept Jasmine from telling Lars about Dave. Faye Gunderson, having sensed it the wrong time to speak with Michael and Alicia about the St. Paul situation, returned to Fargo without divulging Jasmine's secret, but with the promise she would look after the house and the cat in Jasmine's and Lars' absence. Deeply remorseful for what Angela had done, Faye also assigned herself the bitter task of delivering to Susanne and Kenneth the story of their family's sharp-edged new reality.

Not long after Faye's departure, infection in the leg wound caused a ten-day setback in Lars's recovery, until a round of antibiotic finally got a handle on it. Meanwhile, Michael and Alicia Sorenson checked out of the hotel where they had been staying and rented a two-bed, two-bath bungalow near the hospital for themselves and Jasmine.

Days turned into weeks, and soon a month had passed, but Jasmine couldn't bring herself to speak of Dave to her dad or to her grandparents, and the weight of her silence grew heavier. Michael and Alicia began to see worrisome changes in their granddaughter's personality.

"Your grandfather is going to stay with your dad this afternoon. Why don't you and I take a little break and find a salon? I'd like a pedicure. How about you, sweetie? We could get matching toe polish, something fun and glittery and out-of-the ordinary, maybe purple. What do you say?" Alicia suggested over the lunch she noticed Jasmine hadn't touched.

"No thanks, Grams. Maybe some other time," Jasmine said despondently. "I have to log in to my school portal today. I've fallen behind on some of my assignments."

Alicia nodded understandingly and felt another layer of concern build upon the already-high wall closing in around her. It wasn't like Jasmine, an A student, to procrastinate or to miss academic due dates.

"Did you have an opportunity to visit with your friend Rosella last night?" Alicia asked hopefully, to which Jasmine shook her head and stared down at her uneaten sandwich.

During the handful of calls and texts they had exchanged since

Jasmine had been in Florida, Rosella had been supportive, but now Rosella's life was rolling on—school, her on-again, off-again romance with Keon, binge-watching *Stranger Things*, squabbling with her siblings—while Jasmine trudged through this temporary, fragile limbo life where absolutely nothing seemed certain or solid. What could she even talk about right now that wasn't a total downer? Besides, her and Rosella's last conversation hadn't ended on a good note.

"What do you mean by put the relationship on hold? Sage is going to completely freak! He's utterly gone over you, Jas,"

"I know, Ro, but my world is so upside down right now. Everything is purely crazy. I don't even know if *I* can deal with it, so how can I ask Sage to deal with me? He's fifteen. He's supposed to be having fun, not waiting for another distraught, depressing text from a messed-up girlfriend whose mother tried to kill her father."

At that point, Jasmine had fallen silent as she fought back tears, and Rosella tried to console her.

"First of all, *you're* not the one who's messed up, and second of all, Sage's family isn't perfect, either. Remember his sister Cedar's basketball scholarship? Well, that's not happening. Apparently, Mankato State doesn't want a point guard who is going to be eight months pregnant when the season starts. Oh, yes, and then there's the shitshow that is Keon's clan of craziness. What I'm trying to say, Jas, is don't throw away something and someone as incredible as Sage because of your family's drama, because everybody's got family drama."

Jasmine's sadness, or maybe it had been self-pity, swung into irritation, and her words were clipped as she said, "I don't think I'm special or that other people don't have problems. It's just too hard right now. All my thoughts, all my worries, all my energy, it's all focused on what's happening with my dad, what's going to happen when he and I go back to Fargo, how awful it's going to be when more people find out about the shooting and my mom and other things I haven't even told you yet. There's not enough room in my head for everybody right now. Don't you get that, Rosella? Can't you just get that?"

Later, Jasmine had texted her best friend with an apology and Rosella had returned an "I'm sorry, too," but Jasmine still felt as if Rosella didn't understand her reasoning. When Jasmine carefully composed a long message to Sage, explaining her need to roll things back towards "just friends for now," he didn't understand either, but finally, after an hour's worth of texts were exchanged, Sage was forced to accept it. She promised to return the Honor the Earth badge that had belonged to Sage's grandfather.

"Keep it," he had told her. "Maybe it can still help you be brave."

***

Jasmine felt her grandmother's gaze and took a green grape from beside the turkey sandwich, popped it in her mouth and chewed, but barely tasted its sweetness. Alicia's face brightened at seeing the girl eat, but after another piece of fruit and a single bite of sandwich, Jasmine pushed the plate away, and said, "I'm sorry, Grams. I'm not very hungry right now."

Alicia said nothing as she took the plate from the table and wrapped the uneaten portion in plastic. The girl hadn't eaten much in several days, and her once pretty, round cheeks had begun to appear slightly sunken, her clothes seemed looser, and the usual healthy shine of her dark wavy hair had dulled. To ask Jasmine what was bothering her seemed as obtuse to Alicia as asking Lars why he winced when he put weight on his right leg, so Alicia kept making herself available to both, in hopes she could alleviate some of their many discomforts, although she felt she was failing on both counts.

"Can we go to the hospital now?"

Alicia frowned at her granddaughter's request. She had wanted the afternoon to consist of something more normal, more mundane, for Jasmine than more hours of sitting next to her father's bed.

"What about your assignments? You could work on those and then we could visit this evening," Alicia encouraged.

"I can finish them tonight," Jasmine said dismissively. "I would really like to check on Dad."

"All right," Alicia said with a resigned sigh, and hugged Jasmine. "He is lucky to have such a caring daughter. I love you, honey. Everything will be alright."

Later, after Michael, Alicia, and Jasmine had left the hospital for the evening and returned to the bungalow, Jasmine immediately said that she was tired and retreated to her small, home-until-home bedroom.

"I'm concerned about her, Michael. She's not herself," Alicia said quietly when their granddaughter was gone.

Michael nodded solemnly and sunk onto the couch, saying, "I agree. Did you see her reaction when Lars said they're moving him to the rehab facility, and possibly home to Fargo in another week? I thought she would have been more excited, or at least happier than what she seemed. She got so quiet. I could tell that Lars noticed it, too."

Tossing her handbag onto the coffee table, Alicia sat beside her husband. They both were exhausted; why wouldn't Jasmine be under a similar sort of fatigue?

"I don't want to be an alarmist," she said. "Nor do I want to say what is normal or not normal when it comes to her emotions and actions because she is still a child, and her experience in all of this is uniquely hers, but, that being said, I'm seeing signs that, if they become prolonged, we need to address."

Michael turned to his wife. The dark circles beneath her eyes matched the ones he had noticed in the mirror that morning while shaving.

"Situational depression?"

"Perhaps," Alicia replied. "I feel that she needs someone to talk to. She's not sharing much with me, and I sense that she's pulled back from her friends. She's isolating herself. If she's not at the hospital, she's shut up in that little room."

"Lars already mentioned to me that he thought both individual and family counseling would be appropriate when he and Jasmine are transitioning back into their home lives."

Alicia took Michael's hand, gave it a squeeze, and said, "That's good. He's aware that their homecoming has the potential of being rough. Lars will do right by them both."

Michael lifted Alicia's hand to his lips and pressed a light kiss to it before saying, "He will do the best thing. We've raised him right, and now he is the parent and we're the grandparents, which, to me, means Lars is the starter, you and I, we're on the bench, in the dugout. He'll signal if he needs us."

***

Jasmine sat on the narrow twin bed, her back against the coolness of the wall, and took a series of deep breaths before reaching for her phone. The night songs of cicadas and tree frogs and geckos mixed with the rustle of palm fronds and crept lightly into the little room's solace. Although tranquil, the Land of Flowers languid lullaby only served to remind her that time was running out. They all would be returning north soon, and she absolutely had to tell Dad Lars about Dad Dave. So many weeks of omission now had her worried that the news might be too upsetting, might cause a setback in Dad Lars' healing, might cause him to feel threatened, or angry, or possessive. She needed advice. She needed someone just removed enough, just calm and collected enough, just pragmatic enough to give it to her straight. Jasmine knew who she needed. In fact, although it had surprised them both a little, Jasmine had come to seek out this person more and more. She tapped the call button. Three rings in, there came an answer.

"Hi, Jasmine. Good to hear from you. How are things going down there?"

"Hi," Jasmine said, the voice at the other end of the phone a strong, thickly woven lifeline stretching the thousand-plus miles and offering the girl an immediate sense of safety. "I hope it's not too late for me to call."

"No, you're fine. Besides, we're an hour behind you."

"That's right, I keep forgetting that," Jasmine replied and tugged at a loose thread at the hem of her tank top.

"How's your dad today? Is he making progress?"

"Yes, in fact, he's headed to a rehab place soon, and then, if it goes well, home in about a week."

"That's great news. I'm sure you're both more than ready to be home."

Jasmine hesitated, yanking the thread harder until it broke, leaving an inch of hem unfolded and untidy, before she said, "Well, yes. It's good, I know, but that's what I wanted to talk to you about."

"Okay. It sounds like you're nervous about it."

"Yes, I'm nervous, but it's not just about going back to Fargo."

Jasmine continued to pick away at the now-ragged spot of unsewn cloth.

"You haven't talked to your dad about Dave yet, have you?"

It was a statement rather than a question, but Jasmine exhaled and answered, "No, not yet, and now I feel like the clock is ticking. It was easy to put it off up until now."

"Right. You didn't want to add to your dad's stress. You just wanted him to heal. I get that, Jasmine. It was a considerate choice. You love him and were looking out for him."

The approval felt good. It felt good in a certain way that the other supportive people in Jasmine's orbit, although they tried, couldn't seem to make her feel. The feeling came with the specific knowledge attached that if you hadn't truly earned it, you wouldn't be receiving it. No participation trophies here. No niceties for the sake of making nice.

"Listen. It sounds like your dad is a decent distance out of the woods, and, you know, I have real experience when it comes to that, so now it's about your strength."

"What if—" Jasmine began but was cut off.

"Life is full of *what if*. Did you let that stop you when you stole a car and set off to find Dave?"

The thought of being a car thief caused Jasmine to cough out a dry laugh.

"You didn't let it stop you then, and whatever what ifs you have now, I know you're going to take the leap. This risk, like the other, is worth it. My instincts say it is; so should yours. You're not just the daughter of *one* tough-as-hell survivor, you're the daughter of *two* strong men. You've got this, Jasmine. You've got this."

A few minutes later, the call ended, and Cassie Bordeaux laid her phone down and turned to Dave.

"She sends love to you and Davy."

He nodded, his troubled eyes settling back on the televised basketball game rather than face her as he spoke.

"She okay?"

"As okay as she can be."

"She didn't ask to talk to me."

Cassie stretched her legs out the length of the couch and pressed her bare foot against the outside of Dave's thigh, curling her toes, giving him what their son called a monkey hug. She knew his thoughts. Angie had robbed him of Jasmine once, and now her latest act of cruelty could rob him again. Lars Sorenson had just lost a wife, he had almost lost his life, followed by a near-miss when it came to losing a leg. With all that loss, would Lars feel generous enough to share fatherhood? Did Jasmine's loyalty to Lars now exclude any potential for a relationship with *him*?

"It's not personal, Dave. She's juggling as much as she can handle right now. We have to be patient. We have to wait on standby."

Dave smacked the remote against the couch arm a few times, for no other reason that Cassie could see than to vent emotional build-up.

"She's been talking to *you*. Why not me?" he asked, the vaguely-boyish envy apparent in the sharpness of his tone.

"I'm a few clicks off dead center," Cassie said. "I'm close, but not too close. To her, the contact she has with me is her way of keeping contact with you. It's just not as intense, not as complicated. Be cool, give her time, and she'll bring you back in when she's ready."

Dave's face softened, he took Cassie's foot and began massaging it. She sighed pleasurably and offered him the other one.

"You're right, Cass. As usual, you're ten steps ahead of me."

"Trust me, Bordeaux," she said, as she reclined against the couch's collection of throw pillows and watched LeBron sink a three-pointer. "Haven't you and I found a few happy endings together?"

At the mention of happy endings, Dave grinned lasciviously and moved his hand up her calf towards the inner thigh.

"It doesn't matter what we're talking about, you just always go there, don't you?" Cassie chided, but made no motion to avoid his increasingly arousing touch.

"You're smart, and you're tough, and you care about us. That's sexy, damn sexy!"

Cassie stared through the living room's low, screen-lit light until their eyes locked.

"Give me that remote," she commanded and pushed the DVR's

pause button.

With nimble skill, she reached one foot over top of his thigh until her long, slender toes found him. Stroking lightly, she tossed Dave a smoldering smile, and said, "Tell me again how smart you think I am."

Dave's breath caught, and then, in a gritty whisper, he said, "You're a genius."

Chapter Thirty-four: Deep Water

The river looked too wide and deep, its waters roiling, roaring, and rushing ceaselessly before them. The stones upon which to cross were there, but they seemed small, slippery, and too far apart for the way to be truly safe. Regardless of the peril, freedom from the burden of her secret lay on the opposite bank, so Jasmine turned in the chair where she sat next to Lars's bed, faced her father, and spoke. When she was done, Lars expression was placid and full of empathy.

"I always knew one day that you'd want to find him. And now it's no longer a mystery, why he couldn't try to locate you."

Jasmine nodded. The river was behind them, now seeming to be only the narrowest of slow-flowing streams. Cassie had been right.

"There's just one thing," Lars said, his tone becoming serious. "You must promise me you are not planning grand theft auto as a future career choice. I wouldn't want to discover a couple of Saabs and a Jag missing from my sale lots and have to think my daughter might be the culprit."

Despite herself, Jasmine cracked up, saying through her laughter, "No, Dad! It was a one-time crime."

"Did Rosella's parents dole out a heavy punishment?"

"She was grounded for a month and her dad made her clean the garage and she has to mow the lawn all summer. It's her least favorite chore. Mr. and Mrs. Bachman also are considering making Ro wait an extra month to get her license after she turns sixteen."

Lars raised his eye brows, and said, "That's tough, but fair."

Jasmine dropped her gaze to her silver flower beaded flip-flops. Inspecting her bare toenails, she decided that tomorrow she'd take her grandmother up on the pedicure offer.

"Aunt Faye didn't punish me," Jasmine admitted. "She said that would be up to you."

The relationship with Angela's family would have to be worked out sometime down the road, but Lars was certain about one thing: Faye would definitely have an open invitation to remain in his and Jasmine's lives. Running a finger along what were probably now permanent forehead furrows, Lars blew out a breath, patted his daughter's arm, and said, "We've all been punished enough."

***

By the time the Sorensons returned home to Fargo in late April, the snow had melted, leaving behind spears of hopeful green thrusting through the dead brown lawns, the maples and oaks had started to bud, and bird courting songs filled the fresh spring air. Amidst all the vibrancy of birth and re-birth, Lars and Jasmine began their new beginnings. Upon Alicia's request, Faye had prepared for their homecoming, boxing up some of Angela's personal belongings and delivering them to Kenneth and Susanne's house, although, in truth, no one expected Angela to return for them.

"What about the Mercedes?" Faye had inquired, to which Lars relayed his wish to his mother.

"Call Lars' sales manager while you are at the house," Alicia advised Faye. "He'll pick it up."

"Once it sells, I'll bank the money until Jasmine turns sixteen," Lars shared with his mother once she had ended the call with Faye. "I would say take lemons and make lemonade, but I refuse to attach the term lemon to a car that came from my own stock."

Alicia smiled at the return of her son's sense of humor. It was just one more sign of continued healing.

"It's a fresh start," Alicia had replied. "We'll keep all mention of lemons out of it."

Once Lars and Jasmine were settled in and both had given numerous reassurances that they had everything they needed, Michael and Alicia made their tearful goodbyes. As the car accelerated away from the house, Lars looked at his daughter and said, "Does it feel strange to be home?"

She knew the implied meaning beneath her father's question.

"No. I thought it might be weird, but it's not."

Angela had been gone long before she left. Lars moved to a recliner and sat down, laying the cane he still needed for extra stability beside the chair. Katniss had made an appearance as soon as they had entered the house, but in typical feline fashion, she was acting aloof, withholding affection until she decided that her humans had been adequately chastised for their long absence. When Jasmine curled into the corner of the sectional and patted the space beside her, the cat couldn't resist, and, bringing the shunning to its conclusion, leaped onto the leather cushion, bumped Jasmine's hand with her fluffy head, and sprawled out with a contented purr. Jasmine stole a peek at her dad. His eyes were closed. The travel had taken a lot out of him.

In a hushed voice, she asked, "Are you asleep?"

"No," Lars said, and smiled. "Just taking a moment to feel grateful."

"We made it, Dad."

"We did. We really did."

***

Two weeks later, with additional physical therapy and the magnificent medicine that is administered from simply being in one's own home, Lars ditched the cane. A perceptible limp still stuttered his gait, but with the passage of each day, he felt stronger and more surefooted. Not long after, Lars returned to work, where more than a few of the dealership's employee's tip-toed, heads down, eyes averted, when they saw the boss arrive. Halfway through the first day, Lars called a meeting. When all the mechanics, parts department folks, sales people, and secretarial staff were congregated in the showroom, he strode unevenly to the front of the little crowd. Clearing his throat, he thanked them for their thoughts and prayers, their cards and flowers, and their cookies and casseroles.

"My daughter and I appreciate the outpouring of your goodness," Lars said congenially, smiling at each individual as his eyes swept the room. "Now, I would like to clear a few things up, so we can continue to do our jobs here without discomfort."

Some nodded their agreement or gave Lars a thumbs-up. Others frowned a bit, chewed at a fingernail, or grew slightly red in the face. Lars casually pulled something round, about the size of his palm, from the pocket of his suit jacket. With cool, calm, he held it up.

"This is my new paperweight. Inside it are the slugs the surgeon removed from my shoulder and my leg."

Lars noticed a couple of people turn pale, but he continued.

"Yes, my wife pulled the trigger and, yes, we are now divorced and, yes, I have sole custody of our daughter."

He slid the paperweight back in the pocket.

"I believe that opens the way for all of us to get back to work. I know that's what I'm here for. I hope you all are, too."

A mechanic standing next to a Volvo started a slow clap and soon the entire staff was on its feet. When the applause, cheers, and handshakes were through, Lars went to his office and closed the door. He dropped the paperweight onto the desk blotter and sank into his chair. Some probably found the memento Lars had had manufactured for himself macabre, maybe vulgar, at the very least, in poor taste, but he didn't care about the possible criticisms of others. Lars wanted—he needed—a visual, tactile reminder. The physical trauma was nearly gone, and the emotional stuff he knew someday would lessen, but Lars didn't want a return to comfort to lull him into a false sense of security ever again. He stared at the now harmless pieces of metal encapsulated beneath the glass dome and the gun proponents' favorite slogan crossed his mind.

Guns don't kill people, he thought, and then whispered under his breath, "But they make it too damn easy for people to do it."

***

Jasmine's re-emergence into the final weeks of eighth grade proved to come with similar awkwardness: stares, whispers, lack of eye contact, but it also included another component, a component exponentially more insidious than all of Lars' employees' uneasiness combined. Jasmine's first day back included Taylor Vander Schmidt. As soon as Jasmine and Rosella turned the corner and headed towards their lockers, Jasmine spotted Taylor and two of her henchgirls loitering at the end of the hall. When Taylor knew Jasmine was looking, her lips curled into a mean little grin. Shaping her right hand to resemble a gun, Taylor mimed taking shots at some boys who had gathered at the water fountain. Satisfied with the mask of horror that started to spread over Jasmine's face, Taylor pretended to blow the smoke from the barrel of her old west six-shooter and turned to huddle with her cronies. Regan was giggling hysterically at the performance, but Amber frowned, stealing glances at Jasmine and Rosella, as if to indicate that she thought Taylor had gone too far. Bordering on ballistic, Rosella clenched a fist and started towards the other girls. With stoic, unnerving intensity, Jasmine raised an arm and held Rosella back.

"I got this, Ro."

Jasmine lowered her arm and stepped into the center of the hall. She was wearing the bead and quill bracelet Dave, Cassie, and Davy had sent her. The matching earrings that Jack and Isaac had included with the early eighth grade graduation gift swung against Jasmine's neck as she turned to Rosella and winked, before turning back to stare holes into an unsuspecting Taylor.

"Hey, Vander Schmidt," Jasmine called loud enough that the crowded hall of teenagers suddenly fell quiet.

Hoping to find Jasmine in tears, Taylor looked over her shoulder, but Jasmine's cheeks were dry and her expression was frighteningly unreadable. The girls locked eyes and Jasmine reached over her left shoulder. As if slipping an arrow from a quiver, she notched her imaginary bow. With a pulling motion, she drew back, pressed her top teeth against her bottom lip and, with a quick punch of air that made a whizzing sound, Jasmine's arrow hit its mark. Taylor's face went pale, then pink, and then blotchy red, as Rosella exploded in uproarious laughter and several classmates joined her, including Amber, who slapped a hand over her mouth, but not before Taylor noticed and swatted her on the arm. Calmly, Jasmine returned to her locker and grabbed a textbook and her iPad. Rosella slung an arm over her best friend's shoulder, saying with obvious admiration, "Damn, girl, that was fierce! When did you get so fearless?"

Jasmine wished she was fearless, but the truth was she had only learned what and who to *really* be afraid of, and Taylor Vander Schmidt no longer made the list. In the cold, shaky, middle of the night paralyzed, deepest depths of her gut, Jasmine remained afraid. During the earliest hours of morning, as dawn taunted night's thick black into heavy dark blue, Jasmine regularly sprang awake, adrenalin driving her pulse from zero to a hundred while her dry throat choked in the muffled remnants of a scream. Frozen, Jasmine couldn't open her eyes to who she might find in the room, terrified that the images in her nightmares would solidify before her. She would listen and listen, searching for the safety of silence, searching through the quiet for long minutes, until she was sure she heard nothing, until Jasmine was absolutely certain that Angela was not in the room, in the house, not pointing a gun, not pulling a trigger. Once Jasmine did open her eyes, sleep did not return, but the questions always did. Where was Angela now? Would she ever come back?

***

On the Friday marking Lars' first week back at work, a package arrived for him. When his secretary had deposited the small, thickly-padded mailing envelope on his desk with the rest of the mail and closed the door behind her, Lars glanced the return address label. It unleashed phantom twinges through his chest, through his thigh, and caused his hands to shake as he groped for a letter opener. Miami, Florida. It meant she was farther rather than nearer, but that geographical fact did nothing to quell the rising bile that accompanied Lars' sense of impending doom. Pushing the irrational thought of anthrax or some other deadly substance out of his head, he sliced the envelope open and, without reaching inside, dumped the content onto the desk. A black velvet jeweler's box laid partially propped against the domed paper weight. For several moments, Lars stared at the innocuous object before he finally ventured to pick it up. He lifted the hinged lid.

Upon opening the little velvet box, Lars first experience wasn't seeing what was nestled inside, but rather the faint scent of one of Angela's jasmine flower-based perfumes, and for half of a breath, sorrow and longing rode upon his olfactory memories. For that half breath, he let himself miss her. His fingers pressed the crushed velvet, feeling for where Angela's fingers might have recently been, his eyes finally registering what lay inside the box's satin interior. The moment of missing his ex-wife shrank back against the powerful surge of reality. Lars swallowed, his mouth grew dry, and his heart tripped, faltered, and then continued on. He did not take the antique diamond engagement ring from its resting place, but closed the lid; a mourner closing the lid of a loved one's coffin, a man closing the lid on the death of a marriage.

He set the box beside the glass domed paperweight. Why had Angela returned the ring? She could have sold it. While Lars and his lawyers had been preparing the details of the divorce, it hadn't been part of Lars's thought process, and if Michael and Alicia had given consideration to the family heirloom, they had not brought it up, perhaps out of sensitivity to the delicate situation. So what had caused Angela to send the ring back unprompted? Did she possess a residual fleck of decency, a sand grain of guilt, some encrypted moral code that only she could comprehend? Lars wished he could still entertain the notion that Angela may have some redeeming traits, but then Lars shifted his gaze and his thoughts to what sat trapped inside that glass dome. Wherever Angela was now, Lars hoped she stayed there.

***

The yacht motored slowly out of the harbor and into open water. Angie slipped off the stiletto-heeled sandals and curled her bare legs beneath her, sliding the already-short skirt higher along her thigh. Although it was well past midnight, the heavy heat and humidity of Miami still wrapped everything in its weighted stickiness.

"Champagne?"

Angie licked her glossy red mouth and accepted the crystal flute. The tall, muscular, blond man's thin lips curled, the vague smile never reaching his flat, gray eyes.

"Ivan," Angie purred as she patted the cushion next to her and motioned for him to sit.

It wasn't really his name, just the one he had given her, but he obliged her request. He found it amusing to let these women believe that they were in control. Angie dipped a fingertip in the chilled champagne, first running it over her pouty bottom lip before bending her tongue around the wet digit and dragging slowly down its entire length. The man watched, feigned interest, and then, playing his part in her cliché of an innuendo, grabbed her wrist in one large, iron grip. She sighed pleasurably. He took her damp finger, kissed it lightly, and then, viper-quick, snapped his teeth down on the tip. Angie gasped. The man released the finger but kept his hold on her wrist. Again, he kissed it with feather-lightness.

"A little punishment is nice with the pleasure, no?" he said in heavily accented English.

He had told her he was Ukrainian, which he wasn't, but he didn't select women like this one based upon an ear for linguistics. He chose her because it was his game, because she was alone, because she said she was new to South Beach, because she offered that she had no friends, no family. The beautiful, yet hard-edged blonde, who also claimed she was a former Miss North Dakota, batted her blackened lashes at him.

"I agree," Angie whispered, as she leaned in, catching his ear lobe with a flick of the tongue, followed by a nip of her perfectly white teeth.

Sarasota had quickly become just another Fargo, but Angie felt certain that Miami would deliver. The man rose suddenly, pulling Angie to her feet.

"I'll give you a tour of my boat," he said, and let go of her wrist, noting her flash of satisfaction, as if she thought she were back in charge of their course.

The glimmering lights of the coastline were growing dimmer as the yacht moved into deeper waters. The night ocean-cooled air carried a listless breeze, and Angie shivered involuntarily at the subtle shift in temperature. Abandoning the designer heels, she picked up the matching clutch bag. Its content would guarantee that she wouldn't get *too* much of what she wanted. Coyly, Angie took her host's hand and let him lead her below deck. When they entered the master suite and he had locked the door behind them, the man known to Angie as Ivan moved with practiced confidence towards his prey. In an aroused state of silent sadistic glee, he watched her carefully place the clutch on the plush carpet beside the carved mahogany bed. Yes, it truly amused him to let them think they were in control. This one, with the cruel blue stare and the milky skin and the grossly inflated sense of entitlement, amused him more than most. This one actually believed that a gun was still tucked in that fancy little over-priced handbag of hers. The man smiled as he lowered the lights and moved towards the bed. He smiled because she was careless, because he was quick-handed, and because, unlike Angie, he knew that her gun was no longer there.

Chapter Thirty-five: Around the Sun

One year, one earthly rotation around the source of all life, one circle composed of all the circles created by all those circling, searching, seeking someone to hold on to through all the movement. Within those three hundred and more days, Jasmine, her fathers, her family, her friends, did just that. It began with Kenneth Erikson.

Spring had unfurled itself into the fuller, heavy-heated fabric of another unfolding Fargo summer, solstice just having passed, when he showed up on the doorstep. He looked gaunt and older than his sixty years as he stood stooped, hands clasped in front of him, head bowed as if he awaited a judge's sentence. The splotchy, milk-white flesh of his face had given itself over to all the definitions of gravity. His sparse hair had grown thinner and grayer, and the khaki slacks and three-button golf shirt he wore were rumpled and ill-fitting. Lars opened the door to an expression he had never seen on his now former father-in-law's usually stern, self-assured face. Kenneth Erikson looked defeated.

"May I come in?"

Lars nodded and stepped aside, offering the older man entrance. Once inside, Kenneth stopped in the foyer and cleared his throat, saying, "I won't take much of your time."

Lars invited him further into the house, but Kenneth declined and remained planted on the carpet runner just beyond the door.

"I'm here, Lars, because I lost my son, and it appears that, for all practical purposes, I have lost a daughter, as well."

Kenneth's immediate bluntness caused Lars's jaw to clench back the words attached to the harsh response that sprang to mind. Reading it in Lars's emotionless masked, Kenneth said, "And perhaps, on many levels, I am to blame."

Again, Lars stayed silent and civil and let the man say what he had come to say.

"You are Jasmine's father," said Kenneth, his voice cracking at the utterance of his granddaughter's name, before Lars interjected.

"Yes, I am, but I am not her only father."

Kenneth crumpled further into his baggy clothing, the punch of Lars's implication bruising his already wounded conscience.

"I never meant to hurt anyone."

"But you did," Lars replied, matter-of-factly, without malice or condemnation.

Kenneth slowly shook his head and turned to go, saying, "Jasmine will be my greatest loss, but I cannot expect to be given what I took from someone else."

Kenneth's hand was on the door before Lars remembered what he had told his daughter. They all had been punished enough.

"Your relationship with Jasmine," he said, rubbing a hand over the place along his thigh where the nerves, still in their healing, fired erratically, "that's not for me to decide. It's for her to decide."

Kenneth paused, turning to face Lars.

"She loves you, Kenneth. And in time, she'll forgive you. She is the better aspects of all of us."

Tears trickled into the long-dried tributaries that lined the corners of Kenneth Erikson's eyes as he said, "Is she here? Can I see her?"

"She isn't here. She is in Minneapolis, visiting her family."

A sad smile curled the older man's mouth ever so slightly, and he said, "That is good."

Kenneth opened the door and hesitated, the world beyond suddenly seeming less familiar, less favorable than it had to the man he had once been.

"I'll tell her that you were here," Lars said, as Kenneth took a tired step forward. "And what about Susanne?"

"I don't know," Kenneth answered, his countenance hardening. "She and I have separated."

***

Another week's worth of time and distance passed, and Lars was on his way to Minneapolis to retrieve his daughter and, for the first time, to meet her biological father. A University of Minnesota classical music conference had sent Laura Bachman to the Twin Cities ten days earlier and she'd brought Jasmine for an extended visit with the Bordeauxs. Long stints behind the wheel still caused Lars leg and shoulder to ache, but this trip Lars would tough out the three and a half hours and spend the night at Jack Bordeaux and Isaac TwoBears' house before returning to Fargo the following day. During their daily FaceTime calls while Jasmine was in Minneapolis, she insisted that she would help with the return drive. As Lars approached his destination, the last hundred miles built up an achy dull gnaw and mounted the tension he felt about meeting Dave, which convinced Lars that he would accept her help. When Lars pulled up in front of Jack and Isaac's Victorian, Jasmine bounded off the porch, a springy boy, who Lars knew from pictures as Davy, and a chocolate lab not far behind her. With a little wince, Lars unfolded himself out of the Jaguar just in time for Jasmine to wrap him up in an eager hug.

"Dad," she laughed, kissing his cheek. "I totally missed you!"

"I totally missed you, too, kid."

Lars peered over Jasmine's shoulder at the boy and dog who were both bouncing up and down like the swath of green grass beneath them had been transformed into a trampoline.

"Davy, right?" Lars said, and the boy grinned broadly under a Kool-Aid-stained upper lip. "I like your mustache. What flavor is it?"

Davy wiped the area with his tongue and said, "It's a grape, my favorite."

"Awesome," Lars said as he took Jasmine's hand, and Davy and the dog raced back towards the house.

Jack and Isaac were waiting at the door, and although there was a sense, through all of Jasmine's photos and stories, that they and Lars already knew each other, introductions ensued before Isaac directed the group through the house to the back yard. Out back, Cassie and Dave silently sipped iced bottles of beer beneath the shade of the giant old oak tree. Cassie rose from the lawn chair when she saw the door open, and Dave turned the wheelchair to face what had tied his insides in a knot since early that morning. Jealousy tugged the knot tighter when he saw Jasmine holding Lars's hand. The knot loosened a little when she let go and trotted ahead, coming to lay a kiss on Dave's cheek before standing beside him, the same delicate hand now placed on Dave's shoulder. Lars's face was open and kind, but Dave could see that the other man was trying to work tension out of what Dave presumed was the injured shoulder. He also detected the slight limp, the one Jasmine said the orthopedist thought was most likely permanent. With every stilted step Lars took closer, Dave felt the knot untie further, until Lars was directly in front of him and the ground somehow felt oddly even between them. Without prelude, Lars offered Dave a hand, and Dave grasped it, both men exerting more strength than necessary.

"Dad," Jasmine said, neither man knowing for sure to which one she was referring. "This is Dad."

***

The cyclical circle continued on, bringing autumn, Thanksgiving, and the Bordeauxs to Fargo for a turkey feast. Jack, Isaac, Faye, and Faye's famous pumpkin pie were also present. Winter roared in, but Lars and Jasmine found windows in the snowy weather, and spent a jubilant, crazy, chaotic Christmas in Minneapolis, where they met more Bordeaux and TwoBears aunties, uncles, and cousins than either Jasmine or Lars could keep track of, each new relative weaving another thread into the larger family story. Winter relinquished to spring,

Jasmine regularly spent weekends with Dave and Cassie, and occasionally Davy returned to Fargo with his big sister, where the man he called "Uncle Lars" always had plenty of grape Kool-Aid on hand, and liked go-carts, Spider Man, and baseball as much as Davy did. When summer showed up, Laura Bachman phoned Lars and extended an open invitation.

"Our family goes to as many powwow events during the season as possible. It's getting tougher, the older the kids get, but we have a few dates we think will work. There's South Dakota, Minnesota, and one in Wisconsin I've got flagged on the calendar. We would love to have you and Jasmine caravan with us, camp, meet a lot of our old friends."

Lars knew Jasmine would jump at the chance, but a shaky little whisper in his head warned him not to usurp, not to tread into territory he felt belonged to the Bordeaux's culture, and therefore, belonged to Dave. Lars thanked Laura and said that he'd talk to Jasmine.

"They don't do the powwow circuit," Jasmine said when he asked if it might be better she attend with Dave and Cassie, Lars's mind flashing to the framed photo Jasmine now kept on her nightstand—a young Dave Bordeaux dancing, baby Jasmine in his arms.

Considering, Lars replied, "Well, since they don't travel, maybe you would want to go to one of the Minneapolis powwows with them. We can make that happen."

"It's not about traveling," Jasmine said with a slight frown. "Dad and Cassie just don't go to powwows. When I was there last summer, Uncle Jack wanted us to go with him and Uncle Isaac, but Cassie said that we shouldn't mention it to Dad because he would be a hard no on it."

Lars reddened, the sudden, delayed realization that a man, now confined to a wheelchair, who had once proudly danced his infant daughter into the circle would have every reason, every right to avoid that potential grief. The weight of the thought hit Lars full-on, but Jasmine continued to look at him expectantly.

"We'll join Rosella and her family then—if you want."

Jasmine beamed, and threw her arms around Lars, who, despite their daughter's exuberance, still felt hesitant as he wondered how Dave would feel about three non-Native adults taking it upon themselves to expose Jasmine to what some might argue was the very epicenter of contemporary Native culture. Later, when Lars was alone and his conscience wouldn't quiet the question, he finally picked up his cell and composed a text to Dave.

Please give me a call when you get a chance, it read.

Before Lars hit send, a wave of irrational dread, followed by an impulsive urge to bend to cowardice, caused him to add Cassie's name as a recipient. Before he had taken another breath to re-think it, he had tossed the text into the ether, and then paced the living room for a few laps, silently saying little prayers that Cassie would be the first one to respond. An hour passed, Lars leg grew stiff, so he stopped wearing a track in the rug, sank into a recliner, and put his aching limb up on the footrest. Just as he felt the initial nudges of sleep, the cell vibrated loudly against the glass end table beside him. He glanced the screen. So much for meditative pacing and desperate prayer.

"Jasmine okay?" Dave initiated before Lars could get out a greeting, Lars hearing the worry seeping through Dave's words.

Lars assured him that Jasmine was fine and then paused for an irregularly long enough time that Dave eventually cut in to ask what was up. Lars blew out an audible breath, then jumped right to the point. When he had finished, Dave fell into his own prolonged silence. Just when the elasticity of his wordlessness seemed stretched to its breaking point, Dave tried to clear the jagged rock shards of emotion collecting in his throat and spoke.

"Yeah … I get it … She wants that, why wouldn't she? … I suppose this is what's best."

It sounded as if Dave had turned his head from the phone, his voice drifting away from the mouthpiece, his broken-up thoughts seeming more the vocalization of an inner monologue than a response to what he had been told. When Dave again seemed to be addressing Lars, his tone seemed more edged in resignation than approval. It wasn't a blessing, by any means, not that Lars had been expecting one.

"Okay," said Dave before ending the exchange. "Just keep a close eye on her. There's always a lot of young dudes at those things, all prowling to break some girl's heart."

Chapter Thirty-six: Gifts

The heat and dust, fry bread and bison burger, and drums and dancing of June, the strawberry moon, and July, the halfway summer moon, sprang by jack rabbit fast, and with every new powwow grounds, camp site, and crowds of dancers, Jasmine watched and learned. Traditional, fancy and grass, fancy shawl and jingle dress, even the tiny tots; Jasmine studied the dances and the dancers, the rhythms, the motions, the songs, the steps all becoming familiar and beckoning her to join, but although she wanted to, secretly letting her body mimic the movements when she was safely hidden behind her bedroom door, she had yet to participate. Something told her that it wasn't her time yet and that she would know for certain when it was. In the meantime, Jasmine studied each new grand entry with a sense of anticipation and dread; anticipation for the day when she herself would enter the circle and, the deeper of the two sensations, dread for the one person she might spot among the spectacularly regalia-clad young males. Jasmine was afraid of an encounter with Sage Koskinen.

Several powwows came and went, and August, the ricing moon, arrived, along with her sixteenth birthday, but she still had not seen him. By now, Jasmine's fear that she would see Sage became a stronger one: the fear that she would *not*.

"Come on, Ro," Jasmine urged. "What's going on? Isn't it strange that we haven't seen the Koskinens *all* summer? At least tell me it's not something bad that's keeping them away."

After Jasmine had ended her and Sage's relationship, Rosella had set strict boundaries for both of her friends. Neither Sage nor Jasmine was allowed to pump Rosella for information about the other and under no circumstances were they to mention Keon's name. As could be expected with fifteen-year-olds, geographical distance, their best friends' split, and, most significantly, Keon's abundance of brazen Instagram posts that featured him canoodling with different girls quickly iced Rosella's affections. Initially, both Sage and Jasmine respected Rosella's wishes, but when this year's circuit began and Rosella's own Instagram feed overflowed with photos of her and Jasmine living and loving the powwow life, Sage's texts blew Rosella's phone up, to which she replied only with a line of monkey covering its mouth emoji's. As summer stretched forward with no sign of Sage, Jasmine launched her own inquiry. Now, as Rosella and Jasmine lounged in the shade of the RV Lars had rented to bring them to

Shakopee, Rosella rolled her eyes.

"Listen, Jas. I'm *only* saying this one more time. You are my friend, Sage is my friend, and because I would like to keep it that way, he is off limits as a topic of conversation."

When Jasmine looked like she was on the verge of a full-blown temper tantrum, Rosella finally laughed, tossed one of the corn chips she'd been snacking on at her melodramatic friend, and said, "All right! Don't melt down, She-Hulk. No one wants to see that, especially that Ho-chunk kid we met at Leach Lake last month. Wasn't his name Jeff or John or Jake? It was something with a J. Well, anyway, whatever his name is, this will be the fourth time he's walked by and checked you out, girl."

Without as much as a glance at the tall, good-looking boy fruitlessly casting interested signals her direction, Jasmine plucked the corn chip from the front of her turquoise tank top, and lobbed it back at Rosella.

"Talk, Rosella Bachman! Now! She-Hulk angry! Besides," said Jasmine, softening her tactics, "it's my birthday."

"True. That's why I will make this one small exception to my rule, but never again. Got it?"

Jasmine nodded and, turning her lawn chair to face Rosella, she eagerly leaned forward, elbows on knees, and stared her friend directly in the eye, as if an interrogation were about to commence. Jasmine's intensity had Rosella squirming a bit, but she couldn't say a lot; the whole truth was too much of a betrayal to tell.

"He's fine. His family is fine. They have been in Duluth a lot this summer, helping Sage's grandmother. She had a hip replacement."

"Is that all?"

"That's all I'm going to tell you."

Clearly dissatisfied with the miniscule amount of information, Jasmine exhaled, her eyes falling from her friend's face. For a moment, Rosella thought she saw a tear welling there, but Jasmine quickly swiped the back of her hand across closed lids before Rosella could say for certain.

In a wistful voice, Jasmine said, "Thanks, Ro. I guess I don't have to keep worrying whether I'm going to meet up with him or not. He probably wouldn't want to see me even if I did want to see him, which, you know, Ro, I guess I really do. I know I shouldn't want that, but he was *so* great and I was such an idiot."

Rosella kept quiet while Jasmine poured out everything Rosella already knew, or at least, suspected.

"I still have that picture in the beaded heart, the one that you and Sage gave me for my fourteenth birthday," Jasmine continued, no longer bothering to hide the tears, but just letting them splash onto the dust patch of earth that she was staring at as she avoided Rosella's facial reactions. "It's inside my pillowcase. I take it out and look at him and say that I'm sorry. Isn't that crazy, Ro? He's like the perfect guy, and I dumped him. You warned me, but I dumped him. I totally regret it."

Uncharacteristically quiet, Rosella listened as Jasmine confessed: the daily visits to Sage's social media pages and feeds, the countless moments spent composing texts that were never sent, the somersaults her heart did when she saw the photos of Sage holding his sister Cedar's baby, how the sum total of all the adorably luscious boys they had met that summer didn't equal one Sage Koskinen. Rosella was just about to make a joke, try to lighten the mood, about to tell Jasmine that all the mushy-gushy was about to make her toss her corn chips, when Rosella thought she recognized someone. About a hundred yards away, a man with a toddler on his back in a carrier stood in profile, but before she could identify him, he was swallowed up by a swarm of people exiting a food tent. A moment later, the crowd dispersed, a different individual emerged and started walking purposefully towards her and Jasmine.

"Are you listening, Ro? I suppose you've reached your limit about five minutes ago," Jasmine said apologetically, and looked up at her friend.

Rosella was fixed on something beyond Jasmine's left shoulder, her expression frozen into an odd fusion of smugness and low-level anxiousness.

"What is it?" Jasmine asked, to which Rosella's gaze flew to her friend's face.

"You're right, Jas. You are absolutely right about everything you just said."

Stunned and somewhat skeptical, Jasmine frowned and said, "Really?"

Rosella nodded, but her eyes were locked back on whatever was behind Jasmine. What had a grip on Ro's attention? Was that nice enough but kind of pesky Ho-chunk boy lurking around again? Jasmine was about to turn around and shoot John or Jake or Jeff or whatever his name was the most hope-crushing look she could configure when a voice stopped Jasmine cold, and then lit her on fire.

"Hi, Ro."

His voice had deepened, grown rich and warm and intoned with some kind of mystical vibrations that traveled from the ends of Jasmine's hair to the tips of her toes and back again. Rosella grinned one of her most devilish grins, saying, "Hey, Sage. What's up? I think I just saw your dad with your niece."

After the speechless monkey-filled text, her oldest friend Sage had reminded Rosella that June was his birthday month and she should give him the only thing he wanted, so she did.

"Well, at least I don't have to wrap this," Rosella had teased as Sage asked and Ro answered.

Sage's gift had included: one, Jasmine did not have a boyfriend, -in fact, hadn't dated at all since their break-up; two, Jasmine had ignored every flirtatious advance of every guy—there had been more than Rosella could count; three, Rosella was about ninety-nine point nine percent sure that Jasmine still had feelings for him, although Rosella insisted that she had kept him as a forbidden subject when it came to her and Jasmine's friendship; and, four, Jasmine would be at the Shakopee powwow.

In retrospect, Rosella had given Sage better B-day info than she had given Jasmine, but Sage had been pretty vague when Rosella had tried to corner him.

"Are *you* going to be at Shakopee then? Is that why you want to know?" Rosella had asked, but Sage had only given her a semi-solid "maybe."

But there was no maybe now. Sage squatted next to Rosella and, turning on a hundred-watt, lopsided smile, his shiny, brown puppy-dog eyes found the whole reason he was here: the beautiful, complicated, extraordinarily brave and fragile girl that he could not stop thinking about. Her hair was much longer and plated down the back of her head, loose strands dancing playfully around the edges of her light brown, sun-tanned face, a face that more resembled a woman than the girl Sage had last seen in person. She smiled shyly and his mind exploded with the memory of their first kiss and the taste, the feel of those full perfect lips. But that was then, and this was now, and a year and a half could be like a kind of forever. To begin again was the only place to start, so, feeling like the king of the obvious, the king of the idiots, the king of all lame guys in love everywhere, he drank in the warmth and possibility of that smile and said, "Hi, Jasmine. Happy birthday."

Epilogue

"The practice of peace and reconciliation is one of the most vital and artistic of human actions."

~ Thich Nhat Hanh

The aunties combed and braided Jasmine's hair, fastened the quill and bead barrette they had crafted into it, and stepped back to admire their work. It was time for the earrings. A cousin drew out a worn silk pouch and opening it, offered its contents. One auntie carefully lifted the long dangling strands of shiny beadwork and, sliding one and then the other into Jasmine's pierced lobes, said, "Your Grandma Bordeaux made these. I know our mother would be proud if she were alive to see them on her beautiful granddaughter."

A second auntie nodded in agreement while helping adjust the leggings and the yoke decorated with more beads in an Ojibwe floral pattern. The brain-tanned moccasins were slipped on and, as they had been so carefully constructed to do, fit perfectly to every curve of Jasmine's foot. With one final check, the aunties buzzed around, tightening ties, securing all buttons, hooks, and laces before one of them turned and motioned to the cousin who had the crowning jewel of Jasmine's regalia folded over an arm. Unfurling it with a graceful flourish, the young woman brought the shawl to rest around Jasmine's shoulder. Circled around their niece and cousin, the gathering of Bordeaux females smiled, sighed, let loose little oohs and ahs of appreciation at the culmination of their loving efforts.

"Miigwech," Jasmine said, thanking them in Ojibwe.

Grasping the tasseled ends of the bright, multi-colored shawl, Jasmine spread her arms wide and did a slow spin. The women gave quick quiet applause, and one of the spunkier, spontaneous little girls, let loose a whoop of approval, and then proclaimed, "She's ready!"

Outside the tent, the September sky was cornflower-blue and cloudless, a hint of crisp cool mingling with the sun's warmth, reminding those familiar with Mankato's seasonal shifts that night frosts and the color changes of the leaves were just around the corner. For most in attendance, the Makato Wacipi would be the final outdoor powwow of the year and, for its participants, one of the most meaningful and sacred events. Hosted by southern Minnesota's Dakota community, the powwow had come to signify a time of remembrance, reflection, and reconciliation for the Native and non-Native people of the region. In 1862, following a war between the eastern bands of Dakota and the United States during which many Dakota men, women, and children, as well as white soldiers and settlers, were killed, thirty-eight Dakota prisoners of war were hanged. It was the largest mass execution in U.S. history, where, in a gruesome public display, the warriors were hanged simultaneously from a single gallows, as Mankato's white citizenry, their children in tow, watched and cheered. The surviving Dakota men, women, and children were imprisoned at Fort Snelling and later forcibly removed from the land of their ancestors. Over a hundred years later, in the early 1970s, with a rise of Native American pride and power, and Native people everywhere re-claiming culture and a sense of community, the Makato Wacipi, Mankato Powwow, became a focal point for addressing the city's shameful historical significance and remembering what should never be forgotten, while moving towards the possibility of mutual respect.

For Jasmine Bordeaux Sorenson—both Lars and Dave had made possible her wish for the addition to her legal name—the powwow presented a place to examine the parts of herself that still seemed to grind uncomfortably against one another. For nearly two years, Jasmine had gone once a week to a psychologist who specialized in teen and young adult therapy, and although Jasmine liked and trusted the counselor, she continued to grapple with the idea of her identity. Who was she? On good days, she felt secure, she felt certain, she felt the answer firmly in her grip. She was Dave's daughter. She was Ojibwe. She was Lars' daughter. She was Kenneth's granddaughter. She was Jack's and Isaac's niece. She was Davy's sister. These aspects of herself felt rock solid to her, permanent and safe. On the not-so-good days, it was the other ingredient of her makeup that dripped in and eroded Jasmine's stronger foundational building blocks. It was the undeniable fact that Angela, a liar, a thief, a deserter of family, and an attempted murderer, was Jasmine's mother.

"The sins of the mother," Great Aunt Faye had told Jasmine after Angela's disappearance from their lives, "are not the inheritance of her daughter. Your life and your choices belong to you."

This came back to Jasmine as she stepped from the tent into the brilliant September sunshine and joined the scores of other dancers and spectators moving towards where the grand entry would soon begin. As she walked, each step seemed to push the pieces of herself closer together, until the stronger, proud parts fused. The shadowy weaker aspects of her DNA would always be there. Whatever contributing threads had come from Angela were permanent, but they did not have to be prophetic. Jasmine Bordeaux Sorenson held her head high. Today, her rock-solid parts would prevail. Today, she knew exactly who she was.

Along the way, she spotted Sage, dressed in regalia, among the growing collection of male dancers. When he saw her, their eyes met, he pressed his fist to his lips twice and then swung his arm in Jasmine's direction, splaying open his fingers like a starburst. Blushing with pleasure, Jasmine mimed a catch with her empty palm, closed the hand, and touched it twice to her own lips. As had become his custom, he wore his grandfather's AIM badge over his heart. Jasmine pointed to the Honor the Earth badge secured over her own heart. Sage nodded and mouthed the word, "Brave." And then with a wink added, "Beautiful."

Further on, Jasmine felt a tap on her shoulder and turned to find Rosella. Her tall, willowy friend wore a stunning midnight blue velvet jingle dress. Jasmine's jaw dropped at the sight and the usually confident Rosella turned momentarily coy. More of a jeans, leggings, and running shorts kind of girl, Rosella avoided dresses, and hadn't donned one this attention-grabbing since she had worn a much more juvenile version years earlier, when Laura Bachman had convinced her reluctant five-year-old to give the tiny tots powwow dancing a try. By the time Rosella outgrew that first dress, she had come to recognize how many of the other little girls were legacy dancers; their sisters, mothers, aunties, and grandmothers all dancers, too. For little Rosella Bachman, whose white mother stood outside the circle holding a camcorder, these differences caused her to feel *too* different, and the next summer she chose to return to the perimeter with her parents and new baby sister to watch the dancers flow by. But Jasmine's decision had changed Rosella's mind. It was time to return. She laid a hand on Jasmine's arm and, together, they went forward.

They made an odd pair: the blond man with the limp and the man in the wheelchair. As they approached the expansive grass clearing, people moved aside, paying proper respect and observing the challenge the uneven ground presented the determined duo. At the very edge of the circle, the men stopped, the one in the wheelchair taking off a beaded baseball cap imprinted with the words Native Vet just as the drummers at the circle's center began a slow beat.

The drum was in his chest, his heart was inside the drum, and Dave Bordeaux's eyes were riveted to the procession now moving slowly into view. At its head, the honor guard came, compiled of the warriors, elder and young, the military veterans, both Native and, by invitation, their non-Native brothers and sisters. They carried the United States flag, tribal nation's flags, the POW flag, and the tribal eagle staffs, and, among them, Cassie Bordeaux carried a staff of the Navajo nation. She wore black jeans and a military-style short sleeve shirt to which were pinned her medals, including the Purple Heart. On her wrists, she wore simple wide silver cuff bracelets, each etched with the image of a horse. Looped to her belt, she carried a small beaded medicine bag. Her face was shaped by the austerity of the moment and the significance of her place within it, but as she passed, her eyes found Dave's for a single breath, and when she knew he saw it, she touched the medicine bag. He offered her a single knowing nod. Inside that bag crafted by his daughter rode Dave Bordeaux's own Purple Heart.

And then she was there, their daughter, their Jasmine. She flowed past, her feet lightly caressing the earth, her movements as fluid and as mystical as the joining of wind and water and sunlight itself. She had made it clear: Jasmine would not return to the circle unless Dave was there.

"You were with me in the beginning," she had told him. "And I need you there now."

Jasmine's face grew radiant when she saw him and Lars together, each man's expression locked in the masculine myth that they shouldn't let their tears fall. Her fathers, so different and yet so the same in the depth that they loved her.

The MC's voice echoed through the clearness of the Indian summer air.

"We dance for our mother, the Earth."

Jasmine felt her feet land gently on each beat of the drum.

"We dance for our father, the sky, and the sun and moon, our grandparents."

She gazed at the endless blue veil above them.

"We dance for the ancestors."

She could feel the blood of two peoples, of two continents, of two worlds, reconcile and merge into the one roaring river rushing through her veins.

Round and round the great pulsing drum, the living heart of the sacred circle, the people all orbited like the brilliant bright creatures that all too soon, would again circle the wintery edges of the sun.

"We dance for those who cannot dance," the MC's voice pierced through the song of bells and jingles, rustling beads and feathers and cloth and velvet and leather and the sound of the dancers' breaths, and even the singers and the drum itself.

The drum was in her chest, her heart was inside the drum, and Jasmine Bordeaux Sorenson smiled, closed her eyes, and danced for her fathers.

About the Author

Amy Krout-Horn, Oieihake Win (Last Word Woman), is a regular contributor to Slate and Style magazine and was awarded the publication's 2008 fiction prize for her short story, *War Pony*. The publication awarded her again in 2012 for *Trickster's Daughter*. Her essays and stories have appeared in several magazines and journals, including Breath and Shadow, Talking Stick Native Arts Quarterly, and Independent Ink. Additional works are included in the anthologies, *Unraveling the Spreading Cloth of Time: Indigenous Thoughts Concerning the Universe*, *When Spirits Visit*, and *Dozen*: *The Best of Breath and Shadow*. Her writing was also featured in the non-fiction collection, *Spirit Drumming*. She is the co-author of *Transcendence*, which received the 2012 National Indie Excellence Award gold medal for visionary fiction, the autobiographical novel, *My Father's Blood*, and *Dancing in Concrete Moccasins*. *Dancing in Concrete Moccasins* won the 2017 Next Generation Indie Book Award gold medal for LGBT fiction and the 2017 National Indie Excellence Award silver medal for multi-cultural fiction.

Whether she is swimming in the Gulf of Mexico near her Florida home, playing with her brilliant and beautiful granddaughters, or drumming and chanting for personal and planetary well-being, Amy Krout-Horn embraces life with a tenacity of spirit she attributes to her Native American ancestry.

For more information or to purchase books, visit her website.
http://www.nativeearthwords.com

ALL THINGS THAT MATTER PRESS

FOR MORE INFORMATION ON TITLES AVAILABLE FROM ALL THINGS THAT MATTER PRESS, GO TO http://allthingsthatmatterpress.com